Intimate Intentions
by
Angie Daniels

Indigo Love Stories
Sensuous

Genesis Press, Inc.
315 Third Avenue North
Columbus, MS 39701

Intimate Intentions

First Edition

Acknowledgements

To my dear friend, Terraine Saunders for pushing me to follow my dream an constantly asking me "Where's the book?"

To my wonderful hsband, kenneth Hills and my children, Mark, Ashlie and Evan for being so supportive all those months.

To my father, Dennis Daniels for recognizing my talent at an early age and providing me with an endless supply of yellow legal pads.

To my critic team Sherrie Branch, Verl Powell-Williams, georgia Prince, Linda Bosslet & Kim Ashcraft. Thanks for all of your opinions and support.

To my friend Beverly Palmer for providing me with another set of eyes.

To Dr. Luis & Milagros Giuffra for allowing me the opportunity to work in your psychiatric clinic and learn all I could about mental illness.

And to the memory of my grandmother Roxaner may she rest in peace.

Indigo

Sensuous Love Stories

Genesis Press, Inc.

Prologue

Deja Davis pulled her sleek red Mercedes into an empty parking space in front of St. Louis's luxurious Adam's Mark Hotel. She then climbed gracefully out of the car, swinging her purse over her shoulder before shutting the driver's door. After a long day at the studio and a dinner engagement immediately following—to promote her new perfume *Deja*—she was exhausted and eager to soak her weary body in a hot tub of water.

Deja sauntered through the hotel lobby as if she were on a runway—poised and full of confidence. Standing at six feet, she looked stunning in a blue sequined dress with a plunging neckline that complemented her tall shapely body and showed off her long slender legs. Her flawless tawny complexion intensified her dark brown eyes while her dazzling smile, which was girlishly affectionate, softened her features and made her look younger than her twenty-three years. Even though the compelling beauty was looking straight ahead, she was conscious of the desire she kindled in the gentlemen standing around the lobby as she passed. Deja knew she had the kind of looks that made any man or woman look twice, and she used them to her advantage. Her determination was like a rock inside of her and she was not letting anything or anyone stand in the way of her success.

As she boarded the empty elevator a smile emerged. The promotion of her new perfume was going well and next week she would grace the cover of another magazine. Deja giggled with delight. She had a lot to be thankful for. Unlike most girls, modeling had come easy for her. Her mother, Tiffany Spencer, once the world's most sought-after black supermodel, had been able to give her daughter the connections she needed in order to get her career moving in the right direction. That was five years ago. Now Deja was bombarded with a steady flow of contracts and she couldn't be happier.

Deja released a long sigh of relief and stepped out of the elevator. She had the rest of the week to herself before shooting began on a new lingerie catalog and was scheduled to fly to her hometown of Baltimore in the morning. She was looking forward to spending some quality time with her parents, whom she had not seen since the Christmas season.

Deja strolled down the corridor and tossed her thick auburn hair, sending it tumbling carelessly around her shoulders. She stopped in front of room 403 and turned the key in the lock.

"Deja."

She jumped at the sound of his voice and drew in a large swallow of air before turning around to see who had the audacity to frighten her.

"You fool! You startled me," she scolded, although clearly relieved to see a familiar face. Deja dropped her purse from her shoulder, allowing it to fall to the floor before adding, "You're lucky I didn't do some karate on your behind." The man chuckled while Deja leaned over with both hands on her knees as she tried to calm her racing pulse.

"What are you doing here anyway?" she asked between breaths.

The man did not respond.

Surprised by his silence, Deja returned to an upright position, and found that his amused expression had vanished. He was now staring at her so intensely that his unwavering eyes appeared to be looking straight through her.

Deja frowned at the sudden change. "Is something wrong?"

Although there still was no response, his dark eyes told her everything. There was a coldness in them that she had never seen before, and suddenly, she felt uncomfortable. Deja stepped away from him as if he were a stranger. He, in turn, moved forward and was now standing firmly in front of her.

"Well... " Her voice broke in mid-sentence. She slid her purse back onto her shoulder while uneasiness burned at her throat. Taking another step back, Deja reached behind her and placed a hand on the doorknob, suddenly anxious to escape from his disturbing presence.

"I'm tired. I...I have an early day tomorrow," Deja stammered. She turned the knob and pushed on the door. While she backed slowly into the room she watched his lips twist into a satanic smile that caused her to gasp. In a matter of seconds, the door was jerked away from her and a large gloved hand closed around her throat, stifling her scream.

Chapter One

No," Sasha Moore barked irritably into the phone. She strangled the receiver until her knuckles hurt, wishing it were Marcus's neck.

"Sasha, I am your agent or have you forgotten? I know you want to retire from modeling. No one knows that as well as I do, but I don't think your timing is right. So, I'd appreciate it if you would hear me out before you refuse," Marcus said with desperate firmness.

With a long, exaggerated sigh, Sasha rested her elbow on the arm of the couch. "Go ahead, you've got three minutes."

She listened with a deaf ear as Marcus Vaughn gave her—in elaborate detail—all the reasons why she should continue to model. He emphasized the fact that she was still young and appealing and a lot of other hoopla that Sasha didn't care to hear. Instead, she frowned in annoyance and had to fight the urge to keep from hanging up on him. She was determined to stand firm in her decision and wished Marcus would just give up, even though he was acting in her best interest. Or at least he thought so.

Since she had made the decision not to renew her modeling contract with designer Jacqueline Giamanco, her agent had called her weekly to remind her of all of the things that she was missing. Today was no exception. His voice was once again humming in her right ear like elevator music.

Dropping her forehead into her hand, Sasha closed her eyes. After seven years of traveling all over the world, living in hotels and out of suitcases, she had finally realized that there was something else out there for her and had returned home to pursue a dream.

"Hell-oo. Sasha, are you listening?" Marcus asked.

"Mmm-hmm," she murmured, only vaguely aware that Marcus was speaking. Sasha wondered if she should feel guilty for ignoring him every time he called, then shrugged her shoulders and thought better of it. For as long as she'd known him, Marcus had dominated their conversations and had a tendency to rattle on non-stop like a fifteen disk CD player. Even when she used to listen to him, he rarely allowed her an opportunity to get a word in other than an occasional *hmmm* or *oh*.

Before allowing her mind to wander off again, Sasha heard him utter the words *intimate apparels* and shook her head in disbelief. Marcus couldn't possibly think she would be interested in lingerie modeling again. She'd had a contract with a major department store several years ago and nothing had displeased her more than to appear half-naked in front of a camera. Sasha leaned against the comfort of her couch and lowered her thick black lashes. Modeling was no longer what she wanted to do with her life. *There had to be a way.*

Her eyes filled with deep longing as she gazed down at the gown lying across her lap. She stroked the fabric with the back of her hand, enjoying the waves of relaxing pleasure the feel of satin between her fingertips sent through her veins.

Smoothing out the skirt, Sasha examined a row of small gold flowers that she just finished embroidering along the hem. There were fifty-seven flowers. Judith Rencher wanted one for each week since the day her fiancé Eric had walked into her life.

She'd been designing wedding gowns since she was a child. In her spare time, her mother had worked as a seamstress. Nothing had pleased

Sasha more than to retrieve discarded scraps of fabric from the floor of her mother's sewing room and then spend hours creating dresses for her dolls. As a teenager she began designing gowns for friends and family. Today she was adding the finishing touches to a gown she had designed for her cousin, Judith.

While Marcus continued to speak in a language that was now foreign to her, Sasha cradled the phone against her shoulder and held the dress out in front of her. She was proud of her unique, hand-crafted designs. Every gown she created was draped for a custom fit and included a unique train, designed with intricate hand-embroidered thread-work made of the purest silk that Sasha ordered from a small bridal shop she had found while working in Italy. None of her gowns were ever alike, except that they were created to make a woman look and feel the way every bride should feel on her wedding day—like a princess.

Sasha's face glistened with pride. Once again she had brought her creation to life and the finished product was in her hands. Pleased with her masterpiece, she smiled. The sleeveless gown was made of ivory duchesse satin with pleated silk-satin bands at the waist. The fitted bodice was covered in Alecon lace with a low-scooped backline and an A-line skirt where a long row of gold, hand-embroidered lilies extended to the hem of the chapel train. Next week she would complement the ensemble with a floor-length veil attached to a tier trimmed in mother-of-pearl.

Marcus's voice broke into her reverie. "So what do you think?" he asked, sounding out of breath. Sasha couldn't help thinking that it probably had something to do with the long-winded conversation he had just had with her ear.

"No." The word rolled off her tongue without a single thought as to what he might have just asked her. Regardless, her answer would still have been the same.

Marcus sighed heavily. "Come on, Sasha. Don't act like you don't need the money. All they want is six months of your life. You couldn't possibly get a better contract."

Sasha looked up, suddenly aware of the despair in his voice and laid the wedding gown carefully onto the cushion next to her as if it were a newborn baby. For Marcus to sound so persistent, whatever he needed her to do had to be real important, and she owed him quite a bit for his constant support. For years he had taken care of her. The least she could do was listen.

"Six months," she repeated. Curling her legs underneath her, Sasha unconsciously twirled the phone cord around her index finger while she took a moment to think. "Where are you wanting me to travel to this time?" she inquired. Sasha couldn't believe that she was actually considering his proposal.

Marcus chuckled nervously. "You haven't heard a word I've said. You have no idea what I am talking about."

"Yes I do."

"Then I guess you heard me when I said that Deja Davis was murdered." Sasha gasped. Marcus tapped the phone with his index finger. He now had her undivided attention.

"What happened?" she asked. Sasha leaned forward, swinging her legs onto the floor and waited for Marcus to repeat himself. Her eyebrows shot up in surprise. Deja could not possibly be dead. Several years ago they had shared a hotel room while modeling for a benefit fashion show in New York. Deja Davis hadn't been just any fashion model. She had graced dozens of runways from those of Donna Karan to Ralph Lauren in cities all over the world. Sasha just recently had seen her on *Oprah* promoting her new fragrance that she had named after herself. Deja was gorgeous, charming and had possessed a laid-back personality that all of her peers admired.

"I can't believe she's dead." Sasha spoke in a soft, far-away voice.

"It is unfortunate," Marcus added in a somber voice. "The maid found her with her throat slashed. But on a lighter note, her loss is definitely your gain." He chuckled lightly, trying to brighten the mood. "Diva Designs is offering a—"

"Did you say Diva Designs?" Sasha asked hastily. Curiosity quickly replaced the pang of sadness she had felt only seconds ago.

"Yeah, I did. You really weren't listening. I should feel insulted," Marcus said with a note of sarcasm.

Sasha snorted. "Save the attitude for one of those new models of yours that are still wet behind their ears."

Diva Designs was the largest black-owned and operated dress designing corporation in the region. They sold evening gowns and a collection of elegant dresses in an array of styles to complement women of color. They held seasonal fashion shows benefiting numerous hospitals and charitable organizations. The designs were a little too sophisticated for Sasha's taste but her mother owned several. Sasha had tried landing a contract with them for years just so she could stay in the St. Louis area, but each time their fashion director commented that her looks were not mature enough for their gowns. The corner of Sasha's lips curled into a smile. *How ironic.*

"Come on, Sasha. What other contract have you had that has allowed you to work so close to home?"

"Hmmm." Sasha pursed her lips thoughtfully and settled back against the arm of the couch. She hated to admit it, but Marcus made a point that she could not argue.

"You know, I... I am really hurt that you didn't hear a word I said," Marcus interjected.

"You're a big boy. You'll get over it," Sasha said dryly.

"You're very lucky that you're my favorite model. No one else could get away with talking to me like you do," he chuckled. Marcus was used to her smart aleck responses. Sasha always had a quick comeback waiting on the tip of her tongue. No one would ever guess that she was the frightened teenager who had walked into his office several years ago.

"Except maybe your wife?" Sasha hissed back at him. "Marcus, the only reason I am your favorite is because I've made you a lot of money over the years. And if you weren't like a big brother to me, I would have changed my phone number weeks ago just so you'd quit badgering me," she teased. They had been friends long enough for him to know that her teasing was not malicious. In fact, it was an expression of friendship.

Hearing the amusement in her voice, Marcus laughed. "You always were a smart ass."

"Uh-huh, and don't you forget it." Sasha ran a hand through her hair. "So, tell me, Mr. Agent, what does Diva Designs have to do with lingerie?" To her surprise, she was suddenly interested in what Marcus had to say.

"Wow! So you actually heard part of the conversation. Well, I am impressed," he joked. If Marcus had to, he'd drive to her house and make her listen to reason. Diva Designs wanted Sasha and he was determined to get her to see that this was a lucrative opportunity for her, even if it meant knocking some sense into her head.

"Marcus, save the jokes. You know I don't like lingerie modeling."

"I know, I know, but Diva Designs is apparently interested in changing their marketing strategy after losing a substantial amount of money last year. That is why they are launching an intimate apparels division and they need you to get it off the ground. Believe me, these changes are long overdue. Selling designs to a concentrated market, and to a mature audience, might I add, is risky business. They've been limiting their earning potential for years. This new lingerie line might just put them back on the map."

Pressing her lips firmly together, Sasha knew all

too well what he meant about concentrated marketing after having the same disappointing discussion with her loan officer the day before.

Sasha had disappeared from the modeling world a few months earlier in hope of starting her own collection of wedding gowns, *Creations by Sasha.* During her career, she had saved every dime that she made from modeling—short of starving—and turned her savings over to a broker, hoping to receive the biggest return for her money. Instead, she had fallen flat on her face. She had trusted her broker's decisions, but to her devastation, she'd recently learned that he'd invested her savings in several questionable enterprises, causing her to lose a substantial amount of money. Because of that and her father's enormous medical bills and funeral expenses, Sasha had found herself unable to finance her dream. So she decided to seek outside help.

With a great deal of research, Sasha had put together what she thought was the perfect business plan. But the bank turned her down because they did not feel her marketing mix was effective enough nor did they see any immediate return on their investment. Sasha had walked away from the bank feeling defeated. Her mother had offered to help but Sasha knew that the money she offered was for her retirement and Sasha did not have any intention of touching it. Unless she continued to model, she had only one other option, and that was selling the home that her father had left her. But that would have to be a last resort.

"You better be listening."

Sasha's mouth twitched with amusement. "I'm all ears."

"Diva wants you to launch this new division."

"Why me?"

"No one makes love to the camera like you do." Marcus spoke in a low baritone voice that was so out of character for him, that Sasha found herself seized by a fit of laughter.

"Pu-leeze!" She was almost in tears.

Her amusement was infectious and Marcus found himself also laughing at his corny joke. After their laughter died, Marcus gave her the details of the new campaign.

"They have scheduled fashion shows in major cities." Before she could object, he immediately added, "One weekend per month." He then paused long enough for Sasha to disapprove. After several seconds of silence he smiled and continued. "Diva Designs is planning to kick off the campaign with a benefit fashion show in St. Louis next month and all proceeds will go to Children's Hospital. Sasha, think about what this can do for your career. This might be the perfect opportunity for you to network with others in the design industry, and obtain the connections you need in order to get your creations off the ground."

Sasha dragged her knees to her chest and rested her chin. "Hmmm. Minimal travel doesn't sound too bad."

"You would begin shooting immediately for their catalog."

Sasha's eyebrow rose in amazement. "Catalog?" Sasha snorted. "Don't tell me they've switched to discount clothing?"

Marcus chuckled. "No, but they are hoping to reach all economic levels."

Sasha's expression stilled and grew serious as her brain deliberated. Maybe she did need to reconsider, at least until she earned the money she needed, and working for Diva Designs did sound like a piece of cake. Sasha raised her hand to her mouth while she pondered the idea.

"I have negotiated a contract that will make you do cartwheels."

"Sure of ourselves, aren't we?" Sasha gave a dry laugh.

Marcus ignored her comment and cleared his throat. This was one time he knew for certain what was best for her and her future. Sasha reminded him of his younger sister and her success meant just as much to him as it did to her. "At such short notice I was able to get them to agree to pay you a very generous salary." Marcus rattled off a dollar amount that caused Sasha to gasp.

Sasha drew her lips in thoughtfully and sighed. She might as well accept the fact and not deny the inevitable any longer. She needed this job. Her entire future depended on it. The undeniable and dreadful truth was that her back was up against a cold wall and she really did not have much of a choice. What else could she possibly have to think about?

Taking a deep breath, Sasha spoke with little reluctance. "OK. I'll do it."

"That's my girl. You just made a smart decision." Marcus exhaled, relieved that he had finally overcome her resistance. "I don't know why you put me through all of that. I think my hair has turned gray."

"What hair?" she teased. "It's not like you left me with much choice."

Marcus heard the smile in her voice. "Probably because I know you could use the money. I've seen your work. Remember, my wife had the pleasure of wearing one of your gowns on our wedding day and what a vision she was. You are a very talented young lady and I would like nothing more than to see your name on a designer label."

Sasha beamed with pride, remembering the

strapless design his wife wore last summer at their private wedding. "Thanks, Marcus. You always have looked out for me. I guess I can do you this one favor." Then she added in a stern voice, "But no more." She hoped her tone left little doubt in his mind that she truly meant it this time.

"I appreciate it. But this is really for you. Now I can finally go home and spend some time with Joanne. That's if she'll let me in the house."

Sasha giggled. She had never seen two people more perfect for each other than Marcus and his second wife. They were living proof that true love was possible for some people. Sasha frowned. It just wasn't meant for her.

"Drop by my office Friday afternoon and we will go over your contract together."

Sasha thanked him again and told him to give his wife her regards. Hanging up the phone, she rose from the couch, scooped up the gown and carried it down the hall to her sewing room, where she returned it to the dress form on which it had been created.

Maybe this was just what she needed. A modeling contract right here in St. Louis. Sasha stood still for several moments while she considered her decision to return to modeling. She then strolled over to her design table where she had begun sketching a new gown. Suddenly an idea burst into her head that sent her spirits soaring.

"Thank you, God. I knew you would make a way," she whispered, smiling as the plan materialized. She quickly sat down at the table and grabbed a pen and a spiral notebook from her left drawer and began scribbling a few ideas.

If things worked out the way she planned, her designs were going to be introduced to the world by none other than Diva Designs.

Chapter Two

"Spill it, girl."

Sasha looked out into the living room where her best friend and roommate, Honey Love, sat on the couch tapping a freshly-manicured finger-nail on her knee. She had returned home late last night after spending three days in Chicago attending a cosmetology convention.

"The last time I saw you, you were crying your heart out because the bank rejected your loan and today you're wearing a grin a mile long. What gives?"

Sasha walked into the living room and struck a pose in front of the fireplace. "Marcus convinced me to accept one last contract." She smiled, her eyes bright with excitement.

Honey stared at her for a moment with her brow slanted in surprise. "For three months Marcus has tried everything short of giving you his BMW to get you back in front of the camera and each time you've turned him down flat. So why now?"

Sasha crossed her arms and shifted her weight to her other leg. She looked over at Honey, who looked every bit a cosmetologist—sculptured pink nails, long black, professionally styled hair and carefully applied make-up. Even after staggering into the house only a few hours ago, Honey somehow still managed to look as fresh as she would any other morning.

Sasha shrugged and gave a desperate laugh. "What choice do I have? If I can't borrow the money then I have to get out there and earn it."

Understanding what her friend was saying, Honey nodded. "I wish I could help but after that check I wrote to cover my down payment, I am financially strapped."

Last week, Honey had found the home of her dreams and was scheduled to close on it next month. Sasha was happy for Honey but sad at losing her as a roommate. Honey had moved in with her less than five months ago when she had made the decision not to renew the lease on her apartment. Even though Honey was moving less than ten minutes away, Sasha had gotten used to having her around.

"Thanks, but I need to work this one out on my own. My only choices were modeling or selling my home and I am not selling this house."

"Shoot. I know that's right, girlfriend." Honey sucked her teeth. "You've got to do what you have to do. You know I'm proud of you and will stand by whatever you decide."

Facing one another, Sasha gave Honey a slow, secretive smile, an unspoken message that only they understood. She did not know what she would have done without Honey all these years.

While Honey was aggressive, flashy and outgoing, Sasha's style was more passive, practical and reserved. They were like oil and vinegar but to their surprise a strong bond had developed between them.

They had met in high school when Sasha was just an ugly duckling—or at least she thought so. She was taller than any boy in her class and very self-conscious about it. Her mother had enrolled her in charm school in hope of Sasha learning how to walk with confidence and stop slouching and feeling ashamed of her height. By the end of her first year, she had learned to walk with her shoulders back but she still possessed low self-esteem. During her sophomore year, Sasha met Honey, who had skipped class and was sitting on the sink in the girls' locker room with a curling iron in her hand. When she looked up and saw Sasha enter in search of her English book, Honey insisted that she also skip class and allow her to curl her unruly hair. Sasha was too stunned by such a blunt request from the feisty little cheerleader to object. Since then, Honey, who stood at five-two, had encouraged Sasha to put her height to use. It had been Honey who boosted her confidence. Honey spent hours teaching Sasha how to tame her naturally curly hair, and how to dress and feel proud of what the good Lord had blessed her with. Slowly she transformed Sasha into a swan. Honey then decided that Sasha was going to become a model.

Honey entered Sasha's photo in a model search contest that she found on the back of a relaxer kit. Sasha won first place and was offered a one-year contract with Johnson & Johnson. After that, her career soared and Honey decided that she needed an agent. She dragged her to three other agencies before they came to Vaughn's Modeling Agency. Sasha liked Marcus immediately and with a little persuasion on Honey's part, he took Sasha under his wing and groomed her.

For the first year, she did everything from newspaper ads to television commercials. Then Sasha landed a major blue jean ad campaign and moved to New York where she also appeared in several music videos before landing a minor role on a soap opera. Sasha had numerous contracts after that, but her most memorable experience was traveling with a fashion show created by Italian designer Jacqueline Giamanco, which enabled her to travel abroad and learn in-depth about the fashion world.

Honey sighed impatiently, halting Sasha's journey down memory lane. "Are you going to tell me who you are going to be working for or do I have to call Marcus myself?"

Sasha walked over and took a seat in a recliner across from her. "Diva." Sasha smiled and watched Honey's face as she absorbed what she had just told her.

"Oh my God! As in Diva Designs?" Honey's eyes were wide and unblinking.

"As in Diva Intimate Apparels," Sasha conceded as her bright hazel eyes shone with enthusiasm.

"But I...I thought they only sold those fancy dresses that neither of us would buy even if we could afford them?"

Sasha nodded in agreement. "So did I, but apparently they are launching a lingerie line."

Honey chuckled and snorted with exaggeration.

"What are they going to sell, a $100 pair of underwear?"

Sasha shared the telephone conversation she'd

had with Marcus two days ago.

"I was so excited, I didn't get a chance to ask him if they had any murder suspects."

Honey grunted. "Deja Davis probably had some crazy jealous boyfriend like you have."

"*Had*," Sasha emphasized as she shuddered at the thought of her ex-boyfriend, Robby. Even though it had been over six months since she and Robby parted, the pain was still there as if it were only yesterday.

Honey watched Sasha's lips thin at the reminder and immediately wished she could take her words back. Sasha had been through a lot and definitely did not need to be reminded of it. Deciding to steer the conversation into another direction, Honey uncurled her leg and rubbed her palms together. "Now we have an excuse to go out and celebrate."

"Oh no, not again." Sasha groaned and gave Honey a dark look before pulling herself from the chair. She walked in the direction of her room with Honey following close behind.

"Oh come on, Sasha. Let's go out tomorrow night," Honey whined while standing in the doorway.

"I do not want to go out and celebrate. You forgot about the clown I met the last time we went out and *celebrated*." She tilted her brow and looked at Honey uncertainly before poking out her lips with an exaggerated pucker. "Besides, you know that club-

bing is not my idea of fun." Hoping that the conversation was over, Sasha opened her closet door
and scanned her clothes rack. She had promised
Marcus that she would be at his office in an hour.

"This time I am not taking no for an answer."
Honey walked into Sasha's room and took a seat on
the end of the queen size, canopy bed that was covered with a satin comforter. "We have not been out
in months. And it is time for you to get out of this
stuffy old house. Tomorrow we are going to celebrate," Honey said firmly. "You need to learn how to
relax and find time for yourself. How do you ever
expect to find another man?" Purposely avoiding
eye contact, Honey looked down at her jeans, pretending to remove a piece of lint, and missed the
dirty look Sasha gave her before pulling her shirt
over her head.

Honey's words were playful but the meaning
was not. She complained regularly that Sasha
needed a man in her life and lately Honey had been
trying to get Sasha to go with her to a new hot spot
that had just recently opened downtown. Sasha
was not the least bit interested in hanging out at
clubs or finding another man. She would much
rather spend the evening at home reading a book or
sketching a new design. She could not get Honey
to understand that she was not ready for another
relationship. Maybe she'd be ready to try again in a

couple of months, but then again, maybe she wouldn't ever let anyone get that close again. She needed more time to erase the pain that she was still feeling. Sasha didn't care that it had been months since her last date. It had taken her weeks to get over her last relationship and she was not ready to endure that pain again. Honey made it all look so simple but for Sasha it was difficult. She didn't know how to relax and go with the flow and she had never been able to date more than one man at a time. She just couldn't do it. Sasha always seemed to get caught up emotionally. She was a genuinely caring and sensitive person. She wore her heart on her sleeve and someone always seemed to knock it off and step on it. She had been hurt so many times that she had a hard time trusting men and was afraid of getting involved again. After her last disastrous relationship, Sasha had decided she was better off keeping her heart behind an iron door with the key hidden away where no one could find it.

"Honey, why do I have to keep going over this with you?" Sasha groaned." I don't want a serious relationship." Sasha stepped out of her sweat pants. She was tired of meeting men with *drama* in their lives. She'd had enough bad experiences and Robby had been the icing on the cake.

Honey wrinkled her small nose and scooted

onto the bed. "Who said anything about serious? I said you need a man," she responded sharply. "You know, someone to take you out and spend some money on you. You're my best friend and I want to see you with some happiness in your life." She crossed her legs and looked down at her hands.

"And I guess a man is the answer to my happiness?" Sasha asked with her hands on her hips.

"Bingo," Honey said with a note of defiance that Sasha immediately detected. She was not in the mood for another debate.

Sasha leaned against her dresser and blew out a long breath. Honey's idea of happiness was having a date on Friday night. Her friend had a genuine love for life and a passion for excitement that she admired, and sometimes Sasha wished that she could be more like that. Maybe if she possessed some of those qualities it might have made a difference in her life. Honey was her best friend and Sasha loved her for wanting to help her find happiness. It was the way she went about it that sometimes made her mad. Like right now.

"Girl, don't start," she warned with narrow eyes. "You're beginning to sound like my mother. I've been there and done that too many times. Aren't you tired of watching me get hurt? I know I am, and I am not ready to get burned again." She turned around and pulled out her middle drawer.

Honey looked at her friend from out of the corner of her eyes and could tell that Sasha was upset because her jaws were clamped tight. "Sasha, when are you going to start trusting men again?" Honey slid off the bed and halted Sasha's actions with a firm hand to her wrist. "Girl, look at me." Sasha sighed and rolled her eyes towards her. "Don't you even try to get an attitude," Honey taunted with a silly smirk on her face. Then her expression softened as she spoke. "Seriously, all men can't be the same."

"Whatever." Sasha disengaged Honey's hand. She knew that she was probably overreacting, but she was just sick of talking about it all the time. "Yes, they are all the same. I have not met one man that has made me think otherwise."

"Girl, they have to be out there," Honey argued. She had a serious expression on her face that took Sasha by surprise. Seriousness was a rare quality in Honey.

Sasha blew out a deep breath and sat next to Honey on the bed. "Where? Tell me, Honey, do I have 'sucker' plastered on my forehead? I must, because that's what I have been for the last three years!"

"Now you're exaggerating!" Honey fell back onto the bed and threw her arms in the air.

"No, I am not," Sasha argued, shaking her head. "All the men I have ever met were either crazy, insecure, jealous or mama's boys. Otherwise, they were sexually starved and looked to me for some kind of fulfillment or to satisfy their fantasies. Tomorrow will be no different. They'll be standing on the wall at the club waiting to pounce on their next victim, which is usually me."

"Well, think of it this way. When we go out tomorrow I'll wear something sleazy so you won't have to worry about being the center of attention," Honey teased. She sat up and lightly slapped her hand across Sasha's knee.

"That's nothing new," Sasha grunted, pressing her lips tightly together. "I am not going."

"Yes you are, Ms. Thang, so get over it." Honey's voice was firm and final as she draped her arm around Sasha's shoulders. "*I'm* running this. We are going to get our boogie on and then I am dragging your behind out to breakfast. It's going to be just like old times." Honey bounced to her feet and began doing an old dance known as the cabbage patch with a ridiculous smirk on her face. Sasha swung her foot in the air and tried to kick Honey, who on instinct stepped out of reach.

Waving her hands, Sasha tried to dismiss her apprehensions. She was nervous about trusting men again. After each disastrous encounter it took

26

her months to regain the courage to try again and then it was always the same thing, lots of false promises and disappointments. Sasha sighed and got up from the bed. There was no point in continuing the discussion. With Honey as her opponent, she was fighting a losing battle.

"Face it, Sasha, it is the price you have to pay for being a sex symbol. You think Tyra Banks doesn't have problems?"

"If I had her money, I wouldn't care." She reached into her closet and pulled out a black pleated skirt and a white blouse. "Besides, Honey, why are you always trying to hook me up? Where is your man? Or have you already dumped him?" Sasha teased as her anxiety subsided. She reached for a scarf from her top drawer and tied it around her hair to prevent getting it wet in the shower.

"Forget you, girl," Honey mumbled. She appeared irritated, but Sasha knew better.

Sasha laughed. "Whatever, girl, you know I am telling the truth."

"I can't help it if I am not the marrying kind. I enjoy dating." Honey smiled angelically. She was not far from the truth. Honey changed men like she changed hairstyles. Sasha couldn't remember the last time Honey was in a relationship that lasted longer than two weeks. She was not in any rush to settle down and usually ended her relationships before they became serious.

Sasha's laughter slowly faded as her mind wandered back to the time that she had tried that approach. Instead, she had fallen in love. She wished that it was as easy as Honey made it look, but it was not that simple. Honey had told her time and time again that she needed to stop being so serious and learn how to have fun. She was just too practical. Maybe she could blame it on the fact that she spent kindergarten through eighth grade in Catholic schools, in the constant company of nuns, away from immoral thoughts and feelings.

Sasha grabbed her undergarments and walked past Honey to her adjoining bathroom.

"I need to shower so that I can meet Marcus on time. We can talk about this later," she said before shutting the door.

Honey shook her head and spoke loud and clear so her voice would carry through the door. "No we won't because there is nothing else to talk about."

Terraine Andrews swiveled around in the big leather executive chair that once belonged to his grandfather and faced the large picture window behind him. He gazed at the magnificent view of the St. Louis Gateway Arch. Even from his pent-house suite he could not see the windows located at the top of the brilliant structure. As it shimmered in the sunlight, he remembered when he was seven and his grandfather took him down on the riverfront to see the tall monument. He had begged Pops to let him ride to the top so that he could look down upon the entire city. That was when they'd learned he was claustrophobic. He'd wheezed so badly riding in the tram that Pops thought he was having an asthma attack. Terraine chuckled just thinking about it. He had a lot of cherished memories of the times with his grandfather. As the thought echoed in his head, Terraine felt a familiar tightness develop in his jaws. If only the times with his grandfather had always been that way.

Richard Andrews had been the only parent he had ever really known. His mother had died while giving birth to his younger brother, Jay. Terraine remembered her as an affectionate woman who read stories to him at bedtime and who held him tight at night when he was afraid. He remembered her beautiful ebony face that his little hands loved to reach out and caress, and he had not forgotten her heartwarming smile. His father he remembered as being the size of the Jolly Green Giant. Terraine had once believed that if his father climbed a tree, he would be able to touch the sky. One morning while visiting a neighborhood convenience store, he was accidentally killed. David Andrews was the victim of a single stray bullet that was meant for someone else. He left behind a pregnant wife stricken with grief and a three-year-old son. Terraine's memories of his parents were so vague that he didn't know if they were actual recollections or just mental visions of stories that his grandfather had told him numerous times over the years.

Now Pops was gone. After eight-five years he was gone, leaving behind the grandsons that he raised and the multi-million dollar corporation he founded.

Terraine was now CEO of Diva Designs, independently owned and operated by Richard Andrews for over forty years. The concept of designing gowns that complemented women of color had been his grandmother Divanna's vision—a woman he unfortunately never got the opportunity to know. The gowns were exquisite, made of the finest fabric in brilliant colors, sold exclusively at upscale stores such as Sak's Fifth Avenue. Terraine had never agreed on the concept of selling clothing to a selected market and had frequently voiced his opinion to no avail to his grandfather, who did not want to blemish the memory of his wife.

Terraine removed himself from the chair and walked across the plush gray carpet to a mahogany bookshelf that covered an entire wall near the door. He stood in front of the shelves and stared at the clutter of pictures and the memories that they each represented. Most of them were of Jay and himself. There were pictures of their graduations, both high school and college, and pictures of both of them during their military careers. Terraine found this ironic, since Pops was devastated when both of his grandsons chose the army over working with him.

Jay never really had a knack for business and Pops knew that. Terraine, on the other hand, was a born businessman and was groomed at a ripe age to someday step into his father's shoes and work side-by-side with his grandfather.

Terraine had practically grown up in the fashion industry, spending numerous unwanted hours learning about the entire operation. In exchange for the financing his grandfather provided for his college education, Terraine was required to work for the business during all of his summer breaks. This involved working as a marketing assistant, which came with a lot of responsibility. Over the years, he grew tired of his grandfather controlling and manipulating his life. Pops put a lot of unnecessary pressure on him and Terraine eventually resented him.

As soon as he graduated, he joined the army. Following a five-year military career, Terraine accepted a job with a major finance corporation in

Chicago. Terraine and Pops had a turbulent relationship after that, going months at a time without speaking until Pops' health began to deteriorate.

During his infrequent visits, there was tension and Terraine could see the sadness in his grandfather's eyes, but they were both too stubborn to say or do anything about it. He loved his grandfather but Pops had never once asked him what he wanted to do with his life. Instead, he had assumed that Terraine wanted to follow in the same footsteps of the other Andrews' men. Although Diva Designs meant the world to Pops, he did not share in his grandfather's dreams. Terraine wanted to find his own career path, but he never could get his grandfather to understand that.

But even from his grave Pops had found a way. Terraine was back in St. Louis where Pops had wanted him and running the family business the way Pops had always wanted.

Terraine's mind was far away as he reached down and removed his grandfather's picture from the bottom shelf and dusted it off with the back of his hand. He looked down at Pops and saw a look of triumph etched on his face.

For the past couple of weeks, Terraine had been debating if he was going to actually run the corporation or not. He laughed. Who was he trying to fool? Surely not his grandfather. He put the picture back where he'd found it and began pacing a small path in front of the door.

There was no other choice. Terraine knew that it was his obligation as an Andrews to run the family business. Jay had followed his own dreams but would remain partially involved, leaving all of the major decisions to him. Terraine had even pondered the idea of selling the corporation after two interested buyers approached him with tempting offers, but he knew that he couldn't do that. Selling was not even a possibility. What he needed now was time. Time to think about the future that had been decided for him many years ago. But was there really anything to think about? What choices did he really have? Terraine exhaled and slumped his shoulders forward, overpowered by an invisible weight that seemed to have landed on them.

Terraine and Jay were born wealthy. Unfortunately, when their parents died, Pops became their legal guardian and he put their inheritance into trust funds that they were unable to touch until age twenty-five. Terraine believed it was a control tactic that forced him to rely on Pops until he was old enough to obtain his inheritance. Now he had more money than he could ever spend in a lifetime. Terraine could easily sell the business, kick off his shoes and enjoy, but then he would have to live with the constant guilt.

Terraine had directed a major finance company for five years but knew for certain that he had grown bored with the business. He was presently on an extended leave of absence, but even if he decided to let someone else run Diva Designs, he was certain he wouldn't be returning to Chicago.

He was ready for some major changes in his life.

Terraine pushed his hands deep into his pockets and walked back over to the window and placed his forehead on the cool glass, ignoring the congested view below of downtown St. Louis.

Diva Designs had suffered a substantial decline in sales over each of the last four quarters. Two years ago, Terraine had tried talking his grandfather into expanding into other divisions, no longer limiting their designs to evening gowns and elegant dresses. Terraine had even suggested taking the corporation public, but Pops had refused on both counts. So, after acquiring the corporation three months earlier, Terraine had decided it was time to change the marketing strategy in order to reposition the corporation. Research was conducted and Terraine laid the groundwork for a new division, intimate apparels, quality but affordable clothing he hoped to sell in department stores such as Dillard's and also through a mail order catalog. Other than a few minor setbacks, such as Deja's death, everything seemed to be going as planned. If only he could say the same about his personal life.

Terraine ran his hand across his chin. On his way home last night, he had attended a happy hour hosted by one of Diva's largest buyers, only to find out that he was the only one there unaccompanied. The incident made him aware of how lonely he really was. He had not been in a committed relationship since Natalia. He pressed his lips tightly together at the memory of what she had done to him. Terraine cleared his throat and returned the memory to the back of his mind, where it had been buried for almost a decade. He had learned his lesson well.

Terraine moved away from the window and sat back in his chair, resting his elbow on the mahogany desk. For years he had steered clear of long-term relationships. He had been considered a playboy, dating several women at any given time with no desire for commitments.

Now he was older and definitely not getting any younger. At thirty-three, he was ready to start a family of his own. He wanted a big family. Something he never had. He just needed to find the right girl first.

Meeting women had never been a problem. It was meeting the right kind of woman. Recently, every woman that had seemed a possibility turned out to be a gold digger—more interested in what he had than what he was about.

Terraine needed a special kind of woman in his life. A woman that was willing to devote one hundred percent to a relationship and capable of being his friend as well as his lover. Sure, he appreciated beautiful women, but beauty was only an external attraction. He had learned that all those summers while working with gorgeous models that threw themselves at him whenever they deemed it necessary. He wanted more than a passing fancy. He was looking for a woman that was also beautiful on the inside. Terraine longed for compassion, commitment and honesty. Honesty was so important to him. He had to be able to trust her. What he was missing in his life was love. A woman who'd loved him heart and soul, him and only him.

All he had to do now was find her. He was certain that he would recognize the right woman the moment he laid eyes on her.

Terraine was pulled out of his trance by the sound of someone knocking on his office door.

"Come in." He watched as his marketing director, Carl Matthews, entered his office and strolled over to his desk. Dressed impeccably in a dark navy blue suit with a matching tie and shirt accented with gold cuff links and tiepin, Carl looked every bit the executive. He had only been with Diva

Designs for two months, having previously worked for a large cosmetic company that eventually went bankrupt. He had come highly recommended by a business associate.

"Terraine, here is the file you requested on Deja Davis and her replacement, Ms. Moore. She is not a big name, has done more work in Europe than she has in the States but she has the sophisticated appeal that we are looking for." Carl handed him two manila folders. Terraine took the files and opened Deja's, leafing through it briefly before directing his attention back to Carl.

"Thanks. I'll have Geri return these to you in the morning," he said, referring to his executive assistant.

Carl took it as his cue to leave. "Have a good night, boss." He walked back across the room and exited the office.

Terraine leaned back in his chair and opened the other file and unhurriedly studied the photo of the beautiful young woman, feature by feature.

Her facial bones were delicately carved with infinite care and framed by a mass of wavy, honey-colored hair that accentuated a flawless complexion of caramel and illusive copper.

She had naturally red pouting lips. Her amusing grin made Terraine wonder what had created the moment of delight. Her extraordinary hazel eyes were large and magnetic and perfectly positioned around a small charming nose.

Terraine swallowed the lump that formed in his throat as he suddenly felt magnetically drawn to the woman in the photo. She lay leisurely across a beige, double arm chaise wearing a silk charmeuse slip. The material stopped at mid-thigh, revealing long slender legs. And it floated along her curves and full high-perched breasts, exposing ample cleavage. Terraine found the photo dripping with sensuality.

Terraine's brown eyes sparkled with anticipation as he gazed at her face once more before shutting the folder and tossing it aside. He propped his feet on the corner of his desk and clasped his hands behind his head, chuckling lightly to himself.

Terraine could not believe finding her had been so easy.

Chapter Three

Sasha opened the hall closet and reached up high on the shelf, searching for the small beaded handbag that her mother bought her while vacationing in Jamaica the previous summer. Before shutting the door, Sasha stopped to look at her reflection in the full-length mirror and raised a hand to her face. Without the expertise of a make-up artist or her contact lenses, no one could identify her as a fashion model. On a daily basis, she wore only a light brush of mascara and a slight hint of natural color lipstick to accent her already ruby lips. When she was not working, instead of wearing contacts, she wore glasses with thin-rimmed designer frames.

Smoothing down the front of her skirt, Sasha

wondered if her outfit was much too dressy, then shrugged. She would not be caught dead in any of the attention-getting outfits that Honey had tried to get her to wear tonight. Instead, her style of clothing was much more practical and stylish. She was dressed in a lilac silk crepe de chine suit and a long cutaway jacket with a portrait collar. The skirt was also long and slim with high splits on both sides, exposing her shapely legs to the middle of her thigh. On her feet she wore white thong sandals with two-inch heels, exposing toenails painted a pretty shade of purple.

Sasha walked into the living room and laid her handbag across the back of a pastel blue recliner before flopping onto her comfortable new floral couch. She smiled, feeling a sense of satisfaction as she looked around the room.

Sasha loved her home and knew there was no way she was giving it up. It had been her father's until he had died of lung cancer four years ago. Sasha had never been close to him. Her parents divorced when she was twelve and she rarely saw him after that, but when she found out he was dying, she tried to make an honest effort, beginning with visits on holidays and weekends. Towards the end she had cleared her schedule in order to care for him daily. He lived long enough for her to realize that he had always loved her, even if she hadn't seen him much as a child. That knowledge was enough to comfort her.

Inheriting the three-bedroom house had come as a surprise, but Sasha assumed it was a way for him to express his love. Since her father's death, she had removed the drab colors of black and gold and replaced them with splashes of pastels. Her ranch-style home had beautiful, gleaming hardwood floors with numerous colorful throw rugs to contrast with walls painted in ceramic beige. In the living room, two plants hung in a bay window that looked out onto a large front porch. The room was L-shaped with the couch and loveseat comfortably arranged in front of a fireplace with a decorative oak mantel that held several pieces of memorabilia.

Sasha kicked off her sandals and stretched out on the couch while she waited for Honey.

As eccentric as her friend was, it was hard for anyone to believe that Honey was an entrepreneur. For two years she had owned and operated an upscale hair salon. Love Your Hair was a childhood dream come true. Honey usually closed the shop late on the weekends and had carried her clothes with her to save time. As soon as she could manage to hustle their last client out the door, she would swing by to pick her up. Sasha sighed. She was not at all looking forward to hanging out with Honey at a hip-hop club or a "meat market," as she so fre-

41

quently referred to it, but there was no arguing with Honey once she had her mind set. Hopefully, she would be able to cut the evening short.

The telephone nudged her from her thoughts. Sasha climbed off the couch and dashed into the kitchen, hoping Honey was calling to cancel their evening.

"Hello, Sasha."

Her heart dropped like a stone to the bottom of her feet. *Oh no! It couldn't be.* "Robby. How are you?"

"Much better now that I've heard your voice," he said in a velvety tone that she once found sexy. Now the sound made the brown fuzz on the back of her neck stand up.

Sasha snorted.

He chuckled. "I guess I deserved that, but I would have thought after six months my sins would've been forgiven."

There was a short silence, then a deep sigh. "Robby... what do you want?"

"I wanted to let you know I was released last week."

Sasha's face dropped. "But I thought—"

"Yeah, well... " Robby stopped to chuckle again, causing an eerie feeling to crawl up Sasha's arm.

"I... " She struggled to clear her throat. "I'm glad to know that you are better."

"Receiving your cards and knowing that you cared about me made my speedy recovery possible."

"Oh." Sasha stopped, suddenly feeling the need to pop herself in the head. How could she have been so careless? *But he had looked so alone and so fragile that I couldn't help feeling sorry for him.* Big mistake. "Writing you was part of my therapy. I needed you to know that I understand now that you weren't responsible for your own action and that I have managed to get past the incident." Sasha felt flushed. She reached up to touch her nose, making sure it had not just grown twelve inches as a result of the super-duper lie she had just told. But she couldn't possibly let Robby know that he still affected her life.

"I want to apologize again for what I did to you. It was a stupid mistake. I never meant to hurt you."

Sasha closed her eyes, briefly reliving the pain of that final scene. "Thank you. I appreciate that." Though it had been over six months since that terrifying evening, she regularly fought the thoughts that kept trying to filter back.

"Now that the past is forgiven, would it be possible to see you? How about dinner tomorrow night?"

Sasha wanted to scream, "*Are you crazy?*" Instead, she bit down on her lip, forcing herself to remain calm. "No. I don't think that would be a good idea." Months ago, she had finally found peace and had allowed herself to relax, but only because she had thought that Robby was gone and could no longer hurt her. Sasha rubbed her fingers across her forehead. Could her relief have really been that short-lived?

"I think it's a great idea. We have a lot to talk about."

"We do?" Her mouth suddenly felt like sandpaper.

"Yes, I've missed you. Dinner would be good for both of us and it will give us a chance to talk about our future. We do still have a spring wedding to plan."

Sasha felt the temperature rise within her. "Excuse me? Who said anything about us getting back together? You are out of your mind." *Oops.* Wrong choice of words.

A chilled, black silence engulfed them before he spoke again. "Sasha, I said I was sorry." He then exploded with a peal of laughter that sent shivers down her spine. "Did you really think that I was going to let you go that easily? I've had the rare opportunity of possessing something of great value and I will never give that up. You are mine and you always will be. What can I say but that I still love you," he said in a low but very effective voice.

"I wish you wouldn't talk like that." Sasha paused for a moment, contemplating her next move. "Have you been taking your medication?"

"Of course I have," he snapped. Sasha was certain that she had struck a nerve. At this very moment his head was probably spinning around like that of the little girl in *The Exorcist*.

"Robby, I... I am glad to hear that you are doing well. Lord knows that I am. But you need to realize that I have gone on with my life. You and me... we are a closed chapter." Sasha sighed and tried to remain sympathetic while trying to reason with a lunatic. She kept telling herself it wasn't his fault. *Not really*.

"Are you seeing someone else?" he asked in a low voice.

"Well... no," she stuttered, unsure how to answer him except with the truth.

"Good, then I don't see what the problem is. My parents are looking forward to seeing you soon." Sasha could hear the joy in his voice as Robby once again wandered off to that imaginary world in the back of his sick mind. Sasha didn't know what else to say. He just didn't seem to be listening.

"Where are you?" Sasha asked. She walked over to the window and glanced uneasily out into her backyard.

"Close. Very close."

Sasha swallowed. She moved away from the window, suddenly feeling as if she were being watched. Silence then hung heavy between them and just as she prepared to say good-bye, he spoke again.

"Congratulations on your new contract."

"How... how do you know that?" She had just signed her contract with Diva Designs less than forty-eight hours ago. It wasn't even public knowledge yet. "Are you following me again?" She ground the words out between her teeth, trying to hide her anger.

He chuckled with a chilling edge. "Don't ever underestimate me, Sasha. I told you no one will ever outshine you. You are a precious jewel and it is my mission in life to protect and serve you. I'll give you some time to get used to the fact that I am back. Talk to you soon." Sasha heard the dial tone before she could release six months of bottled up frustration from the pit of her stomach.

Leaning against the wall, Sasha swallowed hard, remembering all the weeks she had spent in session with her therapist. As she shuddered, her mind was inwardly overtaken by another mound of painful memories. *Stop it.* She closed her eyes and took several long deep breaths. *Relax, girl. This is supposed to be your moment.* She was not going to let him ruin it for her. Robert Adams III would never get the opportunity to hurt her again.

Sasha heard a horn blow outside. She took one final deep breath and returned to the living room, slipped her shoes back on, and walked towards the door with her chin lifted high. Going out didn't seem quite so bad after all because after that phone call she could definitely use a drink.

Frowning, Terraine glanced at his watch and saw that it was almost ten. He hoped that his brother would be arriving soon. Terraine hated nightclubs, and Jay was now an hour late.

Jay, a successful private investigator, was flying back into St. Louis tonight after working on a case that led him to Chicago. He had called Terraine at the office during the afternoon and had asked him to meet him at Club Rendezvous.

Standing at the end of the bar, Terraine waited another fifteen minutes before finishing his drink. He then tossed onto the bar a more than generous tip and started towards the door, but what he saw made him stop dead in his tracks. Feeling as if he had run full steam into a brick wall, the shock of the impact left him breathless. He had to be dreaming since he had not been able to get her face out of his mind after seeing her photo. Even though she wore glasses, they could not hide her large, almond-shaped hazel eyes. Terraine took a deep breath. This was not a dream. She was real and so close he could have reached out and touched her. Instead, he stood back and watched the newest Diva walk into his life.

"I can't believe I let you talk me into this," Sasha said as she looked around the room. Club Rendezvous was packed with people enjoying the sounds of the latest rhythm and blues hits. She and Honey were standing in a corner not too far from the dance floor.

"Well, you did, so get over it," Honey said with her lips pursed in an exaggerated pucker. "Besides, if you listened to me more often you would have changed our phone number months ago and Robby would not have been able to call you this evening," Honey complained, referring to the conversation they'd had on the drive over.

Sasha suddenly regretted she had even mentioned the call to Honey. She looked over at her friend and held up an open palm, halting any further discussion. "Hold up. I didn't let you drag me out tonight so that we could talk about Robby. I am not going to allow him to put a damper on my evening and neither should you." Trying to appear uncon-cerned, Sasha allowed her eyes to travel around the room and smiled. "So this is Club Rendezvous."

For weeks she had heard people talking about how great this place was, and Sasha had to admit she couldn't help bouncing her head to the music. The club was very upscale with a lively decor. No jeans; everyone was wearing either dresses or slacks. She even saw a few patrons dressed in suits. There were two bars, one located at either end of the room, while the spacious dance floor was surrounded by numerous small, intimate tables and chairs. There wasn't an available seat in the house.

"I have to admit, this is pretty nice." Sasha smiled in approval while she popped her fingers to the sounds of Sisquo.

"Girl, I told you we deserved this. I know I do," Honey said, moving her hips to the beat of the music. Sasha looked over and smiled at her friend who looked great in a melon-colored spandex dress with a seductive, crisscross back and a low V-neck. On her feet were five-inch platform sandals that Honey said made her feel tall. Sasha's feet hurt just looking at them.

When the song ended, the deejay announced that the next one was just for the ladies and to Honey's delight, he played the electric slide. Sasha looked over at Honey and amusement flickered as their eyes met. Honey laced her arm through Sasha's and together they bounced to the dance floor—to the front of the line.

"Let's show them how it's done," Honey shouted over the music. She was dancing with a little added flavor. Sasha joined in with a few extra dips and turns. They knew they were drawing attention to themselves, but they were having too much fun to really care.

"Go Sasha, go Sasha, it's your birthday, it's your birthday!" Honey chanted as they danced simultaneously. Several others joined in. Sasha laughed to hide her embarrassment. Honey really had everyone thinking it was her birthday. She had managed once again to be the life of the party. By the end of three versions of the electric slide and Sasha's favorite, the macarena, they had both worked up a sweat.

"Girl, that was fun," Honey panted as they walked off the dance floor.

"I need to cool off a minute," Sasha managed to say between breaths. She leaned against Honey trying to gather her strength. "You know I'm not used to this. I must be getting old."

As they returned to their spot in the corner, a tall, ebony gentleman walked over and asked Honey to dance.

"See you later," Honey yelled over her shoulder as he took her hand and escorted her back onto the dance floor. Sasha watched them move to a new rap beat. A slender man tapped her lightly on the shoulder and asked her to dance, but she politely declined. She was not into rap music. She preferred R&B groups like Dru Hill and Boys to Men.

Sasha scanned the area looking for a waitress before deciding service would be a lot faster if she went to the bar herself. She needed a drink. There were so many people, she had to weave through the crowd. Several other men tried getting her undivided attention with no success before she made it to the bar. Luckily, a man was getting up from his seat as she arrived and Sasha eagerly climbed onto the leather barstool.

As she signaled, trying to get the bartender's attention, she caught sight of a man sitting at the end of the bar watching her. Sasha tried not to make it apparent that she had noticed, but his dark eyes grabbed her. From what she could see under the dim lights, he was gorgeous with skin that imitated the color of a Hershey's chocolate bar. He offered her a sudden, arresting smile that she found impossible not to return before tearing her eyes away, pretending to look for Honey, who was still on the dance floor. Sasha was so shaken by his penetrating eyes that ordering a drink completely

51

slipped her mind. Instead, she leaned back on the stool and thought about his clean-shaven head and the neatly trimmed goatee that exuded masculinity. Sasha frowned. A guy that good-looking spelled t-r-o-u-b-l-e, and that was the last thing she needed in her life.

"You mind if I join you?" As soon as she heard the husky baritone voice, she knew it was him even before she looked up at the towering figure standing over her. He had to be at least six-two with captivating raisin-brown eyes that left Sasha speechless. All she could manage to do was nod her head as he took a seat on the surprisingly available stool next to her.

"My name is Terraine Andrews." He extended his hand.

"Hi, I'm... Sasha Moore." She couldn't believe she'd almost choked on her words. *You are not interested, so pull yourself together.* She returned his smile and accepted the hand that was offered.

He was good-looking with a complexion that was dark, rich and smooth, just the way she liked her coffee in the morning. Sasha noticed how his expensive charcoal gray suit emphasized broad shoulders that would do justice to a linebacker, and his slacks could not disguise powerful thighs that made his body a work of art.

"A pleasure to meet you." With her hand still in

his, Terraine slowly brought it to his mouth. As his lips touched her skin, Sasha felt her heart leap and her body begin to tremble. She silently prayed that he hadn't noticed. Fortunately for her, it was at that moment the bartender came to take their drink orders, allowing her an excuse to withdraw her hand from his firm grasp. She ordered Malibu Rum with pineapple juice and listened as Terraine ordered a shot of Hennessey in a glass. Sasha bit her lip. It was obvious which one of them had hair on their chest.

"I saw you and your friend out there dancing. You looked great," he said with a wide smile that softened his square jaws. Terraine had watched her as she walked onto the dance floor and had been mesmerized by her moves as she swayed her hips with a little extra oomph, while still managing to look as graceful as a swan.

"Thanks, we were just having fun. Something I have not done in a while." *Oh my God, he has dimples*. Sasha tried desperately to resist his smile but she could not ignore the butterflies in her stomach. She was certain that he was just as intrigued with her because he had not taken his eyes off her since they'd made acquaintance.

"Please forgive me for being forward, but you are the most beautiful woman I've seen all night."

Sasha knew this was the oldest pickup line in

the book, but there was something about the note of sincerity she heard in his tone that made what he said sound genuine.

Their eyes connected again. And this time aroused something in her that she thought had died years ago. She tried to restrain herself from showing him how good he was making her feel but she couldn't stop herself from blushing. Sasha was thankful for the bartender once again as he returned with their drinks.

While Sasha took a sip of the tropical rum concoction, Terraine studied her closely, marveling at the loveliness of her delicate structure. Her long brown hair had bronze highlights that shimmered in the light, complementing her lovely face and mesmerizing bedroom eyes. He was surprised to find himself longing to reach up and push away a wisp of hair that fell over her forehead and to touch her to see if her skin was as smooth and soft as it appeared.

Feeling his eyes on her face, Sasha met his hungry look and was amazed by the tenderness in his expression. She quickly lowered her lashes again. Mercifully the dim lighting hid the extent of her embarrassment.

Terraine lowered his eyes to her round breasts and narrow waist, then descended even further to her slender yet shapely long legs that were visible through the splits in her skirt. Her curvaceous body caused his blood pressure to rise. He liked a woman that took care of herself and she obviously did.

Sasha could track his ravenous appraisal by the trail of heat left on her body. Terraine looked at her with such intensity, she knew he had to be able to see her soul. *Why does he have to look so good?* Sasha felt like a schoolgirl again. How long had it been since a man had made her feel this way?

"So, Terraine, what do you think of this place?" she said, pretending not to be affected by his attention. She crossed her legs and placed her hands in her lap to steady them.

"It has gotten a lot better since I saw you walk through that door." He leaned forward with a mischievous grin. "Actually, with these unbeatable drink specials and the low cover charge, I think this club has a great chance of being a success."

Sasha ran her fingers through her hair. "You speak as if you know a lot about nightclubs."

"Let's just say I've worked at a few in my day." Terraine paused long enough to clear his throat. "I didn't even know this place existed. My brother talked me into meeting him here tonight, but he has obviously been detained. What brings you out tonight?"

Her eyebrows drew together in a frown. "My

girlfriend dragged me out. We're celebrating."

"What's the occasion?"

"I am a fashion model and have just landed a major contract with Diva Designs," she said, not able to restrain her enthusiasm. "Have you heard of them?"

"Sure." Terraine hesitated. This was his opportunity to come clean and tell her who he was. "Don't they sell those gorgeous evening gowns?" *So much for honesty.*

Sasha wrinkled her face. "Don't tell anyone I said this but... " She lowered her voice to almost a whisper as if afraid someone might overhear what she was about to say, then leaned closer. "I think their gowns are old-fashioned and extremely over-priced. I could create a better design." She shrugged her shoulders and tossed her hands in the air. "But what do I care? I am being paid to model lingerie."

Terraine swallowed the lump that formed in his throat. *And what a vision you will be.* He thought about what she said and couldn't help wondering how many other women felt the same way. Carl had made the same comment two weeks ago and they were scheduled to meet with one of the designers on Tuesday to discuss possible changes with the gowns for next season.

"So, are you a designer?"

"Not yet. I hope to be. I designed the suit that I am wearing tonight and occasionally make outfits for some of my closest friends, but what I really want to do is start my own bridal collection." Sasha was amazed at how comfortable she was feeling sharing her dreams with him.

Terraine's eyes traveled over her again and he had to admit he was impressed with what she was wearing, but was equally impressed with the numerous other attributes the good Lord had generously blessed her with. "So, what is stopping you?"

"Money," Sasha sighed. "But not for long."

Terraine admired her determination. "That's the spirit. Let's toast to your success." They lifted their glasses and lightly touched one against the other before they bringing them to their lips.

Terraine lowered his glass to the table. "Don't tell me there isn't someone you'd rather be spending this evening with." He already knew that she was not married but a selfish part of him wanted to find out if she had someone special in her life.

"Actually there is, a good romance novel." Sasha laughed lightly. She was pleased that he was fishing for information about her personal life. *Did I just see a flash of relief cross his face?*

"A romantic at heart, I presume?" he asked.

Sasha chuckled lightly and raised her right hand as if she were on a witness stand. "Guilty as charged."

Terraine leaned forward and in a low voice asked, "So I can safely assume that you are single?"

"Yes, you can." *Why am I eagerly providing him this information?* "If it hadn't been for Honey, I would be at home reading." Sasha stumbled over her words, affected by the sound of his sultry voice.

"Good." Terraine's eyes twinkled as he smiled with satisfaction. "I'll need to thank... what was her name... Honey for bringing you out tonight and allowing me the opportunity to meet you." He gave her a long hungry stare and raised his glass. "I think we need to toast to new beginnings," he said in a sexy whisper that suddenly reminded her of Robby.

Sasha's cheeks burned as she tore her eyes away. *Oh no, not another one.* She wasn't going to even try to fool herself into believing that she wasn't the least bit attracted to this man. Yet, she had been so entranced by his good looks and his charming personality that she had allowed her vulnerable side to surface and now she wasn't sure if she liked the confident grin that he was wearing.

Sasha raised her glass and glared directly into his eyes with her left eyebrow cocked. "My being single is by choice."

"Uh, huh," he nodded with amusement flickering

in his eyes and also evident in his voice.

"And I prefer to stay that way." Sasha's voice shook more than she liked, especially since her flustered reactions seemed to amuse him.

"We'll see." His smile was presumptuous as he ran a hand across his chin.

She returned her glass to her lips and took a long gulp before looking up from her drink just in time to watch him undress her with his eyes. *Another pervert.*

"Are you always this confident with strangers, Mr. Andrews?" Sasha asked, trying to match his boldness. She did not like how her body was reacting. Flirting was obviously as natural to him as breathing. Unfortunately, as much as she wanted to be annoyed by his presumptuous behavior, a pleasant feeling flowed through her body. His disturbing good looks bothered her more than she cared to admit.

"Only with beautiful women like yourself." A stray lock of hair fell onto her forehead again and Terraine could no longer resist the urge to touch her. He reached over and pushed it out of the way, then affectionately caressed her cheeks, knocking Sasha completely off balance with his sudden gesture. Slowly, as his hand descended, he allowed his fingertips to caress her neck, sending a surge of electricity through her body more powerful than she'd ever experienced. Sasha cleared her throat before lifting her glass. She tried to hide behind her drink only to find him watching her with an expression that was simple to decipher. In one long gulp she drained her glass.

"Would you excuse me, please?" Sasha said as a warning light went off in her head. She pushed herself to a standing position and gave him a weak smile before turning around quickly—almost tripping. She was trying to get out of his view because she knew he was watching her. *Where was Honey?* She looked to her left and found her sitting at a table near the back with the same guy she had danced with earlier. "Sorry for being rude," she said to the man with a sheepish smile, "but I need to borrow my friend for a moment." She grabbed Honey by the arm and practically dragged her to the ladies' room.

"You mean to tell me you left him out there all alone?" Honey asked after Sasha gave her the *Reader's Digest* version of what had just transpired. Honey was standing in front of the sink looking at herself in the mirror. "If he is as fine as you say he is, then you better get back out there before someone else pushes up on him." She removed her brush from her purse and Sasha watched as she fixed her hair. Tonight Honey wore a shoulder length ponytail with bangs that made her look younger than her twenty-six years.

Sasha climbed onto the vanity so that Honey had no choice but to look at her while she spoke. "You wouldn't believe how aggressive he is! I probably looked like a complete idiot out there falling all over myself," Sasha said with a note of irritation in her voice.

Honey stopped brushing her hair and pointed the brush at Sasha as if it were a paddle. "Girl, you are trippin'. You needed some positive aggression in your life. You obviously like the attention; otherwise you would not be acting like this. So, why don't you just relax and enjoy the evening? He can't do any more than you allow him to do. Besides, nobody said you have to ever see him again. Just don't give him your phone number." Honey shook her head disapprovingly. Sasha jumped down from the sink and turned on the faucet. She removed her glasses and put them in her pocket before splashing cold water on her face. Honey had to bite her lower lip to keep from laughing. She reached over to her left, tearing off a paper towel and handing it to Sasha.

"Honey, Robby has turned me into a nervous wreck. Terraine is too damn gorgeous, sexier than

Robby and you know I don't trust that kind anymore." She was leaning on the wall trying to pull
herself together. Just thinking about that sexy goatee that captured his tantalizing smile caused her
heart to do somersaults.

"The problem is that you don't trust yourself
around that kind of man. What's wrong, he got your
juices flowing?" Sasha opened her mouth to say
something but the protest died in her throat. Honey
tilted her head and gave her a knowing smile.
"From the way you described him, he sounds like a
chocolate bar to me. Mmmm. And you know how I
like my Mr. Goodbar." Honey puckered her lips as
she reapplied her dark brown lipstick.

"If I had known I was going to spend the evening
sitting with a man that would have me wet between
my legs, I would have stayed at home." She
tossed her hands in the air. Honey looked at Sasha
with her eyebrows arched high and a smirk on her
face.

"Good, I am glad to know that someone has that
kind of effect on you. I was beginning to wonder."
Honey chuckled as she put her brush and lipstick
back in her purse.

"Forget you, girl. You are supposed to be on my
side." Sasha crossed her arms against her chest.
"Seriously. It is the same thing starting all over
again," she whined. Sasha pulled her glasses out

of her pocket and put them back on her face.

"Helloooo, who's the adult here?" Honey said as she pretended to tap the top of Sasha's head. "When are you going to learn that you control your own destiny? What if this man is different?"

"He won't be."   Sasha pressed her lips tightly together and sighed.

"Then...," Honey's voiced trailed off as if she were trying to find the right words, "if you already know that he won't be any different, then what are you afraid of?"   Sasha was silent as their eyes locked.

Sasha was scared. No doubt about it. Plain and simple. She'd given her heart to such a man before and he'd given it back to her in broken pieces. Yes, she had to admit that she was lonely, but it didn't change the fact that she was scared. Lonely and scared, a dangerous combination. Could it be that she was angry because she was enjoying herself for the first time in almost six months? Or was it because she found him attractive and was irritated because her body was responding to him? How was it possible that a total stranger was capable of melting her defenses? *This is ridiculous.*

"Sasha, listen to me," Honey ordered in a stern voice. She turned around and faced her. "You learned how to overcome your shyness in front of the camera, now I think it is about time you conquer your fears with men." Honey walked over to the door and opened it. "Now do me a favor. Get your butt out there and just have a good time." Sasha hated it when Honey was right. She took a deep breath and squared her shoulders before walking out of the room. Sasha then laughed at herself. She was just being silly.

After Sasha left, Honey moved away from the door and leaned back against the cold wall. While allowing her chest to rise and fall heavily, she closed her eyes and took a moment to shake the uneasiness she was suddenly feeling.

When are you going to start practicing what you preach?

Her eyelids flew open and Honey stared straight ahead, her mind reeling behind the impact of the words. How many times had she asked herself that same question? Would she ever have an answer? The restroom door swung opened, and a woman entered, halting any further deliberation. Honey quickly pulled herself together and took one final look in the mirror.

"It's easier said than done," she murmured, regretfully. Then she exited the room.

He liked her.

Terraine sipped his drink, anticipating Sasha's return. He had finally thought of a word to describe her. Natural. There wasn't anything fake about the way she looked. He was pleased to be in the company of a beautiful woman who didn't need the aid of eighteen inches of weave glued to her scalp, or several layers of makeup to be beautiful. Sasha was naturally attractive. Her photo had not prepared him for what he had seen tonight. Even hidden behind glasses he could still see the gentleness in her hazel eyes. And her red lips. They were shaped like a valentine. He could not get them out of his mind. They were full and begging to be kissed. He couldn't help watching her mouth as she spoke and imaging how sweet it would taste. Terraine shifted in his seat. If he had his way, he'd be finding out before the evening was over.

But first he needed to tell her the truth. He couldn't understand why he had chosen not to tell her who he was. He searched for words but came up shamefully empty. Instead, a little voice inside of his head taunted him and told him that now was not the time.

"Sorry I took so long," Sasha said as she slid back onto the stool and rested her elbow on the bar.

"I would have waited all night for you to return." Terraine shot her a crooked grin that sent her pulse racing again.

The deejay decided to slow it down and was now playing one of Terraine's favorite songs, "Spend My Life with You," by Eric Benet.

"May I have this dance?" Shivers of anticipation rippled through him at the prospect of holding her in his arms. He stood up and held out his hand. When she placed her hand in his firm grip, her eyes caught and held his, causing his heart to quicken. Terraine found it strange that he'd never before had this great a sensation with any other woman. The expression in her soft eyes told him that she felt it too. Terraine led her onto the dance floor and placed one arm around her waist and the other across her back and pulled her near. She smelled of exotic fruits. Only a few inches shorter than he, she felt so right in his arms. He wondered how it would feel holding her like this every night. He pulled her even closer against him.

Sasha shifted her hands, placing them around his neck, and looked up at him seductively with her lips slightly parted. Terraine could feel the heat in her hazel eyes. *God, she was a vision!* She moved her hips with him, matching his sway to and fro. As their eyes locked, his body began to respond to the flame that Sasha ignited. Terraine could not help wondering if she moved just as well in bed. The thought of being between her thighs caused his manhood to throb. He hoped it wasn't obvious, but he was on fire. "You feel wonderful," he whispered in her ear.

Not at good as you are making me feel, Sasha thought, resting her head on his chest. The tantalizing smell of his cologne drifted to her nose.

They were glued to each other as they continued to move slowly together, both of them enjoying the way the other felt. Several more slow songs played and they continued to sway their hips in sync with one another. He did not want this moment to end.

Sooner than Terraine wanted, the music changed to a faster tempo. Sasha slowly removed her arms from around his neck and began to bounce to the beat of the music, smiling—almost laughing. He couldn't keep up with her. She was a magnificent dancer. She executed a twirl and broke into a dance move he'd never seen before. Even dancing fast, she teased him. He especially loved the way she looked at him from beneath thick black lashes. *Lord help me!* He dropped his eyes to her legs that were nicely toned and would have liked nothing more than to have them wrapped around his neck.

Stop it. It was torture watching her move. After two more songs, he had reached a boiling point and could not take any more of her abuse.

67

"I give up," he said. Sasha did not realize the effect she had on him. "You are good," he complimented. Terraine placed a protective hand on the small of her back and guided her off the dance floor to an empty table he spotted in the corner.

"Let me buy you another drink. I'll be right back," Terraine said before strolling to the bar.

This was not supposed to be happening. Sasha's brain began racing as she watched him stroll away. But how could she ignore someone that looked that good when the chemistry was so strong between them? Sasha was grateful for a few minutes without him distracting her. It allowed her a chance to pull herself together.

With her head slightly tilted and resting in the palm of her hand, Sasha watched as his powerful body moved with physical confidence and sheer strength across the room. She hadn't felt this alive in years and couldn't believe how comfortable he made her feel. It was also frightening. Part of her wanted to scream and tell him to go away and leave her alone. She didn't want to relax and fall under his spell when she so desperately needed to stay in control. But she couldn't. He was just too darn sexy with an appetizing smile that caused her defenses to melt away.

"You dance as if you've had a lot of practice," Terraine commented when he returned with their drinks. He placed one in front of her.

Sasha took a long sip and nodded her head. "As a child, my mother enrolled me in dance lessons; ballet, gymnastics, tap, jazz, you name it, I took it. I was an only child and she wanted me to have an opportunity to experience things in life that she never had." Sasha leaned back and revealed to him details of her childhood and the close relationship she had with her mother. Sasha still couldn't believe how comfortable she felt talking to him about her personal life. Never before had she spoken so freely with anyone.

"Sounds like you had a wonderful childhood."

Sasha nodded, even though for years she had longed for a brother or a sister, someone to share things with, which was probably why she loved Honey like a sister. Her mother had had two miscarriages after she was born and emotionally could never handle trying again.

"I was fortunate to have a brother."

During the next half-hour, Sasha listened as Terraine talked about his life. He put all his cards on the table except for a key piece of information—who he really was. Her heart went out to him when he told her about his parents' tragic deaths. She felt his yearning to have a family of his own. His sooth-ing voice lulled her and the longer she listened to Terraine talk freely about his life, the stronger her attraction for him grew.

"How does a pretty lady like yourself spend her spare time?" He leaned forward, showing his daz-zling white teeth.

Nervously, Sasha moistened her dry lips before speaking. "Sketching designs."

Terraine found her gesture seductive and had to restrain himself reaching across the table and retracing her lips with his finger. Instead, he cleared his throat, ignoring the rise in temperature in his loins. "What made you decide to become a design-er? Don't you like modeling?"

Sasha smiled over at him. "I've had an amazing career. I've had the opportunity to do a lot of things that some models may never get to do, but when it is all over and done with I want something to show for it. It's like being a child actor, it only lasts as long as you are a child. Designing is a passion of mine. I am happier sitting at home in front of my sewing machine than I am strutting down a runway. There is no comparison."

Terraine stared intensely at her as he heard the excitement in her voice. She had a radiant smile that lit up her face when she spoke. She was intel-ligent with an independent spirit and he was impressed that she was already planning for her future. Terraine leaned back and envisioned her sitting in front of his fireplace, humming merrily while stitching a rip in his pants. He visualized a step further and saw himself sitting on a couch across from her watching television while a little girl with large hazel eyes sat across his lap. Terraine reached up and loosened his tie, suddenly growing uncomfortably warm. "I'm glad I came out tonight," Terraine acknowledged. He reached over and stroked her arm sensuously.

Sasha blushed as his cool fingers caused her blood to boil. Looking down at her watch, she gasped with amazement. "Wow! Where has the time gone?" She lifted her head and peered at him wearing a sweet smile." I have an early day in the morning."

"I really enjoyed talking with you tonight. I would like to call you sometime, if that is okay with you." Terraine watched her expression.

Nodding her head, Sasha smiled. She had enjoyed talking with him also. Terraine seemed harmless but a nagging voice inside her said, *but didn't they all?* Sasha shrugged off the thought. She did not want to listen. She was not going to succumb to her fears. How harmful could he be? If she didn't like him she could always change her number. Sasha pulled an old receipt out of her purse and wrote her home number on the back and handed it to him. He accepted the paper without taking his eyes off Sasha as she rose to her feet.

"Thanks for a wonderful evening and great conversation. I better go find Honey." Her eyes traveled anxiously across the room.

"Here, let me help you, then I'll walk you to your car." He scooted back his chair and stood. Terraine was not ready to let her out of his sight. He had truly enjoyed himself tonight and was in no rush for the evening to end. He also knew he needed to tell her who he was before she left. Terraine took her hand and laced his fingers with hers and together they searched for Honey.

Sasha thought she was going to burst with excitement. She'd never dreamed a man's hands could feel so gentle. She could not believe her luck; to think she had not wanted to come out tonight.

Sasha found Honey on the dance floor and waved her hand in the air to get her attention, signaling that she would be outside. She then allowed Terraine to escort her out the door. He never once let her hand go.

"I think summer is here to stay," he said, breaking the silence. There was a warm breeze present. The sky was dark yet clear with diamond-studded stars.

"I hope so, the weather in the Midwest is so

unpredictable. I wish it were always summertime. I hate winters," Sasha said. Her heart was beating so rapidly that she was sure he could hear it.

"That's because winters require someone special to cuddle close to," Terraine said as they stopped in front of Honey's convertible Sebring. He reached out and swung Sasha around to face him. He leaned her back against the car before sliding his arm around her waist and pulling her close. Sasha inclined her head until their eyes locked with equal intensity. Then he cupped her chin tenderly in his warm hand. She knew what was about to transpire. Her apprehensions resurfaced, yet she was reluctant to do anything about them.

"Sasha?" His appreciative eyes feasted on the loveliness of her curving lips.

Sasha swallowed hard. Terraine hadn't just said her name; he'd caressed it. "Yes?" she responded in a whisper, with her mouth tipped up towards his and her lips slightly parted.

"I'm going to kiss you," Terraine said with confidence and determination. He gave her a second to protest before removing her glasses. He then leaned in and brushed his mouth against hers, causing her to quiver. Sasha could not believe how soft his lips felt. Terraine looked down into her eyes and desire flashed through her like a bolt of lighting before he reclaimed her lips. This time she was open and ready.

Sasha was shocked at her response to the touch of his lips as he plunged his tongue deep into her mouth, causing her to moan with delight. He moved his hands from her waist and locked them against her spine, pulling her closer. His tongue swept the fullness of her mouth, tasting the sweet rum on her lips and then explored even deeper as he found her tongue again and stroked it with his. He wanted her.

Sasha's instincts were screaming at her to resist, but her body refused and she relaxed in his strong embrace. With every kiss, heat built within her and all rational thoughts turned to dust. He pulled her still closer as she arched her body against his and placed her arms around his waist. His lips deserted her mouth and ventured to her neck as he tasted and teased a path to her collarbone before sliding his hands down to her hips and pulling her against his aroused masculinity.

At the feeling of his hardness against her abdomen, Sasha froze. *What am I doing?* Her senses leaped to life as she backed a few inches out of his grasp. She stood shocked by her own reaction. His kisses had resurrected primitive responses that she no longer wanted to feel.

Terraine opened his eyes and saw fear in her eyes. He had sensed her reluctance and did not want to rush her. He was a patient man and had plenty of time, especially when it was something he wanted. Terraine reached up and caressed her cheek with the back of his hand and gave her an understanding smile.

If he had a third leg he would have kicked himself. He should have told Sasha the truth before he kissed her. Now he'd have to wait until tomorrow. The mere thought of seeing her again brought a smile to his face.

"I'll call you tomorrow." His voice was calm. His brown eyes were steady. He reached out and gently placed her glasses in her hand.

Staring up at him, unable to utter a word, she struggled to catch her breath. Terraine opened the passenger door. Sasha climbed in and watched him walk away.

Sasha sat in the car feeling disoriented, her face flushed and her lips swollen and burning with fire. Her heart beat rapidly as the memory of his kiss flooded her mind. She had never been kissed like that before. At least not with the same intensity. She had felt consumed by flames both inside and out and had been powerless in his arms. There were a million reasons why she did not need a man in her life. So why had she not been able to resist him? Physically, she had not wanted a man like that in so long. She had tried with little success to subdue her ridiculous behavior. Instead, he had kissed her and she had liked it. She had completely lost control. Sasha dropped her shoulders and slumped in the seat feeling defeated.

It had to be because he was so good-looking that her body reacted the way it had, plus the fact that she had not been intimate with a man in months.

It was purely sexual attraction. Nothing more.

"Sorry I took so long," Honey announced as she hopped into the driver's seat, bringing Sasha abruptly out of her foggy haze of thoughts. "Oops, I didn't mean to scare you. What are you thinking about or should I say, who are you thinking about?" Honey teased. She knew that those thoughts probably had something to do with that *fine* chocolate brother she had seen sitting with Sasha.

"Never mind," Sasha mumbled. "Let's go. I'm starved." Sasha buckled her seat belt and leaned back against the leather seat, trying to shake off the effects of Terraine's kiss. But her lips still tingled in remembrance of his gentle touch.

"Sasha, that dude I met was the bomb! His name is Jacob and he just moved here from Denver and is opening a men's clothing store at the Plaza," Honey exclaimed as she put her car in drive and pulled out of the parking lot heading to the Waffle House.

"Honey, I am not paying you any attention. They are all *the bomb* for at least a week or two, then I never hear about them again." Sasha sucked her teeth, then yawned.

"What about that brother I saw you with? He sure looked tasty." Honey gave an exaggerated moan. She stopped at a red light and took the opportunity to look over at her friend.

"I know. He was too good-looking," Sasha said sarcastically. She turned her head and stared out the car window.

"And what's wrong with that?"

"He's probably no different than the rest," Sasha sighed before continuing. "I have to admit that I really enjoyed myself tonight, but I won't get my hopes up and make a big deal out of it." Sasha folded her arms across her chest. She was suddenly shivering and didn't know if it was because of the night breeze or that she was thinking about Terraine's arms wrapped around her body. "Besides, I could tell he either has a wonderful job or family money because I know an Armani suit when I see one and he drove off in a Navigator."

"And what's that got to do with anything?" Honey asked. She reached over and pushed a button, filling the car with the sounds of jazz.

"Most men that are that together are either married or gay." *And from the way he touched me, I know he isn't gay.* "Besides, he probably has a woman at home or several waiting in line and you know I am not the one."

"There is nothing wrong with being pampered, even if it is only temporary."

"That's easy for you to say," Sasha said, looking straight ahead. "He probably has some psychotic wife who was probably lurking somewhere in the bushes watching him escort me to your car." Sasha felt puzzled. She knew her fears were premature, but it had happened before and was likely to happen again.

"Girl, you watch too much television. As square as you look in those big bifocals you better be glad he even noticed you," Honey teased. Sasha jabbed her in the side and they both started laughing. "Relax, everything will be fine. He looked like a pretty nice guy. Do you think I worry about every guy I go out with?" Honey asked.

Sasha gave her a knowing look. "You could care less."

"Damn skippy." Honey threw back her head and roared with laughter.

Sasha shook her head. So much for being serious. "I don't have any intentions of allowing another man to get close to me ever again. They change and then have a tendency to become jealous and obsessed." But even as Sasha said it she didn't believe it. At least not this time. She could still smell the faint scent of his cologne on her jacket. She longed to feel Terraine's arms around her again, holding her tight and to feel his gentle lips upon hers once more.

"Sasha, you need something more in your life than that vibrator you've hidden under your mattress," Honey teased.

"What makes you think I have a vibrator?" Sasha asked, flushed.

"We all do," Honey chuckled. Sasha nudged her even harder this time, causing Honey to explode with hysteria.

"Seriously, Sasha, you need a man," Honey said with concern in her voice. "It isn't normal."

"What's abnormal about it?" Sasha asked with her brow raised.

"Do I have to spell it out for you? S-E-X." Honey turned off her car in front of the Waffle House.

"Oh, shut up, Honey. Let's go eat," Sasha mumbled in an irritated voice. She opened the car door and got out.

"Sasha, you are in need of some sexual healing and I think that guy might be the one to give it to you."

Sasha shrugged her shoulders and walked off ahead of Honey. She closed her eyes and instant-

Angie Daniels

ly Terraine's tall frame came into focus. "For once I think Honey might be right," she whispered in the wind. Then quickening her steps, she hurried towards the door.

Chapter Four

Terraine lay across his king-size bed with his fingers laced behind his head, staring at the ceiling as his mind returned to the woman who had danced in his dreams all night.

He knew there was going to be something special about Sasha from the moment he first laid eyes on her. She was ambitious, feminine and beautiful, possessing a unique combination of sexiness and sophistication that was all her own. He remembered how her skirt clung to her curves as she moved gracefully across the room. He could still feel her warm breath against his neck as they danced, smell the provocative scent of her body that made him ache with need, and remembered the softness of her breasts pressed against his

chest. He smiled at the memory of how she unconsciously flirted with the most beautiful eyes he'd
ever come in contact with.

And that wonderfully delicious kiss. Terraine
was not quite sure when aggression had become
his style. He normally practiced a much more laid-
back approach with women, but he knew that last
night there was no way he would have left without
sampling the velvet warmth of her lips. What he
had not expected was the jolt of electricity he'd felt
when their lips touched. It was still hard to believe
that a kiss could affect him so deeply, but it had.
Desire had burned between them and he had
sensed that Sasha had felt as swept away by passion as he had. Today just thinking about her made
his manhood hard with need.

Without being conceited, Terraine knew that he
was an attractive man and was used to attention.
He was not ashamed to admit he'd had more than
his fair share of women in his lifetime. But until last
night he had never met a woman that taunted him
mentally as well as physically. Sasha stirred feelings deep down inside. It was different, a powerful
feeling that was unique and felt right. What he was
feeling was real. And he wanted more.

Terraine had debated calling her when he got
home last night to insure her safe arrival home, and
selfishly, to hear how sexy her voice sounded over

the phone. He wanted to talk to her, thirsted to know everything about her, but he declined. He didn't want to come on too strong. He had sensed her reluctance and he did not want to risk scaring her away.

Rolling on his side, Terraine frowned. Right now there was another matter at hand. Honesty. He gave himself a swift mental kick for his behavior last night. He'd lied to her. Okay, maybe lying was too harsh a word but it did not change the fact that he'd chosen not to be completely honest, and for the life of him, he could not figure out why. Terraine growled and propped his head up with his fist. Now he had to think of a way to fix the mess he'd made without making Sasha think that he was playing games because last night had definitely meant more to him than that.

The telephone rang, interrupting his thoughts. Terraine rolled towards the end of the bed and reached for the cordless phone lying on the plush burgundy carpet.

"Hello?" he answered in a rough voice.

"Hey Bro, what you doing sitting in that empty mausoleum?" Jay joked. He was referring to Andrews Manor, a twenty-room mansion that Pops had purchased over forty years ago. The elegant structure was old, dating back to before the 1904 World Fair. As a child, Jay had thought the house was haunted. Even as an adult he said it gave him the creeps and instead of sharing the monstrous house that they both had grown up in, he preferred the comforts of his plush condominium. Terraine, on the other hand, had always loved the house and was grateful Pops had left it to him in his will.

When Terraine first took over the house, he donated several pieces of furniture to an organization that was hosting a charitable auction. He held on to pieces with sentimental value, such as the vanity that his mother once sat at every evening while she brushed her hair.

"This is a house and it is not empty. There are still several pieces of furniture left and most importantly, I do have a bed to sleep in," Terraine said with a note of sarcasm. "Besides, the movers will be arriving from Chicago with my things on Wednesday. "

"I guess a bed is all you really need anyway, huh Playa?" Jay teased. Terraine hated that nickname. Jay had been calling him that for over ten years. The name was a constant reminder of the type of man he used to be and now he was ready to relinquish the reputation that went with it.

"Sorry about last night man, I was working on a new lead and missed my plane. There appear to be a lot of criminals lurking around our quiet community," he announced in a poor impersonation of his favorite detective, Charlie Chan.

"Give me a break, there is nothing quiet about St. Louis." Terraine rose from his bed, reached for his robe hanging from a hook on the back of his closet door and walked down the hall to a winding staircase. Maybe if he was lucky, he could convince his housekeeper, Ms. Henry, to whip up a batch of her mouth-watering pancakes. She had been with them since his mother's death. Besides the house, she was the only connection he had left to his childhood.

"No hard feelings about last night. As a matter of fact, if you had showed up you would have been in my way." Terraine grinned, as memories of Sasha swam through his mind once again.

"Sounds like you met someone last night," Jay replied with a trace of amusement.

"Yes, I did." Terraine's face lit up. He held onto the railing as he descended a staircase trimmed in rich oak wood.

"So, Playa, did you get lucky or what?" Jay teased.

"As a matter of fact I did, but not the way your perverted mind is thinking," Terraine answered. His voice vibrated with new life. "Jay, this may be hard for you to believe but I am ready to settle down."

Jay hid a bark of laughter behind a cough. "Yeah, it is hard to believe. You are kidding, right?"

Jay's voice rose with surprise. His brother settle down? No way! Jay remembered how they used to compete to see who could obtain the most telephone numbers in one night. Hands down, Terraine always won.

"No, I am dead serious. My playing days are over. I don't want any part of it any more."

"Playa, you are buggin'. I was looking forward to us double dating now that you are back in St. Louis. I can't believe you are ready for the old ball and chain." Jay sounded disappointed and his words lacked their usual laughter.

"I'm not *quite* ready to walk down the aisle," Terraine chuckled lightly. "Let's just say I am no longer running away from it. I'm getting too old for the dating scene. I've recently realized that I am ready for something more meaningful than a one-night stand. Maybe when you get my age you'll feel the same way." *I doubt it.* Jay was a born ladies man. He loved gorgeous women as much, if not more, than the next guy and they all seemed to love him back. He knew how to turn on the charm without letting any one woman get too close.

Jay was also tall, like his brother, with the same signature goatee and raisin-colored eyes. But his complexion was the color of toast, and his thick black hair lay neatly in waves all the way to the nape of his neck. Numerous hours lifting weights at the gym had given him a much more rugged build, however.

After Pops' death, Jay had taken on an active role, running the corporation long enough for Terraine to wrap up his business in Chicago and return to St. Louis. Now Jay was back to the role he loved most—private investigation.

"No way, Playa, I am holding on tightly to my bachelorhood. I'm not ready to wake up and see the same face every morning," Jay proclaimed.

"Trust me, it will pass," Terraine laughed. "By the way, I would appreciate it if you would stop calling me Playa." Terraine walked through the living room towards the kitchen and suddenly remembered that he had given Ms. Henry the weekend off. He swore under his breath. He had his taste buds all ready for pancakes dripping with maple syrup.

"But Playa... I mean Tee, man, you've got to be kidding." He couldn't control his sudden burst of laughter. His brother had changed. He'd either been bitten by the love bug or fallen on his head.

Terraine moved the phone away from his ringing ear and released an irritated sigh. He returned the receiver to his ear. "Are you finished, man?" Terraine asked impatiently as he walked through the dining room to the kitchen.

"Sorry, Tee. Man, you've changed," Jay sputtered as another jolt of laughter erupted from him.

He could tell by his big brother's silence that he wasn't the least bit amused. "All right, my bad." Jay cleared his throat before continuing. "Hey, if that is what you want, man, then I can't do anything but respect you for it."

"I appreciate that," Terraine said dryly. "If you aren't too busy why don't you make it up to me and come over and help me move my stuff in on Wednesday?" Terraine opened the refrigerator, to find only some lunchmeat, a loaf of bread and two apples.

"No problem. It will be a perfect opportunity for you to bring me up-to-date on the new lingerie line." Jay wolf-whistled. "Besides, I want to hear about this babe that has you thinking about turning in your player's card. I'll see you then."

Terraine chuckled before turning the receiver off and tapping it lightly in the palm of his hand. In comparison to pancakes, a ham sandwich for breakfast did not sound the least bit appealing; instead, he had a better idea. He ran up to his room, taking the steps two at a time. He found the pants that he had worn the night before and reached into the right pocket and found what he was looking for. He slid into a chair in the corner of the room, grinning while he dialed her number.

Sasha and Honey were just walking into the house with a bag of groceries each when she heard the phone ring.

"Hello."

Terraine's heart skipped a beat. She had no idea how sensuous her voice sounded on the phone. Detecting a note of irritation in her voice, he hesitated, hoping that he hadn't called at a bad time. "I hope I am not disturbing you?"

Sasha would have known that masculine voice anywhere and it sent tremors down her spine. A wide smile spread across her face as she set the bag of groceries on the floor. "No," she began as her heart leaped with delight. He called her. "You just caught me off guard." She gave Honey a long, meaningful 'get lost' look and waited until she was halfway down the hall before continuing. "I just walked into the house with groceries when I heard the phone ring. There wasn't anything in the house to eat so it was either shop or eat at Denny's. Honey and I decided today would be a good excuse for waffles with lots of butter." Cradling the phone between her ear and shoulder, Sasha leaned against the wall with one foot on the floor.

Terraine's stomach growled, reminding him of the pancakes he had missed out on this morning. Maybe it was time for him to learn how to cook.

"Sounds like my refrigerator, which is why I called. How about going with me to the Black Expo this afternoon?" Terraine asked. *Please say yes.*

Sasha smiled. The Missouri Black Exposition held annually gave black vendors an opportunity to exhibit and sell merchandise while providing economic and cultural growth to the community.

"Well... " Sasha paused, torn by conflicting emotions. She'd had a restless night, spending most of it trying to sort out her feelings. Sasha knew that after the way he'd resurrected dead emotions last night that she should stay clear of him. Yesterday she had not been herself. She had allowed herself to be overcome with feelings and desires that she did not want to feel and she didn't want to encourage him. Yet, she could not deny that when she finally had fallen asleep, he had been the subject of her dreams and the main focus of her thoughts all morning. And to be totally honest with herself, she'd hoped that he would call. In less than twenty-fourhours her willpower had gone out the window.

"I promise to feed you."

Sasha giggled. "That's a tempting offer. Food is definitely the key to my heart... all right, why not?" How could she possibly resist? She would just have to maintain her guard. She was determined not to let the kiss they'd shared and the feelings he stirred override her good sense.

Yes! "Okay, would you like for me to pick you up?" *Be cool, Terraine.* Play it cool. He tried to sound as calm as possible so that Sasha would not detect the eagerness in his voice.

Sasha hesitated as a little voice reminded her of what had happened the last time that she'd given out her address. She wasn't sure if she wanted him to know where she lived. At least not yet. "Why don't I meet you in front of the America's Center at two o'clock?" she suggested.

"Great. I'll see you then." Terraine hung up the phone grinning like a Cheshire cat as he danced to the bathroom.

Spellbound, Terraine's mouth went dry watching the seductive sway of her hips as Sasha walked towards the building. Seeing her again, he realized that his memory had not done her justice. She was more beautiful than he remembered. Her skin looked irresistibly soft and once again free of cosmetics. She was not wearing her glasses today and her extraordinary hazel eyes, flecked and ringed with gold, sparkled with radiance.

"Hi," he greeted her with a husky whisper and a smile, finding her nearness overwhelming as her sweet fragrance filled the air around him.

"Hi," she repeated as they exchanged a long lingering smile.

Terraine eyes wandered over her, pleased. She was wearing a sleeveless rose blouse and a black wrap skirt that tied at her waist and defined its smallness. He could not believe how stunning she made the simplest outfit look. His eyes moved to her parted ruby lips. He had never seen a more inviting mouth, generous and unbelievably sensual. No matter how hard he fought it, he just could not get the kiss they'd shared out of his mind even if his life depended on it.

His hands came down over hers possessively. "Sasha, thanks for joining me today."

Sasha tingled at the sound of her name. Her mind and body were at war over the possibility of being kissed by him again. She knew that she needed to pull her hands away to keep some distance between them, but she simply could not. Instead, she watched Terraine's eyes search her face, trying to reach into her thoughts until a smile found its way through her mask of confusion. Sasha's eye sparkled as she continued to look at him. "Thank you for inviting me."

If she could have read his mind, Sasha would have known that at that particular moment Terraine wanted to scoop her into his arms and take her away to his home—to his bed, and undress her slowly, touching her in places that his eyes had never seen, first with his hand and then with his tongue. Taking a deep breath, Terraine forced himself to look away from her delectable mouth, resisting the overwhelming urge to kiss her tempting red lips and experience the sweet taste again.

He cleared his voice. "We better go in." He dropped an arm across her shoulder to escort her and the hairs on her arm stood up. She had been prepared for much more and was slightly disappointed, but from the look on his face, she wasn't the only one trying to get her emotions in check.

They spent an unforgettable afternoon at the crowded Expo, strolling through hallways that were filled with heavy Afrocentric flavor. Over 600 vendors were in attendance, including musicians, authors, and speakers from all persuasions. There were also numerous booths that displayed African style jewelry and clothing.

Terraine couldn't remember the last Expo that he'd enjoyed as much. Then again, this was the first one he'd attended in the company of an extraordinary woman. He watched with amusement as Sasha sampled everything, like a kid in a candy store. Her eyes were wide with excitement as she tasted international cuisines from the Bahamas, Jamaica, Hawaii, and Africa, along with several local favorites.

The entertainment was provided by the Bahamian Cultural Explosion and Junkanoo Band, which was, in Terraine's opinion, a flavorsome blend of reggae and R&B. Sasha and Terraine talked, laughed and held hands.

While Sasha retreated to the restroom to freshen up, he stood outside contemplating whether to tell her the truth before the night was over. If Terraine had even imagined that he would like her as much as he did, he would have never started the charade in the first place. But how was he to know that in less than twenty-four hours she would move straight into his heart? Terraine frowned. Now that was not completely true. Terraine knew from the moment he'd seen her photo that she would be the one for him. So why was he lying to himself?

His eyes rested on her slim body as Sasha came back around the corner. She stopped at a booth to admire several pieces of jewelry made by a Nigerian vendor. Terraine watched her, as he'd caught himself doing several times throughout the afternoon. He watched the way she walked, the way she spoke with friendly words on her lips and the way she looked up at him from beneath thick lashes framing a pair of mesmerizing golden eyes. There was something about her caramel skin. It seemed to glow as if lit from inside. His heart pounded as she turned around and watched a small fashion show with her right palm on her hip. He couldn't remember when he'd last felt this alive.

Sasha's mind was spinning with ideas as she watched four ladies walk around a small platform stage, modeling caftans created by a Chicago designer. Sasha crossed her fingers and brought them to her lips. If she were lucky, next year she would be ready to display her wedding gowns for all of St. Louis to see. Hopefully, she could convince Diva Designs to add her gowns to their collections. She was confident that if she could get the CEO to listen to her concept and look at her designs, he'd be interested. The more she thought about it, the better she felt about her decision to accept the contract. She hugged herself and then wondered if she should share her plan with Terraine.

Sasha looked across the room at Terraine, who stood against a wall talking to another man. It made her feel good inside to know that he was standing there waiting for her. She eyed him up and down covetously, taking in how handsome he looked in a pair of starched khaki slacks, mustard-colored, button-down linen shirt and brown open-toe leather sandals. Sasha had never really thought about a man's feet before, nor had she ever felt the urge to kiss a man's toes, slowly one at a time. Probably because she'd never seen such an attractive pair before.

Last night her mind had burned with memories of their magical evening. The way that he'd singled her out of a crowd of beautiful women and had given her his undivided attention made her feel like Cinderella. A little shudder of delight ran through her as she remembered the feel of his powerful arms around her as they danced. She had felt as if she would float away if he were not holding onto her hand while his handsome face stared down at her. He possessed so many of the qualities that she looked for in a man. He was affectionate and aggressive, was not afraid to express himself, and had a sense of humor. She already loved the sound of his voice when he complimented her. He made her feel beautiful and special.

She was so mesmerized by the power of those muscular limbs that she was caught off guard when he turned his head and found her watching him. He stared at her with such intensity her temperature rose. *What was he thinking?* Sasha smiled weakly and found herself blushing. Terraine gave her an exaggerated wink before diverting his attention back to the man in front of him. Sasha felt flustered and ran her hand through her hair. Her defenses had evaporated and his dimpled smile was to blame.

What was happening to her? Why was she allowing these feeling to surface? Sasha sighed and walked away from the stage, behind a partition away from his view, and placed her hand to her chest. She had no control over what was happening. Nature had taken over. Something warned her to stay away but she couldn't. She felt magnetically drawn to him and it was wonderful. Deliciously wonderful.

Certainly it would be wonderful to be cared for by such a man, but Sasha didn't even want to entertain the thought of something serious developing between them. She folded her arms across her chest, yet she could not fight the arousal. She had daydreamed about Terraine all morning. She had fantasized that they were lovers and found the fantasy both satisfying and sexually frustrating. Had it really been that long since she had been with a man? She could not afford to be distracted by romantic notions, yet she liked him and part of her wished that she could be that special someone in his life. She could not deny that she wanted more than anything for him to find her desirable. Maybe Honey was right. Maybe it was time for her to give love one more try.

Sasha brought a hand to her brow. Could there be a possibility that Terraine might be interested in more than just a sexual relationship? In her experience, men that looked like *that* pretended to be interested in more than sex but in the end it was always the same story—they were only interested in what was between her legs. She had to admit her needs had not been attended to in some time but she was not interested in just satisfying her sexual needs. She wanted someone who wanted her—who would love and respect her for who she was—and something told her that Terraine might be that man.

Terraine watched as Sasha walked towards him with her honey-colored hair swinging about her shoulders.

"I miss anything?" she asked with an innocent twinkle in her eye.

"I don't know? Did you?" Terraine reached out with both hands and laced her fingers with his own, pulling her closer. Sasha looked up, meeting his dark eyes and saw a faint smile lurking in their depths.

"I...I believe I did," she stammered nervously, moistening her lips.

Terraine had not meant to catch her off guard but he could not deny the enjoyment he received watching the way she reacted by running her moist pink tongue across her ruby lips, a gesture he was beginning to recognize as a habit. A nervous habit that made his groin tighten. He could not get enough of looking at her and seeing her smile. She was so much more incredibly beautiful when she smiled. He liked her. He wanted her. And had every intention of showing her just how much.

"I would love to have dinner with you but after all the food I've seen you consume in one afternoon, I doubt you have room for any more," Terraine joked.

Sasha playfully punched him in the arm and laughed. "I'm insulted. Are you trying to call me a pig?" She was thankful that she had been blessed with the ability to eat as much as she wanted without having to worry about gaining weight.

He stared down at her with his raisin-brown eyes that were dark and powerful. "Sweetheart, there are a lot of things I would call you, but pig is not one of them." Terraine even surprised himself with his next move. He put his arm around her waist and squeezed her affectionately. Her closeness was like a drug, drawing him to her. His eyes traveled to her throat. Instantly he longed to leave a trail of small kisses all around the hollow base of her neck. Terraine tilted his head to meet her eyes, which were as soft as a caress. She parted her lips innocently. The urge to kiss her surged through him and took over his senses. Losing all control, he placed his finger under her chin and lifted her face until their eyes locked. He then lowered his mouth over hers, devouring its softness and touching her lips like a whisper.

Sasha wasn't accustomed to showing affection in public places but there was no way that she was going to object to something that she'd waited over two hours to receive. Though his kiss was gentle, her blood sizzled and her heart pounded against her chest. Opening her eyes, she gazed at him and her eyes met the desire in his. The intimate contact was brief but just long enough for both of them to realize that something special was happening between them.

Terraine broke the silence. "I am not ready to let you out of my sight just yet. How about we go and have a drink?" he suggested in a soft voice.

"Sounds good to me."

Sasha linked her arms with his and together they walked out of the building, both thinking that there was no place they'd rather be right now than with each other.

They agreed to end the wonderful evening on the Delmar Loop, located in University City in the heart of St. Louis and featuring the city's most diverse collection of ethnic foods, along with a number of specialty shops. It was also the home of the Tivoli Theatre, a meticulously restored movie palace that featured international films.

They walked with their hands intertwined down the sidewalk known as the Walk of Fame, where eighty-five stars were embedded the pavement, as well as a plaque containing a short recital of the accomplishments of St. Louisians such as Maya Angelo, Chuck Berry, Miles Davis, and Tina Turner.

Sasha felt like a breathless girl of eighteen all over again. She felt carefree and safe and there was even a bounce in her step. She never dreamed that she could feel or want to feel like this again. Terraine made it easy. He had begun chiseling at the wall guarding her wounded heart, and it was finally beginning to heal.

It was a wonderfully clear evening with no breeze. Sasha draped an arm around Terraine's waist and he snuggled her close to him, pleased to have the warmth of her body next to him.

Terraine kissed the top of her head, inhaling the gentle scent of her hair, which smelled like a strawberry patch. "Sasha, if I could give you anything in the world that you wanted, what would it be?"

Sasha looked up at him and smiled, enjoying being wrapped in the strength of his arm. Terraine had been asking her questions like this all day. This time Sasha exhaled deeply and decided to answer him from her heart. "I'm going to let you in on a secret that I haven't even had a chance to share yet with Honey." She stopped walking and looked down at the sidewalk. "I took the job with Diva Designs for selfish reasons."

Terraine stiffened and placed his hands on her

shoulder, turning her towards him. "How so?"

Sasha continued to look away as she formed her thoughts into words. She wanted—no, she needed—him to understand her intentions. "I gave up modeling months ago to pursue a career as a designer, but that did not financially pan out for me. My agent convinced me to accept the contract with Diva Designs in order to earn the rest of the money I needed, and I did. But deep in the back of my mind I knew why I was accepting the job. I plan to use my contract as a way to convince them to con-sider adding my gowns to their collection." Sasha finally looked up at Terraine, who was staring at her strangely. "It's a stupid idea, isn't it?"

Terraine dropped his shoulders in relief. He'd been almost certain that what she was going to say would put him in a compromising position before he even had a chance to tell her who he really was. This was his window of opportunity. And then sud-denly he realized he had no desire to mix business and pleasure. Not now, not ever. He wanted Sasha to know him as Terraine not as Richard Andrews' grandson. So, now what was he going to do? Intentional deceit was not his style. He'd had three chances to come clean and each time he chose to turn the other cheek. Eventually he was going to have to deal with it.

"No. I think it's a wonderful idea and if your

gowns are anywhere near as gorgeous as you are, you won't have anything to worry about." He meant it. He would order his lawyers to draw up a contract tomorrow based purely on the vision that stood before him if he had to.

Sasha witnessed the compassion in his eyes and her heart did a back flip, causing another stone to crumble. "Thanks. I needed to hear that." Sasha reached up, wrapped her arms around his neck, and kissed his cheek. "Come on. I hear music."

It was happy hour when they walked into Blueberry Hill, a nightclub decorated in rock and roll memorabilia and St. Louis treasures. They found an intimate table in the corner and ordered jerked chicken and a bottle of white wine while they listened to a live jazz performance. Terraine reached across a small table and caressed the back of Sasha's hand with his large, calloused fingers.

Sasha tilted her head to one side and stole a slanted look at Terraine's strong face. His eyes were closed and he bobbed his head to the rhythm of the music. There was something about him, a sense of contained power. Sasha let her glance linger. His handsome features wore a secret expression. Was he hiding something? Sasha flinched and told the left side of her brain to shut up for taunting her with such foolishness. Terraine was different. He was not like all of the others.

"I know you are looking at me," he said from across the table.

Sasha giggled. "How could you possibly know? Your eyes are closed."

"Music does that to me." Terraine turned in his seat and raised her hand to his cheek. "But you do this to me. You feel that? Your penetrating eyes caused my cheeks to warm." Sasha giggled again and Terraine smiled as she traced his jaw with her fingers. "I guess you've noticed my dimples," he said modestly.

Sasha nodded. "Uh, huh. I've noticed."

Terraine's body was on fire. In the course of two days, he'd come to know there was no way he was going to allow Sasha to walk out of his life. Terraine covered her hand with his. "I've noticed a lot of things about you too, Ms. Moore," he said in a low sexy voice.

"Such as...?" she dared to ask.

"That you lick your lips a lot." Terraine's dark eyes twinkled. "Now I figured either your lips are dry..." Terraine allowed his voice to trail off while he leaned across the table and ran a finger gently across her lips. He examined them extra carefully, making it hard for her to keep a straight face. He then planted a small kiss on her mouth and lifted his brow humorously. "Nope. They're definitely not dry.

Could I possibly make you nervous?"

Distracted by his boyish smile, she did not answer right away. She tilted her head to the side. "It's no secret that I'm attracted to you. That was obvious from the moment I laid eyes on you. I...," Sasha hesitated then lowered her head, "I just can't stand to be hurt again."

"Baby." He cupped her trembling chin with his hand and forced her to look up at him. "What I am feeling is not lust nor is it a passing fancy. I am ready for love. I am too old for games, and I know what I want." Terraine gently stroked her cheek. "Something special is happening between us and I want to see where it leads, but only if you're willing. Will you give us a chance?"

Sasha saw that his eyes were brimming with tenderness and passion. Because his proposal had caught her off guard, she stared at him, speechless for several seconds, contemplating an answer. Just as she was about to respond, Terraine leaned over and silenced her with a warm kiss that made her head spin. His lips traveled to her ear and his breath felt hot against her skin.

"Don't answer. Not yet," he whispered. "Because when you do, you should be prepared for the ride of your life." His mouth then traveled back to hers and crushed her lips with burning desire.

Sasha knew at that moment that it was useless

to resist Terraine any longer. It was a moment of exposed emotion more honest than Sasha would have thought any man would ever allow himself to admit. But then, Terraine wasn't just any man. She surrendered.

It was eight-thirty when they strolled to the parking lot with their arms draped around each other's waist. The sun had sunk steadily below the line of trees that rimmed the far end of the lot. The dusky light hummed with cars and laughter, filling the silence between them.

"Thanks for a wonderful evening. I had a great time." Sasha smiled up at Terraine as they stood in front of her car. She'd had a magnificent evening in the company of a wonderful man who was eager to make her a part of his life. Tonight she would sleep with a smile on her face while visions of him would dance in her head. Who could ask for anything more?

"The pleasure was all mine," Terraine said.

Sasha grabbed the handle on her door and was about to open it when Terraine placed a restraining hand on her arm. "Wait." She looked up at Terraine as his hands slipped up her arm, bringing her close against his body. "Aren't you forgetting something?"

Sasha drew in a deep breath before his lips met hers in a gentle kiss that caused her to tingle all over. All the heat and emotion of the evening raced through her and exploded. She enjoyed the way his lips felt once again upon hers, only this time it was private and in a parking lot under the stars. Sasha put her arms around his neck and pulled him closer. Her mouth opened, inviting his tongue, and she moaned from deep within.

He accepted her invitation and savored the taste of wine on her breath. With his arms around her he pulled her even closer. His moist lips moved from her mouth and now covered her cheek and nose with heated kisses. "Kissing you is the most exciting thing I have ever experienced," Terraine mumbled, his breath hot against her ear. He blew a line of goose bumps down the side of her neck. She smelled so good. He couldn't think. Only feel.

She dragged his mouth back to hers. "Don't talk, just kiss me." She spoke in a suffocated whisper. His mouth found hers again, sending an explosion of sensation shattering through her body, igniting her soul.

"I want you, Sasha," Terraine groaned in her ear before he fastened his hand on her breast. Catching a throbbing nipple between his fingertips, he sent warm tingles through her. He nudged Sasha's thighs apart and pressed his manhood against her, causing him to sizzle with desire. It had been too long and right now Terraine needed Sasha to satisfy his needs.

No. Not yet.

Tonight was definitely too soon. He needed to slow down and think with his big head and not with his little one. There was no way he was ruining his chances by rushing into something he knew she was not ready for. Nor was he going to chance losing her by lying to her any further. He wanted to do this right, and right now it was time to tell her the truth.

Reluctantly, Terraine lifted his mouth from hers and sighed. Sasha's eyes fluttered open and she stared up at him, trying to read his blank expression. Terraine dropped his eyes, but not before she witnessed the look of frustration. She knew exactly how he felt. She was feeling it also. Before she could comment, Terraine brought his index finger to her lips.

"We need to talk. "

"Sure. You look so serious. What is it?" Sasha saw the worried look in his eyes and knew that what he was about to say was very important. She braced herself for something that might change the course of their relationship. She had expected something to happen sooner or later. It was probably better that it was happening now.

Terraine dropped his hands and leaned against her car. He was tired of the charade. Sasha deserved to know the truth before their relationship went any further. He had thought long and hard about what he wanted to say while sitting and listening to music with his eyes closed. He just hoped she would understand. If not, he'd have to accept the consequences. Damn it, he was lying to himself again. He was going to do whatever he had to do to get her to understand, because he sure as hell was not letting her walk out of his life.

"I haven't told you what I do for a living."

Sasha raised her left eyebrow in surprise and nodded in agreement. "No, you haven't, but then I failed to asked you." *How careless of me.* She had been so wrapped up in the moment, so mesmerized by him, that she had forgotten.

"I have not been completely honest about my grandfather. There are things that I think you should know." Terraine struggled to find the right words while he cleared his throat. "Well…up until a month ago, I was living in Chicago, working as a financial director. Now I am managing my grandfather's company and trying to decide what to do with it." Terraine tried to laugh but his words sounded strangled. "He recently passed away and left me the family business. It was his entire life." He paused for a moment before he continued. "I am not quite sure how I feel about it yet. It still feels uncomfortable because it is so new to me that it hasn't quite sunk in," he admitted.

Sasha saw the sadness in his eyes and reached over and squeezed his hand. "I'm sorry to hear about your loss. I can tell you really miss him."

Terraine turned away and watched another couple walk across the parking lot. "Yes, I miss him. A lot of things were left unsaid between us." *Like I'm sorry.* Terraine shifted against the car as he felt a knot of emotion tighten in his chest. He was having regrets. Why had he not thought about mending things months ago? He should have been there and swallowed his pride. He could no longer count the number of times he wished that he could turn back the hands of time. "He was a tough old bird. His heart finally gave out but he fought until the end."

Sasha nodded, not wanting to pry any further. She had heard the faint tremor in his voice and hoped that when he was ready, he would feel comfortable talking with her more about his grandfather and his business. Sasha came around in front of him and wrapped her arms around him and gave him a big hug. She knew how he felt. She'd been there. Done that. "I'm sure everything will work out okay. You will probably do a wonderful job with your grandfather's business."

Terraine saw the sympathy and concern in her eyes. "Yes, that's what my brother says." He brought her hand to his lips and kissed her palm.

The mere touch of his warm lips sent a heated shudder through her body as she remembered the sensational kiss that they'd shared only moments ago.

"There is more." He slowly dropped her hand. "My grandfather was—" Before Terraine could continue, a soft chirping sound eliminated the rest of his sentence. Sasha hurriedly rummaged through her purse and pulled out a small cellular phone.

"Excuse me, Terraine. This won't take but a minute." She pushed a button and lifted the phone to her ear. "Hello."

Terraine watched while she listened to the person on the other end, wondering if he should walk away to give her a moment of privacy. Before he had a chance to make up his mind, the expression on her face changed.

"What is it?" he asked, placing a concerned hand on her shoulder. He waited until she closed the flip phone before he repeated the question.

Sasha gnawed on her lower lip and put her phone back in her purse and reached down with a trembling hand into the bottom for her keys. "I have to get home. That was my security service. My burglar alarm went off and the police are on their way." Panic was detectable in her voice. She hoped that it was a false alarm and prayed that it wasn't something else. *Please Lord, not again*. For a second

Sasha, forgot Terraine was there as she opened her car door and proceeded to get in.

"Oh, I'm sorry." She turned back towards him and gave him a faraway smile. "You weren't finished talking to me about your grandfather."

Terraine saw the dazed look on her face and knew that now was not the time. Her mind was already millions of miles away.

"We'll talk later." He planted a small kiss on her forehead. "Get in, I'm following you home." Terraine helped her in and shut the car door behind her, then briskly walked to his Navigator parked a short distance away.

Sasha put her car in gear and drove out of the parking lot with Terraine close behind. She was in no position to argue. Surprisingly, knowing that he was close by was sort of comforting. She smiled and looked up at his reflection in her rear view mirror.

Before turning onto the highway, Sasha reached down and grasped the tiny cross hanging around her neck and prayed that it be no more than a fly that had flown in front of her motion detector.
But her gut told her it was going to be much more than that.

Chapter Five

Sasha and Terraine arrived to find two officers already inside her house, checking for signs of a possible burglary. Bewildered, she listened to a short stocky man, who introduced himself as Officer Slate, inform them that when they arrived, her front door was slightly ajar.

Sasha's ran her fingers through her hair and tried to remember if she had pulled the door tight when she left to meet Terraine. Honey had left long before she did, which would have made her the last person to leave. She shook her head. It was unlike her to be so careless, yet and still, she had been so excited about their date that she might have forgotten.

While Sasha walked around the front of the

house, scanning the entire area for anything out of the ordinary, Officer Slate walked down the hallway towards the bedrooms.

After asking Sasha if there was anything he could do, Terraine stood off to the side feeling in the way and out of place. He watched as Officer Lewis, a young redheaded guy who looked straight out of the academy, examined the front door for forced entry. Terraine then allowed his eyes to wander casually around the room, admiring how lovely, light and cheery her home was. Sasha was talented enough to be an interior decorator, he thought. The pastel colors in the room coordinated well, matching her cheerful and vibrant personality. Then an idea struck him. If he was lucky, maybe he could convince Sasha to help him decorate Andrews Manor and make it look and feel as comfortable as her home. It would also give him an excuse to spend more time with her.

Terraine turned his head and saw Officer Slate coming down the hall towards the living room. He brushed past Terraine as if he were not standing there—only inches away from a collision—and headed towards the kitchen.

"Excuse me, ma'am. I think I found something in the back room." He signaled for Sasha to follow him and Terraine joined them.

The officer pointed to a note taped to the mirror

above her dresser that read, "LOVE CONQUERS ALL."

"Ma'am, do you have any idea what this means?" Officer Slate asked, hooking his thumbs in his belt loops and rocking back and forth on his heels.

Sasha stared intensely at the note and shook her head in disbelief. "No," she responded in a strained voice. Suddenly a little wobbly in the knees, she took a seat on the end of her bed. "I have no idea." *This could not possibly be happening.* Sasha searched her brain for some kind of hidden meaning behind the words. She looked around the room for anything that might be missing or out of place.

Terraine rubbed the back of his hand across his mouth and walked towards her dresser to get a closer look. He noticed that the letters were not typed; instead they were cut out from something like a newspaper or a magazine and then glued to a sheet of paper, in the fashion of ransom notes.

Terraine watched Sasha while the officer asked her a series of questions. She seemed distracted. He followed her eyes around the room and as far as he could tell, everything looked neat and in place, but then, he had never been here before. There were stuffed animals in every corner of the room, from dogs to an oversized honey bear. Terraine began to wonder whose room it was until he discovered the photos of Sasha on her wall above her bed. *A child at heart.* What had he learned while taking a psychology class during college? A collection of small stuffed animals conveys a sense of security.

Moving towards her, Terraine gently squeezed her shoulder. "You okay?"

Sasha nodded without looking up. Nor did she trust herself to speak.

"Would you like a glass of water or something?"

She shook her head and clutched a stuffed bear tightly to her chest.

Terraine caught the officer's scrutiny. He was obviously annoyed that Terraine had interrupted his investigation. *Too bad*, Terraine thought with a frown. It had sounded more like an interrogation to him. Terraine stood tall and looked down into the officer's eyes. Officer Slate was almost a foot shorter than Terraine with a stocky build that reminded Terraine of his old drill sergeant.

"Ma'am, would you like to continue this discussion in the other room in *private*?"

Terraine heard the emphasis on the word and did not miss Officer Slate looking in his direction when he spoke. *He couldn't possibly think that I have anything to do with this.* Terraine glared at him, challenging him to say something and felt the urge to reach out and choke him. He was picking for a confrontation but Terraine refused to initiate it.

Sasha shook her head in dismay and folded her arms tightly across her chest. "N-no. It's okay." Holding onto her shoulder, Terraine's concern grew as he felt her trembling beneath him, and he lightly squeezed her shoulder in comfort.

With gloved hands, Officer Slate removed the note and placed it in a small plastic bag. "We'll take this down to the station and run it through the lab. I'm going to help my partner finish up in the other room and then we will need you to answer a few more questions." He gave Terraine one last hard stare, then did an about-face, turning on his heels and walking out of the room.

Terraine dropped his head and looked down at Sasha, who was playing with her hands. "Are you sure you are okay?" he asked in a quiet, cautious-sounding voice.

Sasha nodded, looking as frightened as a kindergartner on her first day of school. Terraine knew she was vulnerable, but until now he had not realized how much. The gentleness of the kiss they'd shared lingered with him and the very thought of anyone hurting her infuriated him.

"Come here." Terraine commanded. She rose and stood within the boundaries of his soothing arms. Sasha closed her eyes tightly, shutting out her fears and laid her head against his broad shoulder. She felt safe pressed up against his hard body; she felt protected against the big bad world enveloped in the strength of his arms, and she felt aroused in the security of his embrace. How was it possible for her to feel scared, safe and aroused at the same time? All she was certain of was that she wished she could stay in his arms forever. She was not ready to face the problem at hand.

Terraine could feel her trembling like a frightened kitten and held her snugly against his chest while rubbing his hand up and down the small of her back. Eventually he felt her body begin to relax against him. He dropped his chin and placed his mouth near the warmth of her skin. What had caused her such fear? This was a side of her he'd not had the opportunity to witness until now. Fear transformed her face. The emotion was so clearly visible it could have been written on her forehead.

Yesterday and this afternoon, Sasha had appeared confident and in control of her life, wearing a smile that brightened an entire room. Now her entire demeanor projected something else. The laughter was gone and in its place he saw fear. Terraine now felt the need to protect her. He placed a hand on her silky hair and stroked the back of her head. "Sasha, everything is going to be okay," he reassured her. He could feel her nodding against his chest.

"Sure, whatever you say." If Terraine only knew... But he didn't. It was easier to allow him to continue thinking that a burglar had shaken her up, easier than telling him the truth.

"Sasha!" The female voice came from the front of the house.

Sasha lifted her head from his chest. "Back here."

Honey popped her head in the door and Terraine loosened his grip. "Hey girl. "Your security service called the shop and I rushed over to see what was going on." Honey's eyes traveled over the man standing close to Sasha. "Who do we have here?" she grinned. "Excuse my rude friend. She already has you in her bedroom and I haven't even been introduced." She extended a dainty hand that was swallowed up by Terraine's massive one. "I am Ms. Honey Love. My friends just call me Lovely." Honey laughed at her own corny joke. "You must be Terraine. If you're not, then I just stuck my foot in my mouth. I am her crazy friend, the one that dragged her out the other night." Honey then arched her left eyebrow and poked him in the chest with a sculptured index finger. "Keep in mind, if it was not for me, you two would not have met."

Terraine looked down at the small, slender woman in front of him and chuckled. "Thanks, I guess I owe you one." He was glad to meet the woman who was obviously a big influence in Sasha's life. He hadn't gotten a good look at her the other night. On inspection, Honey was petite with the largest pair of gray eyes he'd ever seen, and he would have never guessed that she and Sasha were the same age. She reminded him of Tinkerbell—cute and urchin-like. Terraine almost felt a need to walk over and pinch her cheek. He had a strong feeling that they were going to become good friends.

Honey batted her eyes. "We'll see. My birthday is in four weeks." Honey held up four fingers and cackled before draping an arm around Sasha's shoulder.

Sasha looked over at Honey and cut her eyes. She was such a flirt.

"So Chick, what's going on here?" Honey asked. "Those two bullies in the living room did not want to let me in."

Sasha quickly filled her in on the note that was found. Honey placed both hands on her hips and looked at her through narrow eyes. "You don't think that it was—" Honey was cut off abruptly with a jab in the ribs from Sasha's right elbow. "Ouch!" she moaned.

Sasha chuckled. "Of course not." And with exaggerated eye contact, she reminded Honey what discretion meant. Honey quickly got the message.

Terraine, on the other hand, did not and was certain that something was being left unsaid. He cleared his throat. "Am I missing something?"

Honey and Sasha exchanged glances and Sasha felt the sudden need for air, and privacy. Under Terraine's steady eye she could not think. "Terraine, I had a wonderful evening, but let me walk you to your car." She latched onto his arm and turned to Honey. "Can you entertain the officers for a few minutes?" Honey gave her a thumbs-up signal and Sasha escorted Terraine down the hall and out the front door.

Sasha leaned against him. "I hate to end such a beautiful day on a sour note." She tried to smile despite the nervousness that filled her.

"Not at all. I can't remember when I enjoyed a date quite as much." Terraine leaned against his Navigator and reached up to caress her cheek. "Are you sure you are going to be okay?" he asked with skepticism.

Sasha tilted her head back and stood silent for a long moment, looking towards the dark sky. "There is a full moon tonight," she sighed, and then cast her gaze to him. "I'll be fine. Probably some sick person's idea of a joke. I would not be surprised if Honey did it herself." She chuckled but

Terraine noticed that her laughter did not reach her eyes. She was trying to mask her inner turmoil with deceptive humor. But why? he asked himself.

He observed her a moment more before resting his hands lightly on her shoulders. "I hate to leave you like this." Terraine allowed his hands to slip down her arms and tighten around her waist. He was puzzled by the abrupt change in her mood. Somehow fear and Sasha were two things that did not blend together well at all. He wanted to make everything right again so that he could see the sparkling smile that he had quickly grown accustomed to.

"I'll be fine," Sasha said quietly, pretending to be in control of the situation. She laid an unsteady hand on his chest and attempted to smile up at him but her eyes strayed over his shoulder and swept the entire area as if she were looking for something or someone.

Terraine felt her stiffen and he turned and followed the direction of her golden eyes. "What is it, Sasha? Is something wrong?" Her behavior was puzzling him. She tried to appear calm and in control but her slight tremble gave her away.

Sasha tossed her head back towards the sky and laughed almost hysterically. "Of course not. Relax. N-nothing is wrong. I thought I saw Ms. Ellis's cat running loose again," she said referring to her neighbor. Sasha studied the ground then looked up under her lashes at him with troubled eyes. "Um... I..." Her voice trailed off. "I better get back in the house. The police should be ready for me." She brushed a light kiss on his forehead and stepped out of his reach. Sasha stopped and looked at him for several seconds with her stomach clenched tight. She felt alone without the physical contact. She wanted to lay her head on his chest and share her fears with him, but she hardly knew where to begin. Besides, it wasn't his problem anyway. It was hers.

Terraine looked down into a pair of beautiful hazel eyes. Even if he had not seen the fear, he would have known from her eyes that she was not telling him the truth. He was concerned. But how was he to proceed if she did not want to share her problems with him? "Call me later," Terraine said lightly. Sasha nodded and turned away, dashing back into the house.

Terraine walked around and climbed into his Navigator. He started the motor and leaned forward, resting his arms on the steering wheel.

Something is wrong, he told himself, rubbing a frustrated hand across his shaved head. There was more going on here than a simple break-in. Sasha was definitely hiding something, which Terraine found painfully ironic since he never got around to telling her his own secret. Whatever it was, he planned to find out.

With one last look towards her house, he shifted his car into drive and pulled off.

The man sat in his car two houses down from her home and watched her silhouette in the bedroom window. He had spent many evenings in this same spot watching her activities. Once he even had the nerve to get out the car, walk up and peek in her window, but the neighbor's dog started barking and he decided not to try that again. He didn't want to take a chance of alerting anyone.

He reached over and opened his glove compartment, pulling out a single wilted rose that she'd worn in her hair the last time he saw her. He brought it to his nose and inhaled deeply. It still smelled just like the sweet exotic scent of her creamy skin. "Sasha... sweet Sasha." He moaned as desire race through his blood. He wanted her so bad. She was a beautiful golden goddess. She was his... she'd promised. Soon everything was going to become a reality. All he had to do was wait a little longer, even though it was playing hell with his libido.

"Soon Sasha, we will be together." He had a

plan. With one hand holding the rose and the other stroking an erection, he closed his eyes and smiled wickedly.

Sasha woke up the next morning just in time to make her six o'clock step aerobics class at the YMCA. An hour later she drove home, drenched in perspiration and full of anticipation. Today she began her new career as a Diva model and the thought brought a smile to her face.

It was a gorgeous June morning with a warm breeze that coaxed her into letting down the top on her hunter green Mustang convertible. She drove the short distance home allowing the wind to ruffle her hair while she reviewed the events of the previous night.

After the police left, Honey gave her a thorough tongue lashing for her uncooperative behavior. She spent the rest of the evening in her room with the phone off the hook, not wanting to talk to anyone. She definitely did not want to have to explain herself to Terraine. She remembered his keen probing eyes but she was not prepared last night for any questions. She was ashamed of her past and was embarrassed that Terraine had been there to witness part of it. The worst of it was that maybe he realized that she was a woman with skeletons in her closet and not worth his time or effort. Sasha frowned. She couldn't blame him if he did. She'd reacted poorly last night.

Sasha pushed a strand of hair from in front of her right eye. She was certain that she knew what was going on though she was not ready yet to share it with anyone, including the police. She was not ready yet for any explanations.

Pulling into her driveway, she turned the car off and sat still for a few moments. Last night had been Robby's way of making sure she had not forgotten that he was back and that he was somewhere close by watching her.

A half-hour later, Sasha stepped out of the shower and retrieved an old flannel robe from a hook on the back of her bedroom door. She was padding in the direction of the kitchen with her worries dissipated, feeling fresh and vibrant, when the phone rang.

"Good morning, Sasha," her mother said in a harmonious voice.

"Good morning, Mom," Sasha said.

"Chile, you missed a good sermon yesterday. Reverend Baker had the whole congregation either shouting or down on their knees begging for forgiveness." Roxaner stopped a moment to praise God before continuing. "Rev asked about you."

"I'll try to come next Sunday," Sasha said.

"You said that last Sunday," Roxaner reminded her daughter.

Sasha raised the back of her hand to her forehead and prayed that her mother had not called to wear on her nerves this morning. She was not sure how much more she could handle in a twenty-four hour period. "I promise, Mo-ther." Sasha somehow managed to sound sweet between clenched teeth.

"All right, I am going to hold you to it. Right now guess what I got you?"

"What?" Sasha was almost too afraid to ask. Last month her mother had bought her a pair of the most hideous looking earrings she had ever seen. They were zebras carved out of wood that hung almost to her chin, and she had felt obligated to wear them at least once while in her mother's presence, but wished it could have been somewhere other than around family and friends. Her cousins would never let her live it down.

"A dog."

Sasha could hear the pride in her voice, but that did not stop her from visualizing a large dog the size of a St. Bernard. "What dog?"

"The one you promised me months ago you would get. After that incident with Robby... well... I thought having a dog around would be good and I knew you were going to procrastinate on the issue, so I took matters into my own hand." Roxaner sighed then continued, "I went to the Humane Society yesterday and found the perfect dog for you. I'll have your puppy trained and ready to go home with you in a week. Now wasn't that thoughtful of me?" Roxaner asked in her apple pie voice.

Sasha grunted.

"Sasha, don't think you are too old for me to bend over my knee," her mother warned in a firm yet humorous tone.

"Momma, please!" Sasha gasped before laughing. A flash of humor crossed her face at the mere thought of her mother's petite frame of five-feet, two inches trying to bend her over her knee. "I appreciate your thoughtfulness, but I was really looking forward to going and finding just the right dog for me." *Something small, fixed and already trained.*

"Well, what's done is done. Don't worry, you'll like her." Her? Sasha's eyes rolled up towards the ceiling. All she needed was a houseful of puppies. Now she knew how the man in the movie *Beethoven* felt.

"She's spayed," Roxaner added, as if she could read her daughter's mind. Sasha sighed with relief but was too afraid to ask her mom the breed of the dog. This was not something she cared to discuss this early in the morning.

"Mom, can't this wait? I am trying to get ready. I have to be at Diva Designs in two hours." Sasha could hardly contain her excitement. She'd shared the news of her new contract with her mother several nights ago. Her success meant everything in the world to her mother.

Roxaner gasped. "Oh, I forgot that was today! I am so proud of you, sweetheart, and so is your Aunt Bee. She can't wait to see you at Judith's wedding. We are all so proud. I can't wait to brag to everyone at church that my daughter is going to be on the cover of a catalog." Roxaner started sniffling.

"Mom, don't start crying," Sasha groaned. Her mother could be so sensitive at times. Roxaner was the type of woman who'd speak her mind but she was also the same person who cried while watching reruns of *Lassie*.

"Don't be silly." Roxaner breathed deeply into the phone, trying to regain her composure. "Drop by this week and tell me all about it. Bring Honey. How is my girl doing anyway?" Roxaner was fond of Honey, who'd become a permanent fixture in their lives. At any of their family gatherings she was right at the table with everyone else. Sasha remembered their last family reunion when Honey had pretended to be a distant cousin. She had everyone either fooled or confused until Honey caught sight of Sasha's cousin Dwayne, a professional body

129

builder, and then she didn't want to be related to anyone.

"Wild as ever," Sasha chuckled. She reached into an upper cabinet and took out coffee, deciding she deserved another round this morning.

"That girl has spirit. Reminds me of myself at her age. Getting out would definitely do you some good. Hasn't it been almost six months since you've been out on a date?"

Who's keeping score? Honey and Roxaner. If it wasn't one, then it was the other. No wonder they got along so well. Sasha was almost tempted to tell her mother about her date yesterday but knew if she did, by Sunday her aunts would be planning her wedding.

"Momma, please don't start," Sasha groaned as she set the hazelnut blend to brewing.

Roxaner sighed. "Baby, you are a beautiful young lady and I can't understand why you can't find a good man." She was obviously not listening to anything Sasha said and added, "I want you to find happiness and settle down. I don't know if you noticed or not, but I am ready to be a grandmother."

Happiness? Was this déjà vu? Sasha half listened as her mother went into one of her never-ending lectures on the future of her only child until Sasha decided it was time to end the conversation.

"Momma, my other line is ringing," she lied as

she walked across the room. "I'll be by to see you later in the week." With that she put the receiver down and walked over to the window with her arms folded against her chest.

Children.

She would love someday to have several little rugrats bouncing around calling her Momma. It didn't bother her that it meant losing her slim figure for nine months. Not as long as she was carrying the child of a man who'd vowed to love her through sickness and health. She stared out into her neighbor's neatly trimmed yard. There was no rush. She still had at least ten good childbearing years ahead of her; besides, she had a lot of healing left to do. She needed to first come to terms with her past, forgive herself and move on. Her mother hadn't been there and she did not really know or truly understand everything that happened. Honey appeared to understand but even she really did not know it all. They had not lived through what she lived through. Sasha shook her head. She could still hear the gun going off in her ear, and now her past was back to haunt her.

Sasha hugged herself and then swallowed hard. Today was the first day of the rest of her life and she had something new and wonderful to focus on.

The smell of fresh coffee filled the room. Sasha

grabbed her mug and filled it to the brim before returning to her seat. She slowly brought the hot liquid to her lips and took several long sips before setting the mug down on the table. Sasha then leaned back in her chair and took a deep breath as her mind flooded with pleasant memories of her weekend and Terraine.

Sasha slipped on her sunglasses and steered her Mustang onto the interstate towards downtown St. Louis, to the corporate headquarters located near the riverfront. She leaned over, turning on her favorite R&B station, Magic 105, and listened to The Breakfast Crew's cackling antics before the sounds of Faith Evans filled the car.

Sasha sang along and tapped her burgundy nails against the steering wheel. Other than Roxaner buying her a dog, her day was going pretty well. *Just think positive and the rest of the day will be just as great.* Her smile widened, knowing the radiance that shone on her face had nothing to do with the sunshine overhead; instead it had everything to do with the way she was feeling right now.

She zoomed past a man in a Jeep with a shaved head. How could she have been so lucky to meet someone like Terraine? It was almost too good too be true. The smile faded from her lips and the animation in her eyes dimmed. *And after your behavior last night, he probably won't be anything more than a memory.*

"Oh brother, girl. Get a grip," she muttered. Sasha decided it was safer to sing. It took her mind off things. She turned the music up high and sang along in a loud, off-key voice.

Pulling off the highway, she drove two blocks past the Transworld Dome, the new Rams football stadium. She drove up to a private parking garage and was greeted by an elderly, gray-haired man who was watching a portable television in a guard shack.

He tipped his hat to her. "Good morning, young lady."

Sasha smiled and rested her hands on the steering wheel. "Hi, I am Sasha Moore."

He reached for his clipboard and checked for her name on the list and nodded.

"Pleasure to meet ya. They're expectin' you. I'm Rufus. Been here longer than anybody else. If they give you a hard time, just let Ol' Rufus know." He winked, and then gave her directions into the building before opening the gate. Sasha waved at him and steered into the lot. She parked and took the elevator to the third floor, where her heels sank into plush mauve carpeting. How impressive, she thought as she walked down a long hall towards a pair of huge mahogany doors varnished to gleaming perfection. Sasha paused a moment and smoothed her skirt, then took a deep breath and opened the doors, walking into a large, magnificently decorated waiting room. There were two couches upholstered in splashes of lilac and mauve and between them a large coffee table covered with magazines. Hanging on the walls were several abstract paintings.

"May I help you?"

Sasha whirled around. She had been so fascinated with the decor that she had not noticed the young mousy-looking girl sitting behind a large desk in the corner of the room, who greeted her with a smile that Sasha happily returned.

Sasha walked towards her. "I'm sorry. I'm here to see Natalia Bonaparte."

"You must be Sasha!" she squealed. The young lady sprang from her chair and walked around to where Sasha was standing and shook her hand. "Welcome."

"Thank you. I am glad to be here."

"I'm Tiffany but everyone just calls me Tiff." She wrinkled her nose and lowered her voice as if there were a chance someone else might be listening. "That is everyone but Natalia. She doesn't believe in nicknames. Please have a seat. She'll be returning shortly." She waved towards a couch and Sasha walked over and took a seat across from the reception desk while Tiff took a phone call.

She was probably straight out of high school, Sasha thought. Tiffany's looks were average with a wide nose and dark brown eyes that appeared almost too far apart. Her hair was neatly cut into a short tapered hairdo and she was dressed nicely in a navy blue suit, although the skirt was a little too short for an office. But Sasha quickly found out that Tiffany's personality outweighed anything else. In between phone calls, she asked Sasha numerous questions about her career and listened with delighted interest. Sasha took a quick liking to her. She was warm and—as she quickly found out— a little chatterbox.

"Aren't you excited?" Tiff asked, bubbling with enthusiasm. She was animated, frequently using her hands to get her point across.

Sasha crossed her legs and blushed openly. "Yes. I am very excited."

"I would love to be a model." She shrugged and gave a long, exaggerated sigh. "Unfortunately, I was born too short."

Sasha talked to her about the opportunities that were now available for petite and large woman. Tiffany admitted that as much as she admired modeling, she dreamed of becoming a nurse and was presently attending night school.

Tiff stopped talking long enough to reapply her lip-gloss before she introduced a new subject. "It is too bad about Deja."

"Do they have any suspects?" Sasha was glad that Tiffany had brought up the subject of her death. She had been tempted to ask her earlier but had decided it was inappropriate to do so.

"No, but they are looking for her boyfriend," Tiff whispered loudly. She obviously enjoyed sharing gossip. "She broke up with him two weeks ago in front of everyone. I heard it was an award winning performance." Tiff rolled her eyes. "Deja always did like attention. Alan was so mad security had to escort him off of the premises.

"Tiffany, don't tell me you are gossiping again."

They both turned towards the door where a beautiful, willowy woman stood. Immediately, Sasha noticed her flawless mahogany skin and admired her glossy auburn hair that cascaded in large curls down her back. She had the look of a woman who loved to pamper herself and had to be a model herself, Sasha thought. She watched as the woman examined her with long, inscrutable looks, her slanted, ginger eyes traveling from her face down to her feet. Sasha ignored a feeling of uneasiness.

"Well, it is nice to see that your test sheets did not lie. You are actually as attractive as your portfolio portrayed you to be." Sasha thought she heard a note of disappointment in the woman's voice. She sauntered across the room, extending her hand, and gave Sasha what appeared to be a painful smile. "I am Natalia. We are glad to have you."

"Thank you, I am so glad to be here."

With her raspberry-colored lips pursed, Natalia turned to her receptionist. "Tiffany, please bring a pot of *fresh* coffee to my office."

"Sure thing, boss." Tiffany dashed out of her seat.

"Come." When Natalia led her through a door located behind Tiff's desk, Sasha gasped at the size of the office. Larger than her living room and bedroom combined, it was decorated in mauve and violet with matching blinds and had a large mahogany desk, a sofa in one corner and a small round table next to a small private bath. *Who needs an apartment with an office like this?*

Natalia followed her eyes around the room. "I can tell you are impressed." She placed her hand on her hip and gave Sasha the first pleasant expression she'd seen since they made acquaintance. "I like it also. The founder of this corporation was my godfather and he enjoyed spoiling me."

Sasha stared up at the pictures on the walls,

noticing a poster-size picture of Natalia. She was either vain or a former model. "You were a model?"

Natalia's head snapped around. "I am still a model." Annoyance was visible on her face.

Meow! Catfight.

Natalia named off some of the corporations and designers that she had worked for and Sasha suddenly remembered seeing her face on the cover of *Essence* magazine a couple of years ago. Natalia seemed pleased when she mentioned it.

"They did a five-page spread on Diva Designs but I was the only model they featured."

Vain, Sasha thought, definitely vain.

Natalia took a graceful seat behind her desk and fanned her fingers in the air. "How else do you think I know what we need at Diva Designs? I was one of the first models this company had. I have been directing the fashion shows for the last four years and now I will be working to launch the new apparels line."

Sasha was relieved when Tiff walked in carrying a fresh pot of coffee. While Natalia took the time to swing around her chair and fluff her hair in front of a mirror sitting on a small table behind her desk, Tiff made faces behind her back. Sasha had to put her hand to her mouth to suppress her laughter and hoped that Natalia did not see Tiff in the mirror. Ms. Bonaparte was not a woman to cross.

After Tiff left, they sat at the small conference table sipping coffee, and Natalia showed her the layout and design that they had in mind for the new catalog. Sasha was impressed with the thought that had gone into the project. She quickly learned that Natalia was a brilliant woman, who had a lot of wonderful ideas that were guaranteed to make the new line a success. Sasha was grateful she would be a part of that success.

When she heard a light knock on the door, Sasha swung around and faced a handsome, chestnut-colored man in a beige, single-breasted designer suit.

Natalia looked up and gave her first genuine smile. "Evan, please come in." He strutted across the room to where they were sitting. "Sasha, I'd like you to meet my assistant, Evan Hall." Sasha stood.

"It is always a pleasure to meet a beautiful woman." He took the hand that she offered and brought it slowly to his lips. He then gave her a twenty-four carat smile while continuing to hold her hand.

Natalia cleared her throat. "Was there something you needed, Evan?"

Releasing her hand, Evan quickly returned to his role as assistant. "We have a problem. It appears that our master of ceremony has fallen and broken her leg."

She tossed her hands in the air. "Great, just great!" Natalia rose. "Now what are we going to do without a host." She grabbed a file and strode towards the door. "Do me a favor, show Sasha around while I figure out who is going to speak at our fashion show next month." Then without a backward glance, she exited the room.

Sasha frowned and turned to look at him. "Is she always like that?"

Evan chuckled. "She is usually worse."

The rest of the afternoon breezed by quickly. Evan gave her the grand tour of all five floors that made up the corporate offices and introduced her to the staff. Evan, she found out, was a recent college graduate with a degree in fashion merchandising. Previously he'd done a six-month internship with the corporation, becoming Natalia's assistant in March. He was responsible for all of the prep work for the fashion shows, from reserving the locations to making the travel arrangements.

They stopped by the marketing department and Evan showed her his office and introduced her to the promotions coordinator, Loren Robinson, whom Evan worked closely with. She was a pleasant, dark-skinned young woman who was obviously infatuated with Evan, because throughout the introduction, either her eyes or hands were on him the entire time.

Sasha was then taken to meet Devon, the hair-stylist, who was obviously a homosexual. He wore his hair short and relaxed without a single strand of hair on his beige face. With one hand cocked on his hip, the other moved simultaneously with his head as he spoke in a high-pitched voice.

"Welcome, sista' girl." Devon snapped his fingers, adding emphasize to each syllable. "Oh, my God! Your hair is beautiful!" He reached out and stroked a lock and insisted that she sit down in his chair. He could not wait to get the scissors to her hair. Sasha was hesitant but thirty minutes later Devon had tamed her curls so that they no longer resisted tumbling around her shoulders, and as an added bonus he gave her a facial, which Natalia had insisted on.

It was not until late afternoon that Sasha was ushered into a large studio where photos of former Diva models from over the years adorned three whitewashed walls. The other wall was covered with floor-to-ceiling mirrors and there were lights and props everywhere. There was also a casual lounge with four love seats conversationally arranged around a large coffee table.

Evan received a page to return to his office but before he did, he directed her to the dressing room located behind a backdrop. It was there that she met the other four models.

Sasha walked in and was immediately greeted by identical smiles. Asia and India were twenty-year-old identical twins with slanted, cinnamon-colored eyes that danced while they spoke. Their skin was an even golden bronze that could not be duplicated by any tanning spa. Their copper hair was cut asymmetrically and surrounded their oval faces. Sasha sat down and listened as the two spoke simultaneously with identical gestures. When one started a sentence, out of habit the other one finished it. They were from Birmingham and had a charming southern accent that Sasha found delightful. In a matter of moments the girls made her feel warm and welcomed to the family.

"We are so glad you are here," they giggled before encircling her in a big friendly hug.

Tyler Edwards was next to introduce herself. She was a beautiful Nigerian woman with dark glossy hair cropped short and large opal-colored eyes protected by long thick lashes. She was the same age as Sasha and had been modeling since she was five. She had traveled from Manhattan where she was living with her parents.

Monet Phillips, on the other hand, was about as phony as her breasts. She was sitting in front of a vanity brushing her thick mane of jet-black hair and did not turn around and acknowledge Sasha's presence until her name was called. She then swiveled around and favored Sasha with what looked like a carefully practiced smile that unfortunately did not match the distant look in her dark chestnut eyes. She was the color of pecan pie and had a petite nose, high cheekbones and small thin lips. It was obvious Monet did not want her here and Sasha immediately sensed the resentment as Monet sized her up with her eyes. Monet was taller than everyone else at about six-two. She did not look long and lanky; instead her legs were shapely and sexy. She was beautiful but hard looking. An unspoken message seemed to say, *I am all that!*

Sasha was grateful that she had won the favor of the twins. She was certain that she was going to need the two allies in her corner.

Suddenly a shadow was cast over the room. Sasha looked up and there stood a big burly man with the largest and saddest eyes she'd ever seen.

"Hi, Stefan." The twins spoke in harmony.

"Hello, girls." He then turned and acknowledged Sasha with a swift nod before clasping his hands together. "Come on, girls, get ready to do some test shots. I am anxious to see how beautiful you five ladies look in front of the camera together." He then held up five fingers indicating how much time they had to get ready and disappeared behind the backdrop.

"That must be the photographer," Sasha

observed.

"You bet." Tyler smiled brightly and rose from her chair. "And if I were you, I'd get ready fast."

Sasha spent a fabulous afternoon in front of the camera as they relaxed and clowned around together while Stefan shot several rolls of film. That is, everyone but Monet, who was extremely stand-offish. As the afternoon passed she made sure Sasha knew she was not the least bit interested in being friends. Sasha found herself wondering why.

Tired, Sasha was not sad to see her first day at Diva Designs come to an end. Natalia dropped by the studio to see how well the test shots had gone and rode down in the elevator with Sasha to the garage.

"I hope I didn't offend you earlier about needing a facial. You have to understand this catalog is very important to me. I designed several of the apparels that we are offering," she said in a voice that did not sound at all apologetic. But Sasha figured it was just her way and nodded. "Richard Andrews built this business and now that he has passed, his grandson—"

"Excuse me," Sasha cut in. "D-did you say Andrews?"

Natalia stared at her as if she had just grown a horn on her forehead. "Of course." Just as they reached the garage level the door opened and there stood Terraine.

"Terraine?" she gasped. Sasha saw the surprise and uncomfortable expression on his face as they stepped off the elevator.

"Terraine, darling, I was on my way up to your office." Natalia smiled seductively at him. "Sasha, I'd like to introduce our CEO, Terraine Andrews."

"We've already met." He looked at Sasha apologetically. "I was just on my way up to see her."

Natalia arched a perfectly sculptured eyebrow and watched the exchange of looks between them, not at all pleased at what she saw.

Terraine quickly pointed to the man to his left. "Let me introduce you to our marketing director, Carl Matthews." Sasha looked over at the distinguished, handsome man with the boyish grin.

"It's a pleasure to meet you, Ms. Moore."

She gave him a dazed smile. "Call me Sasha. And thank you very much." Sasha stood stunned while a radar went off in her head. She forced her mouth closed and swallowed. Disbelief and humiliation churned inside her. It took her a few minutes to realize what was going on. "Will you excuse me please?" Sasha spun and stalked off as fast as her long legs could carry her. Terraine dashed after her, catching her just as she was opening her car door. He slapped a hand against it, slamming it shut before she could climb in.

"Sasha." His powerful hand grabbed her arm and pulled her away from the car. "Please, let me explain."

Sasha turned on him, her eyes hot and flashing. "What is there to explain? You played me. You knew all along who I was and never once said anything to me. Joke's on me." She gave a dry laugh. "Tell me, is this some game that you play with all of your models?" Her eyes were full of accusations as she tried unsuccessfully to shake the hand that restrained her.

"No, it was nothing like that. I was going to tell you when the time was right."

Tears sprang to her eyes but she lifted her chin high, forcing them back. "And when would that have been? After you had managed to get me in your bed?" Trembling with humiliation down to the soles of her feet, she ached to slap him in the face.

"Of course not. I care about you. I tried calling you last night to tell you but your phone was busy all evening." Sasha remembered that the phone had been off the hook, but she did not share that bit of information nor was it an excuse. He'd had plenty of time to tell her the truth.

Her cheeks were flushed with emotion. "Terraine, let me go." She tried to yank away but he simply tightened his fingers around her wrist then briskly pulled her into his arms, crushing her breasts against him.

"Does this feel like I'm playing games?"

She felt the pressure of his hand on her neck as he drew her face towards his and kissed her. She needed to resist. Twisting in his arms and arching her body, she sought to get free but Terraine pinned her against the car. Sasha pushed against his chest, trying to ignore the intimacy of his hips grinding against hers while he traced the shape of her mouth with his tongue, sending chills down her spine. When he forced her lips apart and slipped his tongue inside, her resistance halted. She allowed herself a moment to relive the precious time they'd spent together.

"I'd never hurt you," he whispered.

His words broke the spell and Sasha suddenly realized what she was doing. He had made her feel like a fool without giving a second thought to her feelings and there was nothing she could do about it. She needed this job and he knew it. Terraine had her entire future in the palm of his hand. But one thing she could do was not give him the satisfaction of knowing that she'd allowed herself to be used again. Sasha put a hand to his chest and pushed away. Taking a deep, unsteady breath, she stepped away from the seductive scent of his cologne so that she could think clearly and rested her hand on the car for support.

"I guess if I refuse to sleep with you then my career at Diva Designs is over?"

Terraine looked stunned by her question. "Of course not. Our relationship is personal."

Sasha then faced him with a proud tilt of her chin and pierced him with her coldest stare. "Good, then I would appreciate it if you would never touch me again." She grabbed the door handle, jerked it open and climbed in.

This time Terraine did not try to stop her; instead, he stood and watched her speed out of the parking lot.

Chapter Six

Sasha had been sitting in front of her sewing machine for the last hour and still had not finished altering the dress that was staring her right smack in the face. She needed to focus. When Judith came over and tried on her gown this morning, Sasha discovered that the bride had dropped an inch around her waist. Sasha wanted—correction, she needed—to get the waistline adjusted before Judith came back on Wednesday for her final fitting but she could not concentrate. Instead her mind kept wandering back to Terraine.

Staring down at the gown, Sasha found her vision blurring. She was not going to cry. What would be the point? It was painful enough admitting that she had been made to look like such a fool and

149

even harder knowing that she couldn't blame anyone but herself. She had lowered her guard only to
find out that she'd allowed herself to be humiliated
once again. When was she ever going to learn?

Sasha sniffed and once more fought back the
tears that were trying to surface. Crying would be a
waste of precious time and energy. Instead, she
got up from her chair and walked towards the
kitchen, trying to calm her nerves.

Since their embarrassing encounter, she had
managed to avoid Terraine. Sasha had made it
through the week feeling like a zombie, but somehow managing to finish her shoots even though she
was on edge most of the time, certain that Terraine
would walk into the studio at any moment. He had
not. Terraine had heard her silent prayer and had
stayed away.

Terraine. Sasha gripped the edge of the counter top. Even the sound of his name caused the bottom of her stomach to hurt. She had been so certain that he was going to be different. He had
appeared caring and gentle in a way that no other
man had ever been. His kisses had caused her
blood to warm, her toes to curl. With his aggressive
behavior, Terraine had managed to drag her willingly from behind her protective shell and into his
arms. Sasha took long, deep breaths. The joy he
filled her with during the short time they'd spent

together had been special. Though Terraine had made her feel like no other man had ever come close to making her feel, in the end he'd turned out to be just like all the rest. A user. He had used his charm, good looks and unwavering determination to coax her into trusting him. Why had she allowed herself to fall for his dimpled smile? Sasha had been there and done that too many times before, yet somehow she'd allowed herself to be blinded by good looks and aggression and had fallen for the same trick, hook, line, and sinker.

Sasha ran a shaky hand through her hair. She was torn emotionally, as a result, uncertain how she should react. She didn't know if she should be angry with him or cry because of her own personal stupidity. She should have known that no man could ever be that wonderful, that there had to be something Terraine was hiding. But in reality she had not wanted to know. Yes, she should have asked more questions but to be honest, part of her had not wanted to blemish the perfect image she had created of him.

Why me? Sasha reached into the refrigerator and pulled out a cup of lowfat raspberry yogurt, then grabbed a spoon from the drawer and leaned against the counter, shoveling it into her mouth.

Unbidden, Terraine's well-built frame came into focus and a huge ache expanded like a bubble and filled her chest. She was attracted to everything about him. He had been a breath of fresh air, but with the kind of luck she always had, Sasha should have been prepared for something to happen sooner or later.

Sasha walked over to the end of the counter and pushed the play button on her answering machine. Terraine had left her several messages throughout the week, telling her over and over how sorry he was. She had not returned any of his calls. Sasha gave a dry laugh. So excited about the possibility of convincing Diva Designs to consider adding her gowns to their collection, she had even shared her plans with Terraine. God, she felt like such a fool! She was furious that he could have been so conniving that he chose not to tell her that he was the owner.

Groaning, Sasha set her yogurt down on the counter, suddenly losing her appetite. She knew for certain that her situation had definitely turned complicated. If she had not run into him, would he have told her who he was? *Probably not.* Would he have carried on the charade? *Probably so.*

Sasha threw her arms in the air and walked into the living room, flopping onto the couch. She had wanted so badly for things to work out just this one time. She had followed her heart and fallen on her face. Gambled and lost. It had happened to her again. She had allowed herself to be humiliated by another man, just when she was just beginning to mend after her relationship with Robby. No, she corrected herself miserably, Terraine wasn't just "another" man. He was the man who held her entire career at Diva Designs in the palm of his hand, and it hurt her heart.

Curling into a fetal position on the couch, Sasha tried to figure out what had happened to the woman of a couple of weeks ago who was not interested in a man. The woman who managed to stay clear of men for six months. Sasha hugged a small throw pillow tightly to her chest. She knew what had happened to her. She had been kissed by Terraine Andrews.

With a deep exhale, Sasha tossed the pillow onto the floor and leaned back against the couch. At least Robby had not lied to her. Normally, Sasha did her best to draw her thoughts from the dark memories that still troubled her, but today she allowed her mind to race backwards.

First there was Whiny Charlie, who had insisted that he be given the honor of being her first, her last, her everything. His pledge of undying love had lasted about as long as he could hold an erection. Feeling violated and misused, Sasha had fallen into the arms of a male model, Larry the Leach, who always seemed to have misplaced his wallet whenever it was time to pay for anything, including the rent. Then there was Gay Garland, whom she had tried to surprise one evening only to find out the joke was on her when she found him in the bed with her hairstylist, Tyrone. She'd even dated a native of Paris, who turned out to be a starving artist looking for a free ride from a supermodel. How disappointed he was to find out that a supermodel she was not.

Then at the end of yet another heart-shattering relationship with a movie producer, Sasha had met Robby, and she'd thought he was God sent. Maybe if she hadn't been on the rebound she would have seen the warning signs.

It took Sasha two years before she realized that Robby suffered from mental illness. She'd met him one night while finishing up a fashion show in Chicago. He had somehow charmed his way into her dressing room carrying a dozen long-stemmed roses. Surprised, she had not known if she should be angered by his assumption or flattered by his aggressive approach. As she listened to him, she found him charming and extremely handsome. He was a red bone with a light splash of freckles across the bridge of his nose, which she found boyishly attractive. Robby had sandy brown hair cropped close and light brown eyes covered by thick bushy eyebrows. That evening she had been instantly attracted and agreed to have dinner with him and his mother aboard a dinner cruise at Navy Pier. Mrs. Adams had been receptive to her and Sasha enjoyed the evening in the company of both of them, especially the charming Robert Adams III.

Robby was the son of Clarence Robert Adams II, the top defense attorney in the state of Illinois and his wife Victoria, an interior designer requested by the rich and famous. At the time of their introduction, Robby was attending law school and had a promising future ahead of him, working for his father's law firm.

In the course of two weeks, he had swept Sasha off her feet and introduced her to the good life: romantic dinners, Broadway shows, expensive gifts and dozens and dozens of roses. By the time she was scheduled to leave for Dallas, they were in love. After Sasha left Chicago, Robby called her frequently and flew down on weekends or breaks from his course work so that they could be together. Sasha was on top of the world and was certain that this time she had gotten it right. Eight months later, when Sasha was scheduled to tour Europe, Robby had proposed and she had happily accepted. At their engagement party Sasha first witnessed Robby's delusional state.

His mother was generous and held the party at their large home in Flossmoor. Everything was beautiful, including the three-carat marquise diamond that Sasha sported on her finger. Sasha disappeared to the restroom to freshen up and when she returned, Robby boisterously accused her in front of their guests of sneaking off with his best friend. He said that he'd suspected that something was going on between them for a while and threatened to kill her if it ever happened again. Tony had punched Robby and left while Sasha stood flabbergasted by his accusations, especially since she had only met Tony for the first time an hour before. If it weren't for Victoria being an excellent hostess and having a way of smoothing things over, Sasha would have died from embarrassment. Little did she know that evening was only the beginning.

Shortly after, Sasha left for Europe and Robby began calling her every day, asking her where she had been and who she was with. He then began flying over and surprising her by popping up when she least expected and accusing her of having one affair after the other. He then insisted on traveling with her and dropped out of law school. Then things got worse. Robby began searching her purse for phone numbers and condoms, any form of evidence he could use to condemn her. He wanted to keep constant tabs on her whereabouts. He picked arguments and tried to hang out in her dressing room. Eventually his badgering took its toll and Sasha ended the relationship and returned home. A devastated Robby, full of remorse, followed her home and begged her to give him another chance but Sasha refused. It was then he decided to take matters into his own hands.

When Sasha returned from an afternoon at the beauty shop, she walked into her house to find Robby with a gun to his head threatening to end his life if she left him. He put a bullet in the chamber and played Russian roulette, pulling the trigger against his forehead, and scared her to death. Sasha was supposed to have dinner with Honey and when she did not answer the door, Honey became suspicious and called the police. They arrived just as Sasha was wrestling Robby for the gun and it accidentally went off.

After Robby was arrested, he was evaluated by a psychiatrist and was diagnosed with a paranoid disorder.

After the incident, Sasha had been an emotional wreck and sought counseling. She blamed herself for not knowing that something was wrong and for turning her back on him when he needed her most. And now it was happening again.

Sasha sniffed and dragged the back of her hand across her cheek, wiping away moisture. Rising from the couch, she headed to the corner of the room, deciding thirty minutes on her stair climber was just what she needed to relax. Then she'd retreat to the bathroom for a nice warm bubble bath.

"Sly Stone and his son Jacob are here to see you."

Terraine looked up at Geraldine, who stood in the doorway to his office, then threw both hands into the air and sighed. Just what he needed to end his day, another one of his grandfather's friends. Since Pops' death, his so-called friends had been dropping by looking for some kind of hand-out. Sly and Pops went back as far as grammar school, having grown up in the same neighborhood. They'd maintained their friendship for years, even when they did not see eye to eye. Terraine and Jacob had developed a dislike for one another during high school after competing in a basketball tournament in which Jacob was benched after fouling out, leaving Terraine to bring the school to victory. Jacob had resented him ever since. Terraine ran a frustrated hand across his goatee and closed his eyes briefly. After a full day with a non-stop agenda, he was ready to go home.

He and Geraldine—she preferred to be called Geri—had spent most of the morning going over his schedule for the next several weeks. Geri had been Pops' right hand for over twenty-five years. She was a lovely woman in her fifties, who looked like Lena Horne, and was happily married to her high school sweetheart. She had six children and three grandchildren that she adored.

During the six months Pops was bed-ridden, Geri had kept things running smoothly. Terraine quickly found out that she was a great resource in the office. She knew every employee by name—nickname if they had one—and was able to quickly summarize the corporate activities for the last ten years, since Terraine's departure.

Terraine released both buttons on his navy blue single-breasted jacket and leaned back in his chair. He'd had Geri schedule meetings with each division in order to begin building working relationships with his managers. The rest of the afternoon had been spent going over bank statements. Diva Design's revenue had reached a dangerously low level. The company was in worse shape than he'd imagined. Why hadn't Pops talked to him about it months ago? Wasn't finance his area of expertise? Terraine sighed. He already knew the answer to that question.

To top things off, Sasha was avoiding him and there was nothing he could do about it. At least not until shooting was complete. He did not want to risk her quitting the project. He was trying to be patient, but was not sure how much longer he could do that.

"Go ahead and send them in," Terraine said with an irritated twist of his mouth. Geri nodded and walked into the other room. The two walked in and Terraine rose from his seat.

"Terraine, my boy, good to see you again." Sly walked over to his desk with his hand extended. Terraine shook his hand and then turned and acknowledged Jacob with a simple nod of the head.

Wearing his gray hair pulled back with a rubber band, Sly reminded Terraine of a black Steven Seagal. Jacob, on the other hand, looked the same as he had during high school, big and bulky. Terraine resumed his seat, waving a hand towards the chairs for his guests to sit. Sly sat across from Terraine's desk with his hands clasped together in his lap while Jacob sat on the couch near the window.

"How are things going, son?" Sly asked.

"I can't complain." Terraine rested his elbow on the desk. He observed Jacob's smug expression. *I guess he's still holding a grudge.*

Sly smiled. "Glad to hear it. Rich would have been proud. He always wanted you right here with him. It's a shamed that it took a tragedy to bring you back. You look right at home sitting in his chair. How long has it been since I seen you in this office?

160

Ten years? Fifteen? Time sure does travel."

Terraine fingered his mustache and noticed Jacob's lips curl into a smile. Terraine observed both of them and although it didn't show, irritation gnawed at him. Sly was treading on thin ice, touching on a subject that Terraine cared not to think about.

"What can I do for you gentleman this evening?" Terraine leaned back in his chair.

"Oh, yes, of course, the reason for my visit. Well..." Sly stopped to clear his throat, which allowed Jacob an opportunity to intervene.

"Rumor has it that you are thinking about selling Diva Designs."

So that is what this is about. Terraine hesitated before answering. He had given selling serious consideration but quickly relinquished the idea. Now he was glad that he had. Word sure did get around fast.

Terraine leaned forward with both hands on the desk. "You are right about one thing. It is a rumor. I had briefly considered it but selling is no longer an option."

Jacob chuckled nastily as if what Terraine just said was absurd. "Why is that?"

"If you knew my grandfather as well as I thought you did, you would not have to ask that question. Pops spent too many years building this corporation for me to just throw it all away."

Jacob shifted in his chair and began to say something, but before his rebellious emotion got out of hand, Sly cleared his throat, getting his attention. "Son, let me handle this." Terraine glanced at the younger Stone and his eyes conveyed the fury within him.

"Tee, I must agree with you. Rich was proud of this corporation, but it is also the same corporation that you were never interested in," Sly made it a point to add. "I think he would have been pleased if he knew that you were turning it over to me."

Terraine lifted an eyebrow. "To you?"

Sly nodded. "I would like to buy the corporation. I watched it grow over the years. Even loaned Rich a few thousand to get if off the ground." He chuckled lightly. "I think if anyone should have it, it should be me."

Terraine ran a hand across his chin. "Did you ever express an interest to my grandfather?"

"Yeah and the old fart flat out refused to sell it to me!" Sly crossed his legs and waved his hands in the air. Terraine looked at him long enough to see a swift shadow of anger sweep across his face.

Managing to quell his now rising anger, Terraine licked his lower lip. *They must think I am a candidate for the Sucker of the Year award.* "So, what makes you think I will?"

"Because you are reasonable." Sly's voice rose. "Rich always was pigheaded."

Terraine chuckled softly. That point he could not argue. "Actually, I can be pigheaded sometimes myself." Terraine shook his head and slowly blinked his eyes. "I believe that is a quality that I inherited honestly from my grandfather."

Sly smiled at him, a tight smile that wasn't particularly friendly. "Selling the corporation to me will still be like keeping it in the family."

Terraine responded sharply with a dry laugh. "You think so? Now *that* I am going to have to give some thought."

"What's there to think about? If anyone can run this business, I can." Sly's voice rang with pride. He owned a chain of unisex clothing stores in Eastern Illinois. "I am ready to branch out. I want this corporation and I am willing to make you a more than generous offer."

"It is no secret that this business is trying to stay above water." Jacob shifted in his seat and gave Terraine a disturbing look. "I would think you'd be anxious to return to your high class life in Chicago."

Terraine met the anger glinting in his eyes head-on. "I'm not returning to Chicago," he said finally before rising from his chair. As far as he was concerned this meeting was over.

"That's a shame. Chicago is going to miss you."

Jacob's voice was heavy with sarcasm and his eyes were cold and proud. "Come on, Dad, we're wasting our time here." He rose abruptly and walked out the door.

Sly rose slowly from the chair and added, "Give it some thought, son. I'll call you in a few days." Sly smiled weakly and with that, he exited the room. Terraine almost felt sorry for the old man.

Shortly after their departure, Geri walked into the office with both hands posted firmly on her hips. "What the hell did they want?"

Terraine grinned. She had never been one to bite her tongue. "He wants to buy Diva Designs."

"They don't know when to give up. When Rich's health deteriorated, Sly started trying to get him to sell this corporation and he flat out refused. Rich didn't trust him and neither do I."

"Something I should know?" Terraine looked at her, baffled.

"Didn't Jay tell you?" she asked.

Terraine shook his head.

"The night that Pops passed away, Sly was found standing over his bed."

Sasha was sitting on her bed lotioning her legs when Honey arrived.

She walked into the room and leaned against the door. "Hey, girl," Honey said in a bubbly voice. Sasha noticed that she was dressed in a short white tennis skirt, sandals, and an itty-bitty yellow crop top.

"Where have you been all day?" Sasha asked curiously. *Dressed like that.*

Honey grinned mischievously. "You know that guy I met two weeks ago, Will?"

Sasha nodded as her lips formed a tight thin line. *I should have known.*

"Well," Honey started as she walked over and stood on the side of the bed, "he came by and took me to the mall." Honey turned away but not before she held out her arm. Sasha reached over and grabbed her wrist. On it was a diamond and ruby tennis bracelet.

"Ooh! Did he buy you this?" Sasha let go of her arm and gawked at Honey in amazement.

"Yes, he did." Honey started strutting around the room like a peacock.

Sasha raised her brow and shot Honey a defiant look. "You gave him some, didn't you?"

Honey batted her eyes with an astonished look on her face. "What makes you think that?"

"Because I know you, Honey," Sasha hissed. She hopped off the bed and placed the lotion bottle on top of her dresser.

Rolling her eyes towards the ceiling, Honey waved her hand in the air. "Whatever, girl."

Sasha shook her head. "I can't believe you." She turned towards her closet and retrieved a red satin robe from off the back of the door, putting it on and tying the belt loosely around her small waist. "I hope you used a condom," she mumbled under her breath but loud enough for Honey to hear.

"Girl, what makes you think I am having sex? Maybe I just like the attention," she answered in her defense.

Leaning against her dresser, Sasha exploded with laughter. "You expect me to believe that?"

"It's true. Why is it so hard for you to believe me?"

"Because, I don't," Sasha countered.

Following a long penetrating look, Honey dropped her eyes to the floor. "You can't always judge a book by its cover."

"Honey, who are you trying to fool? Face it, you're a tease." Sasha shook her head from side to side before she walked down the hall to her sewing room.

Had Sasha turned around, she would have seen that Honey looked as if she'd been struck in the face.

Swallowing a large lump that rose in her throat, Honey stood in the doorway and stared down the empty hallway. "I'm not a tease," she murmured, then hesitated, tempted to say more but changed her mind. With a resigned shrug, she headed to her room.

Sasha spent the rest of the evening making the alterations on Judith's gown. Then she hung it on the dress form and stood back to look at her work and smiled. Judith was going to be the talk of the town. Sasha yawned and walked over to turn off the lights. When the phone rang, she answered it on the second ring.

"Hello." There was no answer.

"Hello." There still was no answer but she could hear running water in the background.

Sasha gave an exasperated sigh. "Who is this?" The running water had stopped.

"Robby, I don't have time for games." She then slammed the phone down and went to bed.

Chapter Seven

Sasha was curled on top of a bed covered with gold satin sheets when her smile suddenly faded. She was in the middle of a photo shoot but even with her back to the door she knew Terraine was in the studio. She could feel the heat of his penetrating eyes perforating her.

"Concentrate, Sasha!" Stefan yelled.

She tried again to smile into the camera but she could not focus and caught her eyes straying towards Terraine. She found him watching her as if he were photographing her with his eyes, and as she looked at him, a dizzy current raced through her. Sasha had spent an entire week fighting the overwhelming urge to be near him and it had done nothing to lessen her attraction to him. If anything, the attraction had intensified. Sasha took a deep breath, questioning her decision to have nothing to do with him. But before she could manage to gather her thoughts and decide what to do, she found Terraine studying her with smug delight and his eyes flashing a familiar display of over-confidence. *He's basking in the knowledge of his power over me.* Sasha quickly returned her attention to the camera, feeling a shudder of renewed humiliation. It infuriated that she'd even considered for a moment that maybe, just maybe... Sasha shrugged it off; she didn't even want to bring the words to mind. The intensity of his raisin-brown eyes had confused her momentarily.

Her embarrassment changed to annoyance when Terraine leaned against a wall watching her, obviously enjoying her struggle to recapture her composure. It did not help that Sasha felt her confidence level jump out of the window and was suddenly awkward and unsure what to do. She tried to imagine that she was somewhere else but instead, with Terraine's piercing stare and smug little smile— that she wanted to smack right off of his cocky face—she felt completely intimidated.

"Come on, Sasha, loosen up!" Stefan repeated in the same tone from behind the camera.

She took a deep breath, trying to forget that she was half-naked in a pair of black, high cut briefs and a matching demi bra. She rolled over on the bed and tried a different pose.

Out of the corner of her eyes, Sasha saw Natalia enter the room and stroll over to where Terraine was standing. He turned to face her and Natalia distracted his attention.

A part of her was relieved, and Sasha began to relax as music swept over the room, but she could not take her eyes off the two of them. She tried to ignore a twinge of jealousy at the sight of Natalia clutching his arm and pulling Terraine beside her. What did she care? They exited the studio together and Sasha returned her brain to earth, diverting her attention to the camera, and posed. With a smile, she crawled across the bed on all fours like a cat ready to pounce on a mouse.

"That's it, Sasha. Be natural." Stefan shot several rolls of film and by the end of the session she was exhausted and hungry.

Sasha walked into the dressing room and found the twins deeply engrossed in conversation, Tyler on her cell phone with her agent and Monet in the bathroom getting ready for her shoot.

"Sasha, you were great," India said with admiration. Asia nodded in confirmation.

"Thanks. Now I'm ready for bed." Sasha flopped onto the couch and nestled her head amongst the pillows.

170

She couldn't believe that she'd almost ruined a photo session because of Terraine's presence. How was it that she still responded to him as if nothing had ever happened? In the few seconds that she had allowed herself to look at him, his eyes had told her that he had not stopped thinking about her either. The sight of him had reminded her of the taste of his sweet lips upon her, his hands clasped around her waist and the feel of his warm body pressed up against hers. A warm sensation spread through her blood. *But he deceived you.*

"Sasha, the twins and I are going to the Landing for lunch. You want to join us?" Tyler said, rousing her from her trance. Sasha's eyes fluttered open and she found all three of them grinning down at her.

She chuckled. "I'm starving, but I can wait. I want to lie here a few more minutes and then hit the shower." They all nodded in unison and headed towards the door. Asia stopped and turned around with a vivid smile on her face.

"Oh, by the way," she pointed to a beautiful bouquet on the vanity in the corner, "those are for you." She waved and disappeared.

With a gleam of interest, Sasha rose from the couch and walked over to the bouquet, curious to find out who had bothered to send her a dozen white roses. She reached for the card and removed it from the envelope. *Will you give me another chance?* Sasha brought the card close to her heart while the color returned to her cheeks. Begging was not a quality she had expected from Terraine, but after the way he'd humiliated her this afternoon, she'd be lying if she said it did not give her a feeling of satisfaction.

"Now isn't that sweet? You really think you are something, don't you?"

Sasha whirled around to find Monet standing in the doorway wrapped in a towel and dripping water all over the floor, her eyes iced with contempt.

Sasha took a step towards her. "Why would you say that?" she asked calmly, her brow raised inquiringly.

"Flowers, the cover of a catalog, and someone special in your life!" Her voice rose. "How lovely for you." There was a heavy dose of sarcasm in her voice.

Sasha could not believe the jealousy she was hearing! Monet had no reason to envy another woman. She was not only beautiful but rich. *Filthy rich*. "No, I don't think I am any better than the rest of you, but it is no big mystery that you do not like me. Why is that?" The questioned hammered at her.

Monet threw her head back and gave a dry laugh. "Your days are numbered. I'm going to be on that cover," she declared with smug certainty. "I worked too hard to let a slut like you walk in and take it all away from me." With that she turned on her heels and exited the room.

"Terraine, why won't you accompany me to the NAACP dinner?" Natalia pouted.

Shaking his head, Terraine looked up from his desk. "You already know why. I have no intention of starting something that I can't finish."

Natalia ignored his harsh tone and walked around to where he was sitting, stopping only inches away from him. She leaned back on the end of his desk, exposing a slender leg through a split in her skirt. She tapped her French nails lightly on top of his papers. "Terraine, when are you going to face the fact that you and I are good for each other? I think it is high time we put our differences aside and make a success of this corporation together. Pops would have wanted that." She gazed at him adoringly as she raked his tall form.

Terraine looked at the beautiful woman, taking in her perfect appearance and designer suit, and all he saw was a selfish, spoiled brat. Pops had spoiled her, treating her like the daughter he'd never had and she knowingly had him wrapped around

her finger. At one time, Terraine also had been captured by her beauty, until the day she shattered his
entire world.

Natalia had been around all his life. She was
the daughter of Senator McKinley Bonaparte and
his wife Gabriel, who had spent more time fund raising than with their daughter. Natalia became a
rebellious child, starving for attention. Her parents
eventually had grown impatient with her and
shipped off to boarding school. The only person
who had taken a personal interest in her life was
Pops. He felt sorry for her and allowed her to spend
spring and summer breaks at Andrews Manor.

"Don't start," Terraine warned, looking down at
the papers scattered all over his desk. He had a lot
of work to do and no time for her nonsense.

Natalia leaned over and draped her arms loosely around his neck. Her breath was warm against
his nose as she whispered with certainty, "I am
going to win you back."

The scent of her expensive perfume filled his
nostrils. Terraine removed her arms and ignored
her comment. "I thought you wanted to talk about
the catalog."

"I do." Her eyes hid none of the lust she was
feeling. "Over dinner tonight."

"You never know when to quit," he declared.
Natalia was no longer a temptation to him. Their

relationship would never be any more than business.

She lounged across his desk provocatively, blocking his papers from his view. "Let's just say, I know what I want." Her voice was perilously close to a purr.

Terraine put his pen down and leaned back in his chair. He wanted to return to the studio and watch Sasha make love to the camera. He had purposely stayed away from the studio, allowing Sasha her space but the prolonged anticipation became unbearable and today he had not been able to resist the urge to travel down to the third floor. He had done an about-face at the sight of her lying across the bed in her underwear, exhibiting her eye-catching bosom, curving hips tapering into shapely legs and a fine backside. The sight of her made a streak of pure lust race through his body, leaving him tense and hard. Terraine was certain that just for a moment that he'd caught a glimpse of Sasha softening; then just as quickly as it was there, it was gone. In its place he saw the pain in her eyes. Now as he ached with desire, he wondered if he could ever make everything right again.

Filled with resolve, Terraine raised fluidly from his chair and began preparing to leave. It was time to find a way to work things out. He wanted her and he'd be damned if he would let her go. "Natalia, I have things to do. Now if there isn't anything else, please leave. "

Natalia's smile went undiminished by his comment but she did remove herself from his desk and walk around to the other side. There was plenty of time still left to work her magic on him. She was beyond intimidation. After all, she was an intelligent and beautiful woman. Since Terraine's return, they had learned to be civil with one another. She was grateful that Pops had secured her future at Diva Designs in his will; otherwise Terraine would have more than likely thrown her out on her butt by now. Yes, she admitted to lying to him ten years earlier. But they were young then and things like that were to be expected. A girl had to keep a little excitement in her life that added shine to her eyes and color to her cheeks. Now they were both consenting adults and would make a beautiful couple again. And they would be together because she always got her way.

She gracefully sat down in a chair in front of his desk and crossed her legs. "Monet is demanding that she be put on the cover."

Terraine lifted his head and frowned, surprised that Natalia would even present him with such a request. Controlling his voice, he said, "Why am I not surprised? She's been a problem from the start with all of her demands. Sasha is our cover girl. I hope you set her straight." Terraine stood tall and watched her intently.

Natalia flicked an imaginary piece of lint from her skirt before raising her chin and meeting his gorgeous eyes. She shrugged matter-of-factly. "Now why would I do that? For once I happen to agree with her."

"You looked good out there."

Sasha flinched at the sound of Terraine's voice thundering off the walls. He had appeared behind her from out of nowhere.

She did not bother to turn around. "Thanks," she tossed over her shoulder as she continued across the parking garage to her car.

Terraine followed close behind, admiring the way she wore a pair of denim shorts. *Why couldn't my name be Levi?*

Only moments ago, she had stood half-naked in front of him, causing him to throb not with want, not with desire, but with need. A strong pulsating need. He needed Sasha.

He continued to follow her, taking slow, long strides. "Are you going to slow down so I can talk to you?"

"No. I am not going to slow down," she replied without looking in his direction, not trusting herself if she did.

"Sasha!"

He sounded like a wounded animal. She whirled around and Terraine stopped just short of running into her. Breathing in his essence sent the blood rushing to her face. "What?"

Terraine grinned. "It is pretty obvious that I am the last person you wanted to run into but may I have a moment of your time?"

Sasha reminded herself to stay strong and ignore the effect he was having on her. "You think you're really cute."

His smile deepened and a confident light was blazing in his eyes. "So you think I'm cute?"

Sasha's eyes narrowed. "Don't get a big head." She pivoted on the soles of her tennis shoes and strolled to her car.

Terraine followed. "Sasha, I am sorry."

Sasha smiled secretly at his comment. He was wallowing in guilt and wanted her forgiveness. *Too bad.* He wasn't getting it. She reached her car and unlocked the driver's door. "Did you need something?" she asked calmly.

Terraine grinned as he imagined what she would do if he told her what he really wanted. But Sasha quickly chased all thoughts from his mind as she glared at him from behind a sweep of dark lashes.

He leaned back against her car with his hands deep in his pockets. "Can we go somewhere and talk?" Terraine looked at the T-shirt stretched tautly over the heavy swell of her breasts. *An area that he intended to explore.*

Though Sasha inhaled deeply and tried to calm herself, her hands shook and her keys slipped between her fingers onto the ground. They both stooped down at the same time and Terraine's warm hand touched her skin. She looked at his mouth, mesmerized by his sensuous lips surround- ed by thick hair and suddenly remembered rubbing against his face while he kissed the hollow base of her neck. Sasha felt her willpower slipping away. Pulling back, she sprang to her feet and allowed him to retrieve her keys.

Terraine also rose and stood so close she felt on the verge of fainting. Taking her keys from him, Sasha took two steps back so that she could breathe. "Sorry, but I am on my way to lunch." Not trusting her actions any further, Sasha quickly hopped into her car and drove away.

Terraine whistled while he strolled towards his Navigator, remembering what his grandfather had taught him: *You can have anything you want if you want it bad enough.*

Terraine climbed in and chuckled. "I think I'm a little hungry myself."

The hostess showed Sasha to a cozy booth in the back of the restaurant, then went to bring her a glass of water while she looked over her menu.

"I heard the hamburgers here are worth dying for."

Sasha's head snapped up and she saw Terraine smiling down at her with amusement. Their eyes met and dismay struggled with a blossom of excitement before she became annoyed all over again by the satisfied smirk hovering over his face. "Why are you following me?"

Terraine saw her cheeks flare and quickly held up his hands. "Can't a man eat?"

"Yes, but not at my table," she said tartly, lowering her head back to her menu.

Terraine ignored her comment and took the chair across from her. "Actually, I thought this would be the perfect opportunity for us to talk about your gowns."

Sasha looked up suspiciously. "My gowns?"

His steady, raisin-brown eyes met hers while he tapped his chin with his index finger. "Well, if my memory serves me right, you were intent on showing the owner of Diva Designs your collection. As you know, I am the owner."

Humor threaded through his husky voice but Sasha was not amused. Her eyes darkened as if a cloud had moved over them and she rose from her seat ready to storm out of the restaurant. "You arrogant son of a b—"

Terraine stood up and placed a restraining hand on her shoulder. "Hey, I didn't mean to come off like that." His voice lowered. "Relax."

Reluctantly, Sasha closed her mouth and contented herself with glaring at him as she slowly sat down again. She did not want to relax. That was how she got into the mess she was in now. She scowled as she picked up her menu again.

Terraine leaned over and grinned. "By the way, I prefer to be called confident, not arrogant."

Sasha was now seeing red at his need to have the last word. Before she could comment, their waitress returned with a basket of rolls and two glasses of water. Since Sasha was still tight-lipped, Terraine took the liberty of ordering both of them the catch of the day, blackened catfish. Sasha was surprised at his choice but then remembered that during their short time together, she had shared with him her love for seafood.

She was silent while they waited for their food and hoped he would get the hint and move to another table.

He didn't.

Terraine took the opportunity to talk about the progress of the catalog. Sasha had to admit that she was interested in what he said and was

181

impressed with how much knowledge he had about the fashion world. While being careful not to stroke his ego, she shared with him her impression of the project thus far.

The waitress returned with their drinks. As he took a long swig of his drink, Sasha secretly admired how handsome Terraine looked in a dark brown, double-breasted suit. She watched his strong brown throat. A handsome neck. One that she remembered nuzzling close to, smelling the scent of soap and after-shave. *You need to stop staring,* she told herself.

Terraine lowered his drink all too quickly and caught her. He was relieved that she was no longer glaring at him and was at least trying to be civil. Terraine felt that he had made an inch of progress. But being the stubborn man that he was, he did not want an inch. He wanted the entire nine yards.

"How long is it going to take before you find it in your heart to forgive me?" He gave her a smile that would have dazzled a lesser female.

Sasha ran her index finger across her bottom lip. *Damn him for looking indecently good.* "What makes you think I'm ever going to forgive you?"

Terraine took her gesture as a very seductive move. "I hurt you?"

Sasha glared at him. "Like you care?" She sighed. "Let's just drop it."

"I wasn't trying to be nosy." Terraine shook his head apologetically.

Sasha pursed her lips. "Then leave me alone."

"Ouch, girl!" Terraine chuckled and held his hands up, palms out. "You sure know how to hurt a brother's feelings."

"What about my feelings?"

There was an uncomfortable silence as they ate their food but after a while Terraine regained the courage to try again. "What was that all about the other night?" Sasha gave him a puzzled look. "You know what I am talking about. The break in." Terraine leaned back in his chair. Now that she knew his secret it was time for her to reveal what she had been hiding the other night.

Her gaze fell to her food. "I have no idea," she said all too quickly.

"Why are you hiding something? I want to help you if you'll let me." Sasha lifted her head again and met the concern in his eyes.

She shook her head. "It's nothing I can't handle myself," she murmured before placing a forkful of string beans into her mouth.

Against his better judgment, Terraine decided to let it go for now. He placed a hand on her arm. "If you change your mind, remember I'm here." Sasha met his tender expression and nodded.

After Sasha had swallowed her last piece of

broiled catfish fillet she asked, "I'm curious. How could you possibly be interested in my gowns if you've never seen them?"

Looking up from his plate, Terraine stared at her lovely face that was scrubbed free of the cosmetics she wore during her photo shoot. She looked so young and innocent with her hair tightly braided and hanging down her back. He pushed his plate away and leaned over the table. He took her hand possessively. "I have confidence in your ability. "

His eyes were dripping with lust, something that she had learned to identify during years of heartbreaks. It sickened her that he would even consider using her dream of becoming a designer as a pawn to get her into his bed. "Really now," she purred. "So tell me, what would it take for you to not only employee me as a model but also as one of your designers?"

Hypnotized by her dreamy eyes and tantalizing lips, Terraine did not have a chance to think about his answer. Instead, he reacted hastily. "How about if we go back to my house and discuss it?" He smiled and added, "Privately."

Sasha's face reddened and she snatched her hand back. "Just what I thought. You're not really interested in anything other than getting me in bed!" The defensive tone in her voice told Terraine he had made a mistake.

"I'd be lying to you again if I said I wasn't interested in that. But I want more than your body, Sasha. I'm seeking your heart and soul."

Sasha could not take any more of his lies. He was good. She would give him that. Digging into her purse, she laid a couple of bills on the table.

Terraine shook his head. "No, please let me pay for the meal. It's the least I can do."

She rose and glared at him. "You're right, it is the least you can do." She snatched her money back off the table and left before Terraine could summon the waitress to bring him the bill.

When he finally made his way to the parking lot, Sasha was long gone. Instead, he found his Navigator with a brick thrown through the front windshield.

Terraine paid the cab driver and walked up the steps and through his front door, where Ms. Henry greeted him. She handed him a stack of messages from the office. Terraine frowned at the notes and asked her to hold all calls until further notice. He traveled to his office at the back of the house and dropped his briefcase into a chair. Removing his jacket he strolled over to the window, looked out at the gazebo in back, where he spotted a cardinal perched on top.

He should be pissed. *Fighting mad.* But he was not. Instead, Terraine was tickled. If a war was what she wanted then a war she was going to get.

A war in which he would kill her with kindness.

Chapter Eight

The flowers started arriving the next day. Roses. Dozen and dozens of red roses delivered all week, which Honey so graciously placed in Sasha's bedroom. By Friday, every available space was covered with a bouquet and the room was beginning to look like a flower shop. Each card carried the same message, *I'm sorry*, and they were signed *me*. Me? Talk about cocky. Did he really think that he was making an impression?

Well, he was. Only he didn't know it.

Sasha ignored Terraine. She did not accept his phone calls nor did she acknowledge him at the studio. At the end of a week of photo shoots and costume rehearsals, she was exhausted. She thanked God it was Friday. But on the drive home late that afternoon, she decided that she was not ready to go home and spend the evening alone with Terraine slipping through her mind. Instead, she decided to go down to Love Your Hair and see the newest hairdos and hear the latest gossip. Listening to someone else's problems was just what the doctor ordered.

The smell of curling irons and chemical relaxers met her at the front door. The waiting room was packed; every work station was occupied and the room buzzed with chatter and laughter while the sounds of Ginuwine shouted from a stereo system in the background.

Sasha loved Honey's shop. It was designed to create a relaxed atmosphere with four love seats arranged around a large color television in the corner. It offered snack machines, soda machines and coffee made freshly every hour. Two barbers were located to the back, a nail technician near the front along with six work stations with stylists ready to hook up a sista's hair. Honey also had a chair on the floor but it was occupied solely by appointment only. A reception desk was located in the waiting room and in the back was Honey's private office.

"Hey girl." Honey was working on someone's hair and signaled for Sasha to come on back.

"What do you think?" Honey pointed to her own head and Sasha stopped to admire her latest masterpiece.

"It's called a sexy claw cut." Honey turned around so that Sasha could see it from all angles. Bangs were cut to graze the brow line and then flat ironed. A few tracks of weave were added for thickness and combed down around her shoulders. The ends were razor cut to give a jagged look, then feathered with a comb.

Sasha tilted her head to the side. "Unique. Very unique."

Honey beamed. "Thanks. I thought you would like it. Tutti did it this morning. Take a seat while I finish Ms. Taylor's hair." Sasha smiled down at the older lady with long salt and pepper hair. Honey took the rollers out one at a time and the curls bounced like a pogo stick. Sasha dropped down on the stool next to her and swiveled from side to side.

Honey tossed the rollers into a small basket. "You got another dozen roses this morning."

Sasha grinned sourly. "Great. The rate he's going I'll be donating them to the hospital before the week is over."

"These were different. They were all white." Honey looked up in time to watch Sasha roll her eyes. "You can't blame the man for trying." She defended his actions with a sheepish smile.

"If he'd been honest in the first place he wouldn't have to go through all this." Sasha's chin was set in a stubborn line.

Honey wagged her head. "He sounded extremely sorry on the phone."

Sasha raised her brow. "You've talked to him?"

"Yeah, every time he calls. He sounds so sincere." Honey waved the comb in her hand. "Not only is he gorgeous but he has a wonderful personality."

"Don't start," Sasha warned.

"Girl, a good man is hard to find." Tutti was a short round woman in her late twenties who wore her hair short, spiked, and platinum blonde. Sasha turned to the work station to her right where she was putting a finger wave in a woman's hair.

"I know that's right," added Ms. Taylor while Honey hair sprayed her hair. "I don't know what is wrong with you young people today. My Stanley cherished me and we were married thirty years before the good Lord decided to take him away. Men like that are now hard to find. If you get a good one, grab hold of him." She slapped her palms together.

"Speaking of good men." Mercedes was at the work station on the other side of Honey giving a relaxer to an anorexic-looking girl. "Did y'all hear about Sonia and Lamont?"

Silence spread around the room. All heads were turned and patrons strained their ears as they waited for Mercedes to continue. She smoothed the relaxer through the skinny girl's hair, then looked around the room and sucked her horse teeth. "He left her."

"What?"

"The dog!"

"I knew he was too good to be true."

Sasha couldn't help laughing aloud while she listened to voices shouting across the room as everyone added their two and three cents. Half the women in the shop, including herself, didn't even know who Sonia and Lamont were, but it didn't stop them from listening to the juicy details. Being here gave her joy and Sasha smiled with delight. She was glad she'd decided to come down to the shop. It was the spot to be on a Friday night.

Honey handed Ms. Taylor a hand mirror so that she could see her hair from all angles, then focused on Sasha. "Why don't you let me hook your hair up while you're here?"

She shook her head. "And give Devon a heart attack? I don't think so. As long as we are shooting, my hair belongs to him. He doesn't want me putting anything in it but a comb in the morning. I came in yesterday with a rubber band and he faked a cardiac. "

"Whatever," Honey mumbled and planted her hand on her waist. "Who does he think has been taking care of your hair all these years?"

191

Sasha hung around until Honey locked the shop up for the evening. Then they drove their cars and met at Blockbuster's for a chick flick, deciding that *Waiting to Exhale* was just what the doctor had ordered.

While they stood in line at the register, Sasha brushed Honey with her shoulder. "I can't believe you're planning to stay home on a Friday night."

Honey pursed her lips. "That's 'cause you don't know me as well as you think. I don't feel like being bothered tonight, and would much rather hang out with my girl." She draped her arm across Sasha's shoulder.

"How did your doctor's appointment go?"

"It was fine," Honey chuckled. "He was *fine.* You know I look forward to my yearly visits just so I can see my gorgeous gynecologist. It's a shame he's married, but at least I get the pleasure of having him caress my breast once a year."

Sasha laughed. "I can't believe you look forward to breast exams!"

Honey paid for the videos. "Hey, a girl has to take what she can get."

"Let's go." They walked out of the building giggling like teenagers. This was what Sasha would miss most when Honey moved away. "I'll meet you at the house."

Sasha popped two bags of popcorn while

Honey chilled a bottle of White Zinfandel. Then Honey came up with the appealing idea to have a slumber party. They grabbed pillows and blankets and spread them out on the living room floor in front of the television, then ran into their bedroom to find their goofiest pair of pajamas. Sasha found an old baby doll set and a pair of tweety bird houseshoes. Honey threw on a pair of boxers that she'd confiscated from one of her men and a Mizzou T-shirt.

Sasha walked into the living room and found Honey standing in the kitchen with the phone in one hand and the other hand planted on her hip.

"Quit calling here! She is not interested."

Sasha's heart jumped into her throat as she suspected that the caller might be Terraine. She wanted to grab the phone and hear his voice herself but she refused to succumb to her feelings. Then Sasha looked up and saw Honey's eyes roll to the back of her head and knew that she had to be talking to Robby.

"Uh-huh."

"Girl, give me that phone." Sasha snatched the receiver from her hand and put it to her ear. "Robby, what do you want?"

He spoke slowly. "Hello Sasha. Did you have time to think about what I said?"

Sasha sighed. "Robby?"

"Yes, my love?" His voice was dripping in but-

193

ter.

"Leave me alone," she stressed irritably.

"I can't do that. My love for you is a drug that inflames my senses."

Sasha dropped her head. "I'd just as soon you did not feel that way."

"I detect sadness in your voice. Is something the matter?" he asked with genuine concern.

Sasha ran her palm across the back of her neck, feeling the tension of the entire week coming to a head. "No. I just had a long week."

"That's not good. They should be pampering you at the studio."

Sasha remembered her run-in with Monet earlier in the week. "Yeah, right."

"As long as I'm alive, no one will ever outshine you."

Sasha moaned. To think she'd tried to have a normal conversation with him. Robby had never wanted anyone to upstage her. She *always* had to be first. Sasha used to feel flattered, thinking that he was proud of her and wanted to show her off to the world, but that was before she realized how possessive he really was.

"I guess I'll have to show you how much you mean to me."

"Robby, please get on with your life and leave me alone," she pleaded.

"I can't, my love."
"Then try. Goodnight."

Sasha turned the engine off in front of the old two-story home and climbed out of the car. With her purse across her shoulder and both hands resting on her hips, she stared at the house that she had known all her life. Sasha took a deep breath as a warm feeling flowed through her blood. She felt as if she had gone back in time whenever she came home. The lovely brick house looked rejuvenated with freshly painted white shutters and five concrete steps leading to a large front porch with a bench seat. Sasha remembered that when she was a six-year-old, she'd skipped rope and played hopscotch on that same porch because she was not old enough to leave the yard.

Strolling up the walkway, Sasha stopped to admire the multi-color petunias that were growing in neat rows in the flowerbeds on both sides of the porch. The house was located in a neighborhood that was at one time one of the best in North St. Louis. Now the neighborhood was struggling to stay free of the rising drug problems.

Sasha heard music and turned towards the street. Her brow drew together in an angry frown as a yellow Chevy Impala sped by with the car stereo system turned up so loud that its dark tinted windows vibrated. She could not see the driver behind the wheel but Sasha couldn't help stereotyping him to be a young black man probably no older than twenty-three. Sasha shook her head and turned on her heels, strolling to the door.

Sasha had tried convincing her mother to move to north county or even come live with her but she'd flatly refused. This was her home. These were her roots. Her life was wrapped up in this community. Most of the families had lived on this street for as long as Roxaner had, and she felt comfortable right here with her friends.

She walked down the hall heading towards the kitchen. "Anybody home?"

"Sasha, Sasha's here!" A little boy charged down the hall with a wide grin on his face and jumped straight into her outstretched arms. Brian was a neighbor's son. Her mother watched him for Vanessa when she needed to work the evening shifts. He had been around since he was a baby and Sasha enjoyed spending time with him when she was at her mother's.

"Hi, Brian." With a loving smile, Sasha stared into his innocent eyes. She planted a wet kiss on his cheek and hugged him close as he squirmed and giggled simultaneously. "How was school today?"

"Okay." Brian shrugged his shoulders then his eyes flashed with excitement as if he'd just remembered something. "I know nine take away five," he announced proudly.

"You do!" With a look of astonishment Sasha brought a hand to her cheek. Brian nodded with a sheepish grin. Sasha leaned her head back and stared into his eyes. "Are you sure?" she whispered.

"Yeess. It's four." He held up four little fingers.

"All right. You are smart for six." She drew his adorable face to her in an embrace and carried him into the kitchen where the smell of her mom's famous meatloaf filled the room.

"Hi, Mom." Roxaner was standing at the counter whipping homemade mashed potatoes. She turned around with a mixer in her hand and greeted her daughter with a smile.

"Brian, get down off her." He slid down slowly with his lips stuck out in a pout. "Now come over here and sample Nanna's chocolate cake." Brian's face lit up with anticipation as he galloped over to the counter staring up at the chocolate sheet cake that was fresh out of the oven. Nanna grabbed a knife from the drawer, cut him a thin slice and placed it on a napkin before handing it to him.

"Mom, you're ruining his dinner," Sasha scolded, propping a hand on her hip.

Roxaner waved her hands, dismissing the idea. "Shoot. A little chocolate don't hurt no one."

"You are spoiling him," Sasha complained half-heartedly.

"You just let me worry about my godson. And you worry about bringing me some grandbabies into the world." Roxaner looked down at Brian with pride shining in her eyes. "This here little boy is in good hands."

One corner of Sasha's mouth curled into a smile while she watched Brian gobble down the cake. He was definitely a shining spot in her mother's life.

"Ain't that right, Brian?"

"Mmm-hmm," he mumbled with a mouth full of cake. Sasha chuckled and reached down and kissed Brian on the top of his head.

"How is the catalog coming along?" Roxaner reached for an oven mitt and checked on her meat-loaf.

"Tiresome." Sasha sat down, dropping her purse to the floor. "But I wouldn't have it any other way."

"I'm glad that everything is working out for you," Roxaner said as she closed the stove and placed the pan on the counter. Brian put his napkin in the trash and stood in the corner licking his sticky finger. Roxaner turned to him and pointed towards the bathroom. "Baby, wash your hands for dinner." Brian turned and dashed out of the room.

Sasha looked at her fifty-year-old mother with admiration. Roxaner had worked hard for many years as a social worker while raising her and trying to provide her with all of the things she needed. Yet she still managed to look as if she was ready to tackle another twenty years. As a child, Sasha had longed to look like her mother with her mocha brown skin and her dark walnut eyes; instead, she took her looks after her father.

Roxaner turned towards Sasha with both hands on her hips. "My daughter is going to be on the cover of a major catalog."

They shared a smile. "And when it is over, I can finally pursue my dream." Joy bubbled in her voice and shone in her eyes. "I can't believe that it is finally going to happen."

"Why not? I can." Roxaner folded her arms across her breasts. "I always knew you could do it if you stuck with it." She wiped her hands on a dish-towel before walking to the table. "I wasn't going to mention this until later but I guess there is no better time than now."

Sasha looked over at her puzzled at what she was about to say.

Sitting down across from her, Roxaner took a deep breath. "Robby dropped by on Monday."

Sasha's eyebrow shot up in surprise. "What did he want?" She had thought that he was in St. Louis; now she knew for sure.

Roxaner clasped her hands in her lap before continuing. "He wanted to apologize to me for his behavior. He said he needed to do that in order to get on with his life."

"He is so full of himself," Sasha spat bitterly.

"I think it's also time for you to forgive and forget."

Sasha snorted and shrugged her shoulders. "I'll have to think about it."

Roxaner's brown eyes widened with concern. She crossed her arms beneath her ample breasts. "Well, you do that, but keep in mind that God is watching." Sasha started to say something but Roxaner raised her hand and silenced her. "Ever since the incident you have refused to step foot in church. I think it is high time that you stop blaming God for what happened and be thankful that he pulled you through it. You grew up in the church and it is time that you pulled your Bible out and sing to God praises for the exciting career that he has given you and the talent that he has blessed you with," she said in a stern voice. Sasha pressed her lips tightly together and looked into her mother's eyes that flashed a gentle but firm warning. Roxaner leaned forward in her chair and placed a hand to her daughter's cheek. "Now, set things on the table and let's eat." Rising, she called Brian to the table.

Sasha was quiet during dinner as she thought about her conversation with her mother. Life did not always happen the way you wanted it.

"Chile, whatever you are thinking about can wait until later," Roxaner said, arousing her from painful memories. "Right now I want to hear all about this new man in your life that Honey has been telling me about."

Sasha looked over at Brian who grinned innocently with a mouth full of mashed potatoes. Honey and her big mouth. "Actually, there is nothing to tell. I met someone last week and he took me out." Sasha tried to sound as nonchalant as she could manage.

"The way Honey talked, you had a really nice time." Roxaner's dark eyes twinkled with amusement.

Sasha sighed and removed her glasses, rubbing the bridge of her nose. "Yes, we had a nice time." Terraine was the last person she wanted to discuss.

Roxaner pushed her plate away and leaned forward with her arms folded on the table. "Sounds like a nice guy," she said with a light chuckle. "I hope you don't let this one get away."

"Mom, don't start." Sasha settled her glasses back on her nose. "Don't I have a new puppy around here somewhere?" Sasha said, trying to change the subject.

"Ooh! I'll go get her!" Brian dashed out of his chair and down the basement stairs.

"Sasha Renee Moore, don't try to twist things around. Hear your mother out for a change." Roxaner placed a motherly hand on her arm. Sasha braced herself for the lecture she knew by heart. "There is someone out there for everyone and someone is going to sweep you off of your feet. This time let him." Roxaner stood up and began clearing the table. "You ready for cake?" Sasha did not hear her. Her mind was miles away, following in the same direction as her heart.

Monet was exhausted after several hours of lovemaking and wished for the umpteenth time that she was at her condo in Atlanta, lying in her own bed. She had never been able to sleep comfortably anywhere else but at home.

Friends of the family were kind enough to allow her use of their home during her stay in St. Louis since they were away on vacation. Monet refused to stay at a hotel or live out of a suitcase. The

Campbells were retired and spent every summer touring some godforsaken country. This year, it was Turkey.

Monet removed his arm from around her waist and slowly climbed out of bed, trying not to rouse him. As she covered her naked body in a pink satin robe, he stirred and Monet turned and watched as he rolled over onto his stomach and resumed snoring. Her eyes lingered at his firm physique and she licked her lips in remembrance. On his back was a small tattoo of an eyeball and a cross. She had thought it to be a strange combination, but his explanation was that God had his back. He was an interesting man, who did not share much about his past other than that he came from old money. Monet didn't care one way or the other. It wasn't as if she planned on taking him home to meet her parents, not that they would even care. She was becoming aroused once more and was tempted to pull back the sheets and examine his merchandise again but instead she placed a hand to her chest and backed away from him.

Monet sashayed down the long hall, passing all four bedrooms, and descended the stairs and went into the kitchen. She'd had a light dinner last night and a tossed salad appealed to her. She reached into the refrigerator and retrieved a head of lettuce and several other vegetables and placed them all on the chopping board. Pressing her lips together, she imagined what her mother would do if she saw her cooking. Clare wouldn't dream of preparing her own food. That was considered servants' work.

Monet was the offspring of Anthony Reynolds, a multi-billionaire, who twenty years earlier had come up with the brilliant idea to sell medical insurance to pet owners. Clare had had little faith in her husband's success, but to her surprise, pet lovers from across the country were interested in being able to provide the best care possible for their beloved pets.

Because she'd grown up surrounded by nannies and servants, Monet had developed an attitude she was not always proud of, but what else could one expect from a billionaire's daughter? She had an excuse. She was a victim of money. If she was guilty of anything, it was of being rich.

Monet's father had spoiled her. He'd made sure she had everything she wanted, no matter if she needed it or not. As a substitute for his time, something he insisted that he had very little of, he had provided her with a hefty monthly allowance, which had stopped abruptly with her decision to make it on her own. Since then, she had been forced to learn how to survive.

Grabbing for a bowl on the top shelf, Monet reached for a sharp knife from the kitchen drawer.

She had always wanted to be a model. Her father had laughed at the idea while her mother was appalled that she was interested in doing anything other than spending her father's money. So Monet had changed her last name and found herself an agent. It was hard work and over the years she had often run back home to daddy, who was quick to say *I told you so.* Eventually her career had kicked off and she had made a name for herself. But one thing she'd never received was the praise she expected from her parents. She wanted them to be proud of her. Monet thought working with a major black owned business like Diva Designs and being a part of a major campaign was just what she need-ed to gain favor with her dad. But then, she'd found out that Deja was given the cover. Monet thought she was going to have to kill her herself, but lucky someone else had come to her rescue. If she knew who it was, Monet would thank him personally. Now she'd found out that the spotlight had been given to Sasha a model who had unknowingly beat her out of two prior contracts, even after Monet had gone as far as attempting to consummate the deals through sex.

Monet slammed the knife into the cucumber and sliced it in half. Now what was probably her last chance of getting a cover spot had been taken away from her. Or had it? she thought, remembering the handsome man lying across her bed. She had shared her pain and according to him, as long as Monet was good to him, she had nothing to worry about. Monet admired his confidence and was certain that as long as she continued to give him what he needed, he would find a way. She sighed with relief and chopped a small cherry tomato, then placed the knife in the sink. Monet heard movement and knew he was near before his hands warmed her waist.

"Monet, what are you doing out of bed?" he asked as he swung her around to face him.

She grinned up at him. "I was hungry."

"I know what else you're hungry for." He released the belt on her robe and eased it down her shoulders, freeing her breasts. After giving them a long lustful stare, he caressed her swollen nipples with his rough fingertips, forcing a small moan to escape from her parted lips. Waves of pleasure rippled through her body. He leaned against her and stroked her bare thighs. Monet swallowed hard as his hand moved slowly up toward the creamy warmth at her center. She shuddered as she felt his teeth nibbling at the nape of her neck. Parting her legs, she gave him complete access to the most private part of her. He groaned and thrust himself against her. His fingers brushed the softness between her legs before gently parting her and traveling even deeper. He touched her slowly, allowing his hand to move in small, soft strokes against the sensitive bud. She felt an orgasm build and needed desperately to find some release.

"Please," she whimpered.

"What do you want?" he demanded. "Tell me."

"I want to feel you inside of me!" she cried softly.

"Like this?" he asked as he slipped his finger into her wetness, moving inside her with long deep strokes.

"Yes!" she cried, feeling the tension building even higher. "Harder!"

"Whatever you want," he whispered in a husky rasp. He proceeded to slam his fingers inside her, leaving her breathless.

"You'd do anything to be on the cover." His breath was hot against her neck.

"What, baby? What was that?" she asked in a whisper.

"You'd even sleep with the boss if that's what it took," he said with irritation that she was oblivious to.

"Are you jealous, baby? What do I need with another man when I have all this?" She reached down and stroked his manhood that had already risen with desire.

"You don't really love me," he said. Monet

heard the jealousy in his voice and smiled.

"I do, baby, but I deserve to be on that damn cover. I went through a lot to get this job. Now shut up and kiss me." She dragged his mouth back to hers and forced her tongue into his mouth. He returned the kiss and continued to please her. Then as she neared an orgasm, he abruptly removed his fingers. Lost in ecstasy, it took several seconds for her mind to register that his arm was rising with the knife she had just used in his hand.

She shook her head slowly in disbelief. "Oh my God! It was you." Her voice was filled with fear and her eyes bordered on tears.

"Slut!" he screamed as the blade slit her across her throat. "You are no better than the rest. Haven't you realized yet who the real star is?" Each word was enunciated with a stab of the sharp blade to her chest.

Staring up at him, Monet clawed at his arm until she fell onto the floor.

Chapter Nine

Terraine heard knocking on his bedroom door. Had he not given Ms. Henry the weekend off? He rolled over and covered his head with his pillow, hoping whoever it was would go away.

He didn't.

Jay opened the door and walked into his room. "Wake up, Tee."

Terraine groaned at the sound of his brother's voice. "Go away!" After a late night at the office he had hoped to sleep until noon.

"Sorry Bro, I can't do that." Jay strolled over to a large picture window and drew open the curtains. "You've got company downstairs."

As sunshine spilled through the venetian blinds, Jay leaned over and pulled off the pillow that was covering his brother's head. Terraine grumbled and rolled onto his left side, away from the blinding light. He grabbed the cotton sheet and used it to shield his eyes. "Whoever it is, send them away."

Jay pulled out a cigarette and fished in his hip pocket for a lighter. "Sorry, can't do that either."

"Then who is it, for Christ's sakes?"

Jay leaned against the dresser and brought the cigarette to his lips. "It's the police."

Terraine tossed the sheet wildly aside and sat upright with a look of bewilderment. "The police? What do they want?"

Jay blew out a long breath of smoke before he spoke. "They'd like to ask you a few questions regarding the murder of Monet Phillips."

Terraine took his chances by going to Sasha's unannounced. After finding out that another Diva model had been murdered, he couldn't think of anything else but Sasha's safety. She needed him. She just didn't know it yet.

Sasha answered the door after one ring and his amused eyes traveled from the large sponge rollers in her hair to her torn shorts and bare feet.

Her lips parted in surprise. Terraine stood before her dressed casually in shorts, a baseball jersey and cap, looking adorable. Sasha groaned. She knew that she should have looked out the window before answering the door. It would have saved her the embarrassment of having him see her like this.

"Terraine, what are you doing here?"

He smiled in admiration. He did not know many women who would be caught looking the way she was looking, but Sasha's looks were natural and allowed her to get away with just about anything. She could have been wrestling in mud and she still would have managed to look beautiful.

Terraine noticed her uncomfortable expression and squinted his eyes with amusement.

"Sasha, is that really you?"

Sasha was not the least bit amused. "What do you want?"

It was obvious that today was not a good day for humor. He needed to be serious. Terraine stuck his hands in the front pocket of his shorts and spoke in a low voice. "I dropped by to apologize again for my behavior."

Sasha looked puzzled. "But you've already apologized. You've called my house every day for the last two weeks, leaving long embarrassing messages on my answering machine, and you keep sending me all those damn roses."

Terraine shrugged mischievously. "This time I'd like to apologize in person. May I come in?" He leaned against the doorframe close enough for her to take in his masculine scent that left her dizzy. She backed a few inches away and was certain that if she said no, he planned to walk in anyway. But before Sasha could shut the door in his face, Honey walked up and jerked it open, greeting him with a welcoming smile.

"Hello, Tee."

Sasha raised her brow. "Tee?"

"Yeah, it's his nickname." Honey ignored the grim look on her face and escorted Terraine into the living room with a half grin playing at the corners of his mouth. "Make yourself at home. We were just getting ready to have lunch would you like to join us?"

"No," Sasha answered flatly.

"Yes. Wouldn't mind if I did." Terraine followed Honey to the kitchen.

Sasha stared after them with a sour look but remained silent before she stormed down the hall to her sewing room, where she had been ironing her gown for Judith's wedding.

She gritted her teeth and walked over to the ironing board. Why did Terraine have to insist on coming around where he wasn't wanted? She was going to have a long talk with Honey this evening. Terraine was her boss and she was determined to keep their relationship strictly business. Sasha held on tightly to that thought, hoping it was true, knowing that it was not. His nearness always seemed to strip her of her better judgment. Why couldn't he be an ugly or selfish man? At least they were easier to resist.

"So, this is where you work."
Sasha looked towards the door where Terraine stood and nodded. Then she quickly dropped her eyes and tried to concentrate on ironing, but it was difficult with Terraine in the same room, sharing the same air. She wished that she were strong enough to look at him without being affected by him.

Terraine folded his arms across his chest. "Honey tells me you are going to your cousin's wedding this afternoon."

"Yes, I am." Sasha kept all expression from her voice as she made an attempt to mask her feelings. All her life she had worn her emotions close to the surface, and since they met, Terraine had always seemed to know what she was feeling. It was eerie how he always seemed to figure it out at about the same time she figured it out herself. Today was not one of those days when she cared to be analyzed.

Terraine took a couple of steps forward. "Mind if I tag along?"

She quickly looked up with narrowed eyes. "Yes, I do mind," she snapped while eliminating the last wrinkle. "Why are you here anyway?"

Terraine saw anger brewing and walked over

and removed the iron from her hand before Sasha decided to throw it at him. He decided it was as good a time as any to address his reason for coming over. He took her hands and looked down into her lovely eyes.

"Monet is dead." He saw the agony on her face and immediately regretted the casual way he'd broken the news to her.

"Oh, no!"

Terraine looked down into her wide eyes and nodded. "I met with the police this morning. She was killed in the same manner as Deja."

Horror was vivid in her eyes. Her mouth moved as she struggled to make her lips and throat formulate the words. "W-who's doing this?" She and Monet had had their differences and she might have occasionally felt the urge to scratch her eyes out, but she would never have wanted her dead.

"They don't have any clues except that it is somehow connected to Diva Designs."

"How terrible for you." Terraine did not miss the compassion in her voice. He was fully aware that Sasha was a caring woman. What he could not understand was why she tried to hide it.

"I don't want you running around by yourself."

"Why? Do you think the killer will come after me?" she asked in a shaky voice.

He saw the alarm on her face and cursed himself for scaring her. Terraine quickly pulled her into his arms and it felt so good to hold her again. "Not if I can help it."

She felt his fingertips at the nape of her neck and her skin tingled. "Terraine, no." She spun away from him and dropped her eyes. She was upset at the way she'd responded.

Terraine flinched. "Sasha, I am sorry about the way I went about things. Please find—"

Sasha held up her hand. "I don't want to hear it." She paced across the room. "I don't need this right now. Today is going to be the happiest day of my cousin's life and I need to be there for her. I can't deal with this right now." She placed a hand on her hip and looked up at him, trying hard to ignore his beautiful brown eyes as she once again wished that he were not quite so handsome. "Now if you'll excuse me, I have a wedding to get ready for."

"I don't think it is a good idea for you to be going out by yourself," Terraine said, biting the words off angrily. He hated it when she acted stubborn.

Sasha frowned. "Who asked you?"

"Honey did." He watched her anger rise. "She's needed at the shop and asked me to accompany you to your cousin's wedding."

Sasha swore under her breath.

"Did you say something?"

"Yeah, I don't want you going with me!" she snapped with fear mixed with exasperation in her voice.

He was quite aware that Sasha was an emotional woman but stubbornness was one emotion that he could do without. "The intimate apparels catalog can not be completed without you. So consider my escorting you an executive decision," he said with determination. Terraine could care less about that damn catalog but there was no way he was going to allow anything to happen to her.

Sasha could just see walking into the church with her entire family watching, observing, especially her mother. *Hell no*, she thought. There was no way he was going with her. "I don't want—"

Terraine cut in. "Sasha, you've got one hour," he ordered. He had seen her hands tremble. Enough was enough. He was running out of patience with her. "I'm going home to change. Be ready." With that he walked out the room before she could respond.

As soon as Terraine left, Sasha jumped into the shower and tried to get ready as fast as she could. She wanted to be long gone when he arrived but Honey took longer than usual to style her hair and Sasha was certain that Terraine had asked her to stall her as long as possible.

Sasha put her dress in a garment bag and

quickly slipped into a pair of black Capri pants and a white cotton top with spaghetti straps and padded around on barefeet trying to find her shoes that were specially dyed to match her dress. She had been searching for nearly twenty minutes when the doorbell rang.

She answered the door when Terraine arrived and was not prepared for his appearance. He stood outside her door in an immaculate navy suit and an off white shirt. Sasha swallowed.

He frowned at her. "Why aren't you dressed?"

Sasha turned away from his scrutinizing eyes and walked back to her bedroom. "I am dressed. I'll put my gown on at the church. Right now I'm trying to find my shoes."

Terraine stepped into her room. "Your shoes are in my car." Sasha shot him a killer look and bit back harsh words while Terraine shrugged his shoulders. "I had to make sure you didn't try to run out on me."

Sasha grabbed her bag and brushed past him. "Let's go." She walked back into the living room where Honey was lying across the couch reading a magazine. "I thought you had to be at the shop?"

Not looking up from the magazine, Honey answered, "I'm leaving in a few minutes. I want to read this article first." She raised a hand and waved. "You guys have a good time."

Sasha mumbled something.

"Excuse me, did you say something?" Honey looked up from her magazine with an innocent expression on her face.

Terraine was amused by Sasha's reaction and had to do everything in his power not to laugh. Sasha was furious and they both could see that but he was grateful that he had Honey on his side.

"Come on, Sasha, let's get out of here before we're late." Terraine opened the door.

"Yeah." she said, resigned. "Let's go." Sasha walked out with Terraine behind her. He stopped long enough to mouth the words 'thank you' and Honey gave him a thumbs up before closing the door behind him.

Terraine walked down the steps and took Sasha's garment bag off her arm and flung it over his shoulder. "Sasha, I'd like you to meet Cherry."

She looked out towards the street at a beautiful cherry red BMW convertible with a black ragtop. "She's gorgeous," she said with admiration.

"Yes she is," Terraine said with pride. "I don't drive her often but since you threw a brick through the window of my Navigator, I—"

Sasha froze. "I did what?"

"Come on, Sasha, confess. After the way I behaved at lunch the other day...I guess I did deserved it."

Sasha swung her purse at him. "You're crazy, you know that? I never threw a brick through your window! And for you to even think I'd—" She tripped over her words. "You obviously don't know me well!" Sasha was infuriated and stormed back towards her house and caught Honey moving away from the window. She was obviously spying on them. Sasha scowled. Honey better be prepared for an earful.

Before she could ring the doorbell, Terraine scooped her into his arms and carried her kicking and screaming to his car.

Sitting next to him minutes later as they rolled onto the highway, Sasha fastened her seatbelt and stared out the window. Terraine put in an old Marvin Gaye CD and it gave her an excuse not to say much during the ride. It also gave her time to devise a plan of escape. As soon as the wedding was over, she was sending him home and hitching a ride with one of her cousins. Maybe she could get her cousin Dewayne to scare him off.

"Do you know where the church is?" she asked, breaking the silence.

He looked at her out of the corner of his eye. "Of course I do," he answered with a sinful smile. Sasha blew out steam and guessed that Honey had provided him with all of the information he needed.

Sasha rested her elbow on the door and ran her

fingers through her hair, trying to calm her nerves. Terraine smelled heavenly, causing her heart to pound fiercely in her chest. What was she to do? She looked straight ahead, not taking a chance at looking over at him. A girl could only take so much.

"Shoot."

Sasha turned towards Terraine and he gestured for her to look ahead. She stared out the window and straight ahead at the traffic that was at a stand-still. Terraine reduced his speed until he complete-ly stopped and then he put the car in park.

He laced his hands behind his head and turned towards Sasha. "I guess we better not plan on get-ting to the church any time soon."

Sasha crossed her arms against her chest and sank back into her seat. She had hoped that they would get there as quickly as possible so that she would not have to talk to him. *Fat chance*. She turned towards the window and looked at a little boy in the next car making faces against the glass.

"I like you without your glasses on. Your eyes are too pretty to hide." She pushed her glasses on her face. His compliment took her by surprise. "Would you have ever guessed that I also wear glasses?"

Sasha turned and looked at him with surprise. 'You do?"

Terraine nodded. "Yep. Ever since I was seven

year old. I was nicknamed frog eyes for years."

Sasha chuckled, appreciating his humor. "They called me bubble eyes." Before she knew it, she'd allowed herself to relax again and was engrossed in a conversation about their tormented years, growing up with glasses.

Twenty minutes passed before the traffic started to move again.

Sasha looked down at her watch and groaned. "Oh, no. I'm going to be late."

"No, we won't. Just leave it up to me and Cherry," Terraine reassured her as he put his car in gear and sped down the highway. Sasha watched as they whizzed by several cars and whipped in and out of traffic with a skill that made her feel at ease. Maybe he had been a race car driver in another life, she thought. He was an excellent driver and riding with him with the top down and his car moving ninety miles an hour gave her an adrenaline rush. She felt like a kid on her first roller coaster ride. It was great. She leaned back against the leather seat and watched the city of St. Louis fly by her window. Terraine was full of surprises. Was there anything he wasn't capable of? Sasha closed her eyes. Staying mad at him was not going to be easy.

As Terraine sat amongst the congregation at the small Baptist church, he saw an angel so breathtakingly beautiful he could not take his eyes off her.

The only thing missing was a pair of wings. To the sounds of Jesse Powell, he watched as Sasha swayed up the aisle with her slender body encased in a lavender, tea-length gown. In her hands she carried a bouquet of lilies and her hair was swept up high and woven with delicate baby's breath. She looked like a vision. A dream. Once she reached the altar, everyone focused on the five bridesmaids escorted by groomsmen, but Terraine's eyes were still at the altar watching Sasha, who kept her eyes lowered, purposely avoiding his. Terraine rested his elbows on his knees and leaned over. Sasha was still angry with him and his showing up today had not helped his case any. But there was no way he was going to leave her vulnerable for a stalker to prey on. He cared about her too much for that.

Sasha looked over at Terraine out of the corner of her eyes and caught him looking at her again. She was relieved when the congregation rose and Judith and her Uncle Benny started down the aisle, giving her an excuse to look away. If she looked at him too much longer, she would soften again.

Why did he have to tag along? She didn't need a bodyguard and if she did, it wouldn't be him. But his dimpled cheeks and boyish smile kept captivating her. She didn't want to forgive him. She wanted to continue to be angry with him, but her eyes betrayed her and traveled back over to him. Sasha heard herself sigh as her attitude softened and she wondered if she'd ever be able to look at him and remain angry for any long period of time.

After the bride and groom kissed, Terraine tried to make his way over to Sasha. He caught her eye, but before he could get close to her, she was shuffled off into another room for photographs. Terraine followed and stood off to the side watching her interact with her family and her standing close— almost too close for his comfort— to the best man, who had his arm draped around her waist. Whatever he whispered in her ear brought laughter. Terraine had to fight back his feelings of jealousy.

Sasha thought she was going to throw up when Zachary wrapped his arm around her waist. She had never liked him. He was a ladies' man with a string of women waiting at his beck and call, but seeing Terraine's face made it all worthwhile.

Terraine shifted restlessly against the wall and shoved his hands in his pockets. He hated weddings. They were always so long. But as he had watched the bride and groom exchange vows, he knew that if his bride were as beautiful as Sasha, then it would be worth all of the time in the world.

"Hello. You must be Terraine. I've heard so much about you." The woman held out her hand. "I'm Roxaner Moore, Sasha's mother."

Terraine looked down at a beautiful lady in her

fifties, wearing a pink dress with a matching hat. "A pleasure to meet you. I'm surprised your daughter even mentioned my name."

She gave him an uncomfortable grin. "Actually, she hasn't, not really. If it weren't for her roommate I would not have any idea what occurs in my daughter's life." She looked over at the group in the corner still taking pictures and placed a hand to her chest. "Isn't she beautiful?" she asked indulgently.

"Yes, she sure is," he agreed, feasting his eyes on Sasha.

Roxaner cackled. "I wasn't talking about my daughter. Of course she is beautiful. You wouldn't be interested in having her model your designs if she wasn't. I was talking about my niece, Judith." Her eyes brimmed with tears and Terraine felt helpless as he looked around for a napkin. Roxaner followed his eyes and waved her hand. "Oh, don't worry about me. I always cry at weddings." She reached into her purse and pulled out her own handkerchief and wiped her eyes. Terraine sighed with relief. The last thing he wanted was to make a bad first impression. "Did Sasha tell you she designed her dress? Actually, she designed all of the dresses."

In awe, Terraine turned and looked at the exquisite work done on Judith's gown. "I had no idea she was so talented. She said that she was a designer but I never would have guessed the extent of her talent," he said with a high degree of admiration.

"Yeah, it's a shame she couldn't open her own boutique. She was so disappointed when the bank turned her down."

Terraine looked down at Roxaner before his eyes traveled across the room to where Sasha stood with her eyes as large as saucers. Terraine laughed softly. She obviously did not want him talking to her mother. *Too bad.*

"Did she tell you she takes after her mother? Oh! There is Cousin Diana. Come let me introduce you." Before Terraine could protest, Roxaner grabbed his arm and pulled him across the room to meet the rest of the family.

What was her mother up to? Sasha had looked up from the photographer and seen her mother talking to Terraine and groaned. She didn't want him near her and she most definitely did not want him to be introduced to her family. She could just imagine what her mother was telling everyone. Sasha draped a hand on Joe's shoulder to steady herself while she took another look. She wished that the photographer would hurry up so she could get to her mother before she pulled out her baby pictures with those glasses and buckteeth in braces. Just then, Sasha heard Terraine roar with laughter. *Dang, too late.* She stomped her foot.

"Sasha, hold still," her cousin Joe hissed at her.

"Oh, be quiet," Sasha mumbled, then turned her head back towards the cameras and sighed. The damage was done and there was nothing she could do about it now.

After the photographer was finished, everyone prepared to leave for the reception that was being held at the prestigious Ritz Carlton Hotel. Sasha purposely got lost in the crowd and tried to sneak off with the wedding party into the limo but Terraine had scanned the area and found her wedged between two heavy-set ladies. He quickly came up behind her and grabbed her arm, pulling her next to him.

He smiled down at the surprised look on her face. "Going somewhere?"

"Are you going to watch me all evening?" she asked while shaking her arm free of his hand.

"Yes, if I have to," he countered.

"Nothing is going to happen to me," she hissed.

"I am not taking any chances."

"Go home, Terraine!"

He gave her a devilish look. "Not unless you're going home with me. Besides, your mother invited me to the reception."

"She what?" she stammered. Before she could scream in protest her mother walked up behind them.

"There you are. I thought I'd missed you. Tee

so graciously has offered to let me ride with you both to the reception."

"Tee?" Sasha repeated.

"It's my nickname," he smirked.

Roxaner gave her daughter a comforting smile. "This way I won't have to ride with Cousin Frances. You know she never knows when to shut up."

"Shall we, ladies?" Terraine offered an arm to both of them. Roxaner eagerly took his arm while giving Sasha a dead stare—the language between mother and daughter, telling her to behave. Terraine had to look down to keep from laughing at the expression on Sasha's face. It was easy to see who was in charge. He could not have picked a better future mother-in-law.

When they arrived at the hotel, Terraine watched as Sasha stalked off to the other end of the ballroom, furious. Terraine almost felt pity for her after the descriptive stories Roxaner had shared with him on the drive over. Terraine chuckled and went in search of a men's room.

Someone had already replaced Honey's place card with one for Terraine and he was seated across from Sasha. She was pouting. Though she knew that she was acting like a child, she couldn't help it. If she stopped, she was afraid that she'd allow her guard down again.

"Your cousin's dress is exquisite."

His compliment caught her off guard. She had been prepared to give him a smart aleck comment. Instead, he had said something nice. "Uh, thank you."

"I'd like to express an interest in your designs.

"I've changed my mind," she pouted. "They are no longer for sale." Terraine chuckled. "What's so funny?"

"You, my love. Come, let's get some food. We'll talk business later." He placed his hand gently on her shoulder and escorted her to the buffet table.

Sasha noticed the curious looks from her elders, the jealous smiles from her female cousins and her mother's chest stuck out with pride. She was ready to die of embarrassment.

The ballroom was beautifully decorated with long buffet style tables and several expensive dishes with caterers ready to serve guests. Judith's parents had spared no expense for their daughter's big day, Sasha thought as she looked at the swan sculptured out of ice. She piled her plate generously and sat down at her table to enjoy her food. She had been so busy getting ready that she hadn't eaten anything this morning.

"I'm glad to know that I am not the only one that was hungry," Terraine said as he slipped into the seat next her. After the police had left his house he had scrambled into his clothes and raced to

Sasha's house, barely touching the sandwich that Honey prepared for him.

Terraine dug right into the generous portions on his plate. "Mmm," he smacked. "I love these little quiches."

Sasha's face tightened as she listened to him chew like a hungry dog. She put her fork down. He was purposely trying to embarrass her. She kicked him in the shin.

"Ouch!" he cried with a surprised look on his face.

Sasha ignored him and took another bite of her food. She looked to see if anyone else had noticed. They hadn't. She then turned to him and glared. "Quit chewing like an animal," she hissed uncomfortably in his ear.

"Like what?" He looked innocently at her before popping an egg roll into his mouth. He was antagonizing her and was enjoying every minute of it. He'd do just about anything to get her to crack a smile. "Oh! You must mean like this." He began smacking boisterously in her ear. Then suddenly he broke down and started laughing. Sasha tried to keep a straight face but his humor was infectious and she found herself laughing with him. So he liked acting goofy, she thought.

"I was beginning to think you did not like me any more." He placed his hand on top of hers and looked at her with sad beagle eyes.

Sasha snatched her hand back and stifled her laughter. He thought he was so smart. "You are pushing your luck."

Terraine tried to look wounded. Sasha tried to look stern. They took one look at each other's comical expressions and burst out laughing.

That was what Roxaner and her two sisters, Mildred and Beatrice, saw from across the room. They had zeroed in on their table since the moment the two arrived.

Roxaner clasped her hands together with glee. "Ladies, I think we have a fall wedding to plan." They each gave an 'amen' and walked back to their table to begin discussing the arrangements.

When Terraine left to refill their glasses with champagne, Sasha took a moment to rethink things. Part of her desperately wanted him back in her life but the other part of her wished for a continuation of the empty days that she had grown accustomed to. She was so confused.

"Sasha, may I have this dance?"

"What?" she stammered. Terraine was standing over her holding two flute glasses, which he sat down.

He watched the play of emotion on her face. "If you haven't noticed, they are playing our song."

Sasha listened and realized that they were playing "Spend My Life with You," the same song they slow danced to on that magical evening. She was surprised Terraine even remembered.

"Are you going to leave me hangin' and make me look like a fool in front of all of your family?"

Sasha wrung her hands. She couldn't dance with him.

If she allowed him to hold her in his arms again, if she allowed her body to press up against the warmth of his again, her defenses would melt away like a wax candle. Any contact with him would produce potent consequences, for which she was unprepared. Just looking at him set a fire within her. Terraine remained standing in front of her with his hand out, waiting.

"Why don't we wait for a faster tune?" she suggested, giving resistance one more try.

"Let's not." Before she could protest further, he took hold of her wrist and practically yanked her out of the chair. He then leaned near her and whispered for her ears only, "I've been waiting all evening for this."

He escorted her onto the dance floor, wrapped his arms around her and pulled their bodies together as they moved to the music. At the feel of his heart beating against her chest, Sasha felt faint. *Breathe girl.*

"It feels so good to hold you in my arms again,"

he whispered, his breath warm against her cheek. "I don't know if I will ever let you go." He nuzzled her neck with his soft hot lips.

Sasha tilted her head and their eyes tangled. *I wish I could believe you.* His raisin brown eyes raked her face long and slow and seemed to send down a longing caress as he looked into her beautiful hazel eyes. His hands trailed down the narrowness of her waist along the curve of her hips and the air vibrated around them. She was powerless, feeling overwhelmed by his maleness, oblivious to the people dancing around them. A tremor both of fear and anticipation shivered through her and her heart began to race. Sasha had no choice but to interlock her fingers behind his neck and rest her head against his solid chest. The song ended and another began. Sasha closed her eyes, allowing her body to relax against the warmth of his.

Terraine's hand slowly rose to the back of her neck. Her skin was as soft and silky as the dress she wore. He had missed the freshness of her hair, the way she felt, the way she tasted. Having her so close with her body rubbing against him in all of the right places was driving him crazy. Terraine cursed under his breath, suddenly remembering that they were in a room full of people. He wanted to grab her by the hand and pull her away even if it was just for a minute. Fifteen would be even better. He just

needed to be alone with her. He felt that possessive.

"Come with me." He grasped her wrist and
tugged her gently towards the door.

"Where are we going?" she asked.

Terraine laced his hands with hers and Sasha
permitted herself to be led out of the ballroom. With
great effort he managed to keep his normal stride
as they walked down the hall. He felt like a madman. His heart was pounding. He opened the door
of a small coat closet. It was perfect. *Dark and private.* Terraine pulled Sasha into the room and shut
the door. He then took her in his arms, breathing
heavily.

"I want to apologize again. I never meant for
things to happen the way that they did," he said
softly.

Before she could respond, Terraine pushed her
against the door and seized her mouth in a hot hungry kiss. His hands tightened around her waist and
crushed her to him.

She shivered and braced her hands on his
shoulders, feeling the solid muscles shift under her
fingers as he drew her closer. Then with a soft
moan, she threw her arms around his neck. Her
mouth opened and their tongues touched and she
felt an electric shock go through her, down to her
toes. She needed him to kiss her passionately, to

be as hungry for her as she was for him. She pressed her breasts against his chest, her nipples erect and aroused, and the kiss became deeper, more insistent and demanding. Sasha released a low sigh as his large hands slid across her buttocks, moaning again when he caressed them. He kissed and teased her lips, gently sucking, and she met his kiss urgently. She opened her mouth wider, taking Terraine's tongue in deeper, entwining her tongue with his. The kiss seemed to last forever and she was breathless

Leaning forward, Terraine thrust his pelvis gently against her. "Feel what you do to me, Sasha. I'm like this whenever you are around," he murmured. He bent, sweeping his tongue along the side of her neck, breathing hot air. "Every night I lie in bed, hard as a brick, hurting for you. I want to feel you beneath me. I want to be between your legs."

"Yes," Sasha moaned. *NO! NO!* You're falling for it again. It's sex. It's all about sex. Wasn't it just last week that she'd found out who he really was? And now she was in a closet with him pawing her, on the verge of making love.

Sasha staggered away from him and pushed him hard enough to get his attention. "I would appreciate it if you'd leave." She could not see the hurt in his eyes in the dark, but his silence made her anger drain. She bit her lip hard, trying to keep the tears back. Her palms were still warm from holding him and her nipples felt sensitive against the touch of her dress. She could still taste his sweetness on her lips. Sasha wanted so badly to believe him but she could not allow herself to. Not yet. She hated being mean but she hated being used even more.

For a moment Terraine glared at her, frustrated, looking as if he wanted to either shake her or kiss her fiercely again. Then hearing her whimper, he suddenly stiffened. He wished there was some way that he could dissolve her persistent mistrust and anger. "Fine, if that's the way you want it, I'm out of here." He yanked open the door and headed towards the exit.

The rest of the evening passed in a haze. Sasha could not remember whom she talked to or what she might have said. She did not remember her cousin Tanya giving her and her mother a ride home.

Roxaner sat next to her daughter and noticed that her behavior had changed, but did not pry. She knew Sasha would talk to her when she was ready. When Tanya pulled up in front of her house, Roxaner leaned over and gave her daughter a kiss on the cheek and asked her to call in the morning.

The rest of the ride was silent. Tanya knew her cousin did not want to talk and she chose not to ask questions either. The family knew what Sasha had gone through. Tanya had spent years envying her cousin's life only to find out that her own life as a stewardess wasn't quite as bad as she'd thought.

Sasha did not remember pulling up in front of her house or opening the front door. She got as far as the bathroom to find some Tylenol when she noticed a message written across her bathroom mirror. I'M WATCHING YOU.

The entire day came crashing down on her as Sasha crumpled onto the floor. She dropped her head into her hands and cried for the woman that she used to be. Once again, she was quickly embraced by her constant companion for the past year.

Fear.

Chapter Ten

Sasha inhaled the warm summer air as she pulled out of the parking lot to a stop sign at the corner. Before pulling off again, she reached into her purse and retrieved her cellular phone, hitting number two on her speed dial.

"Love Your Hair, this is Honey." Sasha grinned. Hearing the familiar voice was just what she needed right now. "Hey, girl. You got plans for lunch?"

Honey chuckled. "I do now."

"I'll meet you at our spot in thirty minutes." Sasha ended the call and smiled. Everything was going to be all right.

"Well, it seems to me you have two choices: Either you can quit playing hard to get and give Terraine a chance or waste your time feeling sorry for Robby."

The two women were sitting at the St. Louis Bread Factory located in the Central West End. While Sasha poured her heart out, they sipped freshly brewed Irish creme coffee and nibbled on deli sandwiches prepared on fresh-baked sourdough bread.

Sasha looked down at her mug. "I don't see it that way. I'm just not ready yet for another relationship."

Honey lifted the cup of steaming hot coffee to her lips and closed her eyes in appreciation. "And why is that?"

Sasha shook her head before looking across the table at Honey. "You know why."

"Girl, it is obvious that Tee is crazy about you." She pointed her finger at her. "Now what you need to do is to tell that psycho to leave you alone."

"Honey, it's not that easy. I just need to find a way to tell Robby that it is over so that he will understand. Otherwise, he will never listen," she said softly. Sasha knew that trying to explain to Robby that they never would get back together was a big waste of time. She just prayed that he'd find someone else soon and leave her alone.

"Then screw 'em." Honey tossed a freshly painted hand in the air.

"Honey!" Sasha looked over at the couple sitting at the table to her left and gave them an apologetic smile. Honey could be so ghetto at times.

"I'm serious. Enough is enough. I am tired of tiptoeing around this. One day the guy is sane and the next thing we know, he's not. That's the breaks. People are diagnosed with mental illnesses every day and there is nothing they can do about it except control it with medication." She bit into her turkey club and swallowed before continuing. "Robby is not your problem and it's time for you to get over it and get on with your life before you make yourself crazy."

Sasha looked at Honey over the rim of her mug. "I am trying."

"Well, try harder."

Sasha rolled her eyes. Honey could be so insensitive at times.

"I am serious. If you put your foot down, he'll leave you alone."

Sasha was quiet for brief moment. Then she lowered her mug to the table and spoke in a low voice. "Do you think Robby might have something to do with those two murders?"

"You've got to be kidding, that wimp!" Honey threw her head back and roared with laughter. "Robby's not capable of murder." Honey waved her hand. "I'm sorry, Sasha. If you need to be mad at me, then do so, but I will never forget that day when

I came rushing into your house with the police. Robby's mouth was opened so wide he could have caught flies. Then what does he try to do?" Honey leaned forward with laughter in her eyes. "He tries to shoot himself in the head and instead he hits his foot." She stopped to chuckle again. "You've got to look at the lighter side. If it wasn't so serious, it would have been hilarious."

Sasha sucked her teeth. "I don't agree."

"Come on, Sasha. The fool shot himself in the foot! How pathetic can one get!"

While Honey roared with laughter, Sasha gave it some thought and had to admit it was kind of funny. The Robby she remembered would help an injured dog lying in the street. Relief washed over her. She didn't want to think for a moment that Robby was capable of murder and Honey's reassurance made all of the difference. Honey's cackling became infectious and Sasha found herself laughing along with her until the couple to her left glared at them. Sasha brought her finger to her lips and told Honey to "shhh" as another round of giggles slipped out from behind her finger. God, it felt good to be laughing.

"All he is capable of is sneaking into your house and leaving stupid messages on your mirrors." Honey reached for a napkin and dabbed the corners of her eyes and smiled. She was pleased to see Sasha finally seeing the light. "Quit pacifying that man and get on with your life. Robby is no longer your responsibility."

"What you are saying is true but I can't help feeling partially responsible." Sasha shrugged. "Besides, Robby has nothing to do with my relationship with Terraine. I am just not ready for anything serious, whether Robby is harassing me or not."

Honey took another bite. "Why is that?"

"I don't know yet if I can trust him."

"Terraine was just trying to check things out before he dove in head first," Honey defended before bringing her coffee to her lips again. "He told me so." She shrugged. "You know you like him, so you might as well admit it. How much you want to bet Terraine will make you see the truth?"

Sasha rested her chin in the palm of her hand. "Yeah...I like him a lot. So wipe that smile off your face and I am not in the mood for any of your bets." *Probably because I always lose.*

Honey rolled her eyes and leaned back in her chair making tsk sounds with her teeth. "Whatever," she mumbled with the last bite of her sandwich in her mouth. "I'll be glad when you get it together. I want you to settle down and marry someone nice." A silly smirk curled on her lips. "Like Terraine."

After a moment of silence Sasha crossed her

arms on the table and looked directly into Honey's eyes to make sure she understood what she was saying. "All I know for sure is that I really like him but I am not ready for what he wants. Yet at the same time I am not ready to let him go."

Honey lifted her eyes from her mug and smiled mischievously. "Who said anything about letting him go?"

Sasha cradled her head once again with her hands. "I don't know if I can handle being hurt again. Terraine is different. He is special and the more I try to resist him, the harder it gets," she said softly as she stared out the window behind Honey's head. "I am so afraid to trust him but at the same time, I find myself drawn to him."

"No kidding. I haven't seen you like this since big head Darryl." Honey was referring to Sasha's high school infatuation, a relationship that lasted a total of four days. He was now serving time in the state penitentiary.

Sasha snorted. "Thanks for the reminder." She finally bit into her ham sandwich. "I don't think I have ever felt this strongly about anyone. It's scary."

Honey grinned at her friend. "Umm hmm." She studied her nails, antagonizing Sasha with her non-chalant attitude.

"I am pouring my heart out to you and that's all

you have to say?"

"I think it's about time you stop fighting your attraction to him." Honey leaned over, placing both her arms on the table. "So-oo, have you given him some yet?"

Sasha grinned and shook her head. "No."

"No?" Honey's eyes grew large with amusement.

Sasha stared at Honey for a long moment before repeating herself. "No."

"You better do something before it dries up like an old shriveled up prune." Sasha cut her eyes and Honey choked on her own joke. "Instead of taking care of business, you'd rather wallow in sorrow." Honey shook her head. "Sometimes I just don't understand you."

"Yeah, I know," Sasha sighed. "But I know that I am making the right choice. Trust me, Honey. I will take care of everything. If things are meant to be, they'll work themselves out."

"I hope you get it together. I'll be moving soon and I don't know how you are going to be able to manage without me." She looked down at her watch. "Well, that's your session for today." She smiled and rose from her seat. "Excuse me, but Dr. Love has another client to see. A paying customer, that is. I'll see you later." She winked and strolled away.

Long after Honey left, Sasha sat at the table thinking that maybe she and Terraine had reached a point in their relationship that needed resolving.

While listening to Kenny G, Terraine reclined in his chair and looked up at the ceiling fan spinning overhead.

If he had to listen to one more designer complain about Natalia's relentless behavior, he was going to commit murder himself. Natalia's high and mighty attitude was becoming unbearable. She was constantly flaunting her job security in his face and as a result, his lawyers were right now reviewing Pop's will. There were always ways of getting around things.

Terraine threw the irritating thoughts from his mind and let his eyes travel to the catalog layout lying on the end of his desk waiting for his final approval. The corner of his mouth turned up in a grin.

Attending the wedding together had definitely been a start in the right direction, but he still had a long way to go with her. Sasha was more stubborn than he would have imagined. Terraine gritted his teeth. Why did they have to fight whenever they were in each other's presence? It seemed as though she was determined to keep a rift between them. What he needed was to devise a mechanism that would tear down the defensive walls surrounding her. Saturday he had felt that they'd made progress and were possibly growing closer together. Memories flashed across his mind of the passion they'd experienced. He was certain that there was much more to discover about Sasha.

Terraine heard a light tap on his office door and looked up to find Geri walking towards his desk. His eyes came to rest on her worried expression.

"What is it, Geri?"

"You might want to read this." Geri dropped a copy of the *St. Louis Post Dispatch* on his desk. Terraine picked it up and the headlines read DOUBLE DEATHS AT DIVA DESIGNS.

"Damn!" Terraine slammed his fist down hard on top of his desk.

"My feelings exactly. Unfortunately, it made the front page of all the local papers. There was even a small article in the *Chicago Tribune*." She dropped three more bundles onto his desk.

Terraine ran a frustrated hand across his chin as he read the first paragraph of the article. "The media are pointing the blame at us. Saying that the deaths are somehow connected with new management and the corporation's current financial situation."

Geri placed her hand on her hip. "The only paper that seems to have shown us any sympathy is the *St. Louis American*. She dropped the black publication onto his desk.

"I guess we owe them a thank you," he said before tossing the papers into the trash. In one smooth angry motion, Terraine rose from his seat and moved to the door. "I am going to lunch. Find my brother and have someone from public relations get their butt in here, ASAP!" Terraine reached for his jacket and walked out the door.

Sasha pulled into the parking lot and found the twins having a heated discussion with Evan.

"Hey everybody, what's going on?" she asked as she shut the car door.

Asia and India spun around and stormed towards her. "Come on, Sasha, let's go shopping or something!" Asia muttered as she and her sister walked over to their rental car and climbed in. Sasha watched their puzzling behavior and wondered where they were going. They were scheduled to do several group shots this afternoon. Sasha turned towards Evan, who was heading in her direction wearing a gloomy expression.

"Sasha, please try to talk to them. They'll listen

246

to you. If they walk away from this shoot, Natalia will have my job," Evan pleaded. "I'll see you girls back here in two hours!" he shouted after them. He then strolled away before Sasha had a chance to comment. She in turn walked over and climbed into the back seat of their Maxima.

"Can someone please explain what's going on here? I thought we were supposed to be dressed and in front of the camera at exactly one o'clock?"

"We were," Asia answered before she drove off the lot.

"And we would have," India added.

"But something happened to the equipment," Asia said.

Sasha placed her hands on the driver's headrest and leaned forward. "What do you mean, something happened?"

Asia looked at Sasha in her rear view mirror. "Just what we said. Someone came in last night and smashed the equipment. Stefan was devastated."

India swiveled around in her seat and spoke in a soft, sympathetic voice. "I have never seen a grown man cry before."

They took turns explaining. Sasha was flabbergasted. She could not believe this was happening. Asia pulled into the parking garage at the St. Louis Centre, a mall located at the heart of downtown St.

Louis. No one spoke until they all were out of the
car and riding the elevator up to the mall level of the
parking garage.

"We need to talk to you in private," Asia whispered. She latched onto Sasha's right arm and
India grabbed her left.

They escorted her to the accessories department of Famous Barr and Asia pretended to be
admiring scarves while she spoke. "I think someone has been following my sister and me."

Sasha looked over at Asia and then at India,
who nodded in agreement. "When did this start?"

Asia glanced uneasily over her shoulder before
speaking. "A couple of days ago. While we were at
lunch, I saw this man sitting a few tables away from
us. Then yesterday we saw him again when we
returned to our hotel. When we arrived at our room,
we found the contents of our suitcases dumped all
over our beds."

"I think he was responsible," India added.

"W-what did he look like?" Sasha asked,
becoming more uncomfortable by the minute.

"He was handsome. Which was why I remember him. Red bone with freckles."

Sasha swallowed. It was just a coincidence.

"We are scared. After what happened to Deja
and then Monet, well..." India's voice faded.

"We just don't know anymore," Asia concluded.

India gave her a curious look. "Has anything strange been happening to you?"

Sasha nodded. "Yeah, my house has been broken into, but I don't think there is a connection. My ex-boyfriend took our breakup pretty hard."

India tied a scarf around her neck and turned to admire her appearance in a small mirror. "I tried to explain to Evan but all he seems to care about is his job." She sighed, removing the scarf and placing it back on the shelf.

They strolled together out toward the food court. Asia placed a hand on Sasha's arm and looked at her with eyes full of pain. "We don't want to have to leave, but if my dad catches wind of what's going on up here, our career at Diva Designs will be history." Their father was a retired navy pilot, who had not allowed his daughters to begin dating until they were seventeen, and even then he'd tagged along as a chaperone. If it had not been for their mother, they would have never been allowed to become models, not to mention travel by themselves.

"We were hoping to be home before the Fourth of July holiday. Now with another murder, plus the film and the cameras being destroyed, there's no telling when we'll be able to leave," India said with frustration.

Asia shook her head. "I don't know what we are going to do."

The next few days seemed strange and out of the ordinary to Sasha. As a result of the murders, a new state-of-the-art security system was installed, monitoring the activities of everyone going in and out of the building. Badges were assigned, which had to be swiped at the front entrance. Anyone without a badge would have to stop and speak to security before being granted access to the building. Rufus kept his job at the gate but an armed security guard was hired to monitor the main entrance. To top things off, after being off for two days, the twins returned to work with their own personal bodyguard, Duane, a large beefy guy with eyes that were hard and filled with contempt, even though Asia commented that he was really a big teddy bear. Having him around helped the twins relax. Stefan complained about him being in the studio but the twins won the argument. Sasha began to wonder if maybe she should hire her own bodyguard, but decided to postpone the idea since she had not had any problems since the message on her mirror. Surprisingly, not even a call from Robby. Things were quiet. *Too quiet.*

Sasha had hoped to hear from Terraine or even run into him at the studio but neither happened. She felt a twinge of disappointment. But wasn't that what she wanted? If so, why did she feel so depressed? Sasha already knew the answer to that. In Terraine she had found light in her life and without him, her world was dim.

Deciding to take a chance, Sasha went up to the fifth floor to his suite. She had never been on this floor. She'd never had a reason to. Plush green carpet met her as she exited the elevator. She walked down the hall towards two large, carved doors where a secretary was sitting behind a desk, deeply absorbed in something she was keying into a computer.

Sasha cleared her throat. Geri looked up and her eyes gleamed with kindness.

"Hi, may I help you?"

Sasha suddenly felt uneasy about her decision to show up unannounced in his office. God, she hoped he wasn't still mad at her.

"I am Sasha Moore. Is Mr. Andrews available?"

"I'm Geri, his assistant." She rose from her seat and came around and shook her hand. "Welcome, Ms. Moore. I'm sorry I didn't recognize you. I've seen the layout for the catalog. You are beautiful and amazing."

Sasha glowed at her praise. "Thank you so much."

"Let me see if Terraine is available."

She pushed the red button on her intercom.

"Excuse me, Terraine. Sasha is here to see you."

"Send her in." His voice sang over the speaker and through her veins. How she'd missed hearing him speak! His office door opened and his public relations manager, Steven Richardson, came out. Sasha had met him a week ago in the elevator and taken an instant dislike to him. His dark eyes held a strange expression that bothered her. He nodded in her direction before heading down the hall.

Geri stood up and placed a hand on her arm. "Maybe you can cheer him up. He has been a bear all morning." She smiled and pointed towards the door.

Terraine was sitting behind a large desk with his feet parked on the end. She walked into his office and closed the door behind her before turning to face him.

Terraine studied the woman who filled his office with her presence. Seeing her again was like experiencing her beauty and sensual power for the first time. The knit dress she wore accentuated her curvaceous body and clung to her narrow waist. Her brown hair was pulled back, then secured with a clip, giving him a full view of her sensuous neck, and her hazel eyes held a gleam that no makeup could produce.

"Hello, Sasha."

"Hi." She smiled softly at him, looking into his

raisin brown eyes. Sasha's heart seemed to swell at the sight of him. He spelled empowerment sitting behind his desk dressed in business attire, looking devastatingly handsome. Sasha recalled with breathless clarity everything they'd felt and done their last night together. The sudden silence in the room made it possible for Sasha to hear her thumping heart. She watched as Terraine laced his fingers behind his head and waited for her to state the reason for her visit. Sasha swallowed. "I've been thinking about what you said about my gowns and if you are still interested, I'd like to show some of my creations to you."

Terraine dropped his feet and smiled. "That can be arranged."

Sasha ran her tongue across her lip. Her throat suddenly felt parched. "Great." She looked away and surveyed the surrounding area. The deep rich woods of his office looked very masculine. "You have a great view from your office," she commented as she walked over to the window and looked out at the city.

"Yes, I do." Terraine was thinking about the view inside his office as he watched Sasha sashay over and lean against the glass. He rose from his chair and came to stand behind her with his chest pressed against her back. He sucked in his breath as he smelled the sweet scent of her skin that was so much a part of Sasha, a scent that he had missed these past several days. He placed his arms around her waist and planted small kisses on the sides of her neck. "When?"

Sasha was lost by his forward advance. The warmth of his body next to her and the caress of his lips along her neck set her aflame. "When what?" She shivered.

"When do you want to show me your designs?"

Sasha could only shrug and was thankful she had her back to him so that he could not see her face and read her transparent expression.

"How about now?" he whispered as his lips continued to explore the soft caramel flesh at her neck, searing a path all the way to her shoulders.

His lips were a delicious sensation. "Now?"

Terraine turned her around so that she was facing him. His lips had left her weak and confused. She looked up at the man who had tormented so many of her thoughts.

Terraine chuckled softly with confidence. "Sure, why not?" His gaze clung to her face, missing nothing.

Sasha knew she should move away and get out of his office fast, but her heart acted as a weight keeping her in place. Suddenly their faces were close enough for her to feel the warmth and moisture of his breath and she found herself unable to think with such close contact.

"All right."

Terraine raised a hand to her cheek and caressed it. "I'm glad you decided to come to me." He then placed his hands on the window on either side of her head and looked down at her with a lustful stare. "Now we have some unfinished business to attend to."

Her lips quivered and the tip of her tongue darted out to moisten them, which was enough of an invitation for him. Terraine dipped his head down and pressed his lips against hers. Once, twice, then again, enticingly.

This was not why she'd come to his office. Or was it? She felt Terraine's mouth move erotically against her own. The moist tip of his tongue traced the outline of her mouth, then slipped between her lips, which she willingly parted for him. Terraine leaned her against the glass and his tongue explored deeper. She quivered at the gentleness of his kiss. He wrapped his arms around her midriff and Sasha pressed against him, her back arching so that her face could remain tilted up towards his. Terraine's tongue traveled from her mouth to the base of her neck, all the way to the cleavage that was left exposed from her dress. With each kiss he whispered words of need and desire. Sasha tried desperately to remember why she'd come to his office but was powerless against the emotions he stirred within her. He was tormenting her as he slipped his hand beneath the loose neck of her dress and brushed her nipples with long gentle strokes. Sasha was overcome with shock and extreme pleasure.

"Terraine, I am interested in being your business partner, nothing more." Her voice was squeaky as she struggled for a confidence that she did not really feel.

"Who are you trying to convince, me or you? Quit fighting it, Sasha. I know you want me as much as I need you," he whispered.

Sasha moaned and Terraine lifted her as if she was weightless off the carpet. Her arms went instantly around his neck and she wrapped her shaky legs around his waist as he carried her over to the end of his desk.

"Terraine, I didn't come here for this," she whispered breathlessly as his tongue traced her earlobe.

"Yes you did." He lowered the sleeve covering her right shoulder and dipped his head, capturing one of her breasts with his mouth. She gasped as he suckled until her nipple turned hard as stone. His mouth recaptured hers as his hands lifted her dress up around her waist. Then his hands cupped her buttocks, holding her against his grinding pelvis.

Sasha felt him swollen and hot, as he thrust his hips against her thin dress. He rubbed his pelvis against her and set off a series of sharp tremors that turned her muscles into putty before he slipped two fingers into her panties. He was prepared to lower her panties when his intercom sounded.

"Excuse me, Terraine. Natalia is here to see you."

Sasha scrambled off the desk, her eyes large and her face flushed as she straightened her dress. Terraine cursed. "Tell her I'll drop by her office later."

The next voice heard over the intercom was Natalia's. "No, you won't. We have an urgent matter that needs to be addressed immediately." Sasha had barely enough time to straighten her hair before Natalia came barging into the office.

"Well, what do we have here?" Natalia looked at both of them, breathing fire. How dare Terraine even think of being with anyone else? So this was why he wouldn't give her the time of day. Well, all that was about to change. She forced a smile on her face. "Tee, don't tell me you are messing around with our models again?"

Sasha tried to hide her embarrassment.

Terraine glared at Natalia. "This better be important. Have a seat while I walk Sasha to the elevator. I'll be back in a few moments." He knew Natalia had purposely set out to make Sasha feel uncomfortable, so he took her hand to reassure her and exited his office.

"Sorry about Natalia. She can be a little obnoxious at times. If she weren't good at what she does, I would have gotten rid of her a long time ago."

"No problem," Sasha said, even though in the back of her mind she was wondering why he had not responded to Natalia's accusation. Was he in the habit of messing around with his models? Sasha wished for once that she could read him as easily as he seemed to read her.

Terraine climbed into the elevator with her and rode down to the garage. When they reached her car, Terraine gathered her in his arms and kissed her again.

"I have a few things that I need to finish up here, but I can be at your house at seven." He gave her a candid smile that warmed her heart again.
She nodded. "Great. See you then."

He was standing in the garage when he noticed Terraine and Sasha walking hand in hand to her car. He ducked down behind a Lincoln Town Car and moved in closer. What he heard infuriated him. Who the hell did he think he was, trying to spend time alone with Sasha? Didn't he know that it was a sin to covet thy neighbor's wife? It was obvious to him that Terraine had not gotten the hint from the brick he'd thrown through the window of his Navigator. He growled and slapped his knife across his palm. Terraine had everything that he wanted—a corporation and a beautiful woman—and both should belong to him. He pressed the blade firmly against his thumb until he drew blood. Before it was all over, he'd have both. For now he'd have to show them who was boss.

Terraine returned to his office and found Natalia sitting comfortably behind his desk.

"Get out of my chair, Natalia," he ordered in a calm voice but with enough authority that she did not have to question his level of seriousness.

She rose and said merrily, "Can't a girl have any fun?"

Terraine rubbed his hand across his smooth head. "What is the emergency?"

Natalia looked at him as if she was not sure what he was talking about, then suddenly remembered. "Ms. Guccione is being difficult. She refuses to f—"

Terraine's eyes grew large. "Is that your emergency? Our designers are always difficult."

She walked around to where he was standing and stood in front of him, pursing her strawberry-colored lips. "What's wrong, Terraine, you seem a little tense? Did I interrupt something early?" she asked, challenging him with her eyes.

"Stay out of my personal life, Natalia," Terraine warned in a cool manner and strolled over to his desk and reached down for his briefcase.

"How can you say that after all that we have been through?" she pouted.

He placed his briefcase on his desk and opened it, filling it with reports that he needed to review later. He had another long night ahead of him. Seeing Sasha tonight was going to put him even farther behind, but it would be worth it.

"I can say it because of everything we went through." He shut the case. "Now if you will excuse me, I have somewhere to be." As he strolled past Natalia, she grabbed his arm.

"Terraine, I am sorry about everything." She looked up at him with eyes full of remorse.

He gave her a look that was not warm. "It is a little too late for that." He released her fingers and headed out the door.

Terraine arrived just as a patrol car was pulling

away from Sasha's house and practically broke his neck trying to get up the stairs. Terraine found Sasha sitting on the floor picking up pieces of glass from a shattered picture frame. She looked up at him with haunted eyes and then dropped her eyes back to the floor, pretending that he was not there.

"What the hell happened now?" He looked around at the furniture that had been turned over and shattered dishes on the floor. Honey walked into the living room carrying a shirt that had been ripped.

"Hey, Tee," she mumbled. "Grab a broom, stay a while."

Terraine arched his brow, amazed that she could find humor even during the most traumatic experiences.

Sasha had forgotten that he was coming over. She did not want him to be here to see this mess and the bad luck that plagued her life.

Terraine kneeled down on the carpet next to her and placed a hand gently on her arm. "Does this have something to do with what is happening at Diva?"

Sasha looked up at him with tear-brimmed eyes and shook her head.

"I tend to disagree. I'm calling my brother." He turned to Honey. "May I use your phone?" She nodded and he walked into the kitchen.

While Terraine was on the phone, Sasha finished cleaning up the glass and then went into her bedroom to try and pull herself together. It had been a shock to return home and find everything in an uproar.

Shortly afterwards Terraine appeared at her door. He walked over and gripped her shoulders. "Sasha, be honest with me. Do you have any idea who is doing this?"

Sasha shook her head. "I-I don't know. The twins commented the other day that someone broke into their hotel room."

Terraine swore and turned away. Someone was trying to sabotage the success of the new line. He was certain of it. Turning back to Sasha, he saw the fear on her face and pulled her close to him. "I am going to do whatever it takes to protect you." His lips found hers with a kiss that Sasha willingly returned. "I don't know who is doing this, but I promise we will get to the bottom of it." He released her and placed his hand under her chin and tried to smile for her sake. "How about showing me your designs?"

Honey picked the pillows up off of the living room floor and placed them back on the couch. She straightened a large potted plant and scooped the dirt back into the pot. She was heading towards the kitchen to retrieve the broom and dustpan when she heard the doorbell ring. Opening the door, her knees almost buckled from under her. The man standing before her was gorgeous and looked exactly like the one in the other room, except this one's biceps and chest were massive, stretching his shirt well beyond capacity, and instead of a bald head his hair was cut close.

"Hello." He looked down at the beautiful petite woman and immediately hoped that she was not the same gorgeous woman that had his brother turning somersaults.

"You must be Jay." An odd spiraling feeling entered her and gripped by a sugary weakness, she moved away from the door, breaking free of his potent spell. "I'm Honey, please come in." She smiled.

Jay released a long sigh of relief followed by a small chuckle. "You must be the roommate." *Well, well what have we here?*

Honey looked up into his eyes and was disconcerted by her reaction. "Let me go and find your brother." Honey hurried out of the room.

Jay rubbed his fingers across his chin, unable to believe his good fortune.

"I suppose you've noticed how good looking his

brother is," Sasha whispered.

Honey shrugged. "Too much of a pretty boy for me. Haven't you noticed how often he pats his hair? It's like he's afraid that a strand of hair is out of place and then whenever he walks past the mirror in the living room, he stops to admire himself." Honey rolled her eyes with exasperation.

She spoke too abruptly and Sasha looked over at her with amazement on her face. "It's funny how you've noticed." Sasha lifted a vase off the counter and carried it into the dining room. Honey followed with a portable vacuum. Terraine and Jay were sitting at the table discussing what had happened. "Hey, Terraine, the only thing that wasn't destroyed in here is these flowers you sent me." He looked up at the vase of white roses in her hands that she carried over and placed on the mantel in the living room.

Terraine's brow rose. "Sweetheart, I would love to take the credit for those, but I did not send you those flowers."

Sasha and Honey's eyes connected.

Jay immediately became suspicious and rose from his seat. "Was there a card?"

Honey cleared her throat. "Sure. There was a card with each bouquet. I stuck them in Sasha's album so that she could look back on this moment when she gets old and ugly. Let me go get them."

Yesterday was a start for them but ended as a setback. Terraine felt at ease that Jay had assigned twenty-four hour security for Sasha. She'd argued that her life would feel invaded but Terraine had stood firm and she finally agreed to allow him to post a security guard outside her home. She was so stubborn. The only time they seemed to get along was when they discussed her gowns. Then excitement shone in her face and voice. Terraine had to agree that her gowns with their detail and uniqueness were enough to make anyone excited. Her designs were going to bring them closer together. Terraine pressed his intercom.

"Geri, tell Natalia I want to see her."

"She is meeting with designers this afternoon."

Terraine was silent for a moment; then he got a better idea. "Then send in her assistant."

"Yes, sir."

Five minutes later, Evan walked into his office short of breath. "Yes sir, you wanted to see me."

Terraine turned around in his chair and rocked back. "I want to add another designer to our fashion show."

Evan ran his hand nervously through his hair. "But the programs are ready to go in the mail on Monday, the choreographing is almost complete, extra models have been—"

Terraine cleared his throat. "Evan, who is the boss here?"

"You are sir." *But Natalia will put my butt in a sling when she finds out.*

"Good, then I expect you to handle the changes." He handed him a thin manila folder. "I'll handle Natalia. Right now this will be our little secret."

Evan was noticeably pleased that he did not have to break the news to the boss lady himself. He nodded. "Yes, sir." And he quickly exited the office before Terraine asked him to do something else.

Chapter Eleven

Sasha staggered out of bed towards the living room. Who in the world was knocking on her door at this time of the morning? It wasn't even nine o'clock yet. She had spent the last two nights altering gowns and wasn't due in at the studio today. She'd hoped to sleep until it was time to prepare for a meeting this afternoon.

Sasha looked through the peephole and saw Roxaner standing on the other side of the door.

"Oh no!" Sasha collapsed against the door. She wasn't up to dealing with her mother this morning.

Roxaner knocked again. "Sasha, I know that you're in there!"

Sasha groaned, removed the lock on the door

and slowly opened it.

"Mom-my," she whined before being knocked over by a large dog. Not the puppy her mother had bought for her but a large animal that looked to be a cross between a German shepherd and a Chow.

"What...is this?" Sasha demanded on the floor underneath the dog.

"Meet Nikki," Roxaner announced before shutting the door behind her. She faced Sasha with both hands on her hips, grinning blissfully.

"What's a Nikki?" Sasha had managed to get up and was now trying to block the large pink tongue that was slobbering all over her nightgown.

Roxaner patted her hairy head. "Nikki is your new dog."

Sasha's eyes grew large and she sputtered a moment before she could form words. "You've got to be kidding? Where is my puppy?" She tried to push Nikki away but she was strong and knocked Sasha over again, this time onto the couch. "Hey cut it out!" she squealed, trying to sound mad, but her mother heard the laughter in her voice.

"I decided to keep him for myself." Roxaner walked over and took a seat directly across from her.

"Why?"

With worried eyes, Roxaner shook a finger at her daughter. "Honey told me about someone breaking in here. I am disappointed that you didn't tell me yourself. "

"Thanks a lot, Honey," Sasha mumbled to herself. "Because whenever I mention anything unpleasant you get all bent out of shape. When did you talk to Honey?"

"I called you yesterday and you weren't home. After the in-depth conversation I had with her about your near death experience, I went back to the humane society to find you a big dog and *voilà*, meet Nikki." She smiled down at the dog.

Sasha also looked over at Nikki who was now slobbering all over her coffee table. Next she would be chewing on her shoes.

Sasha shook her head. "Mom, I don't want her," she stated firmly

Roxaner reached over and patted her on the leg. "Of course you do, dear. You need protection."

Frustration nipped at Sasha but she managed to conceal it. "And you think this goofy-looking dog is the answer?"

Roxaner nodded. "Big dogs always scare away burglars. You'll probably get more protection out of this dog than you will with that security system you wasted your money on." She frowned. "Not to mention that rent-a-cop you have posted outside your door." Sasha opened her mouth to ask her how she knew that but Roxaner cut in. "Your mother has a good eye. Besides, as soon as he saw me pull into your driveway he stopped me and made me prove I was your mother. Naturally, I showed him your baby pictures." She leaned back in the chair and fanned herself with her hand and did not notice Sasha pressing her lips tightly together to prevent any words from exploding from her mouth. "I've been through worse. Take my word for it. You are better off with the dog."

Sasha scooted over to the other end of the couch, away from the drool that was now dripping on her rug. "I don't think so, Mom." Sasha shook her head. She did not care if she hurt her mother's feelings; she did not want the mutt. Her mother had already persuaded her into accepting a miniature schnauzer, which she really did not want, but she had been willing to make the exception. But she was not agreeing to this amazon that was guaranteed to eat her out of house and home.

Sasha threw her hands in the air with a high degree of exasperation. "Mom, I have a very important meeting this afternoon that I need to get ready for."

"What kind of meeting?"

Sasha hesitated. She was not ready to share her secret with her mother, at least not until everything was finalized. Terraine had expressed a desire to introduce her wedding gowns at the summer fashion show and she had agreed. Sasha was so nervous that she had been on pins and needles for days, but until a contract was signed and in her hand, she did not want to say anything to anyone for fear of jinxing her chances.

"We are going to view the catalog layout today." Actually they had gotten a chance to peek at the layout yesterday and Sasha was ecstatic at the end results. She had never seen a catalog with such beautiful backdrops as the one they had used for the photo shoots. It was definitely going to be an attention getter.

Roxaner clapped her hands together and rose. "In that case, let me fix you something to eat before you leave." She moved towards the kitchen.

Sasha groaned. "Mom, you do not have to do that."

Roxaner turned around. "Yes I do; otherwise you will be stopping by one of those fast food restaurants for lunch. Besides, I need you to humor me and tell me what kind of safety measures Terraine is taking to insure that you aren't the next girl to be found dead. As a matter of fact, maybe I need to pay him a visit," she tossed over her shoulder before reaching inside the refrigerator in search of breakfast food.

Breathe girl. It is only your mother.

"All right. Fine," Sasha mumbled. She looked

down and found herself petting Nikki, who at some point or another had made her way over to her side of the couch and had managed to lay her head in Sasha's lap without her realizing it. "Don't even try it. You are going back where you came from," Sasha murmured while smoothing the hair away from Nikki's somber eyes.

Terraine sat back in his chair and looked around the table at his staff, feeling the team spirit vibrating across the room. Each person had reported on the progress of the new intimate apparels line and even with the bad publicity they had been receiving, everything seemed to be coming along as scheduled. In addition, photographs of the new designs for the summer were passed around the room.

The gowns for the coming year had a sexier design while still managing to preserve their original sophistication. Over one hundred designs were scheduled to be modeled across the stage with the latter part of the show kicking off the new intimate apparels line. Twenty-five models were contracted for the two-night event that was to be held at the historic Fox Theatre. As Loren reported, over seventy percent of their invited guests had already sent an RSVP. Terraine was relieved at the way things were coming together. He had worried that the deaths would cause a decline in customer interest but instead they seemed to have done just the opposite.

"The marketing for this new line is going right along schedule. Advertising is ready. Print, television and radio spots are reserved. Next week we will begin shooting a thirty-second commercial and I was able to get some very good prime time spots. My department has been receiving numerous calls about the show. I think we might have something big happening here," Carl concluded, and he returned to his seat. Applause could be heard from around the table.

Terraine nodded, pleased again with what he was hearing. "Fantastic. Anyone else?"

"Of course we save the best for last," Natalia announced as she rose smoothly from her chair. "The photo shoot was a big success and the catalog layout is ready for review." She passed proofs around the table and drew responses such as "gorgeous," "breathtaking" and "dynamic." The vivid colors blended well with the women's skin and the dramatic background scenes were the perfect touch. Having already seen the proofs, Terraine quickly thumbed through the pages, nodding his head in admiration.

"Even with the murders we were able to complete the shoot with only four women. As a tribute, the families did agree to allow us to use one photo of both of the deceased women on the back cover." Terraine flipped to the photo of Deja and Monet hugging one another while standing in front of a fireplace. Originally the photo was not going to be used. It had been shot just for fun, but given their tragic deaths, he felt obligated to feature both girls by displaying a photo of the two of them together. All the models were beautiful, all six of them, but it was the breathtaking view on the cover that caught Terraine's full attention.

The scene was on a wooded deck. Sasha was sitting at a round table sipping a cup of coffee and wearing a gold and black satin robe that was open at the waist, revealing a gold satin gown with lattice ties up the side exposing long, gorgeous legs that gleamed under the light. Her hair was tousled to give the impression of a good night's sleep or a woman who had recently been made love to. Terraine was pleased. *Very pleased.*

He rose from his chair to address his staff.

"I wanted to take a moment and thank all of you for your hard work and determination to make this new line a success despite the negative reports, which I believe have actually worked in our favor. If my grandfather were here, he'd be mighty proud of all of you. Before we end this meeting, I have something special to share with you." He pressed his intercom. "Geri, you may send them in. Ladies and gentleman, for any of you that have not met our lovely ladies, I would like to introduce our Diva models wearing *Creations by Sasha*."

The back conference room door opened and in walked Tyler, the twins, and Sasha, all wearing satin wedding gowns. Each design was unique, displaying different embroidered threads and beads. *Oohs* and *aahs* were heard as the women modeled around the conference room.

Terraine felt his heart thump against his chest and for the next several seconds he allowed his eyes to devour the beauty standing at the other end of the table. She wore a sexy floral appliqué gown with Austrian crystal beads that hugged the same slim figure he clearly remembered exploring with his hands only days ago. Her hair was stacked on top of her head but untamable honey brown curls fell into feminine wisps around her face and neck. Terraine felt a chill run through his body and in that instant, he wanted Sasha more keenly that he'd ever wanted a women in his life. She looked exactly the way he'd imagined her to look on their wedding day. What was he saying? Terraine's heart stammered in his chest. Could it be possible? With this new discovery his entire body tingled with excitement, sending hot urgent messages from his heart down to his loins as he watched. Terraine had fallen in love with Sasha.

"What is the meaning of this?" Natalia roared. The four ladies stood still at the end of the conference room table in a single line holding their bouquets at an even level.

"What this means is that I plan to introduce these designs at the fashion show next month."

Natalia laughed. "That is impossible! There is too much preparation required, not to mention unnecessary expenses and additional choreographing. The summer fashion extravaganza is only a few short weeks away." She shook her head. "It is too late. We are already way over budget. Besides, the programs are scheduled for delivery on Monday." She reared back in her chair with a look of triumph etched on her face.

Evan cleared his throat. "Actually, I was able to make the change before the programs were printed."

Natalia smacked both hands down onto the table and whirled to face Evan. "You did this without my consent?"

"He had my consent," Terraine answered with thin lips of displeasure.

"I am the fashion director, nothing should have been decided without my knowledge." Natalia tried to sound in control but instead she was fighting mad. How dare he make her look powerless in front of her subordinates?

"And I am the CEO, and I can do whatever I feel will benefit the corporation, especially if it is going to increase our margin." Terraine ended the conversation. He hadn't been at liberty to have disagreements with Natalia in front of his staff and he was not about to begin now.

Terraine turned towards the models with an apologetic smile. "Thank you, ladies, you all look fabulous," he said dismissively. The ladies filed out but Sasha lagged behind.

"Excuse me, Terraine? If you are going to discuss my designs, I would like to stay, if you don't mind, and answer any questions that any one of you might have?" No one knew her gowns as she did, and if there was going to be a debate, she wanted to be present to rebut any negative comments. This was her big chance and she was not about to have the opportunity snatched right out of her hands.

Terraine raised an amused brow. No wonder he'd fallen in love. The girl had spunk. Other than signing the contract, she had nothing to worry about. Their working together was already a done deal as far as he was concerned, but the idea of having her in the same room with him awhile longer strongly appealed to him. "Does anyone object to

Sasha staying?" he addressed the table. Several staff members shook their heads, but Terraine noticed that Natalia sat in her chair tight-lipped.

"Very good. Sasha, have a seat." He pointed to the chair opposite him at the other end of the table, and Terraine watched her move with the grace of a swan. When she sat in the chair and turned her eyes upon him, suddenly no one else in the room existed except for the two of them and the desire coiling between them. Terraine had to force his eyes away in order to resist sending everyone out of the conference room so that he could gather her in his arms and kiss her lips until they were red and bruised.

Clearing his throat, Terraine returned to the matter at hand. "Carl's team will begin putting together marketing plans for this coming fall." He looked over to his left at Carl, who nodded in compliance. "In the meantime, Natalia, you can delegate all the preparations for the addition to the program. Sasha has agreed to the four gowns you just saw in two different colors. Adding eight gowns shouldn't be too complicated to choreograph into the program, especially since we already have more than enough models." Terraine focused on Natalia, who was glaring at him with balls of fire. He allowed a slow smile to curl his lips, then turned and nodded his head at her assistant.

Evan handed out sketches of the gowns around the table while making sure to avoid eye contact with Natalia. Instead he looked over at Sasha and winked. "As you can see, the talented Sasha Moore is more than just a model, she is a designer." Several people agreed as Sasha sat nervously in her seat blushing at their compliments.

"I have to agree her designs are gorgeous but they are going to require a great deal of time," Carl interjected. "It's going to require more than purchasing her patterns to duplicate the quality of these gowns."

"I disagree," Sasha interrupted in her own defense. "Yes, they will lack the personal craftsmanship of my originals, but these designs can be duplicated. The fabric would first have to be woven with the silk threads, and then the patterns could be cut. The beads would be added last."

Debates were heard around the table. Terraine nodded occasionally to give the impression he was following the discussion, but he found himself having trouble concentrating on anything other than his new discovery of love and Sasha's almond-shaped hazel eyes. Terraine chuckled inwardly as he listened to Sasha tangle toe-to-toe with Natalia, who contradicted every idea Sasha presented to the table. Terraine was not surprised. Sasha constantly fought her feelings for him but there was nothing nervous about her when she was fighting for something she strongly believed in.

Eventually it was obvious to everyone who was listening that Natalia felt as if her toes had been stepped on.

Terraine cleared his throat and turned his attention to Tommy Dean, his finance manager. "Tom, I'd like you to begin preparing an expense report. I have put together cost estimates for producing these gowns for the projected year. I would like you to take that information and prepare a financial forecast. I'd like it on my desk one week from today." He handed him a printout.

"Yes, sir. I'll get right on it, sir." He beamed with pride. He was a short and overweight young man with mocha skin, straight out of college and eager to please. Terraine had seen enough potential in him to give him a chance, and Tom was anxious for any opportunity to show him how grateful he really was. Terraine then rose and addressed the entire table. "I'm flying to our factory in Dallas in a week. I believe that will be the ideal location to produce the designs. If there is nothing else, I would like to conclude this meeting."

Terraine met Sasha at the door after everyone else exited the conference room. "You look beautiful."

She blushed. "Thank you. Thank you for everything."

"No problem, I'm glad that I can help you. If you change your mind, I'd be more than happy to market all of your gowns."

Sasha shook her head. "Not on your life. My dream is to create unique hand-sewn gowns that complement each bride as an individual. I can't accomplish that manufacturing 2,000 copies of the same designs." Sasha quickly raised her hand. "Not that I am complaining. You'll be giving me the exposure I need to go at it all by myself."

Terraine beamed down at her with loving eyes. "You are an amazing woman, Sasha Moore. My lawyer will have the papers drawn up in a couple of days."

"Wonderful. I'll have my lawyer review them and get back with you."

"You won't be disappointed," he said with double meaning. Sasha tried to ignore his comment but his eyes revealed his true meaning.

"I'd better go. I'm having a fitting this afternoon." Sasha ignored her traitorous body as desire swam through her. She needed to get away from him— fast.

"Another cousin?"

Sasha smiled. "Ms. Neil. This will be her third wedding gown in five years. She changes men like she changes her oil." *Some of us do not know how*

281

to commit to a relationship.

Terraine chuckled. "That definitely guarantees business for you."

When Sasha hurried off down the hall, Terraine's eyes followed. He felt confident that eventually he would break through her defenses and find that heart of hers, and when he did, he would never let her walk away from him again.

Sasha returned to the dressing room and thanked the girls for all of their help.

"We were happy to help you; your gowns are beautiful," Tyler said with sincerity as she changed into her street clothes.

"Now it's time for the fat lady to sing," India added.

"I hope so," Sasha said softy.

Asia walked over, embraced her in a hug and whispered, "Watch your back. I think Natalia is out for blood."

Her contact lens shifted painfully to the top of her eye and Sasha rushed to the restroom to fix it. She had gently removed it and was rinsing it off in the sink when she suddenly realized that Natalia was standing against the wall behind her. The shock almost caused her to lose her contact down the drain.

"Your gowns are very nice," Natalia commented in a dry tone.

Even in the mirror, Sasha saw the frost in her smile and was not sure how to handle her compliment. "Um...thank you." Sasha popped her contact back into place.

Natalia took that moment to walk over to the end of the vanity and lean against it. "We will have to work extra hard to have them ready for the show." Sasha faced her and nodded. "Terraine explained that it was going to be tough, but I'll be more than happy to pitch in. I even know a great seamstress who would be happy to help. I use her whenever I'm running close to a deadline."

Natalia flinched at the way Terraine's name rolled off Sasha's tongue. She turned towards the mirror and smoothed down her hair with her fingers. "I am curious how you managed to convince him to invest in your designs. Did you discuss it possibly over breakfast in bed?" she sneered.

Sasha noted her tone and was not at all surprised by her comment. "Our relationship is none of your business."

Natalia took a step towards her, "Of course it is. Everything about him is my business. For a while I thought something was going on between the two of you until Terraine assured me that there wasn't anything to worry about. You are no more than a fling." She waved a hand in the air and continued speaking in a bittersweet voice. "Do you really think you are the first model he has found an interest in?" She laughed loudly. "Why do you think he left the corporation ten years ago? He was bedding models every year, looking for that special lady and breaking her heart at the end of her contract. You think you're any different? As soon as Terraine is done playing around, he and I will marry, so enjoy it while it lasts." She swayed over to where Sasha was standing and stopped only inches away from her and tossed her hair away from her eyes. "You see, Terraine has an appetite that only I can satisfy. He promised himself to me years ago and nothing will ever change that."

Sasha didn't know what to say as she struggled with the uncertainty that Natalia had aroused. Could it be true? She took a deep breath and managed to maintain her fragile control as she spoke. "I would prefer not to have this conversation. I really don't care what your relationship is with Terraine because my relationship with him is strictly business."

Natalia's lips curled into a cunning smile. "Of course it is." She then pivoted on her heels and exited in search of Terraine.

Sasha washed her hands, letting the water run while her fabulous day deflated like a hot air balloon.

"How could you possibly agree to take on a new designer without consulting with me first?" Natalia argued from across Terraine's desk.

Terraine leaned back in his chair and placed one hand behind his head. "I guess it comes with being the boss," he smirked.

"You have forgotten that I am the fashion director, not you. Pops guaranteed that I would always hold my position." She reared back on her heels in challenge and placed both hands on her hips.

"According to his will, you have a job as long as you are doing your job. If for any reason I feel that you are no longer capable of handling the responsibility, then I may release you of your duties with three years' severance pay," he announced in a coolly impersonal tone. "Personally, Nat, if I were you, I would take the money and run."

Surprise siphoned the blood from her face. "Are you saying that I'm incompetent?"

"No, I am saying that if you had a eye for quality you would have taken my proposal and run with it. I would be a fool not to grab Sasha's gowns before someone else does."

Natalia could not believe that she'd lost control of the conversation. "Terraine, you couldn't possibly be serious. Wedding gowns! I thought your decision to market lingerie was a bit much, but this idea of yours is ridiculous."

"But your swimsuit line was better," Terraine added with heavy sarcasm. Last month Natalia had approached him with an idea to add a swimsuit line that Terraine had rejected. His feelings were that swimsuits were a seasonal item. "Weddings are year around. Especially now. Most people our age have already been married twice."

"Why now?" she asked in a desperate sounding voice. "We just redesigned our gowns. They are gorgeous and I think they are going to be a big success, so we don't need any additional gowns at this time."

"Let me be the judge of that," he answered in a tense voice that forbade any further questions.

Natalia glared at him as bitter jealousy stirred within her. Why was he suddenly interested in spending more money? The slut! What had she done to get into his good graces? Obviously more than batting her eyes. The thought angered her even more as her imagination ran wild. How dare he sleep under her nose with a model! And the knowledge of it twisted inside of her.

She looked hurt. "You couldn't possibly be interested in her. She's not your type," she whimpered.

Terraine chuckled as his eyes swept over her.

"And what is my type?"

Natalia's eyes sparkled. "Me. No one is better for you than me, Terraine. Why can't you see that?" She looked down at her nails and tapped them lightly on the desk, then looked up slowly with a dull smile. "We are a team. We work well together, and like you, I only want what is best for this corporation."

Terraine stared at her with his rising anger in check. "Natalia, our relationship is strictly professional and that will never change."

Natalia laughed viciously. "Fine. Have your fun with the slut! We'll see how long it takes for you to come running with your tail between your legs."

His eyes flashed a familiar display of impatience. "My relationship with Sasha is none of your business, but no matter what happens, I'll never invite you to my bed. You made sure of that years ago."

Natalia looked as if she had just been struck in the face. "We'll see."

Terraine rose from his seat and leaned across the desk so that she would not miss the mounting fury in his eyes. "As for this corporation, I am the boss, I make the decisions. If you can't follow the rules then quit."

She glared at him with eyes burning with rage. "You are trying to ruin this corporation and I will not sit back and let that happen!" With that she stormed out of his office.

Sasha placed all four gowns in a large garment bag and carried them towards the elevator, pushing the button for the ground floor.

"Here, let me carry those for you." Sasha turned to face Steven's lopsided grin.

"Oh, no, I can carry them myself."

"I insist." Showing no sign of relenting, he took the bag off her shoulder and stepped onto the elevator, leaving Sasha with no other choice but to join him.

It was a long elevator ride down three floors. She was anxious to escape his presence. Steven stood too close for comfort.

"You looked beautiful out there today." His eyes traveled over her face with insolence.

"Thank you." Her voice lowered to a hushed whisper. Biting her lip, she looked away as apprehensions crawled up her spine. He was so close that she could see the color of his eyes, gray with black pupils, and there was something about them that did not sit right with her. Sasha became more uncomfortable by the minute and she practically jumped off the elevator when the doors opened on the garage level. Steven quickly fell into step alongside her and attempted to conduct small talk with her about the quality of her gowns. Sasha answered with short sentences, having no intention of spending any more time with him than needed. She suddenly wished that she had not declined Terraine's desire to provide her with around-the-clock protection even while she was at the studio. She was feeling increasingly uncomfortable around Steven and was anxious to escape his watchful eye. Sasha clicked her tongue. Perhaps it was simply her uneasiness; she felt some relief knowing that twenty-four hour security cameras monitored the parking lot.

Sasha hurried to open her trunk and Steven placed the bag carefully in the trunk and shut it. She then tried to rush around to her door but Steven stood in her way.

"I have been admiring you for some time and I would be honored if you'd agree to have dinner with me." Sasha gave him an annoyed look. He wore a leering smile and his eyes glittered with dangerous intent.

She shook her head instantaneously. "I-I can't. I have a dress fitting tonight. Some other time."

His smile widened. "I'll hold you to your promise." Sasha edged around him and climbed into her car, quickly driving away.

"Mrs. Baker, I found your daughter."

Cries of joy could be heard coming from the other end. "Thank God!" she gasped. "Is s-she—"

"Kim is alive," Jay answered.

She sighed with relief before a second voice rumbled over the line that Jay immediately identified as Mr. Baker. "Where the hell is she?"

Jay swung around in his office chair and looked out at the cloudy dark sky. "She is staying at a Motel 6 in Belleville."

"Is she alone?" her mother asked softly.

Jay reached in his middle drawer searching for a cigarette. "No. She is with Tim." He was referring to her boyfriend, whom her parents were certain that she'd run off with. He was twenty years her senior. Kim was only sixteen.

"The sick son-of-a—"

"Raymond! Remember your blood pressure!" Mrs. Baker interjected.

"I'll have him arrested for statutory rape!" he barked through the receiver.

Jay lowered the phone from his ear. In the two weeks that he'd spent on this case, Jay had gotten used to listening to the two of them arguing to no avail. He was glad to know that his job was done and he'd found Kim in one piece. The last missing person's case he worked had ended in death. He'd have his secretary remind him not to accept any more of these types of cases.

Jay found a pack of cigarettes under a stack of paper. Now that he was done with this case maybe he would get around to cleaning his office. *He doubted it.* He had several other cases to work on. Jay lit his cigarette and interrupted their heated debate, giving them the address of the motel. "You will find them in room 12B. I'll send you my bill."

"Thank you for everything, Jay. I don't know what we would have done without you," Ms. Baker affirmed, gratitude flooding her voice.

"Just doing my job." Jay hung up and rose from his chair. He walked over to the window, carrying his cigarette. The weather forecast was correct for once. Droplets of rain were beginning to fall.

Jay frowned as he suddenly remembered that he had a date tomorrow night with Candace. She was a beautiful lady that he had met on a rainy day like today. She was walking down the street when a car came whizzing by, splashing muddy water all over her pink suit. Jay had immediately run to her aid and after they each introduced themselves, they had made plans to have dinner the next night. Candace was a criminal defense attorney, whose schedule was even busier than his was, but yet and still, they had managed over the next several weeks to find time to spend together. Jay was up front from the beginning about his lack of interest in committed relationships and Candace had agreed that her career was her main priority. Recently, however, Jay was beginning to wonder if she really meant it. Lately she had begun to appear possessive, calling him several times throughout the day and had even seemed to have a tantrum if he called and told her he was too busy to drop by at the end of his day. Now, if his memory served him right, he had agreed to go to her house for dinner tomorrow night. Jay was no longer sure that that was a good idea. Maybe it was time for him to break off the relationship.

Jay puffed on his cigarette and flung the ashes into a nearby trashcan. He knew he would never marry. It wasn't that he had anything against marriage. As far as he knew, his parents had had a wonderful marriage. Instead, the problem was the simple fact that Jay loved women. All women. One woman could only hold his attention for so long and then he suddenly found himself attracted to another beautiful face.

Jay stuck his hand deep into his pocket and his lips thinned. His job left little time for a personal life and he preferred it to stay that way.

Straight out of high school, Jay had joined the army and served a five-year tour of duty with the military police. While stationed at Fort Leonard Wood, he had attended night classes at Columbia College and managed to graduate with a criminal justice degree. At the end of his military career, the St. Louis Police Department had recruited him, and he'd quickly moved up the ranks to detective. But eventually the police department began to feel too much like the military with its identically structured chain of command and protocols that he preferred not to follow. Jay decided it was time to move on. Using a small portion of his inheritance from his parents, he had started his own investigation and security firm. He had never once regretted his decision not to step into the fashion world alongside his grandfather or brother. Solving cases was what he did best.

His office door swung open and Jay whirled around to face Natalia, who looked distraught.

"Jay, I need your help," she said with desperation. Natalia came around and took a seat in an old chair to his left after dusting it off.

Jay raised his brow. "My secretary let you in?"

She waved her hand dismissively. "She must have been on a potty break."

"What is it now?" He put his cigarette out in an ashtray on the end of his desk.

"Why is it you always think the worst of me?" she pouted.

293

"Because you bring that out in me." Jay leaned forward and smirked. "What can I do for you, Sis?" Her face brightened. "You always were my favorite. Why couldn't I have fallen in love with you instead of your brother?"

"Probably because I don't make your head spin like he does." He watched her push her hair off her shoulder and remembered that when they were kids he used to enjoy pulling her long pigtails.

She batted her lashes and placed a small hand on top of his. "Do you know anything about him being involved with one of my models?"

"You mean his models and you need to ask him yourself."

Natalia removed her hand and flung it in despair. "I tried and it didn't work. What can I do to get Terraine to forgive me?" she asked in a small voice.

Jay shook his head. She still did not have a clue. Jay allowed his eyes to travel to the face of the beautiful woman that he'd considered his sister for years and shook his head again. No one was prouder of her success when she had been discovered by a talent scout than he was. Jay had happily traveled hundreds of miles just to see her strut across a runway. Natalia was talented enough to know exactly how to use her body and charm to get what she wanted, but when she tried to use it to trick Terraine, she had made a terrible mistake. One that Jay was not able to help her wiggle herself out of.

"He forgave you years ago. It's the forgetting that he will always have a problems with."

"He has to. Doesn't he understand that our entire future is at stake here?" An intense feeling of sickness washed over her at the thought of losing him for good and she placed her hand to her forehead.

Jay watched her dramatic performance and responded in a voice that was playful but exact. "Why? Because of the murders or because he won't give you the time of day?"

Natalia jumped out of the chair and glared at him with a furious expression that sent him into a fit of laughter. Jay was still laughing long after she left.

Slowly, Sasha lowered her body into the Calgon bath and released a deep sigh. A hot bath was just what she needed to help sort her thoughts. She closed her eyes, allowing every muscle in her body to relax, then drew in another breath as memories flooded her again.

She could not explain what was happening when she was with Terraine. She felt helpless but happy, nervous yet invigorated. She felt like running and hiding one minute and running straight into his strong arms the next. As much as she tried to deny the fact, Terraine was everything she'd always wanted in a man and then some. Passion. That was what had been missing in her life before she met Terraine. She loved the way he made her feel like Jell-O when he touched her. His kisses were warm and welcomed and sent ripples of desire through her entire body, and his dark eyes had a way of zeroing in on her that made her feel as if she were the only person in the world that really mattered to him.

With a large splash, Sasha sank deeper into the water. She liked him. More than she cared to admit. She could not deny that something was happening between them. Something unlike anything she'd ever experienced before in her life. Could she possibly be falling in love with him? Sasha shook her head and raised her hand, wiping beads of sweat from her brow. Not being able to control her growing attraction to him scared her to death. Maybe she needed to just jump right into bed with him and see what happened. Maybe then she would be able to get him out of her system. Then again, maybe she never would. In fact, she felt in her heart that if she allowed herself to give in to her feelings, she was going to lose her heart to him.

As she lowered her eyelids, erotic thoughts entered her mind. The thought of him making love to her aroused her. She bent her left leg and splashed warm water onto her hardened nipples and allowed her fingers to travel sensuously across her stomach. She wanted him desperately. She couldn't help wondering what would have happened if he had been honest with her in the first place. Would they have made love by now? Was she even ready for that level of intimacy? To think that the other day they had come so close. If Natalia had not interrupted, there was no telling what might have transpired. Sasha shook off the thought and opened her eyes. She couldn't think straight when he was around. Terraine made her blood boil and her heart pound as if it would burst out from her chest. *Heaven help her!* She wanted him desperately. His touch made her flesh flame. He made her want to trust in things that she'd stopped trusting in months ago.

Sasha sighed. She could not allow herself to fall in love with Terraine. His desires were merely physical needs and if she was foolish enough to read any more into it than that, she'd only cry with tears of remorse later.

Beaming from ear to ear after signing a lucrative contact with Diva Designs, Sasha was now official- ly a designer, whose gowns would be seen by the entire world! Sasha stood up and shook hands with her lawyer and thanked him for all of his help. Then she strolled over and stood in front of Terraine, smil- ing up at him.

"Thanks for believing in me." She was so happy she did not know where to begin.

Satisfaction pursed his lips as he looked down at her. She looked beautiful in a lemon tailored suit with a cream blouse and matching pumps. "I should be thanking you."

"Why?" she asked with wide-eyed innocence as she watched his smile. Memories of their kiss and the feel of his soft lips upon hers flooded her mind.

His eyes, which were clear and observant, shone bright with joy. Being in love was a wonder- ful feeling. "You are helping me save my family legacy. I believe that both of these new fashion lines are going to make the difference around here." Under the intensity of his narrow eyes, Sasha felt herself blush. "I sure hope so," she whispered. "I better be going. Thanks again."

Standing only inches away, Terraine's nostrils quivered as he caught her aroma and breathed it in like a bouquet of flowers. "How about if we go out and celebrate?"

Sasha shook her head. "I don't think that's a good idea. I need to get home and feed Nikki before she starts chewing the furniture."

"Who is Nikki?" Terraine asked with a frown.

With a sour twist of her lips, she answered, "My new watchdog. Compliments of Roxaner Moore."

"Good idea." A smile returned to his handsome face.

Sasha bit her lower lip. How she loved his dimples. "Well, I'll see you later." Without anything further, she turned and headed for the door.

"When?"

Stopping, Sasha turned around. "When what?"

Terraine's brow was arched high with amusement. "When will I see you?"

Instantly, Sasha shook her head. "I don't think that's a good idea."

"I think it's a great idea. How about this Friday?" When her answer was not immediate, he waited, challenging her with his eyes to go through with it.

"Terraine, please understand that I want to be friends." Sasha spoke with desperate firmness.

"We have gone through too much to go back to being friends." His comment held a note of exasperation. "Why are you afraid of me?" He stepped closer.

Sasha swallowed. "Because I want you too much."

Terraine took a deep breath. Even though she was still running away from him, her words were music to his ears and he was thrilled that she was finally being honest. But as much as it hurt, he was not going to push her. He'd have to be patient and pray that she'd come to him when she was ready. He just hoped it did not take her too long. A man could only take so much.

"I'd like a chance to prove to you that I can make things right between us but I am a proud man so I won't beg. See you soon." He looked at her intently, then strode past her and out of his office. He was at the end of the hall before Sasha caught up with him.

"Terraine!"

"Yes?" he asked, whipping his head back around to face her.

Who was she fooling? Sasha had to know. She needed to know for sure if all the tension between them was the real thing or not. "Friday would be great."

Terraine walked Sasha to her car and returned to his office with a confident smile. He was finally getting somewhere. His private line rang and he walked over to his desk, grabbing it before the third ring.

"Terraine speaking."

"Terraine, Sly here."

The corner of his lips curled with irritation. "Hello, Sly."

"I've been reading the papers. Looks like you are dealing with a lot of bad publicity right now."

"We've got things under control. The police and Jay are handling everything." His response held a note of impatience.

"Oh, yes. I forgot Jay was a private investigator. Well, it is a good thing you have him on your side."

Terraine was irritated by his mocking tone. "Sly, quit the small talk. We both know why you called and my answer is still no."

"Terraine, you are making a big mistake. You are jeopardizing losing everything!" he warned.

Terraine thought about the deal he'd signed today that would market Sasha's creations in the coming year. "I'll take my chances."

There was a moment of silence before Sly responded in a voice that did not reveal a trace of sympathy. "It's a shame what happened to those lovely women. For your sake, I hope no one else comes up dead."

"We can only hope." Terraine hung up the phone.

Chapter Twelve

"It's only dinner."

Honey shook her head at Sasha's comment. "No, I have a feeling this is going to be your big night." She stood back to admire her master-piece. She had rollerset Sasha's hair and after it had dried she teased her curls so they hung naturally around her face.

Sasha was sitting in front of her vanity mirror. "How do I look?" She tilted her head and all of her honey brown hair tumbled onto one delicate shoulder, exposing her long slender neck.

"Seduction is good." Honey smiled wickedly.

"You are bad," Sasha chuckled as she reached down and found a pair of diamond stud earrings and placed them in her earlobes. "What are you doing home on a Friday night anyway? What happened to Tony, or was it Thomas?"

Honey waved dismissively and walked over to the bed. "I dumped him last week. The brother was a waste of time in bed."

"You are nasty!" Sasha screamed with laughter.

"No, just naughty," Honey corrected before quickly changing the subject. "What about this dress?" She reached over and picked up a black dress, one of several that she'd retrieved from her own closet.

Sasha turned in her seat, took one look at the dress and frowned disapprovingly. There wasn't enough material to cover a newborn baby. She shook her head. "I am not wearing that thing."

Honey held the dress out to her. "Here, try it on," she commanded.

Sasha hesitated a moment longer before dropping her bathrobe and wiggling into it.

"Ooh, baby!" Honey sang.

Sasha walked over to her closet door and looked at herself in the full-length mirror. "No way am I wearing this dress!" It captured every curve of her slim figure with cleavage spilling over the edge of the low, scoop neck. She tugged on the dress that stopped way above her knees, trying to see if it would possibly stretch. "Terraine is going to think I am trying to tell him something."

"You are trying to tell him something. That you need some *desperately*."

Sasha raised her hand. "Forget it! I'm changing."

Honey ran around the bed and shut the closet door before Sasha had a chance to find another outfit. "Oh, no, you're not, you look great!" She reached onto the bed and picked up a scarf. "Here, tie this around your neck. It'll cover some of that." Honey clapped her hands and giggled. "Terraine is going to have a heart attack when he sees you!"

Sasha was still standing in front of the mirror indecisively when the doorbell rang.

"Too late to change your mind. You look beautiful." Honey squeezed her shoulder. "Have a wonderful evening. Knock him dead. Just make sure you are back in a week. I do have a new house to move into." Honey giggled again and raced out of the room to answer the door before Sasha could comment.

Of course she would be back before Sunday. If anything, she planned on being back tonight before the clock struck twelve. Sasha rushed to strap on a pair of black open toed shoes and looked herself over one more time before heading to the living room.

Terraine rose from the couch as she

approached him with a nervous smile.

"You look beautiful."

"You don't look bad yourself." *Dang, he was fine.* Terraine was wearing dark brown slacks, a cream-colored rayon top that he left unbuttoned at the top, exposing a patch of wavy hair, and a gold herringbone chain. He gave her the once-over and smiled with an appreciation that erased all uncertainties she had about the dress. His eyes told her that she had made a wise choice. Nervously, Sasha moistened her lips.

"Shall we go? Your chariot awaits."

Sasha took the arm he offered and they strolled out the door. A gleaming white stretch limousine with a black chauffeur waited out front. Her brow rose. "Where's Cherry?"

"I gave her the night off." He placed a hand at the small of her back and escorted her into the limo. Sasha sank into the leather seat and Terraine sat next to her.

"You comfortable?"

He was sitting quite close and the smell of his aftershave surrounded her. *How wonderful he smelled.* Sasha grinned and nodded, feeling like a kid with her hand in the cookie jar. "Very much."

He reached over and stroked her hand. "Good. Then relax and enjoy the evening."

And relax she did. Terraine turned on a little

R&B and they listened and talked softly to each other during the ride downtown. The evening promised tranquility, easing any remaining tension from her body. A half-hour later, the limo stopped and the driver opened the door.

"Ooh! How did you guess?" Sasha exclaimed as she stepped out onto the sidewalk.

Terraine climbed out after her and his eyes twinkled as he looked over at her. "I made it my business to know." They stood in front of Union Station, an historical train depot that had been converted into a shopping mall and hotel. Terraine laced his fingers with hers and led her up the walkway to Landry's Seafood Restaurant. The hostess seated them at a table on the terrace from which they could look out onto a pond filled with large goldfish. A full moon reflected off the water. Sasha took a deep breath. There was crispness in the air and she felt more alive than she had in months.

It was a romantic setting with dinner lighting and candles glimmering underneath globes at the center of each table. Sasha looked off to her far left to where an old train stood. On the other side of the pond a large antique carousel was in operation, its music nostalgic.

Sasha was in a trance. She felt a tingly and peaceful feeling. Tonight was going to be different. She felt it.

Terraine leaned across the table. "You are deep in thought."

Sasha turned to him with her hazel eyes a-blazing. "Guess I'm caught up in the moment. Everything is so right."

"Good. Tonight I want to show you just how special you are to me." The waiter returned with their wine. Tearing her eyes away, she looked down at her menu and immediately knew what she was having—king crab legs with steamed vegetables and a baked potato. Terraine decided on steak and lobster tails.

During dinner the conversation was light but the attraction was strong. Sasha found Terraine staring intensely at her throughout the meal and her body reacted to each and every flirtatious gesture and comment that he made.

The food was delicious, the atmosphere was perfect and his view was breathtaking. Tonight was the beginning of something new for them. Terraine could feel it. Sasha's entire attitude was different, more relaxed and radiant. The defensiveness was gone and the fear had faded from her eyes as well as her tongue. She seemed to take on a completely different character. Did that mean she was finally going to give them a chance?

After dinner, Terraine instructed the chauffeur to take them to Laclede's Landing. They climbed out of the limo and Terraine took Sasha's hand for a stroll up and down the historical cobblestone road, past numerous shops, restaurants and a wax museum. At every opportunity, he pulled her close to him, nuzzling and teasing her neck and cheeks. Sasha found herself wanting his hugs and looking forward to his kisses.

Terraine brought her hand to his lips. "Now your real chariot awaits." He then pointed ahead.

Sucking in a deep breath, she exclaimed joyously, "Oh! A carriage ride." Her eyes were large as he helped her onto an old buggy operated by a blonde woman driving a beautiful white horse.

Within seconds, Sasha relaxed against the deep cushions of the coach. *How romantic,* she thought. They rode around the riverfront with their fingers laced together and stared at the Arch up close as its reflection shimmered on the water. The temperature was cooler near the river and Sasha snuggled comfortably beneath his arm. Terraine leaned forward to kiss her forehead and she looked up as a warm sensation flowed through her breasts. Their eyes met and for several seconds they were encased in a bubble of intensified awareness that shut out everything and everyone but the two of them.

"Come home with me, Sasha," he asked in a low voice. He looked into her eyes that were luminous, highlighted by the flickering of red and green lights coming from the casino boat docked out on the river.

Seeing the tenderness in his eyes, Sasha realized that there was nothing more that she wanted than to spend the rest of the evening in his company. "Okay."

The limo pulled up in front of an enchanting house set back far from the street and surrounded by mature trees and a lush, green lawn. The minute Sasha walked up the front steps and onto the charming wraparound front porch, she knew she was about to enter something special.

The exterior of the house offered a blend of classic architectural details and turn-of-the-century craftsmanship. A stained window on the landing highlighted a huge marble foyer that led off into several different rooms and Terraine guided her through them all. The great room was distinguished by hardwood flooring covered with oriental throw rugs and a fireplace with a hand-carved mantel complete with half moon mirrors.

The kitchen had been updated with modern conveniences such as ceramic flooring, ceiling fans, a large breakfast bar, abundant counter space, a second bar sink and all new state-of-the-art appliances. The center island kitchen even boasted a greenhouse window. *What Roxaner would do for this kitchen!*

Beyond it was the family room, which had four bay windows, a wood-burning stove, track lighting, custom bookshelves, and deep rich burnt-orange carpet. To the left of the family room was a breakfast room with patio doors, which led out into a breathtaking garden and a gazebo. There was also a second living room, a library, several offices, a recreation room and a custom-wood staircase that led upstairs to six bedrooms and three baths.

Sasha was bewitched by it all. "Do you really live here?" she asked as she looked up at the skylight at the top of the staircase.

Terraine watched her expression, pleased to see that she was enchanted and not at all spooked by the size of the manor. "Yes, for most of my life." He loved this house and had always hoped to find a special someone who would love it as well.

"I can't believe that you could possibly live in a house this size all by yourself!" Her home looked like an outhouse in comparison. "It's beautiful."

Terraine came up behind her and locked his arms around her waist. "I am hoping to fill it with my offspring."

Sasha blushed and tried to picture children living comfortably within the walls of a house large enough to hold a whole lot of love.

He turned her around so that she was facing

him. "Would you like to listen to some music?" Sasha nodded, suddenly feeling a little uneasy by the close contact. She followed him into the family room.

While Terraine scanned the CD rack, she walked over to a cherrywood curio that held pictures of Terraine, Jay and an older man who had to be his grandfather. The resemblance was remarkable.

"I hope you don't mind my choice." Terraine gave her a sheepish grin and as soon as the music started, she knew why.

Her lips curled into a nervous smile. "Eric Benet."

He looked over at her with deep longing. "For some reason, I can't get enough of listening to it."

"It's a very nice song," She said in a small, far-off voice. "Spend My Life with You" was their song. He knew it and so did she. Sasha rubbed her hands up and down her arms, suddenly feeling uneasy, and stood in front of the curio uncertain as what to do next. Terraine took matters into his own hands. With his eyes never leaving her, he eliminated the distance between them in two swift steps. He reached out and took her hands, lacing her fingers with his, drawing her near. With his heart banging against his chest, he wrestled for control over his body and over everything Sasha made him feel. Then he released her hands and slowly raised them to frame her lovely face. The texture of her skin beneath his fingertips brought a flash of heat to his body, causing him to tremble with anticipation. He leaned forward and took possession of her inviting mouth, teasing it with nibbling bites. Then Terraine felt his control slipping. He wanted Sasha with a force that stunned him. He wanted her bad, but Terraine wanted her to want him also. Raising his mouth but still cupping her face, he stared down at her.

"You are so beautiful," he whispered, his breath warm against her nose. She sighed as he planted several soft wet kisses down her throat. "Sweetheart, do you feel what's happening between us?" His voice was a deep caress that sent goosebumps down her spine.

Sasha looked up at him and nodded. "Yes. I feel it too."

Under Terraine's look, Sasha's heart lurched. Blood pounded in her brain and her knees trembled. She knew at that moment no other man would ever be able to make her feel this good again. No other kiss would ever feel this good if Terraine were not responsible. She looked at the man who affected her so deeply, wondering where it would all lead.

"I never realized what I was missing from my life until you came into it," Terraine whispered. "I have not been able to think of anything or anyone else but you, all day and all night." Sasha witnessed the desire in his eyes and happiness flowed through her. He leaned down and touched her lips with his again, tasting her with his tongue. A wave of longing swept through him and he moved away again and looked down at her with loving eyes. "Sasha, if you're going to say no, please say it now because once I start, I don't think I will be able to stop." Deep down he was pleading. He was not sure how much more he could take.

She looked up into a pair of beautiful raisin-brown eyes and somewhere in her heart she knew it was time. "I want you too."

She allowed all of her misgivings to melt into raw aching need. Yearning for another kiss, she touched her lips to his, then leaned slightly away from him with a smile, unable to remember when she'd wanted anything as much as she wanted him right now. Though an alarm was ringing in her head, she no longer cared. The more she tried to resist her feelings, the stronger the magnetic pull. She was powerless and did not want to fight anymore. His nearness made her senses spin and caused her to want a man in a way that she had never wanted before.

Sasha leaned into him as he captured her mouth again and their tongues danced together.

She wrapped her hands around his neck and Terraine scooped her into his arms and carried her over to the couch, settling her into his lap. While he kissed her cheeks and teased her neck with his tongue, his fingers began a lust-arousing exploration of her body. He stroked her soft bottom and slender thighs, gently taking her on a roller coaster of pleasure. She wanted so badly for those same hands to explore private areas of her body. When he spoke, his voice echoed her own longing.

"I want to touch you." He wanted to feel the softness of her silky flesh again, to taste her sweetness. Sasha showed no resistance as he unzipped her dress and slid it off her shoulders. Eagerly, Terraine released the front hook on her bra, freeing her breasts. Sasha shivered when his fingers touched her sensitive breasts, caressing them gently before teasing her nipples with his thumb. Sensations rippled through her as they swelled in his hand. Lowering his face, his tongue followed the same path and circled the hardened tips. "Mmm. Delicious," he moaned.

She gasped but did not move for fear he would stop. Instead, she lost herself in the heavenly sensation of his mouth as he suckled her breast, making her body throb with a bittersweet ache. Arching her back, she laced her fingers at the back of his head, pulling him even closer. She could not think of anything other than what he was doing to her body. A desire she never thought she'd feel consumed her. Never before had she so ached for a man. She could no longer deny herself.

Leaving her breast for a moment, he came back to her mouth, kissing her as if she were a delicious meal and he was a starving man. Terraine groaned and cursed. "You make me crazy with wanting you," he said, cupping her other breast in his palm, causing her breathing to quicken. "Do you feel what you are doing to me?" Terraine cried out like a wounded animal. "I have never been so hard before." Terraine did not think he had ever wanted anyone the way he wanted her right now.

He rose and carried her to the other end of the room, gently laying her down on a large silk rug in front of the fireplace. Sasha looked up at him with desire burning feverously in her eyes. He stood over her and she watched as he unbuttoned his shirt and removed it, exposing a dark chocolate, sinewy chest with a fraternity brand across his heart and thick black hair tapering down to his tight, taut belly. The muscles of his well-defined chest and powerful arms left her breathless. Then he lowered his pants and a pair of silk boxers and stood defiantly aroused in front of her. Sasha sucked in her breath at the sight of him. He was beautiful. Rising to her knees, she reached up and caressed a chest that felt like spools of silk. Her hand traveled down to the pelt of hair below his navel and she stroked him with erotic delight.

Terraine shuddered. If she didn't stop things were going to end sooner than he planned. He had not been with a woman in months and wanted this moment to be long and pleasurable for both of them. He captured her wrist and lowered her back onto the rug, raising her arms above her head and straddling her with his knees. Terraine stared into her eyes to make certain that this was what she wanted. Her eyes told him everything he needed to know. He saw the desire that mirrored his. Terraine brushed a gentle kiss across her forehead, then her eyes, and finally her nose.

"We have all night," he whispered. Slowly his hand moved downward, skimming the side of her body, caressing her from her earlobe down to her neck, to her erect nipples and slowly down to her highly sensitive toes.

Sasha thought she was going to lose her mind and moaned as passion pounded the blood through her heart while desire shook her.

Terraine lifted himself and kneeled in front of her to take a closer look. "You are so beautiful." He lowered his head and took a nipple gently between his teeth while teasing the other with his thumb, rubbing it in a circular motion. Sasha squirmed beneath his hand. The scratchy rug rubbed against her back but she did not notice. Involuntarily, she arched as he suckled and stroked. His mouth was a flame on her sensitive skin.

"I need you," he moaned before kissing a path all the way to her belly button. Curling his fingers in the waistband of her panties, he removed them. Raising her hips towards him, Terraine lowered his head and grazed the moistened area between her thighs with his tongue. Sasha gasped at the contact when his tongue probed her tender fold, causing her to cry out with excitement. She angled her pelvis slightly towards him. Eyes fluttering wildly as his tongue flickered seductively, teasing in small, wet circles that caused her to whimper, Sasha arched her back and clenched her fist as the world around her exploded. Yes! Never had anything felt so good! The torture was unbearable. Never had she felt so helpless with a man. His mouth found the tiny nub of intense pleasure nestled in a honey brown nest and he nipped and sucked until her tormented cries filled his ears with sweet music.

Sasha cried out for release. "Oh my God! Terraine, I need to feel you inside of me, now!" she panted as she arched her back. If he did not bury himself deep within her soon, she was going to turn into a madwoman.

"Are you sure you are ready?" he growled.

"Yes, hurry!" She did not want to wait a moment longer. She needed all of him inside her, now. Sasha grabbed his arms, pulling him on top of her, and he positioned himself between her parted thighs.

Terraine lifted her hips to meet him as he entered her in one fluid motion. The heavy surge of sensation almost sent her over the edge. Then he was very still as his eyes found hers.

"Sasha." The look that passed between them said many things. Terraine lowered his head and kissed her fiercely. He'd waited weeks for the opportunity to love her. Then he drew back with a long slow motion and Sasha sucked in her breath as he drove into her again. She wrapped her legs around his back, welcoming his full length deep inside her.

"Yes!" she moaned as her body stretched to accommodate him and she moved her hips beneath him. It had been a long time since she had been with a man. Arching her back, Sasha squeezed his buttocks and forced him even deeper within her. His breath was quick and uneven. He kissed her cheeks and her forehead and then his tongue bathed her nipples. Her hands caressed his buttocks, which were flexing and unflexing with each thrust. His every plunge into her passage took her breath away. Then she found herself meeting his strokes with a fury, trying to match his pace until she thought she'd die with the rapture of it all. Sasha cried out in pleasure, louder this time, as wave after wave of ecstasy hit her.

"Yes, Tee!" she screamed.

Terraine quickened his pace, moving even deeper and faster inside her. Her sudden, fierce tightness coaxed him over the edge, and he found himself crying along with her as he clutched her tightly and they rocked together in a swift rhythm.

Sasha cried out again as she felt him flow into her like warm honey. Shortly afterwards, shuddering and trembling, she screamed his name over and over.

They lay together minutes later. Drenched in perspiration, he held her securely against his chest and Sasha fell asleep instantly. Terraine lay awake and listened to her soft breaths. Kissing the top of her head, he stared down at her as his body slowly began to wind down.

"Now I know what love is," he whispered against her cheek before he too drifted off to sleep.

Hours later his growling stomach awoke him, and he carried Sasha up to his bed. Sighing, he planted small kisses on her forehead. Sasha was fast asleep, her breath even and calm. She looked achingly beautiful with her hair spread across her pillow. His heart flipped as he thought about how much he loved her. How long would he have to wait before he could tell her? He didn't want to scare her off but he knew that was exactly what would happen if he shared his feelings with her before she was ready to hear them. Terraine watched her sleep a few seconds more before he tiptoed to his closet and slipped on his robe. He then crept downstairs in search of Ms. Henry and breakfast.

Shortly after, Sasha woke to sunlight streaming through the windows. She stretched, then suddenly realized that she was lying in an extremely large poster bed that had to be at least three feet off the ground. When had he brought her upstairs? she wondered. Lifting her head, she looked around the tastefully decorated room that had a fireplace embedded in one wall. The floor was covered in thick rich mahogany carpet and custom blinds and drapes were on the windows. Sasha laid her head back on the pillow and stared up at the ceiling.

She had done it. She'd slept with Terraine. But instead of feeling that she had gotten him out of her system, she now felt consumed by him. Last night would not be enough. Her body craved to have him inside her again. Terraine was as addictive as chocolate. Her body was overruling her mind. She craved him and she needed him again. Sasha pulled the covers over her head and groaned. What about Natalia? Was this nothing more than a fling?

"Did you sleep well?"

Peeking out from underneath the covers, Sasha found Terraine standing at the end of his bed holding a tray of food. She returned his smile. "Yes, I did."

He walked around and placed in front of her a tray loaded with coffee, juice, bacon, eggs and toast. Sasha beamed. "You didn't have to go to all that trouble for me."

Grinning, Terraine took a seat next to her on the bed. "I didn't. Ms. Henry did. She was already cooking when I went down, and I'll warn you, she is easily insulted if you don't have breakfast."

"How wonderful! How long has she been with you?" Sasha rested her weight on one arm and the sheet fell away, revealing the fullness of her breasts.

"She's been cooking like this for me since I was a little boy." Terraine's voice was low as his eyes fell to her exposed nipples, and he remembered all the different ways he'd teased them the previous night. "She is like family to me, even though she has a tendency to fuss over me a little too much at times."

"And I'm sure you enjoy every minute of it," Sasha interjected. She followed his eyes to her breast. Seeing the hunger, she blushed and started to draw the sheet up around her shoulders. Terraine halted her actions by grabbing her hand.

"What are you doing?" he asked, clearly tickled by her modesty.

Sasha's lips curled into a shy grin. "Nothing." Terraine moved the tray to the side, then straddled her hips and lowered the sheet again beneath her breasts.

"Why are you hiding them? I've seen them. They're gorgeous. You're gorgeous." He took one in his mouth and she closed her eyes as desire coursed though her again.

"No secrets," he whispered in between kisses. "I want to know every part of your body and I want you to know mine." He lifted his head and his eyes locked with hers. "Deal?"

Looking at him, she remembered everything that had transpired between them last night on the rug in front of his fireplace. She remembered him driving hard and fast inside her, filling her with ecstasy. "Deal."

"Good. Now eat." Terraine rolled off her and placed the tray across her lap. Sasha sat up and leaned against the headboard. As she sipped her coffee, her eyes wandered over to where Terraine was sitting. She noticed that the belt on his robe had loosened and exposed the brand over his chest that she remembered seeing last night.

She took another sip. "What is that on your chest? A fraternity brand?"

Terraine nodded and ran his fingers across his chest as he sat Indian style at the bottom of the bed. "This mark on my chest is something that I hold near and dear to my heart. It is a symbol of how much love I have for my fraternity and my brothers. It signifies that pain is mental and the length that I will go for my brothers. I pledged Sigma and made a commitment to the organization to be a good, upright man and assist mankind, improve myself through scholarship, persevere through triumph and lift others up when able. And thus far, that is the way that I live my life."

Sasha nodded. Then something registered in her mind. "You are a Q-Dawg!" Sasha barked like a dog and giggled hysterically.

Terraine chuckled and frowned. "The dog is the symbol of our loyalty, tenacity and obedience." He shook a finger at her. "You laugh but we are the most diverse organization and one of the most powerful organizations in the world. Power is in numbers; we help kids, people on welfare, the homeless, Boy Scouts, girls' homes, provide assistance and aid to the elderly, provide scholarships, give Christmas in April, and much more. Oh, yeah...we throw the best parties."

Sasha finished chewing on a slice of bacon before speaking, "And to think I thought all of you guys were just a bunch of dogs. I would never have guessed that your fraternity was dedicated to so many causes. I am definitely impressed."

"Not as impressed as I am," Terraine commented with hungry eyes as he crawled to the top of the bed. "You have something on your face." He cupped her chin and brought her face towards his and licked crumbs from around her mouth. "Mmm." Terraine removed the tray from the bed and then grabbed Sasha's thighs, sliding her down onto her back. When he tossed the sheets off her, she was as naked as nature intended her to be. She was perfect and her unclothed body tempted him, causing his muscles to ache. "Now it's my turn to feast." He ran his fingers delicately across her erect nipples and looked down at her with loving eyes.

He was hungry. God help him, he wanted her again.

Chapter Thirteen

Honey allowed her eyes to travel around the home of her dreams while realization washed over her. She had finally done it. Every morning until the day of her closing, she had driven to the two-story brick home. In the quiet, it all seemed so perfect. It was hard to believe that something so wonderful could be happening to her. Having her own home had started out as a childhood fantasy, growing out of a dollhouse that she cherished.

Growing up, Honey had lived hand-to-mouth with two older brothers and a mother who struggled as a housekeeper to provide food for her family after her deadbeat husband walked out on them. She was a good woman who had worked long strenuous hours and still found time every evening to check homework, listen to and snuggle up with her three children on a worn-out living room couch.

Slowly, Honey climbed up the flight of stairs and paused in the hallway that led towards three spacious bedrooms. She'd shared a room with her mother in their tiny two-bedroom apartment until she started junior high. By then her brothers, Rashad and Shaquil, were old enough to work, and finally with their help they had been able to move to a larger apartment.

Her brothers had spoiled her. Rashad was ten when Honey was born and Shaquil six. They made certain that she always had lunch money and nice clothes for school. They provided her with an allowance and drove her to and from any after-school activities. Her brothers personally appointed themselves as her protector. It was because of her brothers' love that she had been able to live a typical teenage life.

Stepping into one of the large size rooms, Honey remembered the comment her real estate agent had made when she first showed her the house three months earlier. "This is a great home in which to raise children." Honey had agreed with her and hoped to fill each of the two extra bedrooms with a little boy or girl. But after the devastating blow she'd received from her gynecologist a couple of weeks ago, having children was one dream that would never come true.

Honey strolled about looking inside closets and touching cold eggshell walls before she traveled across the hall to her bedroom. She was looking forward to decorating and planned on painting all three bedrooms before her new furniture arrived.

Walking over to the window, her pain deepened as she looked out into a large, fenced backyard with playground equipment. It was one of the reasons she'd decided on this particular house and she had insisted that the previous owners leave it behind. *A home intended for a family.* Honey wiped a hot tear from the corner of her eye and clasped her fingers together as she stopped to reflect on a painful moment in her life.

Honey was a victim of date rape during her senior year of high school. She went out with Walter, a football player whom she'd had a crush on since freshman year. And even though Sasha had expressed an instant dislike to his arrogant demeanor, she'd refused to listen.

Honey bit her lip. It was one time she wished she had listened.

Walter took her to see a movie. Afterwards, he suggested that they go for a drive before taking her home and Honey agreed. It was not until he pulled into a dark wooded area that her stomach began to churn with uneasiness. He shut off the car and pulled her into his arms, his lips covering hers hungrily. As the kisses became more urgent and brutal, scorching her lips with their intensity, Walter began fondling her in private areas despite her resistance. Eventually, anger swept across his face and he lashed out at her, calling her a tease. Then he punched her hard in the face with his fist, stunning her with the pain's intensity. "Comply or goodbye." To put emphasis on his phrase, he opened the passenger door, daring her to step out into a pitch-black world that she knew nothing about. Too stunned and scared to fight, Honey allowed him to slide her down onto the seat and shift his body over hers. She didn't even scream when he tore deep inside of her with hard painful thrusts while she lay immobilized. Afterwards, he drove her home as if nothing had happened.

Shaquil was waiting up for her when she returned and as soon as he saw her cracked and swollen lip, he demanded that she tell him what had happened. She swore him to secrecy knowing that if Rashad found out he would kill Walter. And if her mother found out, it would destroy her. The only thing that stopped Shaquil from driving over to Walter's house and beating the crap out of him was the humiliation his little sister would have to endure. Then she missed her period. Shaquil was by her side when she found out that she was pregnant. In deciding to have an abortion, Honey made the hardest decision of her life. Shaquil wanted her to go to a private hospital in Illinois, but Honey refused, saying that it was too expensive, that they needed the money for so many other things. Instead, she found a retired practitioner who had opened her own private clinic. Shaquil went with her and cradled her in his arms when it was over.

Honey sighed and massaged her arms soothingly. According to the gynecologist, she had extensive scar tissue on her uterine wall and would never be able to have children.

Honey felt it was God punishing her for taking a life.

She turned away from the window and walked into the bathroom for a tissue to blow her nose. After her rape, relationships with the opposite sex changed. She went on dates because it was the answer to her loneliness, but Honey found that she could not respond to their kisses and froze up if a man tried to touch her in private areas. Therefore, eliminating any further grief, she ended relationships long before they had a chance at becoming intimate.

For years, Honey had led friends, family and male acquaintances into believing that she was a tease. But now it all had become a game that was no longer fun to play.

Before visiting her doctor, Honey had dreamed of someday feeling whole again and meeting a man who would make her believe in the institution of love. But now that she knew she could not give birth to a child, what did she possibly have to offer? Then she'd met Jay Andrews. And for the first time in years, her mind and body had become aroused by a man.

He was tall with dark wavy hair, and a powerful, well-muscled body. He was gorgeous and looked more than a little untamed as he stood in Sasha's doorway. Everything about him was so masculine it took her breath away. Honey had looked up into Jay's cocoa-colored eyes and seen compassion. Instead of her usual cold shiver, she'd felt a stir of desire.

Honey returned to the hallway and stood motionless against the banister, admiring the view, and suddenly Jay's masculine scent was all around her. Now how the heck did she remember how he smelled anyway? The only time they had been near one another was the moment he brushed past her days before. *But how could I forget?* The scent of his cologne had lingered in the living room for several days.

If things were different, she would go after Jay so fast he would not have time to think, much less run. But one mistake had changed the course of her entire life.

Honey pulled her keys out of her pocket and descended the stairs. Although it was a lot of house for one person, she loved every bit of it. She stopped to take one more look around before she shut the door behind her.

Looking down at the card, Jay flipped it over to the other side. The roses had been purchased at Dierberg's, the same place from which Terraine ordered six-dozen bouquets for Sasha. His gentle laughter echoed against the windows of his car. His brother was pulling out all the stops where Sasha was concerned. After meeting her, Jay could see why. She was a very beautiful and talented lady. *And so was her roommate.*

Jay reached into his breast pocket for his lighter. Honey was gorgeous and so tiny he could stuff her in his pocket and take her home. *Yeah, but she's not interested in you.* Jay had tried on several occasions to establish eye contact with Honey, but she seemed to purposely avoid looking in his direction. A definite blow to his ego. Jay lit his cigarette. It was probably for the best.

Removing his cell phone from his pocket, Jay

punched in a series of numbers.

"Twelfth precinct, Hamilton speaking."

Grinning, Jay leaned back in his seat. "Chad, my man, Jay here."

"Long time no hear. How's it going buddy?" There was a smile in the detective's voice. He hadn't spoken to his ex-partner in months.

"No complaints." Jay puffed on his cigarette. "I need a favor."

"Name it."

"I found out that a dozen white roses were delivered to Monet Phillips on the day of her murder. Last week, another model also received a dozen white roses. Both were delivered by Dierberg's Florist. All I need to do now is find out who sent them."

"No problem. Give me the information and I'll get back with you as soon as I can." Jay gave Chad the dates and locations. "Got it."

"Thanks, man. If my hunch is right another dozen was also purchased on the morning of Deja Davis's death. If so, I think this might be the connection to the murders at Diva Design."

"Robby, what are you talking about?" Sasha asked for the fourth time. She had run home to pack an overnight bag and was on her way back out the door when she heard the phone ring.

"My brother," he answered in a very low voice.

Sasha placed her hand on her hip. "Brother, what brother?" she asked with a hint of impatience. Could he have possibly forgotten that once upon a time she had been an important part of his life and that she knew everything, well, almost everything, about him and his family? "Robby, you are an only child."

He sighed in resignation. "Forget I even mentioned it. I just wanted to warn you. I think he's out to get us both."

Sasha rolled her eyes. "Did you break into my house?" She had been waiting for him to call her again just so she could ask him.

"No, but I think he did. Did he break any of the vases you had all over your room?"

Sasha eyes grew wide with surprise. "How did you...Robby! I am warning you. Stay out of my house."

"I was only trying to protect you."

The past weekend had been a beginning for her and Terraine. And, of course, just as she began to bask in the wonder of it all, Robby had to ruin the mood for her. "Protect me from what?"

"Shhh. Now is not the time. I think he's listening."

"Robby!" *You crazy lunatic.* "You don't have a brother. If you do, what is his name?" she asked with frustration. She was quickly losing her patience with him.

"I can't tell you," he answered in a mysterious voice. "I would be jeopardizing your life. For my silence he promises to spare you. I'd like for us to meet somewhere private. If you have time."

She was about to hang up the phone but felt compelled to help him if she could. Sasha leaned against the wall and prayed for strength. "Robby, you're hearing voices again. I think you need help." She spoke in a calm voice.

"Sasha, don't patronize me! I'm not delusional!" he barked. "I risked my life by calling you...Shhh! Did you hear that?" he whispered. Sasha hadn't heard anything except him rattling on and on like a madman. "I think this phone is bugged."

The pit of her stomach began to hurt. She felt so sorry for him. "Why don't you tell me where you are so I can call someone?"

"I think he likes you and wants you for himself," he said, totally ignoring her request. "I told him I'd never share. It's all my fault. I should have never told him about you," he said with a hint of agitation. "Did you notice the blue bunny I bought you for Valentine's Day was missing?"

"No, I didn't noticed." Sasha put the receiver

down and dashed down the hall to her room. When she looked on top of her bookshelf, intense astonishment touched her face. Sure enough, it was gone. She then sat on the end of her bed and reached for the cordless phone on her nightstand.

"Robby, this has got to stop! You are scaring me," she exclaimed in a choked voice.

"I'm sorry. I won't ever do it again, but promise me one thing."

Sasha tilted her head towards the ceiling and a deep line of worry appeared between her eyes. "What is that, Robby?"

"That you won't see Terraine Andrews again."

Sasha remained silent, knowing that even though she was willing to help, his request was one promise she could not grant.

Sunday morning they had breakfast at Goody Goody's restaurant, a classic diner famous for its delicious down home breakfasts that included grits smothered in real butter. It was small and as usual, filled to capacity. But like every other customer, Sasha and Terraine were willing to wait in line to be served.

They continued their afternoon cycling on Forest Park's five-mile bike trail through lush interior woods, ponds and meadows. It was a magnificent day. Though early summers in St. Louis were often unpredictable, the sun was shining bright and the park smelled of freshly cut grass and the heavy perfume of flowers.

Terraine almost ran into a tree because he was watching Sasha's moves in a pair of yellow cotton shorts that hugged her round bottom so beautifully it made his mouth water. *And her legs.* He shook his head. Her legs were probably the best he'd ever seen—long, shapely and smooth. Beauty and intelligence were definitely a potent combination.

They pedaled the entire trail. To Terraine's amazement, she was able to keep up with him. On the ride back they rode slowly, side-by-side, taking advantage of the chance to talk and laugh together.

Sasha smiled at Terraine. His skin shone like burnt chocolate, and he was wearing a pair of nylon shorts that showed off his athletic thighs and tight butt entirely too well. His well-defined pecs strained against his blue T-shirt, causing her pulse to quicken.

While Terraine loaded their bikes onto his bike rack, Sasha retrieved a large picnic basket that she had prepared earlier that morning and a quilted blanket. As soon as he finished, Terraine took the basket from her and placed his hand on her shoulder in a possessive gesture while they went in search of a shade tree. They walked in silence, both enjoying the surge of excitement radiating between them. They quickly found the perfect spot, a shaded tree near a pond. Sasha spread the blanket and Terraine dropped down beside her and inhaled deeply.

"Mmm-mmm, something sure smells good."

Sasha tipped her head toward the sun with pride written all over her face. "It had better. It's my mom's secret recipe for oven-fried chicken." While Sasha laid out the food, Terraine openly studied her. With her hair parted in the middle and braided on each side, she resembled a young Navajo Indian.

Terraine leaned against the tree, stretching his long legs, crossing them at the ankles, while Sasha removed containers of potato salad, fried chicken, rolls, and chocolate cake. She'd even remembered to bring ice-cold sodas.

"You sure know how to treat a man," he said softly.

"Roxaner trained me well." Sasha handed him a plate of food loaded down with generous portions. He shoveled a forkful of potato salad into his mouth.

Terraine closed his eyes as he savored the flavor. "Delicious."

Sasha smiled and sat cross-legged across from him. She popped a can and took a large thirsty gulp

337

as she observed the way he ate. She chuckled inwardly when he brought his plate to his mouth, fearful that he might drop food in his lap. She liked the way he wiped his lips with his napkin, self-conscious that there might be crumbs around his mouth. It warmed her heart and eased her mind to know that someone that seemed so perfect had his own personal quirks.

"Would you like to go with me to my family reunion next month?" she asked as she spooned potato salad onto her plate, unaware of the stunned expression that was now plastered across Terraine's face.

He dropped the fork that was halfway to his mouth and took a slow breath before answering, still in awe of the fact that she was allowing him to be a part of her life. "I would be honored." While attending her cousin's wedding, he had found her family to be a delight. "Is it your mother's or your father's family?"

"My mother's family. The Moores are my father's family. My mother's maiden name is Simon. When my parents divorced she decided to hold on to her married name so that it would not complicate things for me at school. At least she thought so. Personally, I don't see where it really makes a difference." Sasha shrugged and watched a lady stroll by with a white miniature poodle.

"I guess it is something only a mother would know." Terraine turned and watched the sun reflect on the water. "Do you see children in your future?"

Sasha nodded. "Definitely. I want a boy and a girl."

"And what if you have two girls?"

Sasha raised a hand to her heart. "Heaven forbid! I definitely would need a husband around to keep the boys away." She giggled and then her expression became serious. "I would want to give my husband a son of his own. So I would be willing to try at least two more times."

Terraine continued to probe. "And while you are trying to give birth to a baseball team, what would happen to your career?"

Sasha bit into a piece of chicken and swallowed before replying, "I would continue to design gowns but modeling would become a closed chapter in my book."

"And you would be okay with that?" he asked between chews.

"Being in love and having a family would take precedence in my life. Nothing would ever matter as much as being a mother."

Terraine stared at her intensely as he envisioned her swollen stomach carrying his seed. "You are a very interesting and beautiful woman, Ms. Moore. I want to learn everything about you. Your feelings, desires, everything."

"Under one condition." Her face heated as she met his intense gaze.

"And what is that?"

She watched as his dimple twitched, then she leaned forward and took a moment to speak. "That I can ask you the same."

"No problem." He grinned and his dimples punctuated his amusement.

"So, ask me," Sasha smiled.

Terraine thought for a moment. "I know you like to eat—" Terraine ducked as Sasha threw a chicken bone at him. "What's your favorite food?"

"Seafood, of course," she laughed. "I told you, I can eat fish every day of the week."

Terraine threw his hands up. "Pisces, it figures." Seeing Sasha's amazed expression, he burst into laughter. She had forgotten that she'd told him her birthday was in February.

"Okay, Mr. Smarty Pants, what sign are you?"

"Leo the lion. My bark is worst than my bite. Although I wouldn't mind nibbling on you." Terraine pretended to take a large bite out of her arm.

Sasha giggled as she tried to hide her embarrassment. "What's your favorite food?"

With a dazzling smile he answered, "Chinese."

Sasha tipped her head towards the sun and a ray of sunshine caused her extraordinary eyes to become luminous.   "Good, that is my second favorite."

As they ate they continued their discussion, and the more they talked, the more interesting Terraine became. He hated broccoli, and strawberries gave him hives. They both enjoyed reading mysteries and watching old movies. He had traveled abroad every summer with his grandpa visiting fabulous places such as Europe, Africa and Canada. They discussed cities that they both had visited and were surprised to find out that they both had been in Rome at the same time. Sasha wondered if, had they crossed paths, they would have experienced the same attraction.

Terraine was not afraid to express himself and was open with a great sense of humor. She loved the way his voice sounded. He made her feel beautiful and special.

Sasha wiped her mouth with a paper napkin, then tossed it on top of her empty plate. After sitting in one position for over an hour, Sasha shifted her hips to one more comfortable. She looked over at Terraine while he finished up his second helping of potato salad. Her heart pounded as she watched his face. His eyes were captivatingly gorgeous. *Dark and inviting.* Why did he have to be so fine? *Tall, dark and handsome.* Every time she looked at him, she remembered what it had been like to be in his arms and to have his hands caressing her body. He was a wonderful, caring man.

Terraine saw her looking at him with longing in her eyes and stopped eating. She was so soft and beautiful and so very close. He loved the way she looked, the way she moved and the way she talked with laughter in her voice. Setting aside their plates, Terraine reached for her waist and lifted her onto his lap. Sasha parted her lips in surprise.

"You are a marvelous lady, " he whispered as he lowered his lips to her ear. "Sasha?" He covered her hands with his.

His nearness made her senses spin. "Yes?" she responded with wide eyes that told him everything she was feeling, including uncertainty.

"Sasha, I am not going to hurt you." He planted small kisses on her cheeks and nose. "I love you." This was his first declaration of love and it came out by surprise but he was glad. He no longer wanted to hide his feelings. They needed to be shared. *Now if you could find it in your heart to love me too.*

Sasha's mouth formed a perfect *O* as she was caught up in her own emotion. She looked at him, unable to speak, praying what Natalia had told her wasn't really true.

They spent the rest of the afternoon across the street at the St. Louis Zoo. While strolling through the park, arm-in-arm, he told her he loved her in the monkey house. He told her in the snake house. He told her on the train. And to her embarrassment, he even stood on top of a large rock and proclaimed his love to everyone that was walking by. Her heart flooded with joy.

Was she ready to allow herself to love him back?

Honey slowly jogged around the corner with Nikki on her leash and saw a gray Lexus parked in front of Sasha's house. She slowed down to a brisk walk, allowing Nikki to pull her down the sidewalk. As she closed the distance, she noticed a man leaving the front porch and heading back to his car. Nikki barked, and when the man turned in their direction, Honey realized that it was Jay. To her surprise her heart did a back flip at the sight of him. He leaned against the car, and Honey slowed her pace to take in his physique.

His tall muscular frame was silhouetted against a large shade tree. A pair of cotton shorts clung tightly to his powerful thighs and his T-shirt exposed a muscular torso and molded to his bulky arms that gleamed in the heat of the afternoon sun. Jay Andrews was definitely a crowd pleaser.

He knew it was Honey the moment he turned his head, and he breathed in deeply at the sight of her swaying hips and small, tapered waist. Her hair that was pulled back into a child-like ponytail and bounced as she walked. Jay had not expected her to be home, but he was not in the least disappointed that she was. He inspected her from her head to her spandex shorts and crop top. *Beautiful.* Mesmerized by her enormous gray eyes, he felt his willpower slowly slipping away.

"Hi," Jay said as she moved closer towards him. His mood brightened and he crossed his arms against his chest and settled back against his car. Honey's eyes traveled over his sculptured body and her knees almost buckled. She found herself imagining how his hairy brown legs would feel underneath her fingertips. Honey swallowed and wiped a stream of sweat off her forehead.

"Hello, yourself. What are you doing here?" Honey was relieved that she could use walking the dog as an excuse for her elevated heart rate.

"Actually, I need to talk to my brother. Have you seen him?" Jay realized that his statement was not completely true. As he watched her stroll towards him, he'd begun to question his real reason for coming over this afternoon. If he needed Terraine, he could have called him on his cell phone that was permanently attached to his left hip or paged him on his beeper.

He watched beads of sweat trickle down

between the swell of her breasts. Then he focused on the face of the tiny woman with the slanted, smoky gray eyes and high cheekbones and instantly knew why he was on this side of town.

Shaking her head, Honey looked up, using her hand as a shield from the rays that were beaming down on her face. "No, but I know that they were going to Forest Park today." She clicked her tongue. "No telling what they are planning on getting into later."

Jay grinned. "I think I could possibly come up with a couple of ideas." He squatted in front of Nikki, who was sniffing his feet, and patted her on the head. He was now eye level with Honey's belly button, he watched sweat run from underneath her top and into the pit of her navel. Nothing would have pleased him more than to have his tongue travel that same path. Nothing tasted better than hot and sticky honey. Jay laughed at his own pun. Frowning, she looked down at him. "What's so funny?"

From the look she gave him, Jay was certain she would not find humor in his joke. "Forgive me, but it is kind of hard adjusting to my brother being sprung over one woman." He grinned. "Sasha has really changed him."

Honey smiled and nodded in agreement. "Yeah, he has changed her too. I don't remember when I have seen her so happy."

Jay rose to his feet again, towering over her at least a foot. "What about you? Any special man in your life?" He looked down at her face that glowed with perspiration as a result of her vigorous activity. Honey clicked her tongue and waved her dainty hand dismissively. "Nope, and I like it that way."

Jay raised his left eyebrow in amazement. "Really? Me too."

A teasing smile curled on her lips. "Yeah, I figured you for a playa."

Jay slumped over, pretending that he had just been punched in the chest. "Nah, I'm just not ready to settle down."

Honey was not surprised, men like him never were. She patted the hood of his car. She should have known he wouldn't be driving anything but the best and as fine as he was, he deserved to. "That makes two of us."

With a half-smile Jay turned to her. "Too many headaches."

"Too much drama." Honey met his delicious smile. "I believe it's possible for men and women to be friends without having to be intimate. Just two people that can hang out together without all of the hang-ups that come with relationships."

"I agree," Jay returned, even though in her case he was willing to make an exception. "So friend, think you would be interested in a movie?" He playfully draped a warm arm across her shoulder.

Honey took a deep breath and suddenly felt extremely comfortable with him standing so close. "Which one?"

He shrugged. "Anything, as long as it is sci fi."

She turned and looked at him long enough to tell if he was serious about being friends or if he was just pulling her leg to get close to her. Then she reached down and rubbed Nikki behind her ears as she thought. Honey knew they couldn't be involved and was glad that she and Jay were on the same page. He wasn't looking for a relationship; therefore he would not be a threat.

Honey carried her eyes back up to his and the tenderness she saw warmed her heart. "Make it an action movie and you got yourself a date."

Jay's smile deepened. "Deal." He liked her already.

Chapter Fourteen

Over the next several days Sasha and Terraine were inseparable.

He was so attentive and openly affectionate with her in public that it soon became apparent to anyone who cared to notice that they were a couple. A very happy couple as a matter of fact.

Sasha was so afraid that she was going to wake up at any given moment and find out that it had all been one long, magnificent dream. Never would she have guessed in a million years that someone so wonderful would pop into her pathetic life. As she lay snuggled in the crook of his arm after hours of mind-boggling lovemaking, she thanked God for bringing them together.

One night long after Terraine had fallen asleep, Sasha suddenly realized how deeply she loved him.

The development came as no big surprise. She had known all along that it was just a matter of time. The love he gave her was unconditional without any expectations from her in return. She had been so afraid after her relationship with Robby that she would never be able to risk opening up her heart to another man, but Terraine had taught her how to love again. Her feelings for him were nothing like the love that she thought she'd felt for Robby. Now that she returned Terraine's love, she truly believed that with Robby she had been very lonely and in love with the idea of being in love. But this time it was so very different, so very wonderful. This time it was so very real.

The commercial was shot on Wednesday after twenty-six takes. Then preparations began for the upcoming fashion show. The twins, Tyler and Sasha, quickly stepped back into their roles as runway models. They were scheduled to strut their stuff on opening night and spent every morning at the studio choreographing their moves. Unlike any other show in which Sasha had ever modeled, Diva Designs was popular for their entertaining fashion shows—a parade of smashing designs and as an added treat, coordinated dance routines. A professional choreographer was contracted and the routines were practiced again and again until the girls were exhausted.

During their second day of rehearsal, Sasha noticed Natalia standing off to the side glaring at her. Sasha tried to fight a smile as she watched the choreographer dance across the floor. Mimicking her, Sasha twirled around to her left, soaring with glee. *Face it, Natalia, Tee is mine.* She put extra grace into her moves, making sure that Natalia did not miss for a second how wonderful a dancer she was. Years of practice definitely came in handy. Sasha tapped herself across the hand, scoldingly. *Stop that.* She had never been one to rub her triumph in anyone's face but this was one trophy she didn't mind feeling proud about and it helped her ignore Natalia's hot glares. Sasha danced across the platform and eventually Natalia looked the other way. But the next day it was the same thing again and Sasha began to look seriously at the situation, wondering why Natalia disliked her so much. She approached the problem with Terraine one evening after asking him not to repeat a word of it to Natalia. He planted a small kiss on her cheek and reassured her that Natalia was nothing to worry about.

Sasha raised the idea that had been gnawing at her. "Natalia told me a couple of weeks ago that the two of you were planning to be married."

"*What?*" Terraine frowned, then chuckled. "No." He kissed her cheek again. "Natalia and I grew up together and she is the closest thing I have ever had to a sister, but sometimes her jealousy seems to get a little out of hand." Although Sasha felt relieved by the conversation, the situation remained unchanged. She tried to talk with Natalia on several occasions but her responses were always monosyllables. Finally, Sasha decided to just not to let the situation get the best of her and fell into a daily routine of ignoring her.

Sasha had gotten used to seeing Terraine at lunchtime. He would walk into the room and recess everyone for a couple of hours just so he could steal a few private moments alone with her in his office. She was relieved to get away from Natalia's scrutiny and tickled to find out that Terraine had donated his old leather couch to charity and had replaced it with a sleeper sofa. The next several days were enjoyable. After sneaking off to his office and pulling each other's clothes off behind a locked door, they would lie in the bed for over an hour making love and feeding each other pizza or Chinese food. Their week was unforgettable, more passionate than Sasha had ever experienced. She loved his intelligence, his smile, not to mention his mouth-watering body. She was happy and finally ready to openly admit to Terraine that she returned his love.

Sasha climbed out of the shower and dried off,

then sprayed her body with her favorite body spray from Victoria's Secret. Terraine had complimented her on how wonderful the pear scent smelled against her skin. Wrapping herself in a towel, she stepped into her bedroom and noticed the red light on her answering machine blinking. She pushed the button.

"Sasha, sweetheart, good news. Meet me in my office for lunch. Can't wait to see you."

Shivering at the sound of Terraine's deep, husky voice, she danced cheerfully over to her dresser, singing a merry tune. Then she saw her reflection in the mirror. Her voice faded, and for several seconds, she looked at herself in the mirror. She was glowing, a sign that she was truly in love. Removing several items from her closet, Sasha swallowed. Of course she was, she had been for weeks. She just had not been ready to express her feelings until now. Now, wrapped in a blanket of euphoria, she wanted to shout to the world, "I love Terraine!" Taking extra care in her appearance, she reached into her underwear drawer and found a sexy pink set, which she could not wait for Terraine to see.

The phone rang and Sasha reached for it, thinking that it was probably Terraine wondering what was taking her so long.

She giggled. "Sweetheart, I'm on my way."

Greeted by silence on the other end, her smile slowly faded.

"Hello?" Still no response. This was the third time this week. Chances were it was probably Robby again, she thought. Would he always be a dark cloud hanging over her head? That was a scary thought indeed.

"Whoever this is, quit calling me!" she hissed before she hung up.

Sasha shrugged. There were no clouds in her forecast today. *Only sunshine, sunshine, and more sunshine!* And right now she was anxious to get to Terraine as quickly as possible.

Still no leads. He just could not understand it. The cops were no closer to catching the murderer today than they had been a couple of weeks ago. It just did not make any sense. Terraine ran a frustrated hand across his chin. Two dead models and sabotaged equipment; the problem was just too close for comfort.

Without Sasha knowing it, Terraine had assigned her twenty-four-hour protection. There was a guy posted close by her side at all times. Though uncomfortable sneaking around behind her back, he felt he had reason to. Things had been calm all week, and he was beginning to wonder if maybe things were too quiet. There hadn't even been an article recently in the newspapers. The deaths had quickly become old news. Good, he hoped it stayed that way. Under the circumstances, he should feel a sense of relief that the entire city was no longer focused on the tragedies at Diva Designs. But he didn't. There was too much at stake apart from the tragedies. The future of his grandfather's corporation was riding on the changes and additions that he had made—sexier designs, intimate apparel and now, wedding gowns. Terraine tapped his fingers restlessly on the desk. Jay had reassured him this morning that he had it under control and he trusted his brother, confident in his ability as a detective. *But you just never know.* In the meantime, he was not taking any chances, especially not with Sasha. If anything happened to her, he'd never forgive himself. Never.

Terraine put his feet up on the desk and stretched his arms overhead. He already missed the taste of her warm tender lips.

"What do you think?"

He looked over at his door and his eyes swept disapprovingly over Natalia, who was standing several feet away in a long black coatdress that was completely unbuttoned, revealing a tangerine bra and matching thong underwear, both made of sheer netting that left very little to the imagination.

Terraine pressed his lips together with annoyance. "Natalia, where are your clothes?"

Shutting his office door, Natalia laughed, finding his displeasure amusing. Allowing the dress to fall onto the carpet, she sashayed towards him. "I wanted to show you the latest ensemble by Ms. Guccione." His eyes studied her as she placed her hands on her narrow hips and turned around slowly so that he could see the outfit from all angles.

Terraine dropped his feet and frowned. It wasn't that her body wasn't enticing, because in his opinion, Natalia had always been physically beautiful. It was just that he did not have romantic feelings for her. His attraction to a woman needed to be more than just physical; the mind also had to come into play. When it came to Natalia, she quickly got on his nerves. He was only interested in seeing one lady naked.

Terraine gave her a mechanical grin and returned his focus to the work in front of him. "Very nice. Now I would appreciate it if you'd put your dress back on," he suggested with emphasis.

Natalia's humor quickly faded. She dropped her hands and pouted. "Terraine, you're no fun. Why do you hate me so much?" She could not believe that she was standing in front of him showing him all of *this* and he chose to ignore her.

He greeted her with a bark of laughter. "I don't hate you. I'm just not interested. You fail to realize that no one knows you like I do. I've been around you since you were twelve years old and the same tricks you used then you are still trying to use now. Face it, sweetie, it ain't working." Terraine chuckled again and reached for his pen so that he could make a few notes on Carl's proposed budget for the coming year.

Natalia suddenly felt uncomfortable, unable to believe that Terraine would treat her like that. He had spoken to her in a jesting manner that she did not find at all amusing. She felt a twinge of panic. Maybe it truly was too late for them. "I-I'm sorry, this was a stupid idea."

Terraine looked up, surprised by her words, and met the seriousness in her eyes. His brow rose. Saying *sorry* was not part of her character.

"I just wish that things could be different between us." As tears filled her eyes, she bit her lip and turned away. "Please don't fire me; this job means everything to me. Diva Designs is my entire life."

There was a note of perceptible pleading in her voice. Terraine groaned with uneasiness as he heard the smothered sob. He hadn't seen Natalia cry since her fourteenth birthday when she had been so certain her parents were going to buy her a pony that she had taken all her money out of her piggy bank and purchased an expensive riding ensemble that she wore to her birthday dinner. She had been devastated when she found out they had bought her a pair of diamond stud earrings.

Terraine rose, walked around the desk, and stood in front of Natalia. He watched a tear slide down her cheek, then placed his hands lightly on her shoulders. "Woman, what are you crying for?" He grinned down at her pitiful face, remembering that this was the same girl who used to outrun him to the candy store on Saturday afternoons. He cupped her chin and tilted her face towards his. "We both know that Pops wanted you and me working here together. You have nothing to worry about." Nothing moved his heart more than to see a woman cry. *Even if it was Natalia.*

Blinking fast, she banished the tears that were blinding her eyes. "D-do you really mean it?"

Feeling as if he'd been a heel, Terraine squeezed her shoulder lightly. "Of course I do. Now wipe your face."

Suddenly her entire face did a three hundred and sixty-degree turn. "Oh, thank you!" Natalia wrapped her arms around the nape of his neck and tugged his face towards her, kissing him right smack on his lips.

Sasha exited the elevator wearing a smile a

mile long. She walked to Terraine's suite, and noticing that Geri was not at her desk, she pushed Terraine's door open. Then she came to a screeching halt. Her heart dropped into the pit of her stomach at the sight of Terraine and Natalia sharing a very intimate moment. Terraine's back was to the door and Natalia was standing half-dressed with her arms locked around his neck, the length of her body close against his and their lips pressed together. Trembling with humiliation, Sasha quietly closed the door behind her, silently praying that neither of them had seen her. She quickly ran down the hallway. With the fear of tears threatening to surface and gripped with the fear of being seen, she opted to sneak down the stairwell instead of waiting for the elevator.

Terraine removed Natalia's arms from around his neck and his eyes narrowed suspiciously. "What the hell are you doing?"

She appraised him with wide, ginger-colored eyes that held more than a hint of mischief. "Reminiscing, darling," she purred as triumph flooded through her. She had seen Sasha out of the corner of her eyes. *Perfect timing.* It could not have worked out better if she had planned it. Terraine and Sasha's display of affection all week had been sickening. She had been unsure how much more of it she could take and had been trying to think of a way to show Sasha that Terraine was off limits when opportunity fell right into her lap. Natalia shrugged innocently. "You bring out the worst in me. What can I say?" She reached over and retrieved her dress from the floor.

Terraine was furious that he'd fallen for her 'wounded victim' act. Natalia was purposely trying to get under his skin. "I'm tired of playing games with you, Nat. I think it's about time you decided to grow up," he said in an angry tone.

Natalia looked his demeanor over and instantly knew that she had taken things a little too far. She quickly apologized. "I promise it won't ever happen again." Pivoting on her heels and fastening the last button on her dress before strolling out of his office, she curled her lips in a mischievous smile.

Terraine fell into the chair and blew out a long breath. He was at his wit's end with Natalia. Eventually one of them was going to have to leave the corporation, and he was not so sure anymore if it would be he. He was starting to feel right at home again and satisfied that he had finally found something that challenged his mind in more ways than one.

Terraine straightened his tie and looked over at the clock on the wall, grateful that Sasha had not arrived yet.

Walking into the house with curses falling from her lips, Sasha slammed the front door behind her. How dare he! And to think that she'd almost made the mistake of telling him she loved him. Her stomach churned at the thought of him ever holding another woman in his arms, much less the sight of him kissing Natalia. Sasha scowled. Natalia had tried to warn her in her own selfish way and she'd chosen not to heed her warning. Sasha flopped into a chair and crossed her arms across her chest. For a brief moment, she had been devastatingly close to breaking down right in the parking lot but she had willed herself to hold on until she made it home. Now she allowed the tears to splash down her cheeks.

She had been right. Her first impression of Terraine had been correct after all.

Removing her glasses, she placed them on the table. So why did she feel like her heart had cracked in two and was dragging at the bottom of her feet? Even though she had told herself that this day would come, she was not prepared for the feeling of rejection or being tossed aside like an old scuffed shoe.

Sasha buried her face in her hands and sobbed out the pain and humiliation until there wasn't a tear left. She then mopped her face with her hand, feeling thirty percent better.

Trotting down the hall, Nikki stopped to stare at her. "What are you looking at?" She clenched her jaw to kill the sob in her throat. Nikki whimpered and moved a few steps closer, looking up at her with compassionate eyes. "Oh come here, you big baby!" Sasha mumbled, and Nikki rested her head upon her lap. At least someone loves me.

"Mr. Andrews, she left the house at 1200 hours arriving at your headquarters at 122;5 then she exited the building exactly fifteen minutes later. She stopped for gas at 1255 and returned home promptly at 1340 hours. Her car is parked in her driveway as we speak. Would you like me to knock on the door and check on her?"

"No, no thank you." Terraine replaced the receiver with a thump and hunched over in his seat with his elbows resting on his thighs.

Sasha had seen him and Natalia together.

Sasha opened the door and found Terraine standing on the other side with a boyish grin on his face. Sasha huffed. It was going to take more than a luscious smile for him to get back into her good graces.

He tried to read her blank expression and could not. He sensed her anger but at least she had not slammed the door in his face, which meant she wanted to hear his explanation.

"May I come in?" Without answering, Sasha crossed her arms against her chest and walked away from the door. She took a seat on the couch, hugging her knees to her chest. Terraine took her silence as a yes and followed her into the room. Nikki came around the corner and growled at him.

"This must be Nikki." He squatted on his knees. "Come here, girl." Nikki was first hesitant; then she trotted over to him.

"Traitor," Sasha mumbled as she watched the dog roll over onto her back allowing him to stroke her stomach. What did Terraine want anyway? He had already broken her heart. The least he could do was let her keep her pride. *I hope he gets dog hair all over his suit.*

Rising, he walked over and knelt down on the floor in front of her. "I am leaving for Dallas in two days. I planned to spend that time with you."

He placed a hand over hers, which Sasha quickly removed. He was not getting off that easy.

She's mad at me. Terraine knew that he owed her an explanation but before he made a fool of himself, he needed to first find out for sure what she was angry about. There was always a two-percent chance that she could be angry about something else. Okay, maybe a one-percent chance. Regardless, there was no point in adding fuel to the fire. "Is something wrong?" he asked with a puzzled expression.

She twisted her lips sourly. "You tell me."

Terraine gave a nervous laugh. "I don't know what you are talking about," he said though the look on her face told him otherwise. But still, he needed to be sure. "If I did something, please tell me."

Glaring at him, Sasha was irked by his cool manner. She could not believe he was trying to act innocent. "I saw you and Natalia this afternoon." Watching his face, to her disappointment he did not appear the least bit surprised. He had known all along.

"Oh." He cleared his throat. "I was afraid of that." Terraine had had all afternoon to rehearse his side of the story, but suddenly his mind was blank. He rocked back onto his heels and ran his hand across his scalp. He had hoped that it would be something other than this, but he should have known better.

Sasha jumped up from the couch, giving in to the tension that had been building throughout the course of the day. "You are so full of it."

Terraine moved to where she had been sitting

and leaned back against the cushions. "Are you going to let me explain?"

Her eyes grew wide with accusations. "What is there to explain? You tricked me again and like a fool, I fell for it!" Sasha pressed a hand to her forehead, suddenly feeling a headache coming on. "Why am I so stupid?"

Terraine shook his head. "It's not like that. I was comforting Natalia and she decided to use it as an excuse to kiss me." He had to agree that even though it was the truth, his story did sound lame. But he loved her. Didn't that count for something? But he could tell by her expression that she was not buying it.

Sasha was fuming. *Talk about a weak ass story.* Who did he take her for? He could at least leave her with her dignity. She wanted so badly for him to say it wasn't true or that she had even walked into the wrong office but he had done neither; instead, he expected her to believe that he was the victim. Her mind kept returning to Natalia latched on to Terraine with an orange thong up her butt.

Defensively, she folded her arms across her chest and clicked her tongue. "Terraine, it's over. Please, just leave me alone." She turned and started to walk away.

Terraine rose off the couch and Sasha found

herself being spun around. "What do you mean, it's over?" He couldn't believe that she was really going to end their relationship over something so petty. Well, maybe petty was a bad choice of words. He tried to put himself in her shoes. If he'd found her lip locking with some other dude... yeah, he'd be pissed. Terraine rubbed his hand across his chin. But that was still not enough reason to end a relationship as powerful as theirs. "Is it that easy for you to walk away from our relationship? Did I mean that little to you?" He tried to control his rising anger and took hold of her hands. "I noticed that when I told you I loved you that you never returned the words that I've been waiting patiently to hear. I thought that was because you needed time. Now I am not so sure."

Sasha saw the hurt on his face but what about her own pain? It was high time for her to start thinking about herself for a change and stop being so gullible. Therefore, not trusting her own reaction, she looked up stubbornly towards the ceiling.

Terraine was furious that she would not look at him. He withdrew his hands as intense silence enveloped the room. "I love you but if we can't have trust in a relationship, then I don't know what we have." He pulled a pen out of his pocket followed by a business card and quickly scribbled a number on the back and set it on the coffee table. "Here is the number to the hotel I will be staying at. Call me if you want to talk." He patted Nikki on her head and walked over to the door, where he stopped and looked as if he wanted to say something else before walking out the door.

Sasha waited until she heard the door slam before she lowered her head. She wanted to run after him but her feet would not move. She tried to call his name but the words would not come out, and it was probably a good thing because she wasn't sure what to think anymore. She was glad that he'd left before the tears came spilling down her cheeks. She would not want him to think she was crying because of him. Slowly she reached up and wiped her eyes.

He changed his plans and left for Dallas the next morning, making the next couple of days agonizingly long and unbearable. But he was glad that he had left. He needed the distance. There was no way he was going to be able to work in the same building and not be able to see her. There was no way he was going to be able to sit at his desk and not look at the couch they'd spent so many hours breaking in. There was no way he was going to be able to lie in his bed at night and not have her sensual body lying against him. There was no way he was going to be able to live his life without her.

Terraine sat in his hotel room cradling a bottle of brandy. He had hoped to hear from Sasha by now. He'd even called the desk clerk twice to make sure there weren't any messages sitting in his box that she had forgotten to give him. So much for wishful thinking. In an effort to ignore the longing that he felt, he had been filling his days at the warehouse in downtown Dallas and not leaving until the workday was complete. He was not sure how he was going to survive until he saw her face again. But in his mind he could still see the display of insecurity on her face. What more could he do to convince her that he loved her? Crawl? Beg? When he put himself in her shoes, he had to admit that he would have been suspicious also, but he would have listened to her explanation. He would have believed her because he loved her. So why couldn't she do the same? He loved her, but what good was his love if she did not trust him. Did it mean that she didn't feel the same way about him? Terraine finished the bottle and wasn't sure exactly when he passed out in the chair.

For three nights Sasha tossed and turned in bed, haunted by memories of the two of them mak-

367

ing love. She missed Terraine so much and had to fight her overwhelming need to be with him. Her body craved him, and instead of forgetting about him, her love for him deepened. She missed his magical hands roaming intimately over her, their united bodies sending her soaring to a shuddering ecstasy. Her days went by in one big blur while she tried her best to occupy every second of her day, filling in gaps by working on her designs until the wee hours of the morning, hoping to pass out with exhaustion. *No such luck.* She even took a shot of Nyquil, hoping it would knock her out. *It didn't.* Her heart hurt so much that she cried herself to sleep. For someone who had talent and looks, she sure was dumb in the men's department. She wished she could pretend that it did not matter, that he really did not mean that much to her but then she would be lying to herself. Terraine meant everything to her. The pain was worse than anything she had ever felt in her life. *Because you have never really been in love before*. When was it ever going to end? *When you take him back.* She picked up the phone twice, tempted to call him, but the tightness in her throat and her stubborn pride gave her no other choice than to put the phone back on the hook.

The possibility that she might be wrong began to nag at the back of her mind. Sasha lay awake at night wondering if she had reacted too hastily and if she should have heard him out. What good was a relationship if there wasn't any trust? She began to think that maybe she had made a mistake. But Natalia quickly steered her back in the right direction. Three days after Terraine left, Natalia made it her business to let Sasha know that she saw her watching the two of them together in Terraine's office. She then cackled and told Sasha that she should have hung around a little longer then she would have really seen something on that new couch of his.

By the fourth night Sasha was fuming again.

Tonight, she spent the evening working on Ms. Neil's gown. Her wedding was scheduled for the weekend before the fashion show and Sasha was determined to focus and have it ready.

She headed back to her bedroom to find the beads she'd strung the night before. When she leaned over to turn on the lamp, she froze as a familiar scent filled her nostrils. Sasha turned around slowly and the blood rushed to her head as she saw a dark figure lunge at her, dropping her to the floor. She immediately realized it was a man when a large calloused hand covered her mouth. Sasha swung her arms and they wrestled on the floor. Sasha bit his hand and when he jerked it away from her mouth, she screamed at the top of her lungs until she received a swift blow to her abdomen. She gasped for air, which was a complicated task with his large frame on top of her.

"Please," she whispered slowly, "I can't breathe." The intruder slid off her stomach onto her thighs and pinned both her arms over her head. Sasha took a deep breath. "What do you want?" she asked.

He did not answer. She lay very still, too stunned to cry, and was met with a wave of fear and nausea at once. He slowly lowered his head that was covered by a stocking and pressed his lips against her throat. It was too dark for Sasha to see anything but she could feel the nylon against her chin. With his free hand he reached down and unzipped her shorts. Fear washed over her as she suddenly realized what his intentions were. He planned to rape her.

Then a familiar scent was all around her, but before she could remember where she'd smelled it before, she heard growling. Nikki lunged at the intruder and sank her teeth into his leg. In a deep, muffled voice, the intruder cried out in pain, allowing Sasha an opportunity to wiggle from underneath him. While he continued to wrestle with her dog, she crawled across the floor to turn on her lamp, but before she could reach it, he grabbed her by her ankle. Still, Sasha got hold of the cord and knocked the lamp to the floor. When Nikki lunged at the intruder again, Sasha somehow managed to free her ankle and slam the lamp over his head. The intruder moaned, scrambled across the floor and ran down the hall with Nikki hot on his trail. Looking around her room for something she could use as a weapon, Sasha grabbed an umbrella off the door-knob and tiptoed into the kitchen with her heart racing. Nikki was standing in the kitchen in front of the sliding glass door that stood open. Quickly, Sasha shut the glass, locked the door and then fell into a chair, completely shaken.

"Come here, girl. You deserve a big hug." Leaning over, she embraced Nikki, whose eyes were bright with devotion. "What would I have done if you had not been here?" she murmured as the tears came streaming down her face. She then reached over and grabbed the phone off the wall. Her mind was frazzled, so she hit number one on the speed dial. While the phone rang, she closed her eyes and whispered, "Oh my God, what almost happened here?"

Jay had just pulled into White Castle's drive thru when his cell phone rang. "Jay speaking."

"Jay! Sasha has been attacked!" Honey screamed into his ear.

"What happened?"

"Someone broke into her house and attacked

371

her! I don't know all of the details because she was too shaken up to talk. But I'm in my car and on my way over there now."

"Why the hell is she still—" The phone went dead. "Damn!" Jay swerved out of the drive thru line and sped to the nearest interstate. He slammed his palm down onto the dashboard. What happened to the security guard that he had posted outside her door? If anything happened to Sasha, his brother would never forgive him.

"I'm okay," Sasha said with a pain-stricken face. Jay stood in front of her, Honey on her left. Thawing from her shock, she began to shake. Honey got up and retrieved an afghan from the hall closet and draped it around Sasha's arms.

"Sasha, I think it's time you told the truth." Sasha shook her head and Jay looked at her curiously. Honey squeezed her shoulder. "Sasha! Tell him about Robby!"

Jay leaned against the mantel. "Who is Robby?" he asked.

Sasha shook her head wildly and spoke in a tremulous whisper. "I don't think Robby did it."

Jay looked at the worried expression on Honey's face, then returned his attention to Sasha, speaking with as much compassion as he could manage. "Sasha, listen. One of my men is lying dead in his car! If there is anything you have not told me, I need to know *now*."

The fear was visible on her face as the tears came streaming down her face. Robby couldn't possibly have killed three people. Could he? She bowed her head and began to sob softly. Honey squeezed her shoulders lightly with compassion.

Jay sat down on her right and his soothing voice probed further. "Who is Robby?"

"He's her ex-fiancée," Honey blurted out.
Jay looked at her and frowned. "I was talking to Sasha." Honey cut her eyes and walked towards the door to meet the police officers finally pulling up in front of the house.

"Do you think it was him?" Jay asked.

"No, not really." She dropped her chin in her palm and sniffled. "But it was his cologne," she said with uncertainty. "It was the same kind I bought Robby for his birthday last year. I found it in Italy." He had always worn it when he was around her. But something wasn't sitting right with her. If you loved someone and had planned to spend your life with him or her would you not know how he or she felt lying on top of you? Or even how their hands felt against your skin? She had not recognized either. Even his groans were deeper than she remembered his voice to be.

Jay was certain that he had just stumbled on another clue. He took Sasha's hand and placed it between both of his comfortingly. "Now start at the beginning and don't miss anything."

After speaking to his brother, Terraine was on the first plane back to St. Louis. He rented a car and headed straight to her house. He brushed past Honey and swung Sasha into the circle of his arms. She felt her heart leap with excitement at seeing him again and buried her face against his chest.

"Sasha, life is just too short. You're coming to stay with me," he whispered against her silky hair. It frightened him to even think about possibly losing her. His life would have no meaning without her.

Sasha pushed out of his grasp. "No way." It was one thing for him to hold her but it was another thing altogether to walk in and tell her what she was going to do.

Terraine's eyes darkened. "Quit being stubborn. I am not going let you stay at home by yourself."

Sasha raised her chin. "Honey is here with me."

Standing against the wall, Honey cleared her throat. "Umm... actually, Sasha, I'm leaving tomorrow for a two-day training session in Kansas City but I will be back late Friday night. You are more than welcome to stay with me after I move into my new place on Saturday," she mumbled before she hastily exited the room.

Terraine slapped his hands together. "Then it's settled. You are staying with me."

"I'll go stay with my mom." Sasha folded her arms across her chest and pursed her lips. "I don't want to stay with you. I still have my bodyguards. Besides, I don't think Natalia would like that."

Terraine had to suppress the urge to shake some sense into her head. "Sasha, why do I have to keep telling you there is nothing going on between us?"

Sasha pouted. "Then what was Natalia doing in your office half-dressed?"

"I already told you and you didn't care to listen." Terraine walked over to the couch and took Sasha with him, holding her hands loosely. "Sasha, I love you, even that stubborn streak that is so much a part of you. I don't know what I would do if anything happened to you." Sasha saw the sadness in his eyes and almost believed him. "Please stay with me, at least long enough for Jay to follow a new lead."

She sighed indecisively. Maybe she would be safer at his house. Maybe then her mother would never know. *She doubted it.* Honey was probably on the phone calling her right now. Sasha preferred that Roxaner not find out about what had happened; otherwise the entire congregation would be marching in front of Diva Designs headquarters on Monday morning.

Sasha turned and faced him. "One condition."

Terraine smiled at the small piece of hope. "Anything."

"I need my own space."

Terraine read the message behind her words. She had no intention of hopping back into his bed. He could handle that. *For now.* "You can have all the space you need."

Then Sasha looked over at her furry friend sleeping in the corner and grinned. "One more thing. If I go, Nikki goes too."

Chapter Fifteen

asha and Nikki moved into his house the following evening. To her disappointment, Terraine kept his word and escorted her to a guest bedroom at the other end of the hall. The previous night she had lain awake staring out at the starlit sky as her entire body tingled all over with the knowledge that she was going to be staying with him. Now she felt a shiver of disappointment travel all the way down to her toes.

He set her bag down in the middle of the floor. "I had Ms. Henry prepare this room for you. I hope you like it." Sasha lifted her eyes and searched his face for some clue, something that would help her understand what he was thinking, but was unable to manage eye contact. She had been so sure that he was going to insist that she share his room and was amazed to find herself excited about the possibility. Now she was disappointed that he had not. *But he is a player?* For one weak moment she did not care. She wanted to be in his bed lying beside him and if he had asked, she would have agreed.

He tucked his hands into the pockets of his jeans and turned to face the woman who'd stolen his heart. "If you like, we can pick up your sewing machine tomorrow. There is plenty of room for it."

Sasha nodded and felt guilty at his kindness. She smiled back at him. "I would like that very much."

He looked away from the soft expression on her face, trying to ignore the desire aching in his limbs. Not sure how much longer he could ignore his temptations, he quickly cast his eyes downward. "I'll be down the hall if you need me."

Sasha dug her fingernails into her palm to prevent herself from reaching out and touching him. Instead, she watched as he hurriedly left the room, and shortly thereafter, Sasha heard his bedroom door close. She resisted the feelings of despair and allowed her eyes to travel around the pleasant room. There was a large cherrywood bed and a matching dresser in the corner. An ottoman was next to a window, which looked out on a breathtaking garden. An entertainment center with a television and VCR was on one wall. A large raspberry area rug lent color to the hardwood floor. Nikki had found a spot close to the bed and was now resting comfortably.

Sasha settled on the bed and clasped her fingers together. *Privacy.* Terraine had given her exactly what she had thought she wanted. Now she was not so sure. "Be careful what you wish for," she murmured. Sasha nestled her head amongst the pillows and closed her eyes. Even though Terraine was only a few feet away, she found herself feeling inexplicably lonely.

Terraine paced around his room, for the first time in his life not knowing what else to do. Sasha was only a few feet away and it was killing him. Her stubbornness was driving him mad! He had never known a woman who was worth all the changes she was putting him through. The only thing stopping him from dragging her into his arms was pride. Yes, he wanted desperately to carry her bags to his room and have her share his bed again. He wanted to stroke and suckle her breasts until she shuddered with pleasure. He wanted to hear the sounds she made at the height of her passion. He wanted to see her hazel brown eyes staring at him as they rode the climatic wave together. But instead, he'd given her exactly what she wanted—to be left alone.

Wiping a sweaty palm across his pants leg, Terraine tried to figure out how he was going to survive the torment. He did not want to return to that fantasyland inside his head when the real thing was right across the hall. The past couple of days he'd spent fantasizing about her here, in this house, permanently. He'd fantasized about devouring her soft lips, about waking up curled alongside the curve of her hourglass body, and about the hours of pleasure they would spend as husband and wife. Now that he had her here, he was not letting her go. But first, he needed to bury the hatchet so that he could have a fair shot of convincing her that he truly loved her. Terraine slapped his fist against his palm. He had come too far to give up now, doggonit!

Terraine stuck his hands in his pockets and walked over and leaned against the door as he thought. Then a very simple idea popped in his head. It wasn't much but it was definitely a start. He scowled. Ms. Henry had already left for the day. Terraine shrugged. How hard could it be to steam some vegetables and broil a couple of fillets?

Sasha's eyes flew open and she looked around, suddenly remembering where she was. The instant her head touched the pillow she had dozed off, probably from feeling extremely safe within her surroundings. She had not slept a wink since her attack and had not realized how tired she had been.

As she curled into a fetal ball, she remembered that someone had broken into her home and had tried to assault her. Her home was supposed to be her castle and now she felt uncomfortable even being there. Someone had invaded her privacy and she was determined to find out who it had been.

The smell of the stranger's cologne was imbedded in her brain. It had smelled so much like Robby's. But was it Robby? Even though she had been unable to get a good look, the voice had been much heavier. She was also certain that the heavy body on top of her couldn't have been Robby, unless of course, he had gained an extra fifteen pounds while undergoing psychiatric treatment.

Stretching, Sasha released a loud yawn and looked over at the clock that read six o'clock. She rolled over to the end of the bed and looked down at the rug to see if Nikki was still lying there. Finding that she was not, Sasha sat up in the bed and swung her feet onto the floor. As she allowed her eyes to travel around the room, searching for her beloved pet, she suddenly smelled something burning. She rose from the bed and followed the smell to the door, then moved briskly down the stairs towards the kitchen. When she arrived, what she saw made her smile and stop in the doorway. The kitchen was completely covered in smoke and Terraine was wearing an apron and cursing something fierce while removing something charcoal black from the oven.

Sliding her fingers in the back pockets of her shorts, she cleared her throat delicately. "Need some help?"

Terraine turned to face her and saw the teasing light in her eyes. "I guess I've ruined my surprise dinner." Sasha walked over to the pan and sniffed the burnt item, jerking her head back at the foul smell, and held her nose.

"That must have been salmon." She leaned over the stove, lifting the lid off a pot and looked down at soggy brown asparagus. She raised her eyebrows and turned towards Terraine, who shrugged.

"You can't blame a man for trying."

Sasha could not hold her laughter any longer. "No. I guess I can't," she chuckled. "It's the thought that counts. I appreciate it."

Terraine grinned and turned to face her, pleased to hear her laughing. What would he have done if something had happened to her and he had not been able to hear her laughter or see the radiance on her face again?

He leaned against the counter. "Why don't I clean up and order a couple of pizzas?

Sasha nodded. "Sounds good to me."
They both laughed hysterically and then Terraine became very serious. "Come here," he command-ed and Sasha obeyed. Terraine reached up and brushed her cheek with his fingertips.

"Hear me out." He brought her so that she stood directly in front of him. "Looks are sometimes deceiving. Please believe that."

Sasha looked up into his brown eyes that were dripping with gentleness and felt her defenses weakening. Terralne pulled her into his arms and buried his face at the base of her neck.

"Don't shut me out of your life," he murmured. Her skin felt like satin and he could no longer resist her appeal. He'd missed her too much. His mouth captured hers and she opened her mouth willingly. Without releasing his mouth, he pressed her up against the counter, crushing her soft breasts against his chest. She locked her hands around his neck as their kiss deepened.

"I was going crazy without you," he whispered fiercely before recapturing her lips. "May I love you, baby?" He trailed his tongue along her neck while his hand traveled under her blouse and found her breast. His touch dissolved her stubbornness and left her feeling lustful. She silently prayed that what he said was true. His hand continued to caress her breast, finding her hardened nipple and twiddling it between two fingers.

Sasha arched and moaned as he touched her. "Yes!" she cried. She was pressed against the length of his hard body, immobilized. She couldn't move away even if she wanted to. He nudged her thighs apart with his knee and rubbed himself against her. Sasha was lost as an ache of sexual need coursed through her, reminding her that she had spent too many nights haunted by the memory of the two of them joined together to stop now. She could not deny herself what she was feeling. She knew what was going to happen and she welcomed it.

He slid her shorts, then her panties down around her knees. Sasha wiggled them down to her ankles and kicked them away, anxious to feel him inside her.

She fumbled with the zipper of his shorts, shoving down his boxers. She reached down and stroked his length. He growled against her cheek. Terraine lifted her off the floor, wrapped her legs around his waist, and thrust himself deeply inside her clinging warmth. She clutched him, bracing herself for the stroke after sensual stroke that accelerated into a fast, furious, rhythm.

"I love you," he whispered against her neck.

It ended too soon, in an explosion that jerked a harsh shout from her lips. He pinned her against the counter, feeling her pulsating around him as she screamed shouts of pleasure against his neck. Slowly, she slid down and he set her on her feet and planted small kisses along her neck and face. He then captured her face in his hands and looked at her with the beautiful brown eyes that she loved so much. "I love you because you are beautiful and sexy. I love you because you have a stubborn streak that drives me crazy. I love the way you lick your lips when you are nervous and the way your hazel eye shine when you are happy. I spend every waking minute wondering what you are doing and if you are okay and what you are thinking. The moment I set my eyes on your photo I think I fell in love with you."

"I love you too."

Terraine cupped her face in his hands and Sasha saw the excitement her confession had caused. He then scooped her into his arms and spun around in a triumphant whoop.

Terraine kissed her and carried her to his room where she belonged.

He is going to kill us.

The thought froze in Asia's mind, causing her to groan with exasperation. She grabbed onto the iron banister before climbing the narrow winding staircase, watching her feet as she stepped over crushed beer cans and trash. The staircase was dark due to broken light fixtures overhead; only limited sunlight peeped through the filthy windows.

Asia's dark eyes slanted in a frown as she glanced around at the graffiti spray-painted on the walls—relevant to the gang activity in the building. She hated the low-income building that her sister had been visiting for weeks. India was a part of the Big Brother/Big Sister program and the little girl she sponsored, Bianca, lived here. Asia preferred not to enter a building where the elevator never worked, but she had to talk to India before Daddy did.

India had quickly grown attached to Bianca in a few short weeks. Deana, her mother, gave birth to her at fifteen. Now five years later, Deana was afraid that she was missing something and spent more time chasing men and hanging in the streets than she did raising her own child. Yesterday she'd called India and asked her if she would mind watching Bianca while she went partying, which meant she probably would be sleeping off a hangover and would not be returning until later in the day. India had taken Duane with her after Asia reassured them both that she would be spending the evening with Tyler. Asia had promised to stay put until they returned. But then everything changed.

Asia's steps slowed as she pondered the situation at hand. India was going to be pissed at her and it wasn't even her fault. *Well, not really.* Asia chewed on her lower lip nervously.

How could she have known that Daddy was standing right outside her parents' bedroom door eavesdropping on her conversation with her mother? Asia dropped her shoulders and gave an exaggerated sigh. Her face burned as she remembered her dad grabbing the phone away from her mother and barking into the receiver, "Murders? What murders?"

Now a stab of guilt lay buried in her chest. Asia had promised India that she would not mention the murders to Momma in fear that Daddy would find out. And what had she done? She'd done the opposite. Asia had never been good at keeping secrets, especially not from her mother. Hell. The first time she considered sexual intercourse she called home to discuss it thoroughly with her mother. She had always been a momma's girl. India, on the other hand, was her daddy's girl and he kept close tabs on her. India had always been the wilder of the two but had never managed to pull the wool over their dad's eyes for very long. Now Daddy was

going to be on the next plane to St. Louis to take
both of his daughters back to Alabama. Their contracts with Diva Designs were about to be broken.
India had begged her not to say anything, and Asia
had let her sister down. She felt terrible about it.

As Asia reached the top of the staircase, a wave
of apprehension swept through her again. India
had to forgive her. The thought of her sister being
angry with her caused her insides to turn. India was
not only her only sister but she was also her best
friend. Confidently, Asia recycled the idea as
absurd. She knocked lightly on the apartment door
and gnawed her gum nervously while she waited for
her sister to answer.

After several minutes she knocked harder. She
knew they were in there because India's car was
parked out front with a club on the steering wheel.

"India, wake your butt up!" Her voice rang with
command. She put her ear to the door. Hearing
nothing, she knocked again. Asia reached down
and rattled the knob and to her surprise, it opened.
She drew a deep breath and straightened her
shoulders, quickly setting aside her hesitation. She
would handle the situation the same way she dealt
with any other problems she'd had with her sister.

Humor.

"Hel-lo," she sang as she walked into the living
room. "Goofy, you left the door unlocked. You must

have been really tired last night!" She laughed boisterously as she pulled the door shut, even though
she found it strange that Duane could be so careless. If anything, he had a tendency to be overly
cautious.

Asia stepped into the living room and turned her
nose up at the lumpy gray couch with two missing
pillows pushed in the corner against a filthy white
wall. She could not understand how anyone could
live like this, but the room was neat and tidy for a
change, though it smelled of Pine Sol and urine.
More than likely, India had cleaned it before she
went to bed.

Three cockroaches ran to hide as she walked
down the hall and Asia jumped. She could stand a
lot of things but roaches were not one of them. The
apartment was still except for the faucet dripping in
the bathroom. Asia walked quietly down the hall
past Bianca's bedroom, to Deana's room where
India was apparently sleeping. *I hope she changed
the sheets.* The door was slightly ajar and Asia
knocked lightly on the door.

"Hey girl, you got a man in there?" Asia was
barely able to keep the laughter from her voice as
she teased her sister. But then again, where was
Duane? No! Asia gasped and raised her hand to her
mouth at the possibility of her sister and Duane, the
bodyguard, gettin' it on in the projects. With that

thought in mind, she pushed the door open and stepped abruptly into the room, wondering if she'd catch a glimpse of his naked butt in the air.

"India, are you in..." The words lodged in her throat as shock swept through her body. What she saw made her stop dead in her tracks. In the middle of the room was a full-size bed—completely covered with rose petals—where a crumpled body laid face down in a pool of blood.

"Oh my God!" Asia managed no more than a hoarse whisper as she dropped unconsciously to her knees. Her eyes traveled to a bouquet of white roses sitting on the nightstand and now speckled with drops of blood.

The sounds of her scream shrilled like an echo in an empty tomb.

"I really appreciate all of you helping me move," Honey said as Terraine brought in the last box from the truck.

"No problem. I'm always willing to work for food."

Sasha smiled and shook her head. "Honey, you never should have agreed to cook dinner. It would have been cheaper to hire a mover," she commented playfully. Terraine lightly grabbed her arm and pulled Sasha close to him. They'd spent hours making love and he still could not get enough of the physical contact.

"Did someone say food?" Jay asked as he walked into the kitchen carrying a toolbox.

Sasha giggled. "See what I mean?"

Honey opened another box and frowned. "Well, at the rate I'm going, I probably won't be able to find the pots and pans that I bought. Any objections to me ordering Chinese instead?" Everyone shook their heads. "Good, it's settled. Now all we have to do is find the phonebook."

While they waited for the food to arrive, Jay took several boxes labeled MASTER BEDROOM upstairs. He placed the boxes in the corner of the room, walked over to the window and looked out at the playground equipment in the backyard. *She wants a family.* Why else would she need three bedrooms and a swing set? The discovery made him feel warm all over. Jay frowned. What difference did it really make; they were only friends. *But I thought she was not looking for a commitment.* Jay shrugged. Maybe she just wanted a big house and it meant nothing at all. But family was obviously important to her. During one of their numerous phone conversations, she had mentioned the close relationships she had with her brothers.

Jay wandered across the hall to one of the bedrooms and noticed that it used to be a nursery. There were tiny bears stenciled across the top bordering the room. Jay envisioned a white crib in the corner and a rocking chair not far away with Honey singing a lullaby, while a small infant suckled from her breast. Jay turned and walked out of the room. *What had gotten into him?* Babies, swing sets, stinky diapers, he did not want any part of that. He was a bachelor, for Christ's sake!

"What are you doing?"

Jay turned to find Honey walking up the stairs carrying an oriental lamp. He quickly pulled himself together. "I was looking around. You have a really nice house."

Honey beamed. "Thank you. I always wanted a home of my own."

"What do you plan to do with the nursery?"

Honey's face saddened and she spoke in a low voice. "I'm not sure. Probably make it into a studio." She then stepped into the master bedroom and placed the lamp in the corner on top of her dresser. She stood there for a moment thinking about what he had just asked her.

She did not hear Jay walk up behind her and he witnessed her pained expression on her deep tan face. "Are you okay?"

She turned abruptly and smiled at his handsome face. "Yes, just tired. Today has definitely

been a long day, but it was worth every minute."
She looked around the room and grinned with pride.

Jay was relieved that nothing was wrong. He
never liked to see a woman upset and he definitely
hated to see a woman cry. It broke his heart.

He looked around at the stack of boxes and the
unassembled bed frame. "You need some help
arranging your furniture?"

"What furniture?" She shrugged. "All I really
have is a bedroom set. The rest will be arriving next
week.

Jay's pager vibrated and he looked down at the
number and frowned. "Can I use your phone?"
Honey shrugged. "Like you have to ask. *Mi casa
es su casa.*"

"*Gracias,*" he answered with a smile and a tip of
the hat. He then trotted down to the kitchen.

So, he can *habla* a little. Honey wrinkled her
small nose. Was there anything that Jay wasn't
capable of doing? She reached down to retrieve the
small lamp and she carried it into the other room.
Before she could plug it into the socket, she heard
Sasha scream and the front door slam.

Chapter Sixteen

Asia was crying hysterically when Sasha and Terraine arrived at her hotel room. "It was terrible!" Asia shrieked after the two women embraced. "I have never seen so much blood in my life!" Sasha nodded and a hot tear rolled down her cheek. Ever since Jay got word that there had been another murder, she had been an emotional wreck. In the short time that she had known the twins they had become close like younger sisters to her.

Sasha noticed her red-rimmed eyes. "Where is... " Tears choked her voice.

Asia pointed to the adjoining bedroom. "In there." Sasha dropped her shoulders and turned to face Terraine, who was standing against the wall.

She stepped towards the room and met Jay standing in the doorframe.

Terraine saw the intense look etched on his brother's face. "Did you find out anything?"

Jay shook his head and frowned. "Not much."

Sasha took a deep breath and entered the bedroom. India instantly rushed over to hug her. "I was so afraid he had gotten one of you." Sasha sniffled. India's trembling body clung to her. "He would have if Deana hadn't returned."

The two women parted and Sasha looked at her colorless face before taking a seat on the end of the bed with her hands folded in her lap. "What happened?"

India ran nervous fingers through her hair and paced the floor. "I really don't know. Bianca couldn't sleep, so Duane and I got up early this morning and took her to breakfast at a fabulous little restaurant around the block." She paused and reached for a tissue to blow her nose. "I guess Deanna returned shortly after we left." India saw once again the scene that she would never forget: Deanna's slaughtered body crumpled on the bed and blood dripping onto the floor. She swallowed and found her voice again. "Asia found her body." She sniffled. "I can't help thinking that if we hadn't left, maybe she would still be alive." India sobbed again. "Or maybe that would have...have been me." Her voice had drifted into a slow whisper as she took a seat also on the bed. Sasha handed her a couple more tissues and draped an arm across her shoulders.

India wiped away the tears streaming down her face. "The police have been asking me questions all morning! I just can't understand why this is happening."

A loud voice was heard coming from other room. India rose and looked at Sasha with a look of relief. "Daddy's here."

Monday Diva Designs was swarming with cops. Jay was there to assist Terraine with the three-hour question and answer session. Afterwards, they went to a soul food restaurant in East St. Louis for lunch.

Jay leaned over the table and spoke in a low voice. "This is no longer a coincidence. There is something going on and I think it's personal."

Terraine rocked back in his seat. "Why would someone want to sabotage the corporation?"

"Money. Greed." Jay shrugged. "There are probably a million different possibilities."

"But only one right answer." Terraine sighed, allowing his frustration to show. "I've lost four models. Two to death and the other two to their father who took them kicking and screaming to the airport." Terraine scowled remembering their father, a dark overweight man who spoke so fast you missed half of what he was saying. But Terraine had to admire his love for India and Asia. He would have done the same.

When their food arrived, Terraine thanked the waitress and reached for the hot sauce bottle. "Diva Designs has been financially strapped the last two years. Why didn't Pops talk to me about it?" he asked with frustration.

"You already know the answer to that, stubborn pride. He was determined to make it without us." Jay gave a dry laugh. "Face it. Our grandfather was a jackass."

"Man, he needed me and I wasn't there for him." Terraine balled his hand in a tight fist. "I will never forget that."

Jay growled. "Tee, don't start beating yourself about something we can't change. You made the right choice. We both did. You want to know why? Because they were our choices not his. If Pops had his way, you'd be married to Natalia."

Terraine's eyes grew large. "Heaven forbid! That woman gets crazier by the day."

Jay shoveled a forkful of collard greens into his mouth. "She's just concerned about her future."

Terraine cut his eyes, not at all convinced. He was used to Jay defending Natalia even when he knew she was wrong.

"How's Sasha?"

"She is doing pretty well considering everything that has happened."

"Yeah, I bet that has her pretty shook up," he managed between chews.

Terraine nodded and bit into a piece of fried chicken.

"I've been trying to locate Robby Adams."

Terraine shook his head. "Sasha doesn't think that he is capable of murder."

"I'm not so sure, at least not until I have had a chance to investigate. He is protected by the state so his records or whereabouts are confidential."

"Did they ever locate Deja's boyfriend?"

"Yeah." Jay wiped his mouth with a napkin. "His alibi was airtight."

Terraine pondered another possibility. "What about Sylvester or Jacob Stone?"

"Possible, but right now I think anyone could be a suspect. Even someone working for the corporation." His voice rose an octave. "Any possibilities?" Terraine frowned and Jay shrugged. "Then the only lead I have is a bunch of damn roses."

"We are dealing with a romantic serial killer," Terraine conceded with a scowl.

"Or just a psychotic." Jay took a long swig of his Coke and pointed a fork in Terraine's direction. "Someone knows that you are going to succeed at getting this corporation off the ground and that person is determined to keep you from doing just that."

Feeling flushed, Sasha strolled into Terraine's office and moved over to the window, placing her hot cheek on the cool glass. She looked down on the city while she waited for him to return.

The police had visited the studio earlier that afternoon and Sasha did not feel she had been of much help at all. How many more people were going to have to die before it was all over? She already missed the twins and wished they hadn't been forced by their father to leave, but she understood his concern. Their lives had been in danger.

Fear rose in her throat. "Robby, where are you?" she whispered. Her warm breath fogged up the glass in front of her. Could Robby possibly be involved in all of this? If so, what was his connection? She trembled. What would have happened if Nikki had not been there? Would she have been added to the list of Diva murders? Sasha shuddered and moved away from the window. Death was knocking at her back door, and it too close for comfort. Sasha moved her head from side to side, realizing she was tenser than she ever imagined.

Sasha flopped down on the couch and pushed her hair behind her ear, knocking her gold loop from her lobe and down between the cushions. She reached down, searching for her earring, and was horrified by what she found.

A pair of tangerine thongs.

Terraine took his eyes off of the road long enough to study her face. Sasha had been so quiet since they left his office.

"Are you okay?"

She nodded. "Just tired." Tired of being made to look like a fool.

Terraine squeezed her hand, assuming that the events over the past couple of days had been more than she could handle. She appeared so tough but yet on the inside she was fragile and so freaking unpredictable. He silently groaned. He never knew how she was going to feel or react from one day to the next, but that realization kept their relationship interesting indeed. He stopped at a stoplight and stole a glance at Sasha, who had leaned back in her seat with her eyes shut. His lips spread into a thin smile. It had been a rough day and all he needed now was his woman in his arms.

But instead of following him to his room, Sasha walked down the hall, returning to the guestroom she'd occupied the day of her arrival and closed the door. Terraine stormed in behind her.

"What's going on?" his voice boomed while his eyes flashed with impatience.

Sasha took a seat on the bed and removed her shoes. "Why don't you ask Natalia?" she answered with heavy sarcasm, trying to mask the humiliation. She looked past him and focused on a Thomas Kinkade painting on the wall behind his head.

He was stunned by her comment. "I thought we had already gone over this," he said with outrage. Ignoring him, Sasha lay back on the bed and covered her head with a pillow. Terraine raised his shoulders at the curt way she'd dismissed him. "Forget it," he mumbled, then turned and exited the room.

The following morning Terraine came down to breakfast with Nikki by his side. Ms. Henry was sitting at the table drinking a cup of coffee. She looked up from her newspaper and turned to face him.

"They left about an hour ago," she said, referring to Sasha and Bernard. Ms. Henry brought her cup back to her lips and took a long sip before continuing, "I can assume from the looks on both of

401

your faces that you're having some problems. A shame, too. I was looking so forward to some little Andrews running around this stuffy old house again."

Terraine sat down across from her and reached for a fresh baked buttermilk biscuit and mumbled, "So was I. So was I."

"Sounds fine. Go ahead and run it." Terraine handed the press release back to Steven, then leaned back in his chair with a faraway expression.

Steven caught the look as he turned to leave. "You look like you've got something heavy on your mind."

"Yes, I do." He leaned forward in his chair and placed his hands on the desk in front of him. "But nothing I can't handle."

Steven lingered awhile longer. Terraine's distraction was evident in his behavior. He cleared his throat. "I've seen you and Sasha together on more than one occasion, and I'm curious if the two of you are involved?"

Terraine's eyes quickly focused on the man in front of him, who stood confidently in a midnight blue suit. Terraine was impressed with the calm approach with which Steven dealt with the media, but was now displeased with his inquiry into his personal life, namely Sasha. Terraine spoke in a cool tone, "Why do you ask?"

"Because she is an attractive woman and I would like to ask her out if I am not stepping on your toes," he answered matter of factly.

Terraine felt a tinge of jealousy brewing. He did not care if Sasha was mad at him today, she still belonged to him. His eyes blazed up at Steven and he spoke in as calm a voice as he could manage. "You'd be stepping all over my feet."

Steven raised a hand as a peace offering. "No problem. I just wanted to make sure." With that, he exited the office.

Terraine sat there for several minutes after he left, trying to decide what to make of his comment. Did this mean that he had competition? With rising anger, he began to wonder what Sasha's feelings were towards Steven.

Geri's announcement through the intercom cut the silence. "Terraine, you have a call on line two." He reached for the phone. "Terraine speaking."

"Tee, my man," replied a deep southern voice, which brought a smile to Terraine's tired face.

"Dwight Brown. What's up, brotha'?" He hadn't talked to him since his last visit to Dallas. They had been friends since the third grade, growing into manhood together. Then they had attended the same university, had pledged with the same fraternity and for the past decade they had continued to maintain their friendship.

"I'm coming to St. Louis on business next week and decided to stay a few extra days to spend some time with my parents and maybe even try to kick it with you." The Browns still lived in the same house that he'd frequently visited as a child.

"That's great, I can't wait to see you. We can catch up on old times." Hanging out with his homeboy was probably just what the doctor ordered—something other than murder and his fragile love life to occupy his time.

"Well, get your dancing shoes ready, 'cause I am ready to paint the town red! Y'all know how Dwight likes the ladies!"

"You can have them. I already have a gorgeous woman in my life that will make your mouth water," Terraine conceded with amusement.

Dwight laughed richly. "Not Playa Playa! You mean to tell me someone finally lassoed your behind?"

"Yeah. It seems that way. I'll tell you all about her when you get here. As a matter of fact, why don't the three of us go out to dinner?"

"I can't wait. She got any friends?"

"Yeah, she does." Terraine thought about it for a moment and the corners of his mouth turned upward at the perfect possibility. "I'll see what I can arrange for you. I know how it is when a brother can't manage to get a date on his own. On second thought, I guess I don't." He laughed.

Dwight groaned. "You crackin' on me already."

Terraine cackled. "I'll see you next week." He hung up.

He was still sitting there with a smile when Geri walked into his office carrying two submarine sandwiches.

Sasha walked through the marketing department and waved at Loren, who was chatting away on her telephone. She strolled to the large office at the end of the hall, knocked and waited for acknowledgement before cautiously sticking her head around the door. *You just never know what someone might be doing behind closed doors.*

"Is this a bad time?"

Looking up from his laptop, Carl signaled for her to join him. "No, please come in."

She stepped into his office. Sasha estimated it to be about a third of the size of Terraine's with plush mocha carpet and beige walls. Not nearly the same gorgeous view, but it was still nice. Sasha took a seat across from his desk. He reached for a file that was sitting in a neat pile in his box and passed it to her.

"I wanted you to see the layouts that my staff has proposed to market your designs."

Sasha eagerly opened the folder and looked down at a photo of herself wearing one of her gowns. "I didn't know you planned to use my picture in your advertising."

Carl looked over at her lips that were pursed tightly together. "I hope you don't mind but it was just an idea. I took a couple of the photos that Stefan shot of the four of you in your designs and they were too good to pass up." Carl noticed her right eyebrow rise a tad bit. "It is strictly up to you. But I think every woman wants to look and feel as beautiful as a model on her wedding day."

"Hmm, let me think about it." She did not want to project the message that one had to be a model in order to wear her designs. She thumbed through photos of the gowns from all angles, showing the exquisite quality of the designs. "Stefan did a wonderful job with these photos," she commented and realized *this is really it, kiddo. You have finally done it.*

Carl waved a hand. "You should be giving yourself the praise. These are your gowns."

Sasha felt warmed by the compliment. "Thank you."

"We would like to first try a few ads in publications, such as *Essence* and *Ebony.*"

Sasha nodded while still looking down at the marketing plan. Carl leaned over and pointed to a paragraph on page two. "At that point, we will be ready to hit all of the major bridal shops in each sales territory."

Sasha lifted her head slightly and a scent flooded her nostrils. Her head shot up abruptly as she remembered. She had smelled the same scent only days ago. "*Phaze,*" she whispered louder than intended.

Carl looked at her quizzically. "What?"

Sasha cleared the lump in her throat and met his eyes. "The cologne you are wearing is called *Phaze.*" Just for an instance, Sasha swore she saw a flicker of anger tighten his soft features before he gave her a candid smile.

Carl nodded. "You are good. My wife bought it for my birthday last week." He leaned back and clasped both hands behind his head. "Carmen says it used to be sold exclusively overseas and just arrived in the states a couple of months ago."

Sasha nodded as her stomach churned. "I know. I bought my ex-boyfriend a bottle when I worked in Italy."

Carl rubbed his chin sheepishly. "I thought I'd wear it and beat all the other brothers to the punch.

I guess I can't expect to be the only one smelling this good for too long," he smirked. He met her eyes and was surprised by the pained expression on her face. "Is something wrong?"

Sasha shook her head.

Carl looked over at her for several seconds, still unconvinced, but decided not to pry and to continue with the meeting. "Okay, well, I have two other layouts that I would like your feedback on." He held them out towards her and Sasha shook her head, placing a hand on her stomach.

"Suddenly, I'm not feeling so well, can we do this another time?"

Carl looked worried. "No problem. Is something wrong? Should I call Terraine?"

In all of the time that she had seen Carl in the hallways or even in the studios he had always been cordial and friendly. There was a gentleness about him that she'd seen firsthand, but today she was feeling ill at ease. Maybe it was the mysterious deaths, or the fact that he smelled too much like Robby. Whatever the case, she was blaming it on the cologne.

Sasha shook her head. "No, I just need some fresh air." She then dashed out of his office.

Honey was in her office signing checks for her receptionist to mail later that afternoon when she heard a light tap on her door.

"It's open," she said without looking up from her desk.

"Happy birthday, Honey."

She slowly raised her head at the sound of Jay's low, harmonious voice. He was standing in front of her desk dressed casually as usual in a pair of blue jeans shorts, red cotton T-shirt and running shoes. A smile stole on his face and her heart did a flip-flop. He was too fine. She pinched her leg under her desk in order to regain her composure. It was not until then that she noticed the small cake he was holding in his hands with a single lit candle in the middle.

Her eyes grew wide with surprise. "How did you know?"

He grinned with a cocky smile. "ESP." Honey rolled her eyes and he chuckled. "Truthfully, Tee mentioned that he owed you one and I was more than happy to repay his debt." Smiling, Honey remembered the day she and Terraine had met.

She pushed away from her desk and walked around to where he was standing. She stood in front of him with both hands planted on her waist. "How did you know I liked chocolate?"

"Sasha told me." Jay looked directly at her and

smiled, showing a perfect set of white teeth.

Ignoring the charm, Honey took another step forward, removed the cake from his hand and set it on her desk. "Please, have a seat." She pulled a chair from out of the corner and placed it in front of him. Jay sat down and rested his elbow on his knee. "Let me find a knife and some napkins."

Jay watched her move over to a small sink in the far right corner of her office and reach down into a cabinet. He cocked his head to the side to capture a view at a different angle. Honey was wearing a pair of cream slacks and a soft pink blouse that showed off her cute little curves, and on her feet were the smallest pumps he had ever seen. He ran a sweaty palm across the back of his neck. Why was it every time he was around her he wanted to pick her up and carry her on his shoulders? He had not seen her since the day he helped her move into her new home. He'd missed her and had raked his brain looking for excuses to come by and see her lovely face again. He was glad that they had developed a friendship and understood where the other was coming from, but lately he had to question his motives.

"Here it is." Honey walked back over to the desk carrying a small knife and cut two large pieces. "Mmm, this looks good." She turned and faced him. "Did you make it yourself?"

Jay stared into her beautiful eyes and had to force himself to look down at the cake. He shook his head. "No, Ms. Henry made it for me. Cooking is not something I have mastered yet. All I seemed to be able to do is boil hot dogs."

Honey chuckled and handed him a slice of cake on top of a paper napkin. "Now how do you plan to impress a woman if you can't cook?"

Jay took a bite of his cake before answering. "I prefer to wine and dine her and let someone else do the cooking." Honey nodded her head knowingly while she chewed and took a seat on the end of desk with her feet swinging in the air.

"Are you celebrating tonight?"

Honey shook her head and dabbed her mouth with a napkin. "Sasha and I are going to see a play on Thursday. I planned on spending this evening painting my bedroom." She looked down and brushed crumbs off her lap.

Jay balled up his napkin and tossed it towards a trashcan in the corner, missing by an inch.

"Your shot stinks," Honey commented as he walked across the room to retrieve the napkin. He leaned over, granting her a clear view of his rear. *Too fine.* There wasn't anything that she did not like about his looks.

"You think you can do better?" he challenged as he returned to his chair.

"I know I can do better." She held out her hand. "Give it to me." Jay handed her his napkin and Honey shot it across the room and into the trash.

"Lucky shot."

"Lucky?" She raised her brow and poked herself in the chest. "I will have you know that I was more than a cheerleader. I have brothers and spent many years playing with them in our backyard."

Jay grinned at the image of her running across a basketball court. "How about a rematch tonight? We can go to the 'Y,' shoot a few hoops, then go to your house and I'll help you paint. We can even grab a couple of pizzas on the way." *Just as long as I am spending time with you.* When she did not answer right away, Jay crossed his arms across his chest. "Unless of course you are chicken," he challenged.

Chicken! She wasn't afraid of anything. *Except maybe him.* "It's on." She pointed an index finger in his direction before hopping off the end of her desk. "Now get out. I have work to do." She walked back behind her desk and returned to her chair.

Jay watched her and smiled. "You think you are tough. It is about time someone brought you down a peg or two. I'll pick you up at seven." Without another word, he left.

Honey wore a smile the rest of the afternoon.

He paced with heavy agitation around the small room. He had to protect her. He had to no matter what the cost. They were trying to hurt her and he could never let that happen. No matter what.

Vengeance is mine.

He raised his hands to cover his ears. "No!"

Yes! Yes! She is your entire life.

He nodded. He idolized her and her beauty. He cherished her like a piece of expensive china that was kept on the top shelf. Never to be touched. Only to be viewed and admired.

"But I can't do this."

Yes, you can and you will. Laughter. Hysterical laughter. He pressed his ears tighter, refusing to hear anymore. The voices. The antagonizing voices. He folded his arms across his stomach and buckled over. The voices were driving him mad. He wanted to call her but he was certain his phone was bugged, besides he would know. He knew everything.

"No more, please!" he begged.

A masculine voice roared with a fit of laughter.

Protecting her made him happy and if that meant death, so be it.

Terraine slammed down the phone and slumped in his chair.

Sasha was gone.

Sasha had packed her things and returned to her house. Did she hate the sight of him so much that she was willing to risk her own safety? Ms. Henry assured him that she'd departed accompanied by Bernard, but even so, she wasn't nearly as safe as she had been with him.

Terraine closed the spreadsheet that he had been working on. This was not supposed to be happening to him. He had planned for her to stay with him for eternity. According to Ms. Henry, eternity had ended this afternoon.

Rising from his chair, Terraine took a seat on the couch. Deep in thought, it took his mind several seconds to register something sticking out of the side of the couch. He reached down and pulled out the tangerine thongs and immediately remembered that Sasha had been sitting in this same spot last night. Admitting his own stupidity had never come easily but this was one time he was going to face it head on. Terraine grabbed his briefcase and marched down one floor to Natalia's office.

Tiffany tried to stop him before he barged into Natalia's office but he raised a hand telling her *don't even try it.* He found Natalia sitting at her conference table across from Jacob Stone.

Terraine was seeing red and glared over at him. "What the hell is he doing here?"

Natalia raised her brow. "I thought this was my office and I could invite whomever I wanted."

Jacob crossed his leg and leaned back in his seat. "Hello, Tee."

Terraine ignored him. His temper flared and he tossed the thongs onto a chair. "Try a stunt like that again and you will find yourself in the unemployment line." Terraine turned and exited the office hastily, wanting to find Sasha as soon as possible.

A few minutes later, he climbed into his Navigator and sped out of the lot. Terraine scowled. He had reacted unprofessionally. *Why do I let her get to me like that?* Terraine sighed with frustration and he ran a red light. He had put Sasha through too many changes and he needed to apologize immediately. He had been unfair and he blamed himself for starting their relationship on the wrong foot. He had lied to her and then was caught with Natalia in his arms. Following that, she'd found a pair of undergarments in his office in exactly the same spot they'd made love on numerous occasions. How could he possibly expect her to continue to trust him when he allowed himself to be found in compromising positions? He rotated his neck to release some of the tension. Damn, he was stressed!

He turned a sharp curve, pressing down on the brake and suddenly realized all too late that something was wrong.

"I guess walking Nikki is out of the question?" Sasha looked at Bernard's expressionless face with a sheepish grin. He returned the look with an expression that read, *You're kidding, right?*

He nodded. "But if you'd like to go out in the yard with her, I'll stand by and watch."

Sasha rolled her eyes and opened the slide door. "Come on, Nikki." She was so sick of having Bernard around even though she knew she needed him in order to feel safe. At least he was a nice guy. Sasha stepped out onto the patio, taking a seat in a chair, and watched her dog run around the yard. What a carefree life it was to be a dog. They did not have to worry about being hurt by love.

Drawing her legs up in the chair, she looked up at the beautiful clear sky. The sun lay low and she watched as it set to the west. Sasha dropped her eyes and sighed. She knew she was too stubborn for her own good, but she was tired of feeling like the victim, and most of all, she was tired of feeling that she could not trust Terraine. She loved him, but was love enough to keep two people together?

She turned her head and looked over at Bernard who was standing guard. He was so quiet that sometimes she forgot he was even there, allowing her time to be alone with her thoughts. She looked straight ahead again and watched Nikki dig a hole in the ground and sighed. How much longer was this going to last? After she left the studio she'd had Bernard take her back to Andrews Manor so that she could gather her things and return home. Sasha dropped her head onto her knees. Home no longer felt like home to her. Home was where her heart was and her heart was with Terraine.

The loud ringing of the phone returned her to reality. Sasha dashed into the house to answer the phone with Bernard close behind.

"Sasha, honey, what are you doing at home?" Roxaner asked with a note of exasperation.

Sasha groaned inwardly. Tomorrow she was buying a caller ID box. "I live here, Mother."

"Sasha Renee Moore, I know all about what has been going on and if you don't go back to Terraine's house right now, I am going to—"

"Mom, my other line is ringing, hold on," she said hurriedly before pressing the flash button on her receiver. "Hello?"

"Sasha, it's not wise for you to be there." It was Jay. Terraine must have put him up to calling her. She was not going back no matter how much he begged.

"Bernard's with me."

"There has been an accident. Terraine is in the hospital."

While Bernard drove, Sasha prayed. *Please, God, let him be all right.* She sat with her hands balled into tight white-knuckled fists. Jay had been so vague over the phone that she had no indication of what to expect, except that Terraine had been in a car wreck. Sasha was grateful that Bernard was quiet as usual. As her heart pounded rapidly, she was trembling violently. All she could think about was seeing his beautiful dimpled smile again.

Sasha rushed down the corridor, sickened by the smell of antiseptic, and spotted Jay at the end of the hall sitting on a bench.

"How is he?" Her breath caught in her throat.

Jay nodded his head. "The doctor just returned with his labs and x-ray results. Other than a slight concussion and a few cuts and bruises, he's going to be okay. They are stitching him up right now." He tilted his head towards the door across from them. "We should be able to go in shortly."

"Thank, God!" Sasha felt a shiver of relief run through her and she sat down next to Jay on the bench and waited for her heart rate to slow down.

"What happened?"

"Someone cut his brake line." His voice sounded grim.

"W-what!" She whipped her head around and faced him.

Lines of concern were visible across his face. "I guess my brother was next on his list."

She swallowed hard and blinked. "You think it was the same person that—?"

"I know it was." His voice broke and she witnessed a muscle at his jaw quiver angrily. Without saying another word, Jay rose from the bench and strolled down the hall, trying to recapture his composure. Sasha watched him leave. His brother's near death had upset him more than she could ever have imagined.

Sasha turned towards the nursing station where she heard a familiar voice and looked to see Natalia speaking rudely to the receptionist. Sasha rose and Natalia immediately noticed her and swayed in her direction.

"Where is he?" she demanded.

Sasha pointed towards the door and spoke softly. "He's in there. They'll let us visit him in a few minutes."

Natalia allowed her eyes to travel over her face annoyingly. "That rule only applies to you. Unlike yourself, I am family." She then tossed her a mechanical smile before pivoting on her heels and pushing through the door just as three people wearing scrubs exited the room. Sasha's temper flared and then died. Terraine did not need this right now. Besides, she was not in the mood. She would deal with Natalia's attitude some other time.

With slight hesitation, Sasha followed Natalia and paused outside his room. She just wanted to catch a glimpse of him before she left, just to be sure that he was okay.

Terraine felt as if a ton of bricks had landed on his head. He had a deep gash over his eyebrow where he had hit the windshield on impact and had just endured twenty-three painful stitches. Someone had tampered with his car. He was certain of it. And as soon as he was released he was going to find out who it was.

"You're going to be just fine but I think we need to keep you overnight for observation," the doctor said with reassurance before he closed his chart and headed towards the door, followed by his nurse and a medical student.

Terraine shifted in the bed. *Whoopee!* A night in the hospital. He needed to be at home with Sasha right now in his bed. All he could think about from the moment they'd loaded him onto a stretcher until they stitched his forehead was Sasha and how worried he was. She was not safe at home, especially after someone had tried to kill him. He probably would have noticed something was wrong with his car sooner if he hadn't been so intent on getting to her house and swinging her over his shoulder to carry her kicking and screaming all the way back to his house. Terraine slumped down in the bed. He needed her support right now.

The door was pushed open and in strolled Natalia sporting a lime green designer suit with matching shoes. "Oh, you poor baby!" she cooed. She rushed over to his side and touched the bandage covering his forehead. "I came as soon as I heard." She hugged Terraine, despite his rumbling protest. Natalia was the last person he needed to see. Where did his brother go?

"Natalia, we need to talk."

Her fuschia lips curled. "Not now, Terraine, you need your strength."

"No, we need to do this now."

She dropped his hand and waved hers in the air. "All right, if you insist."

"It is obvious that you feel threatened by my relationship with Sasha."

"Threatened!" She chuckled nastily. "You are out of your mind. One thing I do not feel is threatened where she is concerned." She shook her head in disgust.

"So why the stunts? Why do you insist on playing these games? Showing up at my office in your underwear and when that fails you stuff your panties in the seat of my office couch for Sasha to find."

She placed a hand to her chest and gasped. "D-did she find them?"

Terraine raised his brow at her dramatic interpretation. "What do you think?"

"Well...I didn't mean to cause you problems." She looked at him with an innocent expression but there was no evidence of remorse in her voice. She clicked her tongue. "I just want you to realize what we had."

"Natalia, you and I have never had anything. It was all in your mind. You crawled into my bed one night while I was drunk and the next morning you pretended that we had sex. Lucky for you I was too wasted to remember. Then you took it a step further and faked a pregnancy in hopes of me marrying you. You knew that Pops would be outraged and would not have it any other way. You used us both and caused a ridge between us."

She pouted. "What else could I do? You ignored me and flaunted all of those other women in my face. You wouldn't give me the time of day."

"You were like a sister to me, for Christ's sake!"

"You don't get it? I am sick of being your sister.

I want to be your lover! Don't you see? I want to be the woman that causes that twinkle in your eye."

Terraine's expression stilled. "It will never happen. I love Sasha."

Natalia flinched at the painful words. "Fine... as long as my future is secure."

"It's secure."

She raised her chin with dignity, her face so grim it looked as if it were carved of stone. "Good. Do you need anything while I am here?"

He shook his head. "No. I'm fine." He was not surprised in the least by her quick recovery. It just proved how easy it was for her to toss him aside in exchange for her career.

She adjusted her purse and pulled her shoulders back. "Then I am leaving." She sashayed towards the door, giving him one last chance to look at what he was losing. It was his loss, not hers. She walked out the door and shot Sasha a hostile glare. "I bet you are just eating this up," she sneered before walking towards the elevators.

Sasha tried to calm her racing heart. After hearing everything, she would never forgive herself. She had been quick to judge once again and had almost run the risk of losing Terraine forever. She rushed through the door.

He sat upright in the bed and spoke calmly, trying not to let his excitement surface. She had come to see him. "I guess you heard my conversation."

Adoringly, she stared at him for several seconds. Terraine looked as if the world had turned upside down and had taken him tumbling with it. But he was still gorgeous. Sasha nodded, her eyes bright with hope. How could she have allowed herself to misjudge him?

Sasha stepped closer, her eyes fastened to him, watching his raisin brown eyes twinkle. She sat beside him on the bed. "Are you okay?"

He took her hands in his and raised them to his lips. "I'm fine." She studied him for a moment taking in the bandage over his left eye, the bruises on his cheek and his swollen lips. "Now that you are here."

"I was so scared." Suddenly she had to kiss him. She placed a hand to his cheek and pressed her lips against his. He cupped her face and brushed her lips lightly, experiencing the familiar tingling sensation. She drew in her breath and brought her lips down on his again, more strongly this time.

Moments later, she laid her head on his chest. "Terraine, I think it is time I told you about my past." He slowly stroked the back of her head. "According to my doc, I am not going anywhere tonight, so I have nothing but time." He was glad that she was finally opening up to him. Progress was finally his.

Chapter Seventeen

asha rushed across the street to where Honey was standing in line outside the St. Louis Black Repertory Company.

"Sorry I'm late. I spent the afternoon fitting girls for the show."

Honey shook her head. "I don't know how you find time for modeling, designing and a personal life."

Sasha beamed with happiness. "Where there is a will, you find a way. I have no complaints and couldn't be happier." Terraine had been released yesterday afternoon and they'd spent the remainder of the day in each other's arms sharing their secrets, expressing their concerns and confessing their love for one another. That night Terraine forgot all about his bruised ribs as he made love to her with all of his strength and Sasha clung to him, crying with joy. Today she felt calm and at peace.

"I see." Honey smiled at her starry-eyed expression before looking over her shoulder at Bernard, who was following a few short feet away. She waved at the homely looking man with the super fine body and with a toss of her hair she turned back around. She was going to have to remember to ask Jay where he found his employees.

Sasha handed the lady at the window their tickets. "I tried to call you to wish you a happy birthday but you weren't home. Which one of your friends got the pleasure of spending the evening with you?" she teased.

Honey looked off to her right and answered in a nonchalant tone, "I was hanging out with Jay."

Sasha's eyes lit up. "You two have gotten pretty chummy lately. What's up with that?" She winked and nudged her with her elbow.

"*Nada.*" Honey pushed the double doors open, and Sasha and Bernard followed her into the theatre.

"What do you mean, nothing?" Sasha looked over at Bernard who seemed amused hearing the two of them discussing his boss. Sasha moved closer to her. "It has got to be something," she said in a lower voice as they climbed the stairs to the balcony.

Honey shook her head and gave her a stiff smile. "We have a lot of fun together, end of story." On her birthday, just as Jay had suggested, they shot baskets at the 'Y,' then went back to her house. But instead of painting, they had spent the evening munching on pizza and talking about their lives. Honey truly enjoyed herself. She found Jay to be charming and funny and unspoiled by his wealth. He tickled her with fascinating tales involving cases he was previously involved in. It was long past midnight when he decided to leave and Honey hated to see him go. Yesterday she'd spent most of the day thinking about him after he called her office to see how she was doing. She spent the rest of the evening thinking of all the reasons why she could not be involved with Jay. When she rose this morning, frustrated after a restless night, she came to the decision that she needed to keep some distance between them. She was feeling things that she could not afford to feel and already had a date for the Fourth of July with a resident physician named Chris.

"I can't understand what's wrong with you. He's a great guy." Sasha sealed the statement with a wide smile of approval.

Honey frowned with annoyance. "There is nothing wrong, Sasha. I am just not looking for a relationship. I enjoy being friends."

"Remember I said the same thing several weeks ago," she reminded.

"Yes, but I'm not you," Honey mumbled as they were ushered to their seats.

Bernard sat in the row directly behind them. Having known his boss for over three years, he found the possibility of Jay being seriously involved with any one woman quite amusing.

"Sorry I'm late."

Jay looked up as his old partner, Detective Chad Hamilton, slid onto the bench across from him. Jay took another last swig of his coke and wiped his mouth with the back of his hand. "No problem. What you got for me?"

He reached into his briefcase and removed a manila folder. "I checked out the lead you gave me on the flowers and you were right, a dozen white roses were sent to all three models, including Deja."

Jay leaned forward and looked through the invoices. He was not at all surprised by the confirmation, "Do you have any idea who purchased them?"

Chad shook his head and leaned back on the

bench. "Nope, they were all cash transactions sent through the mail."

Jay slammed his fist on the table. "Damn, this guy is good!" He had been so certain that this was the lead that was going to blow the case wide open. Jay sat back in his seat quietly for several moments while the waitress returned and took their order. "There was one more bouquet sent."

Chad shrugged. "It was probably a cash transaction also."

Jay nodded with a puzzled expression. "Maybe, but check on it anyway just to be on the safe side." He was certain that the roses were the killer's calling card. Jay raised his glass to his lips and looked over to his left. What he saw caused him to choke on his drink. He reached for a napkin to wipe the folder off.

"Hey man, you okay?" Chad asked.

"Yeah... I'm fine." Jay looked towards the door and watched Natalia leaving the restaurant holding hands with Jacob Stone.

Sasha was not sure if his health was strong enough to attend her reunion that weekend but Terraine insisted, deciding that home cooking was just what he needed to cure his splitting headaches.

Fourth of July weekends were always the largest day of the year for reunions and the Simon family held theirs in Forest Park. Following the spread of food and numerous nosey inquiries about her relationship with Terraine, everyone drove down to the riverfront for Fair St. Louis, held annually under the St. Louis arch and hosted by vendors from all across the city. It always featured live entertainment, and this year's performers were the Temptations. There was no way that Roxaner was going to miss them. She pushed her way as close to the platform as possible. Which was no easy task with over one hundred thousand spectators in attendance. They had traveled from as far away as Michigan to hear the live concert, to witness the fireworks display and to sample St. Louis' famous sweet sausage on a stick.

Sasha and Terraine found a comfortable spot under a shade tree and she leaned against his chest as they listened to the crowd sing along with the words to "Just My Imagination."

"Why don't you invite me in?" he asked in a suggestive voice.

Honey held her breath and counted to ten while she tried to remember why she'd decided to go out with this arrogant fool in the first place. *So you'd forget about Jay.*

Honey reached into her purse and retrieved her keys. "Not tonight, I'm tired. Maybe some other time," she said for the fourth time. Chris was either hard of hearing or just plain stupid.

He placed a hand on her waist. "Since you didn't want to go see the fireworks, you could at least let me stay for a few minutes." He gave her a sly grin. "We can make our own fireworks."

She flinched and shoved his hand away. "I said no!" she snapped.

He leaned forward and slurred, "I love it when a woman plays hard to get."

Honey debated using karate on him. After her rape, Shaquil had her take lessons just so she could handle herself in situations like this. Chris had obviously had one too many to drink.

She tried to keep her voice light. "Listen, it is late and I am not in the mood for games." She attempted to wiggle past him but he closed in on her and pinned her to the door.

"Neither am I. Let's go in and get down to business." He lowered his head and planted small kisses on her neck. Honey tried to push his bulky body away but was unsuccessful and was afraid that she might have underestimated him. He was a doctor, for Pete's sake! Honey sighed inwardly and reached down until she found what she was looking for and squeezed really hard until he released her.

"Ow! You stupid bitch!" He buckled over in pain.

"You brought it on yourself," Honey returned coolly before turning her back to him long enough to open her front door.

"I'll teach you to ever touch a man there again!" He lunged for her, but before he could grab hold of her arm, Jay came up behind him and latched on to his wrist.

"You heard the lady," he barked in a deep voice.

Chris swiveled around and faced Jay. "Who the hell are you?"

"A friend." Jay took two steps closer and challenged his glare. "If I were you, I'd leave before I am forced to finish where she left off." Jay stared the guy down. It did not take long for Chris to realize that Jay meant what he said.

"She ain't worth it," he sneered. He strolled quickly down the sidewalk, climbed into his Camry and drove away.

Honey stood on the steps with her mouth wide open in disbelief. Jay had defended her honor, just like her brothers would have if they had been there. Jay turned towards her and climbed the stairs. He stopped in front of her and allowed his fingers to run sensuously down her arm. "You okay?"

Damn, that felt good! Honey shut her mouth

and swallowed, greeting the look of concern in his eyes with a smile.

"Sure." Anxious to break the contact, she turned and walked into the house, tossing her keys onto the table. "You know, you didn't have to come to my rescue. I could have handled him myself."

Jay smirked and followed her into the kitchen watching the sway of her hips. "Sure you could."

Honey turned and faced him with a defensive frown. "You don't think I could?"

"Honey, I don't think there is anything you can't do." He looked her over. She was dressed seductively in a short red dress with thin straps and matching high heels. "But dressed like that you are asking for trouble."

"Dressed like what?" she challenged.

Jay tore his eyes away and pointed to her dress. "Like that. You aren't even wearing a bra."

Honey waved her hand dismissively and walked past him, brushing a firm bosom against his arm. "You don't know anything. You can't wear a bra with this kind of dress." She reached into the refrigerator and retrieved two Cokes, handing one to Jay.

He reached out and took the can. "Then why wear it?" he asked, not at all ready to end the discussion.

"Because I like this dress." Honey shook her head and headed to the living room and kicked off her heels. "You are beginning to sound like one of my brothers."

Jay let his eyes linger over her appreciatively and felt a twinge of jealousy that she had dressed like that for someone else.

Honey sat on the couch with her feet curled underneath her. "By the way, what are you doing over here tonight?"

"I was in the neighborhood." He had driven by hoping to see a light on in her house when he had noticed the strange car. He'd decided to park two houses down and see who it was before he knocked on the door. Then he'd heard her voice and instantly knew what was about to go down.

Her brow lifted. "Jay, you live on the other side of town. How could you possibly just be in the neighborhood?"

He shrugged. "I was working on a case. Besides, I wanted to see how you were doing." He knew that he was probably giving her the wrong impression. He should keep some distance between them but the truth of the matter was that he could not stop thinking about Honey and he'd needed to see her.

"So what do you want to do tonight, Scrabble, Nintendo or *Nick at Nite?*"

Jay took a seat next to Honey on the couch. "*Nick at Nite.*"

She reached for the remote and turned on *The Jeffersons,* then leaned over to kiss Jay gently on the cheek. "Thanks for being there," she murmured with her breath warm against his cheek.

He turned and looked at her with a boyish grin, his heart pounding in his chest. She was so close that he was tempted to turn her face and kiss her again, but this time with passion. "You're welcome." Jay tried to convince himself that it was not desire he felt, that he was only interested in being friends. They sat side by side with their shoulders touching as they passed the evening away.

As she waited for the metro link train, Tyler realized how stupid she had been to attend Fair St. Louis alone. Well... she hadn't really been alone. She had met her girlfriend, Gail, whom she went to high school with in Manhattan. Gail was now living here managing the human resources department of a large manufacturing plant. Gail had stuck around long enough for them to wait in line an hour for sweet sausages on a stick and listen to half of the Temptations' performance before the crowds got the best of her and she left to go home to her husband. Tyler had found a nice spot under a tree by herself and listened to the rest of the act, not mov-

435

ing until the fireworks display was completed. It had been a beautiful declaration of red, white and blue launched through a cannon off a boat on the river. Tyler had boarded the train, glad to get away from the crowded riverfront. The metro link was a lifesaver. It let her off one block from the Chase Park Hotel, where she was sharing a room with her mother. Rebecca had always managed her daughter's career.

Stepping onto the ramp again, Tyler climbed the stairs to the street level, hopped on a shuttle bus that was waiting and rode it down Kingshighway to Maryland Avenue. She loved this area of St. Louis. There was Forest Park on one side, million dollar historical homes to the west and to the north St. Louis city, which was infected with drugs and poverty. She took a deep breath thankful for the things the Lord had blessed her with and was suddenly in the mood for a latte from Lakota's.

She strolled up the well-lit street patronized by dozens of college students that lived in the apartments in the area. There was Latino music playing in the cafe and several young people were swaying their hips to the beat.

Tyler ordered a turtle latte and took a seat out front enjoying the evening breeze and taking advantage of the opportunity to clear her head.

The entire situation at Diva Designs had the makings of a motion picture. That was for sure, but she didn't worry about death. She believed that only God knew when it was time for her to go and when she did, it would be His way. She did not need a bodyguard to watch over her shoulder everywhere she went.

"Hey stranger."

She looked up at his mysterious eyes and her face split into a wide grin. "Steven, what a pleasant surprise."

"I should say the same for you." He pointed at the chair across from her. "You mind if I have a seat?"

She waved her hand. "No, go right ahead. As a matter of fact, I would enjoy the company.

He smiled across at Tyler as he sat down. "Good, so would I."

Chapter Eighteen

Terraine slammed his fist on the table and barked, "What do you mean someone is following her?"

Rising from his chair, Jay walked over to the kitchen counter and returned with several photographs that he placed in his brother's outstretched hand. "This car was seen following her from the theatre. That same car was seen the next day parked out front of her house."

Terraine gritted his teeth and looked down at pictures of a blue Ford LTD parked only a few feet away from Sasha's home. "Why didn't one of your men question him?" He ripped out the words impatiently.

Jay leaned against the wall and rubbed his chin.

"And let him know that he is being watched? No way! We need proof first. I don't think he even knows yet that she is staying with you."

Terraine set the photos down on the table and turned to his brother with a look of frustration. "Did you get a license plate?"

"Yes, it is a rental registered to a Mr. Leon McKinley."

A combination of anger and fear knotted inside him at the possibility of someone trying to harm Sasha, his woman. The thought tore at his insides. "Do we know who he—" Terraine stopped and propped his hand under his chin. "Why does that name sound so familiar?"

Jay took a step forward. "You think you know him?"

"I don't know but I heard that name just recently." He looked out at the dark sky. "I just can't put my finger on where."

"Try to remember." Jay took his seat again. "In the meantime, I have a friend at the precinct checking on it for me."

"Oh come on, Honey. You owe me big time!" Sasha spat into the receiver.

"How do I owe you?" Honey asked suspiciously.

"How soon we forget," Sasha mumbled as she lay back onto the bed. "You could not have possibly forgotten all of the blind dates I let you talk me into."

Honey twirled the phone cord around her finger. "Yeah, I guess."

"You guess!" Sasha laughed with a hint of hysteria. "What about Darryl with the big forehead?" Honey chuckled. Several years ago, Sasha had done her a big favor by going out with the cousin of a guy she was dating at the time. Honey hated to admit it but he was ugly with a capitol 'U'. "Yeah, I forgot about him."

Sasha clicked her tongue. "And buck-tooth Byron. His teeth stuck so far out of his mouth, I thought I was having dinner with Bugs Bunny."

Honey smiled and propped her feet on the coffee table. "I forgot about him too."

"And country Calvin, with the weak rap and the big gap. Don't forget big lip Robert, and—"

"You've proved your point," Honey cut in with a snort.

Sasha smiled at the animosity she heard in her voice. "So, should I take that as a yes?" she sang merrily.

Honey sighed. "Yeah, sure."

She knew her best friend would not let her

down. "Great, we'll see you at six!"

Honey hung up and groaned.

"What's eating you, boss?" Geri asked as she strolled into Terraine's office with a stack of checks for his signature.

Terraine rocked back and forth in his chair in dazed exasperation. Ever since he'd met with Jay at his condo last night, he could not get the name Leon McKinley out of his head. In fact, long after Sasha had fallen asleep, he lay awake trying to figure out the connection. "I am trying to remember why someone's name sounds so familiar."

She walked over towards his desk. "What's the name, maybe I can help you." Names were one thing she was good with; numbers were a different story.

Terraine's eyes traveled to her concerned face. "Leon McKinley."

Geri let the name roll around in her head for several moments, then shook her head. "No, I'm afraid it doesn't ring a bell with me. But I can run it through our database if you'd like."

Terraine rubbed the back of his hand across his mouth, then sat forward in his chair and clasped his hands together. "Yes, please do."

441

"No problem, boss." She smiled, hoping to ease his mind. She was worried about him. With all of the tragic events happening that were connected to the corporation, she was even beginning to doubt its future. But she was proud of Terraine for stepping in after Richard died, just as Richard always wanted. He would have been pleased, because in spite of their differences, he had loved his grandson dearly. She had tried so many times to get Richard to mend his fences with his grandson, but he had been too stubborn for his own good. "Here, these checks just came up from accounting." She placed them in his in box and exited his office.

Terraine's frustration level had reached its maximum level, and he would be glad when all of this was over. He decided to remove his worries from his mind and began signing payroll checks. While Pops was alive, checks were processed and printed through accounting, then stamped with his signature block. But until their current financial situation was under control, Terraine wanted to keep a tight rein on all transactions and double check everything financial before processing, including payroll.

He reached over and took a long swig of his cola, looked down at the name on the paycheck in front of him, and nearly choked. Staring at him was a payroll check made out to Leon McKinley.

Humming softly in front of her sewing machine, Sasha took several minutes to realize that someone had entered the room. She turned around in her seat and faced the brothers' grim expressions. Her heart sank as she planted her hands tensely in her lap. *Please, Lord, not another murder.* The first person to come to mind was Tyler. Sasha had tried reaching her without any success for two days and was beginning worry about her. *Then that would only leave me.*

"What's wrong?" she managed to ask in a shaky voice.

Terraine moved in closer. "Jay found out who sent India those flowers."

Sasha exhaled and placed a hand against her rapidly beating heart. *Thank God!* "I thought the flowers were all cash transactions?"

Jay shook his head. "Not this time. He used his credit card."

"Who is he?" she asked with rising uneasiness.

Terraine came over and dropped a large palm to her shoulder. "Robert Adams," he answered with emphasis.

Sasha eyes grew large with surprise. "R-Robby bought those flowers?"

He nodded. "He has also been working at Diva

443

Designs for the past several weeks as a janitor
hired under an assumed name."

Sasha barked with disbelief. "You've got to be
kidding." For a long moment Sasha looked at
Terraine expressionless as she found herself
searching for a believable explanation. Robby
could not have possibly been responsible for all
those deaths. She shuddered inwardly at the
ridiculous thought. No way!

Jay walked over and leaned against her sewing
machine. "No, I'm afraid not. I spoke to his supervisor this morning and he described his appearance, which is identical to your description of
Robby. Then I took the social security number off
his application and had it run through the DMV
database. It came up with Robert Adams. We
know him as Leon McKinley."

Sasha slid down in her chair and lowered her
lashes. "Oh my, God! I can't believe this."

Terraine's brown eyes came up to study her
face intently. "Neither can I, sweetheart."

Her eyes shifted nervously from Jay to Terraine
as she searched their expressions and noticed their
identical long faces. They should both be wearing
smiles for cracking the case, unless of course...
She quickly sat upright again. "Have you arrested
him yet?"

Jay dropped his shoulder and his expression

hardened. "No, unfortunately we have not. He must have known that we were on his trail because he has not reported to work in three days. We do have an APB out on him and his rental car but nothing has turned up yet."

Terraine knelt down beside her, placing his hand lightly on her knee. "Right now I am concerned with your safety."

Sasha shook her head wildly. "Robby would never hurt me," she defended.

Terraine stared at her with disbelief. "How can you say that after he attacked you in your home?"

She chewed nervously on her lower lip and mumbled, "I still am not sure it was him."

Terraine reached for her hand and stroked it lightly. "My housekeeping supervisor described Leon with a bulkier body than you described." His eyes widened with concern. "Does that help to convince you?"

Sasha was quiet as what he implied began to register. Robby a killer! It was hard to digest. She had been so sure that she knew Robby better than anyone else and that there was no way he could have killed those people. Sasha swallowed the dismay that was lodged in her throat and she rose slowly from her chair. "I need to lie down."

Terraine saw the pain in her eyes and felt a second of jealousy as he knew her thoughts were centered on a man who had once captured her heart. He couldn't understand his own reaction, especially when he knew it was painful for her to believe that a man that she once loved could be responsible for such a hideous crime. Sasha was a compassionate and caring woman and he wouldn't expect any less from her. Disappointed by his reaction, he quickly nodded in agreement. "Sure, sweetheart. Let me help you to the room."

The next afternoon after a vigorous workout in the weight room, Terraine and Jay headed to the locker rooms to shower and change.

Jay unlaced his shoes. "How's Sasha holding up?"

Taking a seat on the bench, Terraine answered, "Trying not to act scared. She puts on a brave front but I see through it."

"That's understandable."

Terraine wiped his towel across his head, catching beads of sweat that were streaming down his face. "But she's tough. Besides, I've found ways to take her mind off her fear." He rubbed his chin with a cocky smile.

Jay returned the grin. "I'm sure you have. Things seem to be working out in your favor."

"Besides that nut running loose, everything is great. As a matter of fact, after all of this is over, I am going to try and convince Sasha to stay with me permanently."

Jay turned his head abruptly. "You're serious?"

Terraine gave him a crooked smile. "Couldn't be more serious. I'm prepared to spend the rest of my life with her if she'll have me."

Jay whistled. "Wow. This is serious."

Rising, Terraine walked over to his locker. "Yes, and I can't wait to introduce her to Dwight tomorrow."

A gleam of interest shone in Jay's eyes. "Out-of-sight Dwight is stopping through?" Jay had known Dwight almost as long as his brother and was well aware of his reputation as a lady's man.

Nodding, Terraine dialed his combination. "Sasha and I are taking him to dinner tomorrow night."

Jay chuckled. "I doubt he is going to want to spend an evening watching the two of you all over each other."

"Believe me. He'll be preoccupied." Terraine gave him a mischievous grin.

Jay couldn't imagine Dwight traveling accompanied by a female unless of course, like Terraine, he had changed. "How so?"

"Sasha has arranged for Honey to be his date

for the evening." Slamming his locker shut, Terraine headed towards the shower with his towel and a bar of soap. The look of disappointment on Jay's face went unnoticed.

"You've been quiet ever since we left the showers. What's up, Lil Bro?" Terraine looked at Jay with concern. He'd known him long enough to know when something was bothering him.

"Nothing." Jay shook his head, unaware that his brows had drawn together in an angry scowl. "I was just thinking about the case." It was none of his business whom Honey went out with. They were just friends, nothing more.

"How much longer you think it'll be before he's found?"

"I don't know. Right now all we can do is wait. Robby can't hide forever. He'll eventually show up." He slipped into a pair of sweats. He needed to snap out of it, maybe even go out on a date himself. "Maybe I need a night on the town. A little relaxation might do me some good," he said more to himself than to his brother.

Terraine stuffed his sweaty clothes into his gym bag. "You know you are more than welcome to join us tomorrow. We'll probably dine at Max's Steakhouse."

"Nah, I don't think so. But I will try to catch up with Dwight before he leaves town. I'll talk to you tomorrow." Swinging his bag onto his back, Jay walked out the locker room without another word.

Terraine climbed into his car minutes later, still puzzled by his brother's behavior.

He was cute. No, he was handsome. Medium brown complexion, light brown eyes, a sexy smile with perfect, pearly white teeth, and a small, neatly trimmed mustache. He was tall with a solid build and dressed nicely in a pair of khakis, a peach polo shirt and brown loafers with designer socks.

Honey decided to drive her own car so that when she was prepared to leave she could, and Dwight rode to the restaurant with her. She picked him up at his parents' house and he greeted her with a single red rose. He appeared to be the kind of guy that any woman would be dying to take home to momma. So why was she not the least bit interested? Honey blew her breath on the window. She knew why, she just was not prepared to admit it.

Terraine had already made reservations for the four of them, so they were escorted to a large table in the back. Sasha sat directly across from Honey and tried to get her attention. Honey was well aware that Sasha was dying to find out her impression of Dwight, but instead of easing her mind, she picked up her menu and hid behind it.

"What are you going to have?" Dwight asked. Turning in his seat, he smiled down at Honey.

She shook her head indecisively. "I'm not sure. Probably prime rib and steamed vegetables."

Closing his menu, he placed it lightly on the table. He turned to study her face and gave Honey another dazzling smile. "That sounds good. I might have the same."

Honey looked up at him. "What's wrong, you can't handle their porterhouse steak?" she teased.

Dwight beat on his chest like Tarzan and his smile deepened into laughter. "I can handle it."

The waitress arrived with water and granted them a few more minutes to look over their menus. Shortly after she left, Terraine rose from his chair. "Dwight, it looks like Jay made it after all."

Honey lowered her menu and glared over at Sasha, who shrugged, looking just as surprised as she was. Honey turned as Jay came over to the table and Dwight rose to grabbed him in a bear hug.

"It's good to see you again." Dwight smiled and gave Jay the once-over.

"You too," Jay said to Dwight, and then his eyes moved over to Honey.

His smile radiated across the table and she greeted it with a smile of her own. She was instantly taken by his dress attire. When they went to the movies or out to lunch he wore shorts and a t-shirt but tonight he looked as if he came straight off the cover of *Ebony Man* magazine. He wore a royal blue rayon shirt that was tucked neatly into a pair of navy blue dress slacks. Honey's eyes traveled up to his neck where he'd left the top two buttons of his shirt undone, exposing a solid chest tastefully decorated with a gold Turkish chain. Honey's mouth watered and she was about to ask him to sit to her right when she realized he was not alone.

Standing next to him was a beautiful female with prominent Indian features: broad nose, bronze skin and long, silky black hair that was pulled into one long braid that hung halfway down the middle of her back. She wore a white dress that looked as if she'd been poured into it. It hugged every curve and emphasized her ample bosom. When she placed a possessive hand on Jay's arm, Honey dropped her eyes to the table.

"Why don't you guys pull up a chair?" Dwight suggested.

Sasha and Terraine moved over so that Jay and his date, that he introduced as Nina, could sit next to each other. Jay was now sitting directly across from Honey.

All through dinner Honey's eyes were on Nina, who laughed at every joke Jay told and made it her business to whisper in his ear any chance she could. Jay seemed to enjoy the attention, smiling back at Nina and patting her hand, which was still clutched on his arm. What did she care? Honey thought. She played with her food, overcome by a sinking feeling in her stomach. She sneaked an occasional glance at Jay and looked away quickly when he caught her. Several times during the meal Honey felt Jay's eyes on her, and though she tried to ignore him, eventually she would look up and their eyes would lock. Then his luscious full lips would curl into a smile. She dragged her eyes away and turned for the tenth time and half-listened to a conversation that Terraine and Dwight were having about a fraternity party they held during college.

She was jealous. Plain and simple. *Didn't you make it clear that you were only interested in being friends?* But she suddenly realized that somehow during all of the time that they'd spent together, Jay had somehow become an important part of her daily life. She had gotten used to him coming around fixing a latch on her door or helping her put up shelves in her living room. Why did things have to change? Couldn't things stay the same without feelings coming into play? Unfortunately, it wasn't that simple and she did not like it.

"Will you excuse me, please?" she whispered. Dwight rose and pulled Honey's chair out for her so that she could escape to the ladies' room.

"Thanks." She walked quickly away and entered the room, finding it empty. She leaned against the mirror, briefly shutting her eyes, and took several deep breaths. Certain that Sasha would be following her, she then rushed to an empty stall and closed it, counting to three. Sure enough, she heard footsteps.

"Honey, are you in there?"

She quickly rattled the toilet handle. "Yes, Sasha. Where else would I be?"

"Are you okay?"

"Not really." *I'm just jealous of Jay's date.* "My stomach has been bothering me all day. Don't worry about me, I'll be okay."

Sasha was quiet for several seconds and then cleared her throat. "I guess this is a bad time to ask you what you think of Dwight?"

Honey forced a laugh. "Yeah, I would think so, but your timing has always been a little off. He's gorgeous."

"That's all I needed to know." Honey could hear the smile in her voice and was pleased. "I'll see you back at the table."

Honey listened to the door shut behind her. She unlocked the stall and walked over to the vanity and stared at her reflection.

Because of life's funny tricks, she would never be able to give a man the thing that he'd want most in life—a son. She had come to terms with that weeks ago but lately it had really begun to bother her, and seeing the friend that she had grown attached to in the arms of someone else was making it even worse. Honey gave a dry laugh and reminded herself again that she had a lot to be thankful for, a booming business, a beautiful new house and her health. Honey straightened her hair and forced a smile on her face before exiting the room. Startled, she found Jay waiting outside the door.

"I thought I would check on you." He gave her a curious look. "Sasha said you weren't feeling very good."

"I am okay now." Honey tilted her head and saw the heartrending tenderness in his expression.

"Good. I couldn't have anything happen to my homegirl."

Honey smirked. "Funny." Jay stepped forward, placed a hand to her shoulder and squeezed it lightly. Honey looked up and searched his beautiful chocolate face, feeling her control slipping away again.

Jay eyes moved over her body seductively and back to her eyes, taking in the tasteful pink dress that was cut above her knee and draped her breast and trim hips. There was so much he wanted to say to her. There was so much he wanted to do. He had watched her every move during dinner as if committing it to memory and knew he should have come alone. Bringing Nina had been a last minute decision. He did not want to be the only one without a date. But as he looked down at Honey, he felt a rush of desire and a strong, agonizing need to pull her into his arms and remove the sadness from her large gray eyes. He tried to assess her unreadable expression. Something was bothering her. She said it was her stomach but he was sure it was something else. Could it be that it bothered her as well to see him with someone else? He looked down at her and watched her eyes search his with equal intensity. She smiled but something in the set of her shoulders and her downcast eyes told him she was sad.

"Honey..." He stopped, not really sure what he was about to say to her, but knew it was time that he said something. Then he noticed Nina swaying over towards them with a tight smile.

"Jay, darling, there you are." She draped her arm around his waist, staking her claim, and turned fixed, frosty eyes on Honey before smiling up at Jay again. "Your food is getting cold," she cooed.

Jay gave Honey an apologetic smile and allowed Nina to lead him back to their seats. Honey stood against the wall and watched them for several moments after they left, trying to pull herself together.

When she returned to her seat, Honey engaged in idle conversations with Dwight but did not miss the jealous, sideward glances that she was receiving from Nina. Honey wasn't worried. She could handle Pocahontas; it was Jay she found herself up against that scared her. She was in no way blind to his attraction nor her own.

Honey made it a point to talk to Dwight privately every chance she got and did not object when he draped his arm across the back of her chair. She knew that Jay was watching her and her face flushed, but she made it her business to ignore him.

Jay and Nina were the first to depart. Honey felt a certain sadness as she watched them leave the restaurant. While Terraine took care of the bill, the rest of them prepared to leave.

Sasha watched Honey's face as they walked. "What's gotten into you, girl?" she whispered in her ear. It was so unlike Honey to be so withdrawn.

"Why does everyone keeping asking me that? I said I was fine!" Honey snapped. Sasha pressed her lips together. She wasn't buying it. There was a lot more bothering Honey than a stinking old stomach ache, but until she could get her alone, she would have to accept her answer.

On the ride to his parents' house, Honey was quiet, but Dwight kept the conversation going. He owned a hotel chain in Dallas that was branching out east. She was glad he dominated the conversation because she did not feel like talking. Instead, she kept picturing Jay and Nina together.

Honey pulled in front of the house and left the motor running. "It was a pleasure meeting you tonight, Honey," he said in a deep baritone voice. "I would like to see you again before I leave. If that is possible?"

"Sure, I'd like that," Honey said with little enthusiasm. Here she was sitting in the car with a fine black brotha' and all she could think about was Jay.

"I'll call you." He leaned over to kiss her, but Honey cleared her throat and lightly patted her chest.

"I think I'm catching something."

He caressed her chin. "Next time."

By the time Dwight shut the car door and strolled across the grass, Honey had decided she was being ridiculous. Dwight would be a perfect diversion. Lightly tapping her steering wheel, she watched him close the door behind him. Hmm. Maybe she hadn't really given him a chance. "I don't think so," Honey muttered after a second. She pulled the car back on the street and shook her head as she reached the corner.

Across town, Jay shut the door to his condo and tossed his keys onto his coffee table. He could not believe he'd survived another evening with Nina. She was really nice but usually wore out his nerves before the evening was over. She had been highly disappointed when he took her home instead of back to his place. Tonight he was not in the mood for sex. Being with her did not appeal to him as it once would have.

Jay kicked his shoes off in the living room and sat down on his black leather couch, lighting a cigarette, and suddenly conscious of the silence of the room.

Going out tonight had been a bad idea. He had never known what jealousy felt like until tonight. Seeing Honey sitting next to Dwight had burned him up. No, he was not interested in being anything but friends with Honey, but he found himself not wanting to see her with anyone else either. But the more he said it to himself, the less he began to believe it. He liked everything about her from the top of her head all the way down to her manicured fingernails. He was never bored around Honey. She breathed light into his dull life.

He rose and walked back to his bedroom, hoping for a decent night's sleep without dreaming about Honey the entire night. But he was certain that task would be damn near impossible.

Sasha slipped off her pantyhose and hung them over a chair as Terraine was coming out of the bathroom.

"Dwight seems like a really nice guy."

"Yeah, we've been friends for years," he said as he placed his watch onto the dresser. "He seemed to really hit it off with Honey."

Sasha frowned over at Terraine. "Hmm, I don't know. She seemed a little distant tonight, not her usual self." She unzipped her dress and it fell to the floor.

"She seemed okay to me." Terraine walked over to Sasha in time to help her unhook her bra. "Baby, let me do that." Standing behind her, he freed her breasts, then curled his fingers around them gently, teasing each nipple between his fingertips. He pressed his body against the curve of her back and rotated his hips against her buttocks, making Sasha aware of his need. With a low giggle, Sasha twirled and wrapped her arms around his neck as he continued to caress her breast with bold gentle strokes.

"I'm going to have to call her tomorrow," Sasha whispered as the heat rose between her legs. Then all her worries about Honey passed right over her as she concentrated on Terraine's hands that had traveled down past her navel.

"You do just that," he mumbled. Terraine dropped to his knees and began kissing the insides of her legs. She released a moan. He then parted her thighs and found himself lost in paradise.

Chapter Nineteen

Sasha pulled her Mustang in front of her house, then peered out the window with skepticism before reaching over and patting Nikki on the head.

"He shouldn't be too mad. At least I brought you with me," she muttered, but thinking about how Terraine would react if he found out gnawed at her confidence. *He won't ever know.* In any event, Sasha looked carefully around on both sides of the street before she climbed out of her car. The coast was clear. Blowing out a whistle of relief, Sasha laughed out loud. It was the middle of the day, for crying out loud! Besides, she wasn't really alone. She had Nikki with her. Yet and still, tearing at her insides was the lie that she'd told Bernard this

461

morning, informing him that she planned on spending the day at Andrews Manor and did not need his services. Now she was beginning to wonder if maybe she should have brought him along. After all, a murderer was still on the loose.

Sasha shrugged the apprehensive thought aside and pushed her shoulders back. "Come on, Nikki." Obeying her command, the dog jumped off the seat of the car and followed Sasha up the steps. They entered the front door together. It wouldn't take more than five minutes for her to grab the bag of vanilla silk threads that she needed to finish a tea-length gown for this weekend's show.

Sasha walked into the living room and stopped in her tracks, overcome by emotion. Her house looked tiny in comparison to Terraine's spacious home. But it was still her home. Not being able to be here was ridiculous.

Nikki trotted into the kitchen straight to her water bowl. Sasha followed and laughed.

"You miss home too, don't you, girl." Sasha poured fresh water into her bowl and then reached into her refrigerator where a six-pack of diet soda was sitting on the top shelf. She popped a top and quickly put the can to her lips. It had been a scorching afternoon and she'd reneged on letting down the top on her convertible—something Nikki had quickly grown accustomed to—because of the ninety-degree weather forecast. Sasha brought the ice-cold drink to her lips again, then walked over to the table and quickly flipped through her mail lying on the table. Jay had assigned someone to patrol her home, which included bringing in the mail each day.

She strolled down the hall to her sewing room and immediately found the plastic container under a bolt of fabric. Sasha propped her hands on her waist and shook her head. No wonder Terraine had missed it. When he came to remove her sewing machine, she gave him instructions to bring two plastic containers filled with embroidery needles and thread. He had only been able to locate one and now she knew why.

She picked up the container, returned to the kitchen and found Nikki running around in the backyard. Puzzled, Sasha set the container on the counter and walked over to the patio door.

"How did you get out there?" she asked aloud.

"I let her out."

Her eyes widened and her mouth dropped open as she swung around, completely caught off guard at the sound of his silky voice. There he stood against the refrigerator, looking as handsome as ever. His face was fuller than she remembered, and just as Jay had informed her, he was carrying about fifteen extra pounds. She sucked in her breath and had to admit it complemented his physique quite well. His sandy brown hair was still worn short and faded on the sides. He was also dressed much the same as always, freshly starched khaki slacks and a white button down shirt. The only difference was in the way she felt. No longer was there that deeply painful longing. Her feelings of love had been replaced with pity.

For some reason she stood insanely still and everything was quiet, so quiet that she could hear her own heart hammering in her chest. She had waited for this moment, curious as to how she would react to seeing him for the first time in almost eight months, and now the moment was here. Fear, no, she was not afraid; instead, what she felt could be categorized as surprise. She wondered why, especially since Robby had always been unpredictable.

"Robby,...how did you get in?" She spoke in a low, uneasy voice.

"It wasn't hard." His eyes traveled the length of her, unhurriedly, before returning to her face. He frowned. "I don't bite, Sasha. Please, have a seat."

Sasha slowly lowered herself into a chair at the kitchen table without taking her eyes off him. They were finally face to face and she wasn't sure what to say.

Robby walked over to the counter and rested against it. "We need to talk."

No kidding! Sasha nodded in agreement. "I think so too." She placed her hands in her lap and her anxiety level increased while she waited for him to stop staring at her intensely and begin speaking again.

Robby smiled as his dark round eyes drank up the presence before him. "You look as beautiful as ever."

"Thanks," she responded with a crooked smile of her own. His comment in some strange way relaxed her for what was to come. A part of her still did not want to believe that the handsome man standing across from her with the boyish face that she once loved could possibly be a serial killer. *There had to be some kind of reasonable explanation.*

Robby pushed away from the counter and for several seconds paced a small path a few feet away from her with his right hand pushed deep inside his pocket before speaking in a troubled voice. "There have been a lot of things happening lately." He stopped and looked over at her with eyes brimming with passion. "And I feel partly responsible, especially when all I have ever wanted was the best for you, nothing less. I hope you can understand that." He looked at her from under a sweep of long lashes that women yearned for.

Sasha searched anxiously for the meaning

behind his words but turned abruptly toward the sliding glass door that Nikki was now beating her paws against.

Robby strolled over to the door and slid it open, allowing Nikki access in the room. "I see someone else cares about your welfare as well." He knelt down and stroked the back of her head.

Sasha watched his exchange with her pet as if they were already long time friends. *How strange.* Then Sasha remembered the anonymous notes taped to her mirrors and swallowed while realization washed over her. Maybe they already knew each other.

"Robby, did you kill those people?" Her voice had dropped to a whisper but he heard it.

Robby chuckled and stood up, placing his palm to his chest. "Sasha, I am hurt. I thought you knew me better than that."

Sasha folded her arms across her chest. "You didn't answer my question."

Robby took one look at her stubborn expression and burst out in a hearty laugh. "Sasha, you haven't changed a bit."

"Neither have you," she mumbled. Still the charmer, Robby had always had a way of getting around giving her a straight answer.

He smiled and his eyes glittered mysteriously. "I'll make a deal with you." He leaned back casually against the counter again and crossed his ankles. "You tell me about your relationship with Terraine Andrews and I will tell you whatever you want to know."

What did her relationship have to do with this? In Robby's case, everything. "My relationship is none of your business," she snapped. His expression stilled and she knew he wasn't going to give her anything if she didn't cooperate. She studied him for a long moment, then her eyelids lowered and she looked down at her hands. "I don't feel comfortable talking about Terraine."

"Why not?" He laughed bitterly. "You *are* living with him."

Sasha sighed, sounding exasperated, not at all surprised by his actions. "You've been spying on me."

Robby made tsking sounds with his teeth. "Sasha, Sasha, you are underestimating me again. I love you."

She darted her tongue across her lips and spoke from her heart. "And I care about you." She rested her chin in the palm of her hands and stared up at his face, praying that this time he would understand. "Once you were the most important person in the world to me, but I've moved on and you need to understand that."

He gave her a distasteful look. "How can I when

I need you in my life?"

Against her will, Sasha's hazel eyes misted. "I don't want to be needed. I need to be wanted."

Robby folded his arms across his chest and sulked like a child, a habit that Sasha once found cute, but now obnoxious.

"I hope we can stay friends."

"Friends listen to one another. But you chose not to listen to me when I warned you to stay away from Terraine." His voice rose an octave.

"But why, because I care about him?"

"No, because the Andrews men are a bunch of murderers! Now heed my warning and stay away from him," he demanded.

Sasha blew out a deep, irritated breath.

Robby scowled at her reaction. "Who do you think killed those woman?"

"W-who?" she asked quickly.

He looked a little surprised by her question. "An Andrews of course!"

"What!" she screeched, frustration ringing in her voice. "This is getting ridiculous. Two models, a security guard and a young mother were all murdered. Terraine survived a car accident and someone tried to rape me in this house!"

"What?" It was Robby's time to be baffled, and he looked as if the wind had been knocked out of him.

"You heard me." She was still trying to sound tough while hot frustrated tears streamed down her cheeks.

He eliminated the distance between them and knelt down beside her. "I am so sorry, Sasha. He promised me he would not touch you."

Sasha quickly wiped her eyes. "Who is he?"

Robby shook his head. "I am so sorry. This is all my fault." He kept shaking his head and reached for her hand. "All I wanted to do was protect you from all the people who were trying to hurt you." He raised his left hand to her cheek and wiped away a single tear. "You are so beautiful. I would give my own life to spare yours," he said in a soft, desperate sounding voice.

Sasha looked at his glassy eyes and snatched her hand back. "Okay Romeo, snap out of it! I want some answers and I want them now!"

Robby looked as if he had just awakened from a bad dream. "What do you want to know?"

"Who killed those women?"

There was a long painful silence and Sasha knew what his response was going to be before he even turned to face her with the saddest look she'd ever seen. In an attempt to block out the truth, she raised her hands to cover her ears but not before she heard his confession.

"Me."

Before she could question him further, Jay and several uniformed cops came rushing though her front door.

Jay walked up to Robby. "We got you." Robby's hands were handcuffed behind his back.

Robby took one last look at her before turning away. "Sasha, I never thought anyone would get hurt."

The officer tightened his hold. "You better watch what you say without your lawyer present. You have the right to remain silent. Anything you say..." While his rights were read, Robby was hauled out the door and into the back seat of a patrol car.

"You okay?" Jay sat next to Sasha and patted her hand.

She nodded, then chewed on her lower lip. "Yes, I'm okay. But Terraine is going to be mad at me."

"Being mad is an understatement," Terraine barked as he came through the front door. Sasha smiled innocently, and rushed into his comforting embrace. "Thank God, you are okay."

She pulled back so he could see her face. "How did you know?"

"Sorry, Sasha." Jay wore a sheepish grin. "I called him when I saw your car in the yard.

I've been following Robby all day and when I

found him parked in front of Terraine's house this morning, I knew he was up to something."

"I am glad that it's all over." Terraine squeezed her tightly to him.

Was it really? Sasha just wasn't sure. Why did she have to always feel so sorry for Robby? Sasha stepped out of Terraine's arms and faced Jay. "Are you certain that Robby is responsible for the deaths?"

Jay nodded. "We are positive. We had him identified by the twins. His fingerprints were all over your house. The roses were purchased by him and he was seen in Deja's hotel the day before her death." He strolled over to her coffee table and removed a small device from underneath, holding it up for her to see. "And thanks to this little device, we now have a confession."

Sasha sighed, still feeling unconvinced. Maybe it was just the stress catching up with her.

Sasha and Terraine went to the Hill, an Italian community on the city's south side for dinner. Terraine believed a celebration was in order. Sasha tried not to think about the sadness she felt over Robby's arrest, but she was having a difficult time picturing him as a killer.

On the drive home, Terraine glanced over at her with a concerned frown. "Are you going to be okay?"

"Yeah, I guess. I just wish..." She sighed with resignation. "It's over. Why am I dwelling on it?"

Terraine nodded with a relieved smile and reached over and caressed her cheek. "Yes, it is. Now we can celebrate the projected success of the new lingerie line." Sasha shivered. The fashion show was only three days away. "I'm hoping that I will finally be able to pay my dues to my grandfather."

Sasha stroked his hand. "Terraine, I'm sure that he is in heaven smiling down at you right as we speak."

He touched the side of her face, letting his fingers stroke through her hair. Her words had touched his heart in a way that he needed most. "That's why I love you so much." His expression conveyed the seriousness of his words.

Sasha slid her hand sensuously across his thigh. "Actions speak louder than words." Feeling wicked, she wrapped her arms around his neck and left a trail of kisses down his cheek, neck and around to the opening of his shirt.

"Sasha, I can't drive! You are dangerous," he cried with the intensity of his own desires.

"You just keep your eyes on the road and let me

take care of the rest," she purred, feeling an over-whelming sense of power. Sasha unbuttoned his shirt and lowered her mouth. Her tongue seared a wet circular path around his nipples. Terraine released a throaty groan that caused her heart to flutter in her chest.

Her fingers moved slowly and arousingly. She was slowly killing him and his body was screaming at him. Not able to control the car, he pulled over on the side of the road and reached for her, kissing her hard yet tenderly.

"I haven't done this since high school." Excitement apparent in her voice, Sasha reached down and unbuckled his pants, releasing him and stroking his pulsing length slowly and effectively. Terraine threw his head back against the headrest and gritted his teeth as he tried to control his rising desire while her fingers sent tantalizing jolts through him. Though they had made love this morning, already he felt passion rising in him like an erupting volcano. He wanted to bury himself deep inside of her again. With Sasha he would never have enough.

"Come here," he commanded. He placed his large hands on her waist and lifted Sasha into his lap so that she faced him, her thighs straddling him, and on contact, he groaned with anguish.

Terraine reached for the buttons on her shirt and

undid them, opening her blouse to her waist. He leaned in and suckled her breast gently, bringing it quickly to a hardened peak. She could not bite back the shriek released from her lips. Terraine then bunched her skirt up around her waist, wanting unbarricaded access to her most private area and reached down, ripping her panties off.

Sasha gasped. "Terraine!"

"I'll buy you another pair," he murmured before capturing her other nipple between his lips. Sasha arched her body and her breath came in long, sur- rendering moans as her heart hammered against her ribs. Terraine grasped her buttocks and pulled her close. Sasha ground against him until Terraine thought he was going to burst. His hands moved downward, skimming both sides of her inner thighs, finally finding the moist core between her legs. The soft dampness tempted him beyond measure. He was rock hard, the blood pounding in him so fierce that he felt it throbbing throughout his entire body. Not able to bear it any further, he lifted Sasha up and buried himself inside her deep embrace, caus- ing a tidal wave of passion to rage through both of them. Their bodies met in magnificent harmony as a shudder rocked them both to a private world of ecstasy.

It had been too easy. He could feel it in his bones, Jay thought as he crossed the street in the direction of his car while puffing on a cigarette.

Nothing was that easy. Even though Robert Adams, a.k.a. Leon McKinley, was behind bars, he had a strong feeling that there was still some unfinished business. The reason was motive. What did Robby stand to gain by murdering models or sabotaging Diva Designs? His only connection was Sasha, and she had not begun the ad campaign until after the first murder.

Jay moved swiftly, taking long strides. He should have headed home hours ago. Now the moon was perched on a tree overhead. It was no wonder why he didn't have a personal life. But this was personal. Diva Designs business. Next time something happened, he'd be ready.

The next morning Sasha pulled into the parking lot late in the afternoon. Terraine had already been at the office most of the day. Following the intimate evening they'd spent in each other's arms, Sasha had decided to take the morning off and now was running late.

She climbed out of the car and removed several dress bags from her trunk. Dress rehearsal would begin in an hour, and she was looking forward to the entire thing coming to an end. It saddened her to know that Deja and Monet would never get to see the success of the new product line, and it bothered her to know that both of their deaths had been senseless. There had to be something Robby was not saying and she needed to find it out. If anyone could get Robby to talk, it was she.

The elevator door opened and Sasha collided with Steven.

"Oh, I am so sorry!" she gasped, then groaned inwardly. She did not want to repeat riding in the elevator with him again. Thank goodness, he had ridden down and was probably on his way to lunch.

She stepped into the elevator and pushed the button to the third floor. Steven moved to the side and lingered inside the elevator.

"Weren't you getting off?" she said, not trying at all to mask her dislike for him.

If he noticed, he sure didn't let it get to him. "No. Actually I forgot something in my office. So, I'm riding up again." The doors shut.

Lucky me. Sasha looked up at the numbers that indicated each floor and prayed that they would get there as quickly as possible. Something about Steven was unsettling and she wanted to be as far away from the man as possible.

"I saw two of your designs earlier; they were gorgeous," Steven complimented.

"Thanks." She managed a small smile for his benefit.

"If I were getting married, I'd want my bride to wear one of your creations."

She nodded with a plastic smile. When they reached her floor, Steven used his hand to block her departure. Sasha bore her eyes into him as he gave her a slick smile.

"Terraine told me you were off limits. What do you have to say about that?"

She met his eyes unflinchingly. "That I am off limits." She pushed his hand aside and passed.

"Shucks, my loss, I guess," he smirked as the elevator doors closed.

The models were preparing for rehearsal and Sasha decided to shake off the feelings of uneasiness, determined not to let Steven's arrogant behavior get the better of her. Besides, something serious had invaded her mind. She was standing in the corner of the dressing room wearing a worried expression when Stefan came racing by her, and she latched onto his arm, slowing him down.

"Have you seen Tyler?"

He saw the worried look on her face and instantly knew why. "No, Sasha, I haven't seen Tyler in days."

477

Sasha dropped her hand. "Neither have I," she mumbled. She walked over, reached for her purse, and removed her cellular phone. She dialed the number that she had on redial and there still was no answer.

After Terraine left early the next morning, Sasha had a cup of coffee out in the gazebo. Her eyes clouded with visions of the past.

She remembered sitting with Robby in the gazebo behind his parents' house planning their wedding. It seemed like only yesterday. Now he was locked in a jail cell. Life definitely had a way of playing tricks on you. Sasha wanted Robby out of her life once and for all, but not like this. She would never wish any harm to come to him. Was she just that blind that she had not seen the signs? First, that he was ill and second, that he was capable of murder?

Sasha brought her cup to her lips once again and stretched her legs out in front of her. Until she understood, the puzzle of Robby would drive her nuts.

Robby was not a killer and even though he'd said that he'd done the killing, she still did not believe it because the man who had attacked her was not the same man who'd stood before her in her kitchen only days ago. She knew this in her heart. The night she was attacked left her with an eerie feeling. The same type of feeling she had when she was around...Steven.

Sasha jumped out of her chair, quickly changed and drove off in her car. She remembered her brief encounter with Steven and was more certain than ever that Robby was not responsible for the deaths.

He could not have done it.

Chapter Twenty

Sasha sat down at the table and waited. The door opened and Robby entered wearing an orange jumpsuit and escorted by two uniformed officers. He smiled at her.

"Missed me already," he commented as he stepped away from the officer and took a seat across from her at the table.

Sasha grinned. "Yeah, right." She leaned over, placing both palms down onto the table and looking directly into Robby's oval eyes. "I need some answers."

Robby shrugged. "What do you want to know?"

His cheerless expression crushed her heart. *This is not right. There has to be something I can do! I once was engaged to this man.*

"Have you contacted your parents?"

He gave her a painful laugh. "Funny you should ask that. My dad disowned me the day I was admitted to that mental hospital."

"I didn't know."

"Yeah...well..." He leaned back in his chair and glanced over at her, his sadness still apparent. "You did something different with your hair."

Sasha looked at him, astounded that he could care about something so insignificant as her hair at a time like this. Did he not realize that they were trying to pin four murders on him?

"Robby, I want to help you but you have got to tell me the truth. Are you responsible for those murders?"

"No."

She clamped her hands and sighed. His response removed the last iota of doubt that she might have had. Now she just needed to prove his innocence.

"Then who is?"

Robby scratched the top of his head. "I'm sorry, but I can't reveal that."

His answer was absurd. "What do you mean, you can't reveal it? Don't you realize that your butt is in a sling?"

"Yes, I am quite aware, but I still can not tell you."

"Why?" If he could give her some logical reason, then maybe she might be able to better understand. He was silent for several seconds before he looked away quickly. Sasha followed the trail of his eyes over to the officer standing in the corner. "What is it?" she asked softly.

"If I say anything, I will be putting your life in danger," he whispered.

"M-my life?" She tried to swallow the lump that was forming in her throat.

He nodded. "Your life, and I can not have that happen."

"So you'd rather go to jail for murder than tell the truth?"

"If it should come to that, yes." He looked serious for several seconds and then his face relaxed. "But I think my lawyer will be able to cop an insanity plea on my behalf."

Sasha placed her hands in her lap and wrung them nervously. Was she supposed to feel grateful for his loyalty? "Robby, please tell me."

He shook his head. "I'm sorry, but I can not. I love you too much to allow anything bad to happen to you." Robby then rose from his seat and the officer moved over towards him.

"Wait a minute! I'm not done talking to you," she shouted desperately.

"Good luck, Sasha. Remember everything I told

you and watch your back. It will all be over very soon." He turned towards the door and exited the room before she could say anything else. Robby was trying to protect her and in order to do that he was willing to sacrifice his freedom for her safety.

Sasha quickly exited the building and reached into her purse for her phonebook to look up a number that she had not used in almost a year.

"Adams residence."

Sasha tried to ignore a sick feeling and forced a smile. "Hello, is this Laura?"

"Sasha, is that you?" Sasha grinned remembering the way Laura used to stand behind her chair until she cleaned her plate, thinking models were too skinny for their own good.

"Yes, it's me. How have you been?"

"Good. We all miss you."

Sasha's mood soured in remembrance. "I miss all of you also." She paused before addressing the matter at hand. "Is Victoria available?"

"Sure, dear. Let me get her for you." Within a few short minutes, Sasha heard someone pick up the other line.

"Sasha, darling. How are you?"

"Good." They quickly caught up on the events of her life since they'd last spoken before Sasha redirected the conversation. "Victoria, Robby has been arrested."

His mother sighed. "Is he harassing you again?"

"No. Not this time." Victoria was silent for several seconds while Sasha explained what had been going on.

"Do you believe Robby is innocent?"

Sasha did not hesitate with her response. "Yes, I do. Robby isn't capable of murder."

"That means a lot coming from you. If you believe in him, then I believe in him also. I do love my son very much. Let me see what strings my husband can pull to have him released. I'll contact our lawyers right away."

"Thank you so much."

"I should be thanking you. Please keep in touch. We all miss you very much."

Sasha promised to call and headed home, feeling more hopeful about Robby's future.

Arriving at her house an hour later, Sasha was surprised to find Terraine there. He was sitting on the couch staring down at his laptop. Nikki was lying down at his feet.

"Hi." She walked over and planted a kiss on his cheek.

"Hello." Terraine did not look up when he spoke, but instead pretended to be engrossed in his work. Sasha sat down next to him and noticed he was unusually quiet. Something was bothering him.

"Is something wrong?"

Terraine peered up at her, then lowered his head again. "Why were you visiting Robby?"

Sasha almost choked on her gum. "How did you know that?"

He closed his laptop and looked up at her again. "I've been having you followed by a detective."

Sasha's nostrils flared with fury at his matter-of-fact tone. "You what? How dare you!"

He looked at her as if her statement were ludicrous. "I was worried about your protection."

"You had no right doing that without asking me first."

Terraine's face was expressionless. "It doesn't change the fact that you went to visit him in jail today. Why did you do that?" Sasha rose and exited the room in a huff. Terraine followed close behind.

"I asked you a question," he said.

Sasha stood outside the kitchen and turned towards him with thinned lips. "Because I believe he's innocent." She then continued into the kitchen and removed a grapefruit from the refrigerator. Terraine stormed into the room behind her.

"How could you say that? All of the evidence points to him," he said with contempt.

"He'd never hurt me," she said with anger flowing through her veins. "He's harmless."

"How can you be so sure?"

"Because I was once engaged to him. We were together for two years."

"But you said yourself that it took a year before you realized he was ill." Clenching his teeth, Terraine was furious.

"That was only because I was traveling so much. The warning signs were there. I just chose to ignore them."

"The man is unstable and completely fixated on you." He spat out the words. "Why are you being so stubborn about this?"

Sasha held her chin up and gave him a cold stare. "Because I know that I'm right."

There was silence for several seconds until it became too unbearable for Terraine, and he ran a frustrated hand across his bald head. "I don't know why we're even having this conversation. Let's just forget it and let the judge decide." Terraine drew Sasha into his arms and began kissing her neck and face, but Sasha stiffened against him. He released his hold and backed away. "What is it going to take for you to realize the man is crazy?" Terraine pounded the counter. "A knife across your throat?"

"You can be so simpleminded at times." She turned on her heel and exited the room.

Terraine reached her before she stepped into

the hallway and grabbed her arm, swinging her around to face him. He looked down at her stubborn face. He had seen it often enough in the past several weeks to know that she was not going to give in; his efforts were futile. "Dammit! Stop being so stubborn!" Sasha pressed her lips tightly together and glared up at him. After several seconds of silence, Terraine released her arm and watched her walk away again. His heart was beating frantically. If he hadn't realized it before, he definitely knew now. Sasha's mind was made up.

"You need to leave," she said without turning back.

"Fine. I'm out of here." Before she reached her room, Terraine stormed out the house, slamming the door so hard that every window in the house rattled.

"Tee, you are sprung," Jay chuckled while popping the tab on a can of beer.

"Save the wisecracks." Terraine rolled his eyes at his brother and gave him a hard, cold stare.

After leaving Sasha, he'd gone directly to Jay's condo to avoid going home and being alone. He was starting to agree with his brother. The Andrews Manor was too big for him. If he couldn't have a bunch of kids and fill the house with love and laughter, then there wasn't any point in keeping the house. He might as well buy a condo like Jay.

Jay whistled softly. "My big brother is in love. Never thought I'd see this day."

"A lot of good it's gotten me."

"Tee, I have to agree with her."

Terraine jerked his head around and witnessed the serious expression. "What?"

"I've been thinking about it and either Robby is stupid or innocent. Now who in their right mind orders flowers using their own credit card and then kills the person they send them to?"

"Yes, but we are talking about someone that suffers from mental illness."

"Yeah, but don't forget Robby was at the top of his class before he dropped out of law school. He's not stupid." Jay paused long enough to watch his brother scowl at his comment. "I think you need to listen to what Sasha has to say."

Shaking his head, Terraine mumbled, "I think she is being stubborn or still has feelings for the psycho."

"I think you're being stubborn. I've seen the way she looks at you. Sasha is crazy about you."

Terraine leaned forward and briefly shut his eyes as the impact of Jay's words hit home. He knew she loved him. Hell, he loved her. Maybe it was the frustration of everything coming to a head. Was Robby really a threat? He hated that he was jealous. There were no if, ands, or buts about it. He didn't want her feeling anything for anyone but him. She was his and he'd be damned before he ever shared her with another man. Terraine rubbed both hands across his scalp. Now he was being selfish.

Jay parked his Lexus and left the motor running. Why was he here? He had several cases that he needed to begin investigating, but his mind refused to cooperate and instead, he was wasting his evening sitting out in his car thinking about Honey.

She had gotten under his skin, and no matter how hard he tried to hide from it, there wasn't a damn thing he could do about it. Tonight he didn't want to lie awake staring at the ceiling nor did he feel like another cold shower. There was no sense in pretending. Tonight he wanted the real thing.

Jay shut his motor off and flicked a cigarette butt out the window. It was now or never. He took a deep breath. Why did he feel like he was about to confess to murder? He had not seen her since Dwight's visit and missed her. He could not put off talking to her any longer. He had to tell her how he felt.

His eyes traveled to her bedroom window, and he saw that the small lamp was on next to her bed. Honey was probably sitting up reading. His breathing increased as he envisioned her lying beneath her sheet dressed in a satin nightie.

Jay threw his head back with bottled up frustration. This couldn't possibly be happening to him. He didn't want there to be anyone special in his life. He didn't want to think about a woman all day and all night. But he couldn't stop thinking about Honey. He wanted to kiss her, to touch her.

The truth caused him to react hastily as he jumped out of his car and slammed the door harder than he intended. It was only a matter of seconds before Honey was looking out her bedroom window. *Damn*! He wasn't ready to face her yet.

Honey raised her window and stuck her head out. "Jay! What are you doing out there?"

"Would you believe I was checking my oil?"

Honey laughed. "You are crazy!"

She was suddenly quiet and Jay stood silent, wondering what she was thinking.

"Would you like to come in?" she finally asked.

"Sure, just for a few minutes." He was relieved that she had offered and that he didn't have to ask. Maybe somehow he could get her to meet him halfway, but with Honey he wasn't putting too much faith in it.

Honey lowered the window, and Jay strolled slowly to the door, trying to get his emotions in order. A few moments later she opened the door dressed in a lavender satin robe with matching gown tied at the waist. Just looking at her and imagining what she looked like underneath made his heart slam against his ribs.

Honey noticed his focus was locked at her cleavage. "What you looking at?" She rolled her eyes and walked away from the door. Jay shrugged and followed her into the living room and took a seat. Honey yawned and reached over to turn on the lamp.

"Long night?"

"Yeah." He shifted uncomfortably on the couch. "What do you have to drink?"

Honey clicked her tongue. "You're not a guest anymore. Go see for yourself." Her saucy words made him feel good, knowing that somehow he had become a part of her life also.

When Honey reached over to turn on the television, the belt to her robe came loose. Jay had risen to raid her refrigerator, but he stopped in his tracks. Honey froze under his intense eyes. Jay was looking at her in a way that she had never seen him look before, as if he had just realized at that very moment that she was a woman.

He came over to her and took her in his arms,

holding her immobilized against his muscular frame. Honey gave him a strange look.

"What are you doing?" she asked with wide-eyed surprise as she realized what was about to happen. Shocked at the depth of his feelings, which were readable, she had mere seconds to stop him if she dared. But she didn't. She trembled a little but didn't move away.

Jay reached up and curved his hand around her delicate neck, stroking her jaw with his thumb. Emotions leaped like flames in his eyes. "What I should have done a long time ago," he said in a voice husky with desire. "You are driving me crazy." He dipped his head low and touched his lips to hers briefly, then again, experiencing their softness for the first time before he gently slid over her mouth with his tongue and sent a shocking trail of flame curling deep down inside her. He gathered her small frame against him snugly, and her soft curves molded perfectly against him. Slowly his hands memorized the texture of her skin and the shape of her body. With her robe agape, he felt her warm flesh through her satin gown. The heat of her body seared through his clothing, causing his skin to tingle. So many nights he had lain awake dreaming of holding her like this, and it was finally happening. Was he possibly still dreaming? If he was, it was one dream he did not care to wake up from.

He placed his hands inside her robe and allowed them to roam up her smooth thigh all the way to the middle of her back, never imagining she would feel as soft as silk. He continued to kiss her, finding her so delicate and her kisses so fresh. Honey began to gasp against his mouth, and she tilted her head back as he teased the skin across her jaw and along her collarbone.

She reached for him desperately, abandoning all resistance, instead enjoying how wonderful it felt to be held and kissed by him as he took her mouth in a hungry kiss that literally paralyzed her. In her wildest dreams she'd imagined this happening between them but never expected it to come true. Delight flowed through her as he coaxed her lips apart and sought refuge for his moist tongue. His lips were persuasive, weakening her senses, and confusing her mind.

When he lowered the strap of her gown and cupped her breast in his hand, a shiver rippled through her body and she found herself arching up towards him, inviting his waiting mouth. His lips magnetically lowered and captured a sensitive nipple. Honey gasped at the contact and felt her knees weaken beneath her. Her body was completely dominated now by his lips. Jay scooped her weightlessly into his arms while his lips continued to caress a hardened nipple and carried her over to the couch. A soft moan escaped her as Jay gently lowered her onto the cushion and knelt beside her on the carpet. Then he found her other breast, which surged with fullness at the contact with his warm breath.

Honey found herself lost between reality and fantasy as Jay took her further than she had ever gone. As his tongue seared a path all the way to her abdomen, causing desire to pound through her blood and travel to her heart, she couldn't think straight. He exposed her hips and Honey was stunned when she felt the flame heat between her thighs as his fingertips brushed her nest of brown hair.

Suddenly the memory of being pushed down onto the front seat of a car flashed in her mind. "Comply or goodbye," her attacker had hissed, with every intention of making her walk the ten miles back into the city down a dark road in the middle of nowhere.

Her eyes flew open and she scrambled upright onto the couch, pushing him away. Jay saw the terror in her eyes and reached out for her again, but she quickly rose from the couch and walked away, covering herself.

Honey leaned against the television while her thundering heart slowed down to a normal pace. She had been so close to doing something that she'd vowed to never let happen again. A terrifying realization flowed through her veins. *You can't give him what he needs.* Since that terrible night, she had never allowed anyone to get that far or to even put her in such a compromising position. Jay had almost shattered the last piece of control that she had. What was wrong with her?

Jay saw the fear etched on her face and wanted to reach out to comfort and reassure her that there was more going on between them than just sex. But Honey looked ready to race across the room if he tried to touch her again. Finally, he thought he'd figured out the sad look that he had witnessed numerous times in her eyes. Honey had been hurt badly, possibly even scarred. Her pain made his blood boil. Somehow he needed to let her know that something special was happening between them.

Jay broke the silence. "We need to talk." He stepped towards her and tried to embrace her, but Honey backed away, not trusting herself to be touched by him.

She shook her head. "Not right now. I need time to think." She knew where this conversation was heading, and she was not interested in venturing down that road.

Jay muffled a curse. He had blown things between them but he could no longer hide his feelings for her. Hadn't they just shared a magical experience? They could work through whatever it was. "I'm not leaving until we talk."

Honey looked at him and felt suddenly tired, so tired that she did not even care if she hurt him. "Please Jay, not today."

Jay saw the pain and against his better judgment, he gritted his teeth and nodded. He would follow her wishes for now, but they were going to talk. And soon. He'd see to that.

Honey turned and headed up the stairs, instructing him to shut the door on his way out.

From her bedroom window, Honey watched as Jay drove away. When Jay had kissed her, she had not become stiff in his embrace as she had done with others. Even before she pushed him away, she felt the desire he kindled. Jay made her want things that she'd never yearned to have: sex, love, marriage. How could it be that it had taken seven years for a man to awaken her senses? *But are you ready?* No, she sadly admitted. She still held years of pain inside of her. She still had an open wound. *Face it, girl, you need help.* Until she eliminated the person that she'd become, she could never completely give herself to Jay. But now she knew a different person existed deep inside herself. She prayed that when she was ready, Jay would still be available.

Jay lifted his glass to his lips and finished it, then pointed it towards the bartender. "Give me another," he commanded in a louder than normal voice.

The bartender frowned. "Buddy, I think you've had enough." He'd watched Jay sit in that same seat for almost three hours, staring at the floor and downing drinks as if they were Kool-Aid.

"I said, I will have another."

The bartender looked at him for a long time and then shrugged and went to make him another gin and juice.

"I should have known that was you starting trouble."

Jay turned his pounding head to face Kendra, a dentist that he had dated on several occasions but had not seen since first meeting Honey.

"Hey, Kendra," he slurred and tried to toss her a smile but the painful throbbing at his temples made it close to impossible.

She slid onto the barstool next to him and swung her voluptuous chest right under his nose. "Why haven't you called?" she pouted.

Because your name isn't Honey. "I've been busy." To put a little distance between the two of them, he turned his stool, anticipating the bartender's return, and found himself comparing Kendra's build to Honey's petite frame. Honey was proof that good things came in small packages. Jay scowled, trying to forget the scent of her hair and the warmth of her tiny frame against his. When feelings of desire washed over him again, Jay flinched with annoyance and had to catch himself before he slid off his seat and onto the floor.

Kendra snatched up his keys that were lying on the counter and dropped them safely into her purse. "I think I better take you home with me." She was concerned for his safety but also felt a twinge of delight at the possibility of having him in her bed again. For once she would be in control.

Jay shook his head and looked at the blurry figure in front of him. "I wouldn't be responsible for my own actions."

Her lips curled into a wicked smile, and she leaned forward and lightly stroked his neck with her index finger. "You don't hear me complaining." She then rose and slid her purse onto her shoulder. "I've been looking for an excuse to get you back in my bed," she said bluntly, knowing what she wanted and determined to get it. She crooked a finger at him, signaling for him to follow and swayed her ample hips across the room and out the door.

The bartender returned with his drink and Jay tossed several bills on the counter. Maybe he had been wrong to approach Honey tonight, he thought as he brought his drink quickly to his lips. She was only interested in being his friend and he should have respected her choice. Instead, he had thrown himself at her and made a fool of himself. Then he remembered Kendra sitting out in her car waiting to take him home with her. Maybe her showing up tonight was some kind of test delivered from above to find out if he was really ready to commit to one woman. Was he really ready? Or was he only interested in Honey because he knew that he could not have her? After all, he was always the first to admit that he loved a good challenge. Jay looked at his reflection in the large mirror hanging behind the bar, seeing the dark circles under his eyes, and did not like what he had done to himself. *All because of a woman.*

Patting his pockets, Jay remembered that Kendra had his keys. Managing a weak smile, he rose from his stool, went outside and found her sitting in her Range Rover. Jay climbed in and leaned back in the seat. "To hell with love," he moaned as he felt the onset of one heck of a hangover. But one thing he knew for sure: After tonight, things between him and Honey would never be the same.

Chapter Twenty-One

Champagne bottles were carried to the table and shortly thereafter the sound of glasses clicking against one another echoed around the room. Terraine offered the members of his staff who were sitting around the table a warm smile. "To guaranteed success." He toasted with his glass lifted confidently in the air, then swiveled to his left and extended his arm, tapping his glass lightly against Steven's before bringing it slowly to his lips.

"Customer service training ended today and I can say not a minute too soon. The orders for the new intimate apparel line have been coming in non-stop." Excitement was apparent in Evan's voice as he grinned across the table at Terraine, who in turn shifted his eyes to Carl and eased into an appreciative smile.

"Job well done," he complimented, even though he never expected any less from his marketing director. He was very impressed with Carl's ideas for marketing all phases of the new product lines and his ability to keep within budget. The man had definitely proved he had a creative mind.

Carl drew back in his chair and acknowledged the compliment with a wide grin. "Thanks, boss, but I can't take all the credit. He tilted the mouth of his glass towards the end of the table. "That lady sitting over there is the one who pulled this all together."

Natalia's brow rose in amazement before she tossed a lavender fingernail in the air dismissively. "I appreciate the compliment, but this is one time I can not take all the credit. We were all willing to work together to save this corporation and the end will definitely be the result of a team effort."

Caught off guard by her unselfish response, Terraine nearly choked on his champagne. It was the first time he'd ever heard her speak with a positive attitude about anything, not to mention team spirit. What had gotten into her? They were dining at Houlihan's, having a pre-celebration dinner, and since their arrival, she had been quiet and more reserved than usual. Lowering his glass, Terraine observed her for several seconds, trying to read her unusual behavior. He hadn't seen much of her since telling her he wasn't interested in being anything more than friends and was certain that Natalia had made it her business to stay clear of him. It was a relief that she was no longer dropping by his office three to five times per day.

Carl leaned back leisurely in his chair, lacing his fingers behind his head. "The fashion show is going to be a smash. Both performances have been sold out for nearly a week."

Steven rubbed his knuckles across his chest as if polishing a new red apple. "I guess my PR work might have had a little to do with that."

"Maybe just a tad." Carl's eyes sparkled with humor as he spoke jestingly.

Terraine chuckled before clearing his throat and addressing his staff. "I am pleased with everyone's work. It's great the way we all pulled together and stuck through a very difficult situation. Now that we have a suspect in custody, maybe we can move Diva Designs to the next level and hopefully take the corporation public in the foreseeable future," he said with a glint of determination in his eyes.

Natalia took a quick breath and sat back in her chair. "Are you serious?" Her voice rose with astonishment.

"I am very serious." Terraine rubbed his chin and leaned forward, placing both hands on the table. "I think that is where we should have been a long time ago."

"I agree," she spoke softly. Her mouth curved into an unconscious smile as she glanced at him. As she relaxed in her seat, Terraine saw no traces of her former animosity. Her attitude was becoming more puzzling by the moment. They exchanged one final smile, then he turned to face the rest of his staff.

"I have also decided to stay on as CEO." Stunned expressions touched all their faces. Everyone grew quiet and exchanged questioning glances, which came as no surprise to Terraine since he had made It clear the first day he arrived at Diva Designs that his leadership was only temporary. But somewhere during the planning, the long hours of preparation, not to mention the multiple deaths, he had finally come to his senses and had decided that this was where he belonged. *Where he should have always been.* His throat burned as he remembered the love he'd had for his grandfather and the love that Pops had always had for him. "Do I hear any objections?" He spoke to all, his open expression inviting honest responses.

Without further hesitation they shook their heads, and each congratulated him for his decision to stay on.

Terraine clapped his hands together. "Good, I'm

glad we got that out of the way." He took a moment to stretch comfortably in his chair. "Everyone better be ready for tomorrow," he joked.

"I couldn't be any readier," Evan interjected. "All of the garments are beautiful and Sasha's gowns are going to be the icing on the cake tomorrow night."

Cheers rang around the table, followed by a round table discussion about the positive impact the two-day event would bring to the corporation.

Terraine's thoughts wandered off as he sat there thinking that it had been two days since he'd last heard from Sasha. Was she really that angry with him? He had hoped that for once she might come to him and say, "I am sorry," but he knew that hope was fruitless. He missed her like crazy and felt a sharp twinge every time he thought about what life would be like without her. He decided he never wanted to find out.

The meeting adjourned an hour later and as Terraine strolled across the street towards his car, Natalia quickly fell into step alongside him.

"You got a minute?"

Terraine was amazed that she even bothered to ask. "Sure." When he stopped and turned towards her, she dropped her head. Bewildered by her behavior, he thought whatever she was about to say was going to be hard. "What is it?"

Looking up at him, her ginger eyes glittered with mist. "I was thinking about what you said about the corporation. I'm glad that you want to see things move forward." She spoke softly, "All I have ever wanted was for this company to be a success. Pops meant the world to me and I could not stand by and watch anyone destroy what he worked so hard to build."

Terraine tucked his hands into his pants pockets. "I'm disappointed that you expected any less from me. I know now that Diva Designs is where I belong."

Natalia smiled. "Good, I'm glad we cleared that up." They turned and walked quietly side by side with Natalia moving swiftly to keep up with his long strides. Finally after years of animosity, Terraine felt at peace with her. They would always have a common bond—their love for Richard Andrews.

When they neared her car, Terraine gave her a sidelong glance. "I hear you're seeing Jacob."

She halted, shocked by his comment, and blushed. "Yes. I have been fighting my feelings for him for years," she admitted openly. "Your last rejection made me wake up and smell the coffee, and I finally realized what loving a man truly means." Terraine noticed the way her eyes sparkled with truthfulness, her feelings obviously genuine. Love does strange things to people. He would know.

Terraine playfully pinched her cheek. "Be careful. You know I've never liked him."

Chuckling, Natalia threw her hands in the air. "Men! You sound like Jay." She leaned back against her Mercedes. "I would think you'd be glad to be finally off the hook."

"Sly wants the corporation." Terraine remembered Sly's proposal to purchase the corporation and Jacobs's reaction.

Natalia frowned. "Sly has terminal cancer and is not expected to live much longer. He was re-admitted to the hospital yesterday."

"So that's why I haven't heard from him." Sly had never been one to give up a good fight. Now he knew why. "Then why was he trying to buy Diva Designs?"

"You know as well as I do that Pops and Sly spent all of their lives trying to outdo one another." She shrugged. "He was just trying to secure Jacob's future, which is ironic since Jacob isn't the least bit interested in the fashion business, never has been." She planted her hands on her waist and smiled. "He wants to start his own software company."

Terraine rubbed his chin and gave her a puzzled look. The evening was full of surprises. "I still don't like him."

"I know. Why else do you think I am with him?" she joked. With a brisk wave she climbed into her car.

Sasha stepped into the shower and allowed the warm water to massage her body. She'd just lathered her washcloth and was rubbing it against her skin when the shower door opened. He climbed in and stood behind her, wrapping his arms around her midriff and sending shivers down her spine.

"Mmm," she moaned and leaned back against him, enjoying the warmth of his body. His hands rose slowly to her breasts and he worked in the lather with his fingers, sliding across her sudsy peaks. Her breathing quickened as Sasha realized how much she had missed Terraine and was glad that he had found it in his heart to compromise.

He brought his arm around her neck and took the cloth from her and finished washing her. With slow caresses, his hand lowered and lingered between her thighs. She closed her eyes and relaxed her head against his throat while his breath softly fanned her face. He then turned her around, and Sasha's eyes fluttered open and she stared up at him in shock. It wasn't Terraine but Steven. There he stood with a glistening knife in his right hand. When she tried to back away, he roughly reached for her, pulling her head back as he raised the blade and brought it in contact with her throat.

Sasha screamed and sat upright in her bed, her heart pounding rapidly. She took several deep breaths and lowered her head onto her pillow.

What did her dream mean? Was it a warning that she was next in line? That Steven was their serial killer?

The morning of the fashion show finally arrived, and Terraine rose early and quickly showered. After he slipped on his shoes, he paused long enough to review what he was about to do and smiled with complete confidence. He still hadn't seen or spoken to Sasha. But he could not—would not—live without her. After thinking it over, he'd realized that she had a right to her own opinion. If she believed that Robby was innocent, then he needed to respect her decision. With a wide grin he reached for his keys and a few minutes later, shut the door quietly behind him. He was about to change the course of the rest of his life.

An hour later, Sasha stirred, awakened by the loud ringing of her phone. At the sound of Tyler's raspy voice, she sat up, pulling the receiver close to her ear.

"Girl, you scared me! Where have you been?" she asked with a high degree of intensity.

Tyler groaned, although amused by Sasha's reaction. "You sound like my mother," she chuckled. "My father was sick so I went home to see him."

Feeling a sense of relief, Sasha rolled back onto her pillow. She had been so afraid that something had happened that she'd made Jay promise two days ago to begin investigating her disappearance. "Is he okay?"

"Yes, just a touch of the flu. I didn't realize anyone was looking for me until my mother received a call yesterday from a Jason Andrews." Tyler remembered her mother pulling her to the side yesterday so as not to disturb her father who was sleeping in the other room and demanding to know why a private investigator was searching for her. "I am surprised Steven didn't tell you."

"Steven?" Sasha's brow rose.

"Yeah, Steven." Tyler giggled. "I did a shameful thing."

"What?" Sasha asked, curious as to what Steven had to do with any of this.

"I slept with him," she confessed, relieved to finally be able to get it off her chest.

Sasha shot straight up out of bed. "You...you what? How could...when did all this happen?" Of all the people she could have chosen to sleep with, she'd picked that pervert!

"It sort of happened," she sighed. "But don't say anything to anyone. I promised him I wouldn't tell a soul." She paused again, long enough to yawn. "He sort of has a wife."

"A wife?" The snake had a wife? Sasha groaned inwardly. Why was she not surprised? Could Tyler possibly be that naive?

Tyler heard the insinuation in her tone and quickly tried to defend his actions. "He's trying to divorce her but Steven has a lot at stake. He comes from family money."

Big freaking deal. "I see," Sasha responded in a low voice. How could she tell Tyler that she despised her choice in a man?

"Anyway, Steven was supposed to tell Natalia where I was."

Sasha frowned. Natalia had probably considered it privileged information. She was not sure what else to say. Should she tell Tyler that she didn't trust Steven, that she even wondered if he could be responsible for the murders?

"Anyway, quit worrying about me. I'll see you at

the show tonight." Then she added at the last minute. "I'm flying back home the day after tomorrow and taking Steven with me to meet my family." She giggled with delight. "Let's get together and have lunch before then."

Sasha hung up the phone, needing to talk to Jay to share her suspicions. But before she could pick up the receiver again, the doorbell rang. Climbing out of bed, Sasha reached for her robe and tied it tightly around her waist. She then walked down the hall to the front door, where a deliveryman greeted her with a bouquet of white roses. Sasha looked down at them, and accepted them reluctantly, remembering the flowers delivered to the other three women. Slowly, she removed the card and exhaled with relief as she read it. *'Till death do us part. Will you be mine? I'll swing by in the limo at six.*

Pressing the card to her lips, Sasha's heart did flip-flops. Did this mean that Terraine was planning to propose? Because of her stubborn determination to stick to her guns, she hadn't spoken to him in days. Did this gesture mean that he was ready to support her decision to help Robby in any way that she could? Sasha turned and faced the clock on the wall. In less than an hour his bail hearing was scheduled to begin.

Terraine walked out of the bathroom and stood still for several seconds, certain that he had heard the phone ring. Deciding after a period of total silence that it must have been the water in his ears, he strolled over to his dresser and splashed after-shave across his chin. Several minutes later, he slipped into his black suit jacket, then opened his drawer and pulled out a small black box. He opened it, looking down at the three-carat marquise diamond surrounded by amethysts, and smiled. After the show, he planned on asking Sasha to spend the rest of her life with him.

The doorbell rang, indicating that his chauffeur was early. Terraine put the box in his left jacket pocket, then strolled purposefully down the steps and through the foyer, full of confidence. He could not wait to see her face. Terraine took a deep breath and smiled broadly. He was ready. Sasha was his life.

He opened the door and before he could see who it was, something struck him and his world turned black seconds after his head hit the ground.

Jay pulled in front of the Springfield Psychiatric Hospital and climbed out of his Lexus. Something still nagged at him about Robby being the murderer. Hoping to find the answer, Jay had decided to visit the facility where Robby had received treatment. Adjusting his tie, Jay strolled up the sidewalk and through the double doors.

An hour later Jay was racing down I-55. He tried calling Terraine again and scowled when he was connected to the answering machine. He clicked the phone off and tossed it on the seat beside the photograph he'd borrowed from the psychiatric hospital. Glancing down at the familiar face in the photo, he cursed himself for being a fool and overlooking the obvious. They were all in trouble. Pressing down on the accelerator, he prayed that he would get there before it was too late.

Sasha saw a pair of headlights pull into her driveway. Terraine was early, but she was glad because it would give her a chance to talk to him before the fashion show. She took a few seconds longer to check herself in the mirror. Even though she would be spending most of the evening modeling designs, she was dressed for the celebration afterwards in a strapless sarong, yellow floral dress, which defined all her curves. Quickly, she slipped into a pair of three-inch white leather slides. The doorbell rang and after reaching for her purse, Sasha rushed to the door and was greeted by the chauffeur.

He tipped his hat to her. "You ready ma'am?"

Sasha smiled. "Yes, I am." She locked the door behind her and allowed him to assist her into the limo. Settling back onto the seat, she realized Carl was sitting on the seat across from her.

Sasha's mouth gaped open. "Carl, what are you doing here? Where is Terraine?"

He wore a worried smile. "He had an accident and asked me to escort you to the theatre."

"What happened?"

He hesitated. "He was struck over the head."

"What?" she shrieked.

Carl raised his palms. "Don't be alarmed. He's okay, Steven is with him. They were called to an emergency at Diva Designs."

Her heart pounded in her chest. Steven. He was with Steven.

"What kind of emergency?" There was an irritated tone in her voice.

Carl shook his head. "I don't know, Sasha. Terraine and Steven should already be there. I received a page and was picked up about ten minutes ago." He shrugged. "I'm just doing what I was told."

Sasha crossed her arms firmly against her chest in an effort to keep Carl from seeing her hands shake. This could not be happening to her. "I want you to take me to Diva Designs."

Carl dropped his shoulders. "But Terraine said—"

Sasha's eyes clouded and she spoke with rising irritation. "I don't care what he said," she snapped. Nodding, Carl picked up the phone. "Nick, take us to Diva Designs," he instructed the chauffeur while Sasha leaned back against the seat and closed her eyes, remembering Robby's warning that it would all be over soon.

Chapter Twenty-Two

Honey was standing in the bathroom brushing her hair when Jay came barging in. He startled her, and she wagged her brush at him.

"Don't you believe in knocking?" she sputtered as her heart hammered against her ribs, not from fear but from standing so close to him, close enough to make her head spin. Though they had not seen each other since their uncomfortable encounter, she had thought about him repeatedly the past several days, wishing that she could be everything he wanted her to be, and disappointed with herself because she was not.

He shot her a penetrating look. "Next time lock your front door," he countered.

Honey raised her stubborn chin and turned

away, brushing her hair again. "I left it open for my date." She wouldn't necessarily call Mark a date, but he was escorting her to the fashion show tonight. She'd known him forever but Jay didn't need to know that.

Jay's jaw flexed at the thought of her being with someone else, but he brushed the thought aside. "Where is Sasha?"

She turned to meet his handsome face again. "On her way to the fashion show. Terraine was picking her up."

"She hasn't arrived. And I can't find my brother. Something is wrong."

Honey lowered her brush and asked quickly, "What do you mean, something is wrong?"

Jay took a deep breath, quickly regretting that he had said so much. "I mean...Robby didn't kill those women."

"What?" Astonishment touched her pale face and filled her luminous gray eyes. "Then who did?"

"Someone who is probably after Sasha. I've got to go." He quickly pivoted on his heels, heading towards the door.

"Wait one minute, Jason Andrews!" Honey yelled after him. She quickly slipped her feet into a pair of flip-flops and reached for her purse. "You are not going anywhere without me!" She fell into step alongside him.

"Stay here, Honey," he commanded without breaking his stride.

She rushed down the stairs. "Not on your life! That's my best friend we are talking about."

Jay remained silent as Honey ran after him to the car.

Terraine regained consciousness just as Jay and Honey pulled into the driveway.

Jay spotted his brother sitting on the bottom doorstep and hastily climbed out of the car. "What happened to you?"

Terraine rubbed his palm across the back of his head and flinched with pain. He was in for a killer headache. "I was hit over the head."

Honey raced around the car and stooped down in front of him. "Oh, my God! He's bleeding!" she exclaimed. Blood trickled from the side of his forehead.

Terraine tried to stand but was light-headed and lost his balance. Jay quickly reached down to assist him to his feet. "I have a first aid kit in the car. Right now, we need to find Sasha. Think you can ride?"

"What!" Terraine tried to stand up straight but the pounding in his head sent him stumbling forward. Jay caught him just before he landed in the grass. "Where is Sasha?" he demanded.

"Take it easy, Bro," Jay said, trying to speak calmly.

Terraine shot daggers at Jay. "What's going on?" He turned to look at Honey for some kind of answer, but she was too close to tears to speak.

Jay steadied him. "Come on, hop in. I'll explain on the way." They tried to assist him towards the car, but Terraine pushed their hands away and stood straight up, ignoring the pulsating pain.

"Dammit, Jay, if you don't tell me what's going on right this minute, I swear I am not going to be responsible for my actions!" Chest heaving, he glared at his brother.

"Robby isn't our killer."

Terraine was flabbergasted and his eyes darted back and forth from Honey to Jay and back again. Sasha had warned him, and yet he'd chosen not to listen. Terraine briefly shut his eyes and took a moment to collect his thoughts before opening them again. "Do you know who is?"

Jay reached for his arm again. "Yeah, Bro, I do."

The limo driver pulled up in front of Diva

Designs headquarters and within minutes, Sasha and Carl hurried through the building to the security desk.

Sasha frowned at the empty station. "Where's the guard? Shouldn't there be someone at the desk at all times?"

Carl nodded. "The way Steve was carrying on, I expected to smell smoke. Come on." He signaled for Sasha to follow him down the hall and they boarded the elevator. Sasha tapped her leg lightly and shook her head.

"Something is not right," she murmured. It was just too quiet. There weren't even any identifiable cars in front of the building. Sasha found herself wondering again if Terraine was really here. Thank goodness, she had not come alone. "Do you think Terraine has already left for the show?"

"There's only one way to find out." Carl pulled his cell phone out of his pocket and dialed, then almost immediately began speaking. "Evan, Carl. Have you seen Steven or Terraine?" His eyebrows furrowed as he listened. "All right, if you see either of them have them call my cell phone." He swore out loud after ending the call, then tucked the phone back in his breast pocket, avoiding her eyes. "No. I am afraid the show is about to begin without us. They must still be here."

Sasha wore a look of horror. "They can't start

the show without me!" Carl gave her a sympathetic look while she chewed angrily on her bottom lip. She hadn't meant to sound conceited, but Roxaner was going to be in the audience, along with as many people she could manage to load in her car, and she was going to be worried if she didn't see her daughter strutting across that stage.

Sasha quietly observed Carl for several seconds before speaking. "When Terraine called, what did he say exactly?"

"I didn't exactly talk to him."

Sasha swung around with both hands planted firmly on her narrow hips. "What do you mean, you didn't talk to him? How else did you know to come and get me?"

Carl loosened his tie slightly. "What I mean is that I received a page." He reached in his pocket. "Look for yourself." Sasha read the message on his pager and sure enough, Terraine had sent him an urgent message to pick her up. "Then Steven called, ranting and raving about an emergency."

Sasha followed him off the elevator, not completely convinced. Anyone could have sent the message. Including Steven.

They walked down the long, dim hall and Sasha frowned. Terraine couldn't possibly still be here.

Carl read her thoughts and nodded. "I have to agree with you, Sasha, something does not seem right." Slowly opening the door to Terraine's office, he walked in.

"Sasha, take a look at this!" Carl barked, stepping around an overturned file cabinet.

Sasha moved in behind him. Shocked, she saw that the office was completely trashed. Cabinets had been pushed away from the wall and their contents dumped onto the carpet. Her photos were tossed all over the place and across his desk was one of her gowns. But where was Terraine? She suddenly became frightened thinking about the numerous possibilities.

"Where's Terraine?" she said out loud. She then walked over to the gown and examined it more closely. It was slashed, as if someone had taken a knife to it repeatedly. She shuddered and moved away. "I thought you said he was here?" she accused with rising frustration.

"Maybe he left already." He reached down and retrieved a large photo of Terraine's parents on their wedding day, then sat at Terraine's desk.

Sasha was too busy picking the photos off the floor to notice. She had her own problems and felt sick as she tried to figure out all of the possibilities. Where was Terraine? Was Steven with him?

As she kneeled down on the floor and reached for several of the photos that were scattered all over, she realized some were from her portfolio.

How had they gotten in here? "I think we had better leave," she suggested as she grabbed a fistful of photographs and tried to place them in a neat pile. Something was unsettling about the entire thing.

As if he hadn't heard her, Carl spoke, "My mother had a wedding gown just like this that she kept hanging in the hall closet for years."

Sasha looked up from the floor and noticed him stroking the gown. "She must have been proud." She picked up several more photos, then rose from the floor and dusted off the front of her dress.

"No...," he briefly hesitated, "she was stupid."

Startled, Sasha's brow rose. "Excuse me?"

Carl shook his head and looked out the window in a dreamy daze. "They said that she waited all day for my father to come but he never came. Even after the guests left, she waited. The Jell-O mold was ruined, the champagne had gone flat but she insisted that he was coming." He rubbed his nose before continuing. "My grandmother had to pull her away from the church kicking and screaming in that same stupid dress that she made me look at every day of my life until the day that she died."

His voice rose at the end, and Sasha began to have that uneasy feeling again. "Wow, that is deep." She didn't know what else to say.

As if suddenly remembering that he was not alone, Carl turned his eyes on Sasha and stared at her long and hard before he began to laugh hysterically. Sasha couldn't figure out what was funny and stood frozen a few feet away, clutching the photos to her chest.

Carl then leaned back in the large chair and fingered the leather. "I always wondered what it felt like to sit in this chair." He swiveled from side to side and smirked like a cat before pointing over at Sasha. "I was standing exactly where you were standing the first time I came into this office, and I looked him straight in the face. You know what he did?"

Sasha shook her head, afraid of where this conversation was heading.

"He laughed at me!"

"Who are you talking about?" she asked softly.

He glared at her, angered by her ignorance. "My father!"

Sasha squeezed the photos. "Your father?"

Carl fingered the armrest again as he spoke softly. "Richard Andrews."

"Pops was your father! I-I don't understand." Sasha's mind whirled as she tried to take in what he was saying. Why hadn't Terraine mentioned that Carl was his uncle?

Carl rose slowly from the seat and came around to the front of the desk, resting on the edge and crossing his feet at the ankles. "It's quite simple.

I'm Richard Andrews' love child." He stopped to laugh boisterously at his poor choice of words and placed his palm to his chest. Then as quickly as he started he stopped laughing. "He never loved my mother. He used her and refused to acknowledge me as his son." His jaws flared as he remembered the day he introduced himself to his father. "He told me I was crazy just like my mother and to get out of his office, that he already had two heirs and what in the world did he need with another."

Sasha's heart went out to him as she witnessed his wounded expression.

"I am so sorry."

"So am I." Carl smiled, then cracked his knuckles. "Now it's time to finish this." He stood up straight, walked from behind the desk and her heart stopped beating for a second.

"Carl, what's going on here?" she asked while the pieces of the puzzle slowly came together. Could she have been wrong all along?

"It's time." He shook his head with uncontrollable agitation and stepped forward. "Fortunately for Tyler, she was a preacher's daughter. The thought of burning in hell did not appeal to me so I spared her life. But you, my sweet, are my victory cigar."

Sasha stepped away as a green light in her brain flashed. Oh my God! Steven wasn't their killer. *It was Carl.* "You killed all those people!" Sasha exclaimed. "But why?"

"You don't know?" he smirked. "Girl, you better ask somebody." He laughed and stepped closer. "Come on, Sasha, you are brighter than that. Revenge. Richard Andrews denied me my legacy. Diva Designs should be mine." He shrugged and looked at her with a long face. "And if I can't have it, then no one will. The same rule applies to you."

"You are crazy!" Sasha made a dash for the door in her high heels but Carl's legs were longer. He grabbed a fistful of her hair and snapped her head back to where he could see her frightened expression.

She screamed and tried to free herself. "Let me go!"

"This would be a lot easier if you would just go along with things," he whispered near her ear. "You should show a little gratitude. I got everyone out of your way so that you could shine and be the star. I think it's about time you thanked me." He grabbed her wrist, then threw her down onto the carpet and lay down on top of her.

Sasha struggled as she realized he had every intention of raping her. He held her hands, ignoring her pleas and pulling up her dress. Hot tears flooded her eyes as he spread her thighs with his own legs and closed his mouth over hers. Sasha tried thrashing her head from side, but he caught her chin painfully. Then he lowered his face onto hers. "That last time I tried to do this, your stupid dog stopped me. This time we won't have any interruptions."

Renewing her struggle, Sasha tried to cast off his weight. "Terraine will find me!" she vowed. "The limo driver even knows that we are here." She smelled his cologne again and her stomach churned.

"It doesn't matter, it's all over after today." He pinned her arms to the floor. "You are a feisty thing. I have no problem giving it to you rough if you prefer." When he lowered his mouth to her lips, Sasha clinched hers tightly together. *Please, Lord, not this!*

Suddenly Carl was flung away from on top of her. Sasha scrambled up off the floor and looked to see who had come to her rescue.

Robby!

He stood over Carl with his fists clinched tightly. "Leave her alone!" Robby demanded.

Carl realized who it was and laughed. "Well, well, if it isn't my old roommate."

"Roommate?" Sasha asked, becoming more confused by the moment.

Carl rose from the floor. "Yes, my roommate. You see, we spent fourth months in a psychiatric hospital together and during that time I learned a great deal about you. Robby decorated our room with your pictures and magazine articles. Why else did I decide to have you come to work for Diva Designs? It was to get you close to me so I could have you all to myself. Someone stupid like Robby would never know how to love you the way I do." Suddenly, Carl began to frown. Sasha and Robby watched as he began shaking his head vigorously. "No! Shut up! You want to ruin everything!" Carl exclaimed.

Sasha looked at Robby, wondering if Carl was speaking to him. Robby in turn shrugged his shoulder. "What are you talking about?" she asked.

"It has to be done!" Carl shouted. He raised his palms to his ears and turned his head from side to side, trying unsuccessfully to drown out the voices. Sasha suddenly realized what was transpiring as she listened to him debate with the voices in his head. She'd seen this before—schizophrenia.

Suddenly Robby lunged at Carl, and as the two men rolled around on the floor, Sasha seized the moment to grab the phone. It was dead, and her heart sank. Just then, Carl landed a solid punch to Robby's stomach and knocked the wind out of him. Robby was no match for Carl. Sasha frantically looked for an umbrella or something large that she could use to slow Carl down. She spotted a large paperweight on the end of the desk, reached for it, crept up behind Carl and swallowed hard before slamming it down on his head. Carl staggered forward and sank against the wall. Breathing hard and assuming the fight was over, Robby turned his back to Carl and moved towards Sasha.

Behind him, Sasha saw Carl reach into his jacket and pull out something shining. She immediately knew what it was and tried to scream a warning but nothing came out. Robby saw her look of panic and started to turn just as Carl reached him and raised the knife.

"Robby watch out, he has a knife!" she yelled, finally finding her voice, but her warning was too late. Carl plunged the knife into Robby's back and his knees buckled.

"Run!" Robby managed to yell.

Sasha screamed and made a quick dash towards the door but Carl caught her and tossed her onto the carpet again. Sasha screamed again and quickly scrambled over to Robby and cradled him in her arms. His shirt was soaked with blood and Sasha felt sick inside.

Carl placed a hand on his waist and made a loud tsk sound. "Isn't this a pretty scene?"

Sasha sobbed against Robby's hair. "What have you done?" She cried, then broke into sobs as she buried her face in the curve of Robby's neck.

"Sasha...," Robby whispered, then coughed while his eyes remained closed. "I'm sorry."

Sasha cast narrow misty eyes upon Carl. "What do you want with me?"

"What?" He looked confused for several seconds as if he was pondering an answer before speaking.

Carl began to pace with agitation in front of her. "I have to do this; otherwise they won't leave me alone."

Sasha opened her eyes and looked up at him. "Who won't leave you alone?"

"The voices." Carl flinched his shoulder and left eye in unison.

"No, the voices are trying to confuse you. Ignore them. What you are doing is wrong." She controlled her fear and managed to speak in a calm voice, trying desperately to get through to him.

He shook his head wildly. "No! You're trying to trick me!" he shrieked with rage. Carl swiftly moved towards her, yanking Sasha off the floor and striking her hard across the face.

They pulled into the parking lot and spotted the limousine immediately. Terraine was out of his seat before Jay came to a complete stop.

Jay shut off the engine and left the key in the ignition. "Stay here, Honey."

She reached for the door handle. "I'm going with you."

"No, you are not!" he ordered. "Can you for once not have things your way?" Jay cursed under his breath. He loved her fire, a woman like her could challenge him in every way, but this was one time he was not willing to budge. "This is not a game." He pulled a revolver out of his glove compartment and filled the chamber with bullets.
Honey's mouth snapped shut, stunned by his outburst.

Jay opened the door and slid out his seat, then tossed her his phone. "If we aren't out in fifteen minutes, call the police."

Sasha slowly opened her eyes and tried to look around the room, unable to ignore the throbbing pain in her lower lip where Carl had struck her. Her hands were bound tightly behind her back.

"Welcome back, princess." Carl stooped down in front of her so that she could see him without having to strain her neck. "You had me worried that I might have hit you too hard."

Sasha lowered her head again as the smell of

his cologne overpowered her. Then the reality of the entire sick situation hit her like a ton of bricks.

Finding the elevator stuck on the top floor, Terraine raced up the stairs, taking them two at a time. Sasha was a brave and stubborn woman who was probably raising hell with Carl at this very moment. But she was in serious danger and he hoped she for once would keep her mouth shut.

Grabbing the railing for balance, Terraine increased his speed. He heard his brother scrambling up the stairs behind him but he didn't have time to wait. He had to get to her as fast as he could. *Please God, let me be in time.* He pushed his rising anger at himself away. If anything happened to her it would be his own damn fault. What kind of man was he that he could not stand by his woman?

Terraine reached the landing, opened the door and peered around the corner. He heard voices coming from the direction of his office and slowly slid against the wall towards the room until he could squint through a crack in the door.

The first thing Terraine saw was Sasha sitting in his chair with her hands tied behind her back. *She was alive.* He sighed with relief. She looked frightened but he told himself to remain calm. Then he noticed the blood smeared across the front of her dress. After a heart-stopping moment, he saw a crumpled male body in the corner and realized the blood wasn't hers. It looked like Robby. What was he doing here?

Jay came up slowly behind him. "Can you see anything?" he whispered. Terraine nodded and moved away so that Jay could get a good look. When Carl turned his back to stand over Sasha, Jay nudged the door open with his foot.

"Well, well, the cavalry is all here." Sensing their presence, Carl quickly swung himself behind Sasha and placed the knife at her throat. "I must admit, Jay, that you figured things out sooner than I expected."

Terraine took a deep breath through his teeth. "Let her go."

Carl stared blankly at him. "I'm afraid I can't do that."

Sasha drew comfort from Terraine's deep baritone voice. *He had come.*

Jay stepped forward, pointing the gun towards Carl's chest. "Carl, don't make me shoot you."

"Now why would you want to kill your own flesh and blood?" He gave a peal of laughter at the puzzled reactions on both of their faces. "I was your grandfather's little secret. The son he rejected. I guess since my mother was a waitress that meant she was not good for anything but a quick romp in the sack." He eased behind the large leather chair so that it was impossible for Jay to get a clean shot. "She tried to tell him about me, and he called her a liar, refusing to allow me to be a part of his world. Diva Designs is mine! I should be the heir to this empire. Not you!" He waved his arms wildly in the air and shot them a look with ugly eyes.

"You think you are so smart! Well, let me tell you, your grandfather was a fake! He pretended that his entire world revolved around the memory of his dead wife and that he spent the rest of his life worshipping her. Well, I am sorry to say it isn't true. He had an affair with my mother for over five years until she became pregnant with me. Then he was outraged and didn't want to have anything further to do with her. I guess he was ashamed for anyone to know that he'd bedded a waitress." Carl stopped to stroke Sasha's hair as he remembered the woman he'd called mother. "To keep my mother quiet, he sent her money every month but that was never enough for me." Carl's eyes grew dark and cold. "I wanted the Andrews name and the power that came with it, but he was never willing to give me those things." He smiled with pleasure as he related his story. "A couple of months ago I came and visited him at the hospital and asked him again to acknowledge me as his son, but even on his deathbed he refused. So I decided not to prolong his suffering any further. I pulled his oxygen tube and exited the room only seconds before Sly Stone arrived. By then he was already dead." He laughed wickedly before continuing, still holding the knife tucked closely underneath Sasha's neck only inches away from her jugular. "I then set out to destroy the corporation. It was easy."

"Did Robby kill anybody?" Jay asked.

"That coward?" He threw his head back and laughed. "I did it all myself. Killing Deja was fun. She was a snotty bitch and hearing her beg for mercy was rejuvenating. Monet was a slut, willing to crawl on all four if that's what it took. And the little girl's mother—that was a case of being in the wrong place at the wrong time." He waved his hand in the air again, then placed his palm on his forehead as if in pain.

"If I can't have this company, no one can. The same goes for the beautiful Sasha Moore." He turned a malevolent look on Terraine. "I've seen the way the two of you look at one another. I've followed you since day one." He bent his face close to Sasha's and licked her cheek. She groaned, nauseated.

Speaking calmly, Terraine stepped forward. "Carl, can we talk about this? We are, after all, family."

"Why? Do you think you deserve to be happy? Well, you don't!" Carl screamed. For added emphasis, he traced the knife across Sasha's throat, drawing blood. Sasha screamed and Terraine stepped closer with his fist clenched tightly. "Take one step further and I'll be forced to do some real damage."

"If you hurt her, I will kill you myself," Terraine threatened. Feeling helpless, he watched Carl become increasingly agitated. "Toss the gun over here, Jay," Carl ordered. Jay hesitated but lowered his arm a few inches. "Do it now, or I will cut a hole in her throat the size of my fist!" he screamed hysterically, causing Sasha to flinch with fear.

With horror, Terraine observed the unfamiliar look of pure madness. He nodded to his brother to follow instructions. Jay squatted, never taking his eyes from Carl, and tossed the gun to his right, where it slid over near Robby's body.

Sasha's heart raced wildly. She tried to reassure Terraine with her eyes that everything was going to be all right. She did not want him to try anything stupid, especially not on her account. An opportunity was going to come for all of them to get away, she could just feel it. She bit her lower lip. Had they come alone or were the police only minutes away?

Terraine never once took his eyes off Sasha.

He would do anything Carl asked in order to save her life. There had to be a way to get to her without risking her life. He had to think carefully about his next move. One false step and she would be lost to him forever. He felt totally helpless. Then he remembered Honey waiting downstairs in the car and he hoped by now she had decided to call the police.

Honey climbed the stairs, stopping on each floor, uncertain where they were, but certain that she would hear voices sooner or later. As she reached the top level, she heard chilling laughter. Heart pounding, she followed the sound down the hall. She had contacted the police and they were on their way. Despite Jay's instruction, she had to know if they were all right.

Robby's eyes fluttered open. Tormenting pain in his back had left him practically paralyzed on one side of his body. But he had to somehow get up off the floor. Sasha was in trouble and she needed him. His lips curled. For once, she really needed him. If he did nothing else in his life, helping her would be it. With that in mind, Robby gathered his limited strength and picked up the pistol he saw near him. He slowly rose to his feet. Carl's back was turned and he was crowing so loud that he did not even notice him, but Terraine did. He sighed with hope when he saw Robby stir. He had believed him to be dead. Jay also noticed and pre-pared himself to dash across the room the minute Carl turned his head.

"How do we want to end this?" Carl asked, more to himself than to anyone else. He tapped his chin lightly, contemplating what to do next. Burn the place down or kill Sasha and then commit suicide right before their eyes. He nodded. Then and only then would the voices stop. Maybe then he could go on to a better life. Yes, yes! A better life and join his mother in heaven. Maybe his father would final-ly accept him as his son. Carl smiled, pleased at that idea and tightened his grip on the knife at Sasha's throat.

Honey entered the conference room side of Terraine's office and placed her ear to the door, only to find out that it was slightly ajar, causing her to stumble into the room.

Robby had just risen to a standing position and braced himself against the conference room door. When the door slammed into him from behind, he lost his balance and collapsed to the floor, but not before firing a single shot.

Epilogue

It was a beautiful Sunday morning as Sasha and Terraine exited the church with their arms entwined.

"My girl can sing," he praised. "I knew you were talented. Is there anything you can't do?"

"I don't know, but when I do, I'll let you know." She stuck out her chest proudly. It had felt good being back in church again amongst friends and family. They rounded the corner and walked down the sidewalk towards his car.

She had to admit she was happy. Everything was finally behind them.

Robby's single shot had found its mark. Carl had been killed instantly. Feeling it was his duty, Terraine had made all of the necessary arrangements and buried him near his grandfather.

Robby had spent a week in the hospital following his near fatal stabbing but had been released a day earlier. After giving his statement to the police, he returned to Illinois with his parents.

Following the fashion show, Terraine had taken two weeks off and he and Sasha took time to really get to know each other. In a short period they built a relationship that now included trust. Sasha loved him more than ever.

The fashion show had been a huge success and orders were coming in by the hundreds. Terraine had hosted a barbecue and invited everyone involved to Andrews Manor. Honey and Roxaner helped with preparations. The twins, who had returned for the fashion show, attended, as well as Tyler, escorted by Steven. Sasha had found him different, and by the end of the evening felt more at ease with their relationship. What was even stranger, Natalia had greeted her with a smile. The only person missing was Jay, who at the close of the investigation, took an undercover assignment that sent him to the East Coast. "I want to give somebody time to sort things out," he'd said by way of explanation.

When they approached her car, Terraine took her into his arms and leaned down, kissing her cheek lightly, and Sasha, flooding with happiness, wrapped her arms tightly around his waist. Terraine then released her and took her hands, wearing a serious expression on his face. Suddenly, she realized what he was about to do before he knelt down. She looked up towards the church and saw her mom and two aunts moving quickly towards them, wearing warm, knowing smiles. Before he even opened his mouth, Sasha began to shake with anticipation and the tears came streaming down her face.

Terraine spoke in a deep voice. "Sasha, I never knew what love really was until you walked into my life. Will you make me happy and become my wife?" Sasha remained silent for a breathless moment, savoring his words as they filled and surrounded her.

Finally able to trust her voice, she looked deeply into his eyes. "I guess if I want our baby to have a father, I better not say no."

Terraine rose slowly. "Our baby?" he repeated.

Sasha nodded her head. She had suspected it for days and after a quick trip to the drugstore, she'd confirmed her suspicions. "Yes, I am pregnant."

Terraine shouted at the top of his lungs and lifted her into his arms, kissing her passionately. He lowered her to the ground and placed a palm to her stomach. A part of him was now growing inside of her.

"You still haven't answered my question."

"Oh, Terraine, I love you so much," she said in a tremulous tone, ignoring the tears of happiness streaming from her eyes. "Yes, I will marry you." She nodded, smiling and crying at the same time, while looking deep into the eyes of the man she loved. Roxaner began to cry with tears of joy and the others clapped with excitement.

Suddenly remembering they had an audience, Terraine blushed, then turned to Sasha. "Let's go home." His eyes twinkled.

"Mmm. What are your intentions, Mr. Andrews?" she asked in a sensuous voice.

He pulled her close to him and brushed her ear lightly before whispering, "I have intimate intentions."

INDIGO
Winter, Spring & Summer 2001

January

Ambrosia	T. T. Henderson	$8.95

February

The Reluctant Captive	Joyce Jackson	$8.95
Rendezvous with Fate	Jeanne Sumerix	$8.95
Indigo After Dark Vol. I	Angelique/Nia Dixon	$10.95
In Between the Night	Angelique	
Midnight Erotic Fantasies	Nia Dixon	

March

Eve's Prescription	Edwina Martin-Arnold	$8.95
Intimate Intentions	Angie Daniels	$8.95

April

Sweet Tomorrows	Kimberly White	$8.95
Past Promises	Jahmel West	$8.95
Indigo After Dark Vol. II	Dolores Bundy/Cole Riley	$10.95
The Forbidden Art of Desire	Cole Riley	
Erotic Short Stories	Dolores Bundy	

May

Your Precious Love	*Sinclair LeBeau*	*$8.95*
After the Vows	*Leslie Esdaile*	*$10.95*
(Summer Anthology)	*T. T. Henderson*	
	Jacquelin Thomas	

 June

Subtle Secrets	*Wanda Y. Thomas*	*$8.95*
Indigo After Dark Vol. III	*Montana Blue/Coco Morena*	*$10.95*
Impulse	*Montana Blue*	
Erotic Short Stories	*Coco Morena*	

OTHER GENESIS TITLES

A Dangerous Love	J.M. Jefferies	$8.95
Again My Love	Kayla Perrin	$10.95
A Lighter Shade of Brown	Vicki Andrews	$8.95
All I Ask	Barbara Keaton	$8.95
A Love to Cherish (Hardcover)	Beverly Clark	$15.95
A Love to Cherish (Paperback)	Beverly Clark	$8.95
And Then Came You	Dorothy Love	$8.95
Best of Friends	Natalie Dunbar	$8.95
Bound by Love	Beverly Clark	$8.95
Breeze	Robin Hampton	$10.95
Cajun Heat	Charlene Berry	$8.95
Careless Whispers	Rochelle Alers	$8.95
Caught in a Trap	Andree Michele	$8.95
Chances	Pamela Leigh Star	$8.95
Cypress Wisperings	Phyllis Hamilton	$8.95
Dark Embrace	Crystal Wilson Harris	$8.95
Dark Storm Rising	Chinelu Moore	$10.95
Everlastin' Love	Gay G. Gunn	*$10.95*
Forever Love	Wanda Y. Thomas	$8.95
Gentle Yearning	Rochelle Alers	$10.95
Glory of Love	Sinclair LeBeau	$10.95
Indiscretions	Donna Hill	$8.95
Interlude	Donna Hill	$8.95
Kiss or Keep	Debra Phillips	$8.95
Love Always	Mildred E. Kelly	$10.95
Love Unveiled	Gloria Green	$10.95
Love's Deception	Charlene Berry	$10.95
Mae's Promise	Melody Walcott	$8.95
Midnight Clear	Leslie Esdaile	
(Anthology)	Gwynne Forster	
	Carmen Green	
	Monica Jackson	$10.95

Midnight Magic	Gwynne Forster	*$8.95*
Midnight Peril	Vicki Andrews	$10.95
Naked Soul (Hardcover)	Gwynee Forster	$15.95
Naked Soul (Paperback)	Gwynne Forster	$8.95
No Regrets (Hardcover)	Mildred E. Riley	$15.95
No Regrets (Paperback)	Mildred E. Riley	$8.95
Nowhere to Run	Gay G. Gunn	$10.95
Passion	T.T. Henderson	$10.95
Path of Fire	T.T. Henderson	$8.95
Picture Perfect	Reon Carter	$8.95
Pride & Joi (Hardcover)	Gay G. Gunn	$15.95
Pride & Joi (Paperback)	Gay G. Gunn	$8.95
Quiet Storm	Donna Hill	$10.95
Reckless Surrender	Rochelle Alers	*$8.95*
Rooms of the Heart	Donna Hill	$8.95
Shades of Desire	Monica White	$8.95
Sin	Crystal Rhodes	$8.95
So Amazing	Sinclair LeBeau	$8.95
Somebody's Someone	Beverly Clark	$8.95
Soul to Soul	Donna Hill	$8.95
The Price of Love	Sinclair LeBeau	$8.95
The Missing Link	Charlyne Dickerson	$8.95
Truly Inseparable (Hardcover)	Wanda Y. Thomas	$15.95
Truly Inseparable (Paperback)	Wanda Y. Thomas	$8.95
Unconditional Love	Alicia Wiggins	$8.95
Whispers in the Night	Dorothy Love	$8.95
Whispers in the Sand	LaFlorya Gauthier	$10.95
Yesterday is Gone	Beverly Clark	*$10.95*

All books are sold in paperback form, unless otherwise noted.

You may order on-line at www.genesis-press.com, by phone at 1-888-463-4461, or mail the order-form in the back of this book.

Shipping Charges:

$4.00 for 1 or 2 books
$5.00 for 3 or 4 books, etc.

Mississippi residents add 7% sales tax.

Tango 2 Romance

Love Stories with a Latino Touch

Hearts Remember	M. Louise Quesada	$15.95
Rocky Mountain Romance	Kathleen Suzanne	$8.95
Love's Destiny	M. Louise Quesada	$8.95
Playing for Keeps	Stephanie Salinas	$8.95
Finding Isabella	A. J. Garrotto	$8.95
Ties That Bind	Kathleen Suzanna	$8.95
Eden's Garden	Elizabeth Rose	$8.95

RED SLIPPER

Romance with an Asian Flair

Words of the Pitcher	Kei Swanson	$8.95
Daughter of the Wind	Joan Xain	$8.95

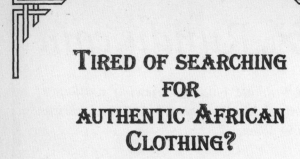
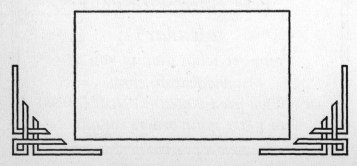